THE GIANTONIOS

FAMILY MATTERS

Other Books by Gerard R. D'Alessio

Dr. Cappeletti's Chorus
Iraq Dreams

THE GIANTONIOS

FAMILY MATTERS

Gerard R. D'Alessio

iUniverse LLC
Bloomington

THE GIANTONIOS: FAMILY MATTERS

iUniverse books may be ordered through booksellers or by contacting:

iUniverse LLC
1663 Liberty Drive
Bloomington, IN 47403
www.iuniverse.com
1-800-Authors (1-800-288-4677)

ISBN: 978-1-4917-1588-8 (sc)
ISBN: 978-1-4917-1589-5 (e)

Library of Congress Control Number: 2013921265

Printed in the United States of America.

iUniverse rev. date: 12/20/2013

I take great pleasure in dedicating this book to my children, stepchildren, and grandchildren, who have given me so many wonderful family experiences.

Acknowledgments

I want to acknowledge my daughter, Carla LaVoy, and my friend Jeff Goldman for their very important encouragement and support. I especially want to thank my wife, Susan, for her unceasing support and for the invaluable contribution she made with editing and suggestions.

TUESDAY

MARCH 2, 2004

CHAPTER I

GRADY

Although the temperature was around forty degrees, the wind and rain made the morning seem much colder. Grady stood outside of the Doughnut Shop, his long, blond hair and drooping moustache contrasting with his black leather jacket. He shifted back and forth from one foot to the other, taking his hands out of his jeans pockets only to flick the ashes off his cigarette or to remove it from his mouth to give his eyes a rest from the smoke. He'd already spent almost two bucks for a coffee and a doughnut, and he felt funny hanging out inside without buying anything else—not that anyone would mind. It just didn't feel comfortable. Grady checked the clock on the wall inside. It was almost eight o'clock. Uncle G. should be along pretty soon. It couldn't be too soon. It was freezing.

It wasn't long before Grady saw the big, black Town Car turn onto Washington Avenue and come toward him. Grady flicked his cigarette away, waited under the awning for the car to pull up to the curb, and then hurried over and got into the back.

"Good morning, Grady. You look a little cold and wet this morning, huh?"

"A little bit, Zio."

"That's okay. We'll get some breakfast, something hot to warm you up. All right?"

"Sure. That would be great." Zio Gennero always took him out to breakfast on these mornings when he'd asked Grady to meet him. It was a treat, given Grady's lack of funds. But it was also a treat to spend time with the man. It felt good just to be in his company. He was gracious, generous, and considerate, but Gennero was no Boy Scout. Grady didn't know for sure whether he was a "made" guy or not, but Gennero knew and had influence with just about everybody who mattered. It wasn't simply because people liked Gennero. That was definitely not Grady's view of how the world worked. Gennero had juice. He oozed power, although of an understated kind. Gennero was never anything but respectful to others, but Grady knew that there had to be a rougher side, though he had never seen it in all of his thirty-four years.

Grady caught the eye of Sal, the driver, in the rearview mirror and gave him a nod. Sal nodded back and returned his eyes to the road. Sal had been Gennero's driver for at least these last five years, and he never spoke unless it was necessary. In many respects, Sal looked like an average guy. There was nothing remarkable about his physical appearance, but there was something about his bearing and his attitude that gave the impression that he was totally reliable and dependable. Grady had no doubt that in any kind of emergency, Sal would come through for Gennero.

Gennero grabbed Grady's knee. "I see you're still smoking, eh?"

"Yeah, you know I'm never going to give them up."

Gennero pressed his lips together and looked out the window. "Well," he said, "I guess it's good that you get to choose your own death. That's not a bad thing, to be able to choose how you want to die. You choose smoking. And me, I choose eating." He laughed heartily, patting his belly with both hands.

"What are you talking about? You ain't fat. You look pretty good for your age."

"Well, it could be a lot worse, but it could be a whole lot better too. Not just the weight. I should eat more healthy too."

Grady looked at the man beside him. Grady was six foot two and towered over the much shorter man. Whereas Grady was slender and muscular, Gennero was thick and powerfully built. At seventy-four, he still emanated strength and, despite his lack of height, was still an imposing figure. Gennero, with his thick, gray hair combed straight back, and his expensive suit and coat, gave the impression of being a distinguished gentleman, an educated and successful businessman—which he was. Grady felt admiration and love for this man who was like a blood uncle to him. Even more, although he called him "Zio," Italian for uncle, Gennero felt more like a father to him. Grady would do anything for him—would lay down his life for him—and not give a second thought to it. Gennero was the only man Grady trusted. Not another soul.

Sal pulled the car up in front of the familiar South Philadelphia brownstone where they usually went, the home of Gennero's older sister, Maria. It was a place where Gennero felt comfortable when he wanted to talk privately. Sal got out with an umbrella and walked Gennero up the steps to the front door where Maria was waiting for him. Grady waited and then got out and bounded up the stairs. He went inside where Gennero and his sister were exchanging hello kisses.

"Good morning, Grady. How are you today?" Maria greeted him, her twinkly eyes and warm smile making him feel welcome. Her thick, black, gray-streaked hair and short, compact stature made it obvious that she was related to Gennero.

"I'm good, Maria. A little cold, but good."

"And hungry too, I hope," she answered, laughing.

"Yeah." Grady smiled. "And definitely hungry."

"That's good. Come in. Everything is waiting for you."

Maria helped them hang their coats on the clothes tree in the foyer and led them into the dining room where their places were already set. Grady could smell the bacon and the coffee. He loved coming to this house. It was a comfortably warm and cozy home. With its heavy and solid furniture and varnished wood trim, it seemed to be furnished more for Gennero than for Maria, although he had his own place with his wife, Theresa, while Maria had lived here alone for over twenty years.

"So," Gennero started, "how are you doing?"

"I'm doing good. I'm still clean. Smoking is my only vice now. I'm getting by."

"You doing any work at all?" This was a reference to his music. Grady had been a musician, on his way to a good career. People were still asking him to play or sing with them or help them in producing records, but he usually declined. He had been so outraged by the dishonesty in the music and record industry, the exploitation and lack of standards or integrity, that he'd been afraid he'd lose his temper and kill somebody. It was while he was performing that he had started abusing alcohol and using drugs. Now he didn't trust himself enough to go back into that scene. Rarely did he allow himself to do a gig to help out a friend. When he did, he discovered that all of his talent and energy was still there; riffs just poured out of him. He was a born performer. But he was terribly afraid of where it might lead him.

"No." Grady frowned. "You know I can't go there anymore."

"I understand. I do. Forgive me for asking. It's just that I know it used to give you so much pleasure. Music seemed to be your whole life. It makes me sad to see you without pleasure in your life." He paused. "Is there anything I can do for you?"

Grady smiled. "I know you want to help out. You do more than enough for me. You always have. There's nothing more you can do. I just don't have the tolerance for that world anymore, Zio."

Gennero studied him.

"There's just so much bullshit in that world," Grady continued, "so much pain. Everybody is fucked up, and rather than deal with their own shit, rather than being honest with themselves, they pass it on. Pass on the pain. They dish it out to whoever's in front of them. I tell you, Zio, one of these days, the wrong person is going to fuck with me, and then they're gonna end up dead!" The words came out sharply through his teeth, and his eyes were wide.

Gennero put his hand on Grady's arm. "Calm down, Grady. Relax."

Grady let out a sigh and sat back on his chair. He guessed at what might be going through Gennero's mind. One time, Grady nearly beat to death a couple of hoodlums who were stupid or unlucky enough to try to mug him. And then there were three separate occasions when he put himself in the hospital; he had given himself a concussion by socking himself in the head. Later, he said that he assumed that he'd done it as a way of trying to control his rage, hitting himself instead of somebody else. Fortunately, each time there were people around to witness what happened and to call for medical help. But Grady wasn't totally sure what had happened because he had amnesia for each of those events. From his perspective, it had felt as if somebody else had done it to him.

"Grady, I know there are a lot of mean assholes in the world, lots of bad people. But everybody isn't a bastard like you say. There are some good people, like Maria, for instance, or Tessie and Nina, or even you and me. Not everybody's the enemy, you know."

"Zio, you may just have named the only exceptions: your sister, your wife, and your daughter. I'm not sure I'd even include the pope." They both laughed. Maria had been bringing out their breakfast: juice, eggs, bacon, potatoes, Italian bread, coffee, and sweet rolls.

"This is wonderful, Maria," Grady said, seeing and smelling the food. He turned to Gennero. "You know, it's amazing. A couple of minutes ago, I was close to feeling suicidal, seeing everything and everybody—almost—as so screwed up that life was hopeless. But right at this moment, being here and soaking all this up, makes me feel good." He laughed at himself. "I'm such a wacko. Every time I get down, I tend to think that that's the way the whole world is all the time. But right now, I wish life could always feel just like this."

During breakfast, the three of them made small talk, caught up on one another's activities, and commiserated about Philadelphia's politics and its sports teams. When they finished eating, Maria cleared the dishes and excused herself to go upstairs. Grady said to Gennero, "What a nice, old lady Maria is." Gennero smiled and then asked Grady about his mother, who was living in an apartment in Florida, limited in getting around by a bad case of arthritis and some heart problems. Fortunately, she had made friends with a couple of women in her building, and they looked out for each other. Grady visited her about once a year.

"You've been a good son to her, Grady. From all that you've told me, maybe even more than she had a right to expect. Still, it's good that you keep in touch with her. If you ever need some money to go see her, don't be too proud to ask me, eh?"

"Sure, Zio. Thanks. I'll remember." Grady paused and looked at the older man while they sipped their coffees. "You've always been so good to me, more than anybody else. You're like a father to me; I wish there was something that I could do for you. So I also want you to not be too proud to ask if there's anything, I mean *anything*, that I can ever do for you."

Gennero glanced at Grady as he put his cup down. "Grady, I know how you feel about me, and your feelings are very important to me. You hold a special place in my heart too. I know you feel that." He paused. "There's only one thing I've ever been able to think of to ask of you, other than that you take good care of yourself, and that's to ask you about Richie. But I've never asked you because I suspect that it'd be difficult for you to talk about and because it might mean that you'd have to violate some confidences."

Grady remained silent, staring into his cup.

"But someday, if you could help me understand what happened to my grandson, I'd appreciate it very much."

Grady struggled silently within himself. He had just committed to doing anything that Gennero might ask of him, and now he had been asked to do that which would be the most difficult. Finally, he said, "What would you like to know?"

"Well, to begin with—how and why he got into drugs. What really happened and why? Who's responsible? Am I responsible?"

Grady leaned back on his chair, sighing. He and Richie had known each other since they were four years old, when Grady's family moved into the South Philadelphia neighborhood. Nina and her husband, Joseph, lived downstairs in a basement apartment with Richie and his older sister, Rosalie. He and Richie had gone all through school together, starting up a band when they were fourteen, and playing in clubs by the time they were seventeen. It was during that time that they started drinking heavily and doing drugs: pills, pot, and then snorting cocaine, then heroin, and finally mainlining. Grady knew that Gennero was aware of some of this, but he wasn't sure how much. He knew that Richie had never confided in his sisters (Andrea, his baby sister, was born when Richie was eight) or in his mother. Richie's father had died in a work accident. He was working under a car and hit a wrong release button or something, and the car dropped on top of him. He died on the spot.

"No, Zio, you're not responsible. Nobody is responsible for Richie being dead. Nobody and everybody. Me and Richie got addicted to drugs. Other people get addicted to other stuff. You got addicted to food. Most people are addicted to things or money and power. That's life. The business we were in, people wanted to use us. They were glad we were on drugs. They wanted us on drugs. That way they could get what they wanted from us, control us, manipulate us. It got to us. I couldn't take the bullshit anymore and got out of the business. Richie kept working. But it took its toll. I think he needed to use more and more to be able to continue to put up with the crap. Finally, he just took too much, overdosed." Grady stared into his empty cup. "There's nobody to blame, Zio. It's just the way life is."

"I know you and Richie started using when you were still in high school. But I don't understand why. Why? Why did two bright and talented kids, smart kids, get sucked into that kind of shit? Demeaning yourselves, destroying yourselves? I don't understand."

"I've thought a lot about this, Zio. You know, as part of the programs that I've been through, working with my sponsors, going on retreats, talking to shrinks, I think I have a pretty good understanding, but it's complicated, and there are no simple answers." Grady looked up, and Gennero leaned forward, resting his elbows on the dining room table, the remaining dishes having been pushed aside. It dawned on Grady that Gennero had prepared for this conversation. For some reason, he was ready to ask the questions he'd never asked before and ready to find out what the answers might be.

Grady proceeded to tell Gennero how he and Richie started to play in clubs where they were exposed to drugs, alcohol, and prostitution. "It was dangerous. There were some tough dudes hanging out in those clubs." Although they were only seventeen and underage, there were some people who watched out for them. Still, they had easy access to women and drugs. It was a heady and overwhelming mixture of danger and excitement where alcohol, drugs, and sex were pushed onto them. "We couldn't have said no even if we'd wanted to. It seemed to us that if we were going to survive in that scene, we had to be accepted as being part of it. To be honest, Zio, it wasn't exactly a hardship to join in."

"Why do you think your parents and Richie's mother let you kids be in that environment? Staying out all night, missing school, coming home drunk?"

"Well, you have to remember, our band was pretty popular at school. We had a following even then and were seen as special, and people wanted to cut us a break. Also, I don't know how much you know about this, but at my house, my parents had lost all control over me. My father was always half in the bag with his medications." Grady shook his head at remembering. *God, I want a cigarette*, he thought. But he knew there was no smoking in the house.

"Your father . . ." Gennero prodded.

"He was a junkie. He'd never admit it, of course. Nor would my mother. God forbid she'd ever acknowledge anything like that about him, or anybody else in the family for that matter. Yeah, he was always stoned on pain medications or tranquilizers.

He retreated into the zone to get away from her, I think. My mother ran everything. But who knows what reasons he had."

"I think I remember Richie always liked your father."

"Sure, why not? He did all those magic tricks for us when we were little kids, and he was easygoing and soft-spoken. Everybody liked him. But as a father, he wasn't there for me. He was weak. He never stood up to her. No matter what she said or did, no matter how outrageous she was. Everything revolved around her. 'Don't upset your mother. Just do what she wants. Keep the peace.' What a fucking waste he was! What a poor excuse for a human being!"

"So your father couldn't or wouldn't provide you with any discipline or guidance. No . . . support?"

"Right. You got it. And my mother . . . if she couldn't have full and total control, she didn't want any part of it. So when I got too big to smack around, she just gave up. I lived there, under the same roof, but it was as if I was no longer part of the family, more like a boarder. And that suited me just fine. And she retreated into the church."

"I remember Richie referring to your mother as 'St. Catherine.'"

"Yeah. She passed in the neighborhood as a 'good woman' because she went to church every day, worked in the Rosary Society, whatever. But she was never a mother. Her idea of being a mother was being a mother superior. She should have been a freakin' nun!"

"So," Gennero offered, "it was in these clubs that you and Richie got introduced to drugs?"

Grady grimaced. "Not exactly," he said. "The truth is . . ." Grady paused, reluctant to admit that Richie had sneaked alcohol from his house and Grady had taken some of his father's medications. Then he described for Gennero the ready availability of drugs at school. "So, no, we weren't exactly virgins when it came to getting high. But once we started working the clubs, it went to a whole other level."

Gennero said, "Tell me. Didn't the two of you know what you were doing, the risk you were taking, getting addicted?"

"I don't know, Zio. We didn't think about it. We didn't care. We didn't think it was such a big deal. Getting high was fun. It felt good. We couldn't see the downside. We didn't know . . . or we didn't believe how bad it could get. Everybody we saw seemed to be doing great. All those warnings, 'just say no' and all that crap, we just chalked it up to adult propaganda. What did they know? I guess we didn't have any confidence in anything adults had to say. There was no reason to pay any attention. It took us a long time before we had any idea of how it was fucking us up."

"How bad did it get, your habits?"

"Well, we spent a lot of money, that's for sure. But a lot was made available to us, given to us by people—friends, hookers, groupies. I think it got to the point where we were high on something almost all the time. It didn't seem to affect our music. I don't know if being high helped us to perform better, but I don't think it made us play any worse. But . . ." He paused and looked at Gennero. "It did affect us . . . our judgment."

Gennero cocked his head. "How so?"

"Well, we were in heavy demand then, making what seemed like a lot of money. Richie and I were both writing songs. We started making demos, you know, looking for a recording contract." Grady stopped and seemed to stare off into space. Gennero sat back in his chair and waited for him to continue.

"Those fuckers. Just because we were young, they thought they could manipulate us. They didn't care a fuck about us or our music or our songs. They only wanted to make money off us. Chew us up and spit us out." Grady had that wild glare in his eyes again. Gennero waited silently.

"But," Grady said with a sigh, "thinking back, if we had been sober—if I had been sober—I think I could have dealt with all of it better. Between being young and full of myself, I think the booze and the coke helped to make me a cocky and arrogant hothead. Hell," Grady laughed, "I may still be a cocky and arrogant hothead, and I've been sober for two years now. But I think I would have been a little smarter, more mature, if I hadn't been all coked up."

Grady stretched and leaned forward. "But that's not the most important part." He paused, looking at Gennero. "You sure you want to hear all of this, Zio?"

"Grady, I've been waiting these last two years to ask you what you know. I knew some of this before, of course, but only the tip of the iceberg. Now, it's important that I know as much as possible. I know this is difficult for you, dredging up memories and feelings that you would rather keep buried and to yourself. But as I said, this is important to me, and I'd appreciate it if you would spare me nothing. Agreed?"

Grady nodded and, taking a big breath, continued. "After a while, we'd met just about everybody in the business, and everyone wanted us to play for them. We began to make some real money then, even without the records. I was never home. In fact, I had moved out. Richie still lived at home with his mother when we were around, but I didn't have to see my mother and put up with her attitude. Then, a little over two years ago, we were playing here in the city, and Richie found out that the girl he was going with was stepping out on him. Tracy—you remember her?"

Gennero shook his head no. "I could never keep up with all of the women in Richie's life. I knew they broke his heart a couple of times, but no, I never knew the details, the particular women."

"Well, they were pretty serious. At least Richie was. And one night we're not playing, he calls her, expecting them to get together. She makes some excuse, I don't know, got a headache, has to wash her hair. Who the fuck knows? Anyway, Richie says fine, and he calls me, and we go out by ourselves to have some drinks."

Grady went on to describe how Richie thought he saw Tracy passing by outside the bar where they were drinking. The two of them followed Tracy and the man she was with and saw them get into a car and drive away. However, Richie still wasn't sure if it had been her, so they went to her house and parked across the street. They waited to see if Tracy came home or, if it hadn't been her, she'd emerge from the building in the morning to go to work.

"Sure enough, about seven o'clock, a car pulls up with the two of them in it. They smooch a little, and then she gets out and goes inside. Richie is devastated. Just blown away."

Hesitantly, Grady related how he and Richie decided to follow her that night and devised a plan for Richie to confront the dude she was seeing. After following her to a club in Old City and confirming that she was with the same guy, Grady went in and took her aside for a chewing out for cheating on Richie. Meanwhile, Richie induced the guy to go outside with him.

"After I left Tracy in the bar, I went to the alley behind the bar, and Richie is beating the shit out of this guy. A couple of bozos start to interfere, but I wave them off. They take one look and know not to mess with me. Also, they see what's going down with Richie. I mean, he's viciously beating this guy to a pulp."

Grady paused and took a deep breath. His eyes were watery. "We should have known better. We should have . . . but we were so full of dope that even if we didn't use one day, we'd still be high from the night before. That night, we left that poor son of a bitch for dead. We expected him to die. We thought he would die. He should have died. I mean, Richie was hitting him with a pipe." He shook his head again in disbelief. "No sane person would have done what we did. I look back, and I don't believe we would have done it unless we were high. Sure, Richie was in love, and she cheated on him, and he was royally pissed. But that wasn't the first time he got his cherry broke. We'd both been down that road before and were always able to handle it. But that night, we both thought he'd killed a guy, and we believed that he deserved it. We actually felt glad, like we'd done a good thing."

Grady shifted his position in the chair. "We found out the next day that the guy, I think his name was Brian, a junior exec in some bank or something, was in the hospital in serious condition, maybe critical condition. I don't remember. He was in there about three or four weeks. The papers said that he'd suffered a concussion, broken teeth and cheek bones, fractured ribs, a punctured spleen. Afterward, both Richie and I felt bad about it. I don't think either of us ever got over it. That's when I decided to stop using. I figured if Richie, who was so good-natured, so easygoing, could go off like that, then what the hell would I be capable of? I knew what I could do if provoked, but I didn't want to be responsible for killing or crippling somebody who didn't really deserve it. Seeing what Richie could do scared the hell out of me. I'm out of control enough as it is, on a good day, without taking that kind of risk.

"Richie, I think, never forgave himself. Between the heartbreak over Tracy and the guilt over maiming this guy for life, he must have started doing more drugs." Grady paused. "It wasn't too long after, before he overdosed."

Gennero raised his eyebrows. "You mean you think it was deliberate?"

"I really don't know, Zio. I really don't . . . but, yeah, it's possible."

Gennero covered his face with his hands and leaned back in his chair. Then he rubbed his eyes and his cheeks as if to wake himself out of some dream. The two men avoided looking at each other for a while. Finally, Gennero spoke. "Grady, does anyone else know about this, know what happened with that beating?"

"No. Richie couldn't even talk about it with me, and I would never rat on him. Besides, I was just as much a part of it as he was. I always thought of it as something we both did, not just him. So, no. No one else knows. I don't know if Tracy ever put two and two together, but she never said anything to anybody that I know of."

"Is there anything else that I should know?"

Grady shook his head. "No, Zio. I don't think there's anything else. I think that's pretty much the whole story about what happened." Grady looked up at Gennero. "I'm sorry to have had to tell you. I know how much you loved him. He never would have wanted you or Nina to know. He was really so ashamed. He made me promise not to ever tell you or his mother or anybody."

"Grady, I know you didn't want to tell me all of this. I hope you won't feel like you've betrayed a trust. And although I can't say that this makes me happy, it's a great relief to know what happened. In a way, knowing the truth of what Richie went through allows me to feel closer to him . . . and to you, Grady. I feel like we're sharing something intimate, a secret about somebody we both still love. Thank you." Gennero pushed himself up from the chair and went to Grady. The two men hugged awkwardly. "Come. Let me have Sal drive you home." He walked Grady to the front door, where he helped him on with his jacket. "Tell Sal to go have lunch when he's done dropping you off and then to come back here for me."

"Okay," said Grady. "You okay?"

"I'm fine," said Gennero.

"I love you, Zio. I'm so sorry."

They hugged each other again. "It's all right," said Gennero. "Everything's okay. Take care of yourself. I'll see you soon."

"Sure," said Grady. "Tell Maria thanks for me. She outdid herself this morning."

"I will. I'll tell her."

Grady walked down the steps. It had stopped raining. The wind had died down, and it felt a little warmer. Sal was waiting in the car reading. The two men nodded at each other. "Home, James," Grady joked.

Sal looked at him and smiled. "Yeah, sure. Mr. G. not coming?"

"No. He said for you to take me home and then go have lunch before you come back to pick him up." Grady sat back into the soft comfort of the limo. He thought about all that he'd been talking about. His whole life. Where had it gone? He felt drained and tired, like an old man.

Chapter II

Gennero

Gennero watched through the curtains of the living room windows as Grady climbed into the back of the limo. He saw Grady and Sal banter for a few moments and watched as the car pulled away and moved off down the street. His hands in his pockets, Gennero slowly walked back through the dining room, where the empty coffee cups remained, and into the kitchen. He went to the sink, took a knife from the drain board, and tapped a few times on the radiator pipe that led up along the wall and disappeared into the ceiling. Then he opened the refrigerator and took out the little bag of espresso coffee and brought it to the sink. Hearing footsteps on the stairs, he went to the kitchen table and sat down. Soon Maria came in.

"You want some espresso?" she asked.

"Yes, please, Maria. I already took it out."

Maria proceeded to make the coffee, using the battered aluminum espresso pot she'd used forever. "So how did it go?" she asked.

Gennero rubbed his chin before answering, still trying to think of what he was going to say. "Good," he said. "Grady turned out all right. He's still screwed up, of course, but he tries hard to do the right thing."

"So what did your fine, young man have to say about our Richie? Did he tell you why Richie died?"

Gennero knew that, after two years, Maria was still upset and angry about Richie's death. *Not knowing who to blame, she blames me. After all, she thinks that I'm the one who's responsible for everything that happens. If I'm the boss, I must be to blame for this too, unless someone else can be found who's even more responsible, like Grady. The two boys had always done everything together; how could it be that Richie could die from an overdose of drugs without Grady being involved?*

"Yes, Maria, he did." Gennero looked at Maria, and his voice was stern. He was letting her know that he was not about to let her blame him for everything. He had also determined that he would say as much as he had to, but that he wasn't going to volunteer anything he didn't have to. "It seems that Richie had been dating a young woman with whom he was quite serious. He wanted to marry her. I'm not sure, but they might even have been engaged. And"—he paused to make sure he had Maria's attention—"he caught her cheating on him. He was very upset. Grady said that after that, Richie began to use more drugs, and that's apparently how he happened to accidentally overdose. Richie's overdose scared the pants off of Grady, and that's when he decided to get clean."

"That's it?" asked Maria. She stood by the stove and looked at Gennero.

"Of course that's it. Isn't that enough? What more do you want? He was in love. He had plans to get married, probably have a family. He was upset. He was furious. Grady said Richie was in a rage. He must have been totally depressed to get out of control and immerse himself in drugs as a way to get relief. An accident was bound to happen. He wasn't paying attention to himself the way he should have. Isn't that bad enough?"

The water in the espresso pot began boiling, so Maria turned to invert it and let the boiling water drip down through the coffee. She remained silent while she brought the pot over to the table and then went to get the little cups and saucers. Finally, she sat down. Gennero watched her through all of this, waiting, trying to keep his face impassive and calm. Maria looked at him. Gennero was unsteady in meeting her gaze.

"You may be the big man to all of your friends out there, a *pezzo grosso*, but in here, I am still your older sister. Look at me,

Gennero. Don't disrespect me in this, in my own house. At this time in my life, with this sickness growing inside of me," she said, bringing her hand to her right breast for emphasis, "I don't need you to play games with me. When I tell you that I need your help with something, then I ask you. Right?" He nodded. "All those years ago when I needed your help, I asked you, right?"

"Yes, you did. And I was always there for you."

"Well, now, Gennero, my little brother, I'm *not* asking for you to protect me. I'm asking for you to be truthful with me."

"Maria, I have been truthful with you. I have told you the truth."

"Maybe," she said. "You've told me some of the truth, maybe a version of the truth." She looked into his face. "Gennero, I need to know the whole truth. You understand me? The *whole* truth!" she said, banging the table for emphasis. Maria poured out the two cups of coffee, spooning some sugar into each of them from the bowl on the table. When she looked up again at him, there were tears in her eyes. "Gennero," she said, "please . . . the whole truth, everything that Grady told you."

Gennero looked at her, at her watery eyes, and nodded. "Richie found the guy she was cheating with. He beat the bastard up pretty good." Maria leaned in closer, trying to maintain eye contact as Gennero looked away. She waited. "He beat him up pretty bad. Put him in the hospital."

"So? Sounds like the bastard had it coming to him."

"Yes, he probably did. Probably the girl deserved something too, deceiving him like that."

"Gennero, I don't understand. A girl leads Richie to believe they might get married, and then she cheats on him, and Richie gives the louse a good beating. What has that got to do with his ending up dead from an overdose of drugs?"

Gennero shrugged and turned up his hands. "Maria, Richie wasn't that kind of a person. He was more gentle and . . . always in a good mood. He liked everybody. As they say, he wasn't a fighter, he was a lover. You said that, remember? It wasn't like Richie to get violent. That would have been Grady's way. It might even have been my way . . . or your way if you were a man, like our Zio Dominic." Maria rolled her eyes toward the ceiling at the mention of their father's brother, known within the family to have been a fearsome hit man.

"But it wasn't Richie's way," Gennero continued. "In fact, the more I talk about it, the more unbelievable it seems. Anyway, what Grady said was that Richie was so upset by what he had done that he couldn't forgive himself. He was heartbroken about the girl and was ashamed about beating up her boyfriend. Maria, he had been using drugs heavily for a long time, both of the boys. You remember; we talked about it. We suspected that he was smoking marijuana or experimenting . . . but it was a lot more than that, much worse than we ever thought. He wasn't in his right mind. He never would have ended up like he did if it wasn't for those goddamned drugs in the first place. Maria, the drugs just took over. They ate him up, consumed him. And finally, they killed him. Now, that's it. There is no more." Gennero felt his eyes filling up, and he waved his hand to signal that he didn't want to discuss this anymore. "*Basta*," he said. "Enough."

"Bullshit!" Maria waved her finger in his face. "So Richie did drugs; he got high. His girl stepped out on him, and he beat up the bastard who dishonored him. What the hell has that got to do with his being dead?"

"Because Richie almost killed the guy! Because he was so fucking angry that he tried to kill him. You know who Richie is, for Christ's sake! He's not like the rest of us. You think of Richie, you don't think of a murderer. Richie didn't think of himself as a murderer. Richie wanted to be different from everybody else. He must have been horrified when he discovered that he could be a killer. Apparently, it was just luck that this guy survived because they thought they'd killed him."

"They?"

"Grady was with him when Richie beat up that guy. Grady, apparently, kept some other people away, kept them from interfering. Grady feels responsible too. That's why he stopped using drugs. He saw what they did to Richie, and he was afraid of what they would do to him too."

"I knew it. I knew Grady was involved. Don't tell me he wasn't responsible for this. He's the one. He's the one who's responsible for killing my Richie. I knew it. The bastard!"

"Maria! Stop it!" Gennero shouted. "Now!" Gennero glared at her, and she sank back onto her chair. "Stop this goddamned nonsense. You're talking like a crazy woman. Grady didn't kill Richie. Richie killed Richie. Nobody made him use drugs. Nobody told him how much to use or how often. Nobody is responsible for giving him a sense of honor so that he'd feel justified in seeking revenge and then feel ashamed of himself for attempting to beat someone to death. That's who he was. And who he was is what killed him. Don't demean him by taking away his responsibility for himself. He chose the course of his life, and the course of his life led him to an overdose in his own bedroom. It's not your fault, it's not my fault, and it's not Grady's fault. And it's not that bitch's fault. It was a goddamned accident. That's all that it was."

Gennero poured himself another cup of coffee, and his hand shook as he stirred in some sugar. He took a deep breath and averted his eyes.

"Gennero," Maria said, more quietly, "how do you know it was an accident?"

"You mean Richie? What else could it be?"

"Could he have done it deliberately? Killed himself?"

Gennero explained that Grady was sure that Richie's death was accidental and not a result of suicide, although no one could give a guarantee that that was the case. It was something they had to accept as the most logical explanation. Drugs had clouded his mind, and he'd made a horrible mistake and died because of it. It was nobody's fault, Gennero insisted. Just bad luck. Maria laid her head in her arms on the table and began to sob. Gennero put his arm around her shoulder, trying to soothe her as best he could. After a while, she sat up and wiped her eyes and blew her nose.

"Gennero," she said, "do you think there's anything that I could have done . . . should have done?"

"No," he said softly. "I don't think there's anything that either of us could have done differently that would have prevented this. You did everything—we both did—that seemed to make sense at the time. You can't live their lives for them, these kids. What do you think should have been done? Lock Richie up so that he couldn't live his life? It's the times, the way the world is, that's all. There's nothing else you could have done other than what you did."

"You think I did right? Giving him up? Letting Nina raise him as her own with me just being his *zia*?"

"Maria, of course it was the right thing to do. You were over forty years old, single. What were you going to do? It's not like today when nobody wants to get married, and everybody, even gays and lesbians, want to have kids. It was different then. And you were so angry about being pregnant. Don't you remember? Nah, this is crazy. Of course you did the right thing. At least he had a family with Nina and Joe. He had parents, sisters. No, Maria, you did the right thing. It's not your fault this happened. Lots of parents go through this with their own kids. I'm sure they ask themselves the same questions. Maria, you have to let them live their own lives, and sometimes it just doesn't work out the way you'd like. You just have to accept it.

"Listen," he said, "I've got to make some calls, and then Sal is coming to pick me up. Are you going to be all right?"

"Are you going to say anything to Nina?"

Gennero pushed himself up from the table and stood, his hand on her shoulder. "I don't see any reason to say anything to her. I think she knew that Richie was using more drugs than we thought he was. She may even have talked to Grady about that. She's not asking any questions. No, there's nothing to be gained by opening old wounds. We were the ones who were having the problem. And," he continued, catching her eye, "no need to say anything to Tessie, either. Understood?"

"Go inside and make your phone calls. I'll clean up everything here."

CHAPTER III

MARIA

Gennero left the kitchen, and Maria heard him slowly climbing the stairs, heading for the bathroom. She proceeded to clean up the mess from breakfast, going over the conversation in her mind and remembering. Maria wanted to believe him that she wasn't responsible for her son's death. Still, she wondered if what her brother said was entirely true. Maybe being exposed to Joe's binge drinking had had an impact on Richie. And what about Richie's sense of honor and the idea of justifiable revenge? Didn't she and the family have any responsibility for that? And all those many years ago when the boys had been underage, playing in after-hours clubs, could she have done more than she had done to make sure that Gennero had someone looking out for them?

As she stood at the sink, washing the dishes in a kind of reverie, she thought back; it was in November 1938 that she, Maria Anna Giantonio, had turned ten years old. Her huggable little brother, Gennero, had already turned eight, and she loved him dearly. Outside, they had their own groups of friends, and they did not often play with each other. But inside, they spent long hours together and were very close. Maria never needed dolls to play with. Gennero was the best toy imaginable, always willing to be whatever she suggested. They would play house or school or work, pretending that they were in Pop's store, selling groceries. Sometimes she would be magnanimous and give in to his requests for something a little more physical—playing cops and robbers, or baseball using newspaper wrapped up in string so as not to break anything. Once, while playing football (using a small pillow as the ball) in the living room, Gennero banged into a floor lamp, and when the upturned glass shade hit the wall, it shattered. A pointy shard came down and cut him along the side of his head, yielding what seemed like a huge amount of blood all over Mama's rug. And Maria still carried a scar in the palm of her right hand where another pointed piece of the glass impaled itself when it fell. There was no hiding the damage they'd done, of course, but Mama had been so upset about the blood and the frightening thought of what might have happened that the expected punishment never came.

A few times each year, Pop drove them down to Philadelphia to their grandparents' house. Because it was such a long ride from New York City, they often stayed for the entire weekend, and Maria loved those visits. She loved the big family dinners, seeing her relatives—aunts, uncles, and cousins. She loved the time the women would spend in the kitchen, cooking and preparing the wonderful, big, tasty meals—the smells, the laughter, even the arguments. She loved cooking with her *nonna* and her mother and her aunts, once in a while getting to have a sip of their wine. Younger cousins would run screaming and laughing all through the house, chasing the dog. Older cousins would be out in the small backyard or out front with other neighborhood kids, going off to the store or to the movies, where she was sure they smoked.

Maria remembered the mystery of the men in the living room with fondness, their deep voices rumbling from behind the closed French doors. Behind those doors were her *nonno*, whose voice was the deepest and most gravelly, her father, and his two brothers, her Uncle Dominic and her Uncle Tony. No women and no children were allowed near that front parlor. Maria found out later that the business being discussed often was illegal, and Gennero told her that once he'd seen them cleaning guns in there while they sat around talking, smoking cigars, and drinking wine. During dinner, children and adults sat at different tables in different rooms because of the lack of space. But after dinner, there was often singing, and Nonno would bring out his mandolin and guitar, and everyone would participate in singing the old Neapolitan songs.

It was in the following year, although before she had turned eleven, that her family made the move from New York City to Philadelphia in order to be closer to the rest of the family. Pop opened a grocery store in the Italian market, and they moved into the very house in which she was now standing, just a few blocks from where her father's store was for so many years. She still loved this house. It smelled of family and intimacy, and for her, it had a cozy feeling of security. Although some of the neighbors had died or moved away, she still knew a number of them, and she cherished the close feeling of community that she experienced here.

After Mama died in 1952, Maria continued to stay in the house, taking care of Pop, running the house, and gradually taking over his business as well. In fact, he essentially retired from the store the year following Mama's death, only occasionally coming into the store to "supervise" and lend a presence, more for company and for the socializing than for anything else. Pop was only sixty-two then. She was only twenty-five. They lived together in the house for another twenty-six years until his heart finally gave out in 1979. When Maria turned sixty-five in 1993, she sold the store to the children of a Korean neighbor and let herself rest for the first time in her life.

Maria had been washing the dishes and cleaning up in the kitchen while her mind reviewed all these old memories. She hadn't allowed herself to think of them for many years, but now it seemed they were coming back on their own. She spread out her dishtowel on the drain board to dry, went upstairs to the bathroom, and washed up. Only then did she realize that Gennero had left and was no longer in the house. She couldn't recall whether he'd said good-bye or not, so lost had she been in her recollections.

After drying her hands on her apron, Maria went into her bedroom and got some boxes down from the shelf in her closet. Here were all the pictures from earlier in her life: pictures of her, her family, schoolmates, friends from school and from the neighborhood, family gatherings from the holidays. Maria searched through them until she found what she was looking for, pictures of Richie. There were pictures of Richie as a baby with Nina, Joseph, and Rosalie; birthday pictures taken at his first birthday with Richie standing on wobbly legs, his hand in the birthday cake; pictures of the family when little Andrea was born; countless pictures of the three children together at holidays and birthdays, communions and confirmations; Richie's graduation picture from eighth grade, so handsome, she thought, despite his long hair; pictures of Richie and his friend Grady and the rest of their high school band, Onfire. There were high school graduation pictures and family pictures of Richie with various dates he'd brought home. Maria took each picture out, studied it, slowly put it back, and deliberately took out the next one. It was a slow and unhurried process.

There were no pictures of Richie's natural father, of course. Maria didn't need any pictures to help her remember him, but she had some anyway in her high school yearbook. She and Artie hadn't paid much attention to each other then. Neither one had been active in school activities, each having to work in their parents' store after school. While Maria worked in her father's store, Artie was just a block down the street in the middle of the Italian market, working in his family's butcher shop. Artie's father owned the store with his two brothers. About three of Artie's cousins worked there with him. Even after high school, while they continued to work just a block from each other and often saw each other on the street or when shopping in each other's store, they never socialized. Later, Artie said it was because he didn't have the courage to approach her. She had smiled at that but hadn't believed him for a moment. And, in truth, Maria had never been interested in him.

In 1966, their high school arranged a twenty-year reunion. Both Artie and Maria were persuaded to be on the organizing committee, and that's when they first really got to know each other. Despite the fact that Artie was married, Maria found herself becoming more and more attracted to him. He was full of energy, a real force. He was of enormous good spirits and seemed to take a primitive delight in life. The whole committee, a group of eight, met frequently, often in restaurants around the city, as well as in some of the homes.

Artie loved music and was a gifted dancer as well as a more-than-passable singer. Maria was enchanted by his extroversion, so different from herself and most of her family. Artie took her out of herself. She felt like she was experiencing life for the first time. Maria loved the rascal and rogue part of Artie, his childish and uninhibited way of spontaneously embracing life, even as she recognized that he was unstable and undependable. He was, in fact, at the age of thirty-eight, working on his second divorce. Maria easily saw that Artie drank too much and eventually learned that he had been physically as well as verbally abusive to each of his wives, although it was also true that he had picked women who seemed to enjoy provoking and waging high-pitched battles with him.

Maria sat back on the bed and remembered one incident she had witnessed at a dinner-dance given by the Ninth-Street Association, made up of all of the shopkeepers on their block. Artie was there with his second wife, Virginia. Both were drunk and sitting at a table with his cousins and their wives. Gradually their voices became louder until they reached that threshold where everyone suddenly became aware that Artie and Virginia were in the middle of a major argument.

Virginia screamed at him, calling him a lousy son of a bitch and a poor excuse for a man, and then she threw her glass of wine in his face. Artie, at first, sat back, surprised. Then he took his plate, something with a lot of tomato sauce on it, and threw it at her chest. She screamed and cursed, "You motherfucker. You prick," and ran off to the ladies' room. Artie followed her and grabbed her. They slapped each other in the face, and in trying to get away from him, she twisted her ankle on her high spike heels and fell down. Artie kicked her in the ass while she was down. Some of the men grabbed Artie and pulled him away.

Then Virginia got up and walloped him from behind with the heel of her shoe, giving him a concussion. If the men hadn't been holding him, he would have collapsed. The police came, and both were taken away.

Artie's entire family was embarrassed, but of course, they blamed it all on Virginia. Maria shook her head and smiled at the memory. Yes, she was well aware that Artie was one of those men who might make a good brother or cousin, maybe even a good friend—certainly a wonderful date and a very knowledgeable lover—but not good family material, not a good husband or father.

Still, for three years she carried on an affair with Artie, and it was the most fun she had ever had in her life. She felt no guilt about him cheating on his wife. She knew that he and Virginia would eventually get a divorce, and it wouldn't be because of her. Artie's lack of responsibility toward his two children from his first marriage and toward Virginia's daughter from her first marriage had nothing to do with her either. When she discovered she was pregnant, she told Artie that it was time for them to call it quits. They were both disappointed to see a good time come to an end, but there were no tears. She never told him she was pregnant.

Maria discussed the pregnancy with Gennero and her father, and they decided it would be best if no one locally knew that she was pregnant or that Artie Palucci was the father. Instead, Pop would run the store, and she would take a vacation. She considered going back up to New York to take some courses and maybe stay with some family there. But she decided instead to spend eight months in Italy, taking some cooking classes and learning more about the land from which her family had emigrated. When she came back with the baby, Nina and Joseph took him and raised him as their own. Later, Rosalie would chalk up her lack of memory about her brother being born as being due to the fact that she was only six and probably hadn't been aware of her mother's pregnancy.

As Maria thought about all of this, she realized that Gennero had been right again. It had been better for Richie to grow up in a complete family, even if Joseph had been an asshole. He hadn't been the worst father in the world, and he had been a reasonable male model for Richie. Better, thought Maria, than Artie would have been, and she found herself nodding her head for emphasis. Artie! He did get divorced from Virginia, who moved away, and he was still down the street, working in the butcher shop and living a few blocks away. *He has slowed down a bit,* she thought, *but he's still just a great big kid.* And she smiled a wide happy smile, remembering him as she drifted into dreamy sleep.

Chapter IV

Gennero

When Gennero came down the stairs into the foyer, he turned into the living room where, while looking out of the front windows, he made some calls on his cell phone. It wasn't long before he saw Salvatore park the limo in front of the house. He called his good-bye to Maria, put on his coat, and went down the front steps. Sal was waiting with the back door open. "Thank you, Sal. Did you have a nice lunch?"

"Yes, thank you, Mr. G. I went home for lunch." Gennero settled himself in the backseat, and Sal closed the door and went around to get into the front. "Where to, Mr. G.?"

"Downtown to Nina's office," he answered and settled back, thinking about the encounters to come during the rest of the day, Nina, and Tessie, as well as some other items of business. In a few minutes, Sal pulled along the curb in front of Nina's office building where she ran a management-consulting firm. "I shouldn't be too long," he said.

"I'll be right here, Mr. G.," Sal replied.

Inside, Gennero took the elevator up to her floor. The elevator opened into her reception area, and the receptionist immediately buzzed Nina to let her know that her father was there. By the time he approached the receptionist's desk, he saw Nina coming out of her office down the hall, a big smile on her face. "Hi, Pop, how are you?" she said, giving him a big hug. Seeing Nina always made his heart smile. *What a joy she is. Never a moment's heartache.*

"I'm good, excellent. How about you?"

"Oh, me too. Things are great," she said, taking him by the arm and leading him down the hallway to her office. As he entered it, he felt the same surge of pride he always did. The large office, with its view of the Center City skyline, was nicely decorated with good taste and style. It conveyed her success and her level of competence, while still allowing clients to feel comfortable and not intimidated. "So what's up? Anything I can do for you?"

"No, nothing. I was just thinking about you and thought I'd drop by. I had breakfast this morning with Grady Power." He paused while taking off his coat and sitting down in one of her comfortable chairs, but he noticed that she didn't change her expression as she poured some water for them and came and sat down.

"Wow," she said. "I haven't seen Grady Powers for ages. How's he doing?"

"He's getting by. He's keeping himself clean and healthy. That's the important thing."

"Yeah, I'm glad to hear that. Grady was always such a good kid, but"—she paused, searching for the right words—"he's always been so idealistic. He doesn't have any tolerance for the world the way it is. He gets enraged when people don't behave the way he thinks they should. But he and Richie were always so close; Grady used to be over to the house so often it was like having another son."

"I know," he said. "I still have those same feelings about him. But," he shrugged, "you can't live their lives for them, can you?"

"No, and thank God I don't have to. Living my own is difficult enough, what with the business and the girls."

"And how are Rosalie and Andrea?"

Nina took a sip of her water. "Okay, I guess. Poor Andrea's working her butt off at the hospital. I still don't understand why they make interns work those horrible hours. But she'll be done with that in another couple of months, and then it's on to a residency."

"Has she decided where she'll go for that?" he asked.

"No, but she has to make up her mind pretty soon. Anyway, she's so busy that I hardly get to talk to her, never mind actually see her."

"And Rosalie?"

"Oh, Pop." She sighed. "She's doing all right, I guess, but I don't know . . . I'm still having trouble with this relationship business. I mean, Denise is a sweetheart. Really, she's a lovely person. I'm just having trouble thinking of her as a daughter-in-law." Nina turned up her hands and rolled her eyes to the ceiling. "I mean, I'm just not sure how to act. I'm not used to this lesbian stuff."

Gennero smiled. "Yes, it takes some getting used to. But Rosalie, she's happy?"

"I think so. She seems to be, certainly a lot happier than she was with Rob." Nina practically shuddered at mentioning her former son-in-law's name. "Christ, I'm thrilled that she finally divorced that bastard. Even her boys are glad that he's out of the house. But that's part of it. I don't know if Rosalie is with Denise only as some kind of experiment, a reaction to what she went through with Rob, or if this is something deeper, something about who she's always been." She paused, reflecting on this question. "Anyway, yes, she seems happy, and I know that's what's really important. The funny thing is the boys really like Denise and tease her, saying that they're glad to finally have an older brother." Both she and Gennero laughed.

"Finally, I get to hear about my great-grandsons."

"Well, the latest is that Bobby, who'll be turning seventeen next month—don't forget, is looking forward to getting his driver's license and is pestering me for a car. I told him not to hold his breath. And Brian is such a charmer. He keeps getting phone calls from the girls at school. I'm going to have my hands full with him. I think I'm going to have to lock him up in a chastity belt or he'll get every girl in school pregnant." They both laughed, and it was clear that she took a lot of pride in both of her grandsons. "Listen to me," she said, "I'm talking like they're mine. Anyway, all four of them come over to the house a lot, so I get to see them, and we end up doing a lot together."

Gennero smiled and nodded enthusiastically. "I guess you would have had even more grandchildren if Richie had gotten married like he planned."

Nina sat up and raised her eyebrows. "Huh? What makes you think Richie planned on getting married?"

"Oh," Gennero muttered, "maybe I misinterpreted something Grady said. Somehow I had the impression that Richie was going with some girl who he was very serious about."

Nina furrowed her brows, thinking. "You mean Tracy Malatesta? Is that who you're thinking about?"

"Maybe. I'm not sure if Grady mentioned a name. It might have been her. Was Richie serious about her?"

"Tracy was a tramp. Richie would never have married her in a million years. She was pretty, that's all. Beautiful, actually. But I'm sure she had a bad drug problem. Not that Richie actually said that, but everything pointed to it. Richie, I know, drank, and sometimes he smoked marijuana, but I'm sure she was into cocaine, maybe even worse. She was trouble, and I told him so. No, he would never have been serious about her."

"I guess I must have misunderstood Grady. No, you're right. Richie had more sense than to get too involved with a girl like that. Anyway," he continued, "I have to tell you that I always love coming into your office. It's so comfortable and yet very professional. You've done very well, and I'm very proud of you."

Nina beamed. "I know you are, Pop. I couldn't have done it without you."

"Eh, I'm glad that I could help. But you made it into a success. This is your doing. You. You made it happen." Nina smiled again, reaching out her hand to his.

"I love you too, Pop."

Gennero pushed himself up out of the chair. "Well, I have to be going. I hope I didn't hold you up too long."

"No, not at all. Listen, why don't you and Mama come over this Sunday for dinner? The kids always love to see the two of you."

"That sounds like a good idea. I'll ask her and have her call you to let you know for sure."

"Great," she said, giving him a big hug. Then she walked him to the elevator where they said good-bye.

Gennero was thoughtful as he stood in the elevator. He'd discovered that Nina didn't know that Richie had been addicted to hard drugs and that she didn't think that Richie had been serious about Tracy, possibly because the girl was a tramp. *But,* Gennero reasoned, *if Nina was right about Tracy having a drug problem, then Richie might not have wanted his mother to know how serious he was.* The door opened, and Gennero stepped out into the lobby area. *Maybe none of this makes any difference,* he thought. But he found himself wanting to know for certain what had gone on between Richie and that girl, and it would do no harm to find out. He saw Sal spot him coming out of the door and smiled in appreciation as Sal hurried over with an umbrella, for it had started to shower again. "Turned out to be a lousy day," Gennero mumbled as he got under the umbrella.

"It'll be this way on and off," answered Sal as he opened the back door for Gennero and held the umbrella for him as he got in. When Sal got into the front, he looked into the rearview mirror, raising his eyebrows in question.

"Looks like this is a day for family visits, Sal. Let's go over to my cousin Dom's place."

"Sure thing, Mr. G.; Villa Contursi, it is."

Gennero often talked to his cousin on the phone, but he didn't usually visit Dom at his restaurant. The Villa was owned by Dominic, although his youngest son, Nick, now managed it. It was here that his own granddaughter, Rosalie, worked as a bookkeeper. Dom was often hanging out up front, greeting old friends and generally keeping an eye on things without straining himself. It would be relatively easy for Dom to have one of his friends take a look into this Tracy girl and see what turned up.

Soon, the Town Car pulled up in front of the restaurant. "Sal," Gennero said, leaning forward, "park the car and come on in. Have something at the bar while you're waiting. Tell whoever's that it's on me." After a moment of surprise, he thanked Gennero and then quickly got out with the big umbrella to escort him to the front door.

CHAPTER V

NINA

Nina blew Gennero a kiss as the elevator doors closed and then returned to her office down the hall. Pop still looked good for his age, but she thought she was beginning to notice a little bit of a stoop in his shoulders. *Well, it's not surprising if this business with Ma is beginning to get to him.* She sat down at her desk, checked that there were no messages waiting for her attention, and then turned her chair toward the window as she thought about her mother.

Her mother would probably not agree to a Sunday visit. *Every time I talk to that woman, it turns into an argument*, she thought. *All she wants to do is complain about how people are trying to hurt her, stealing her stuff, and sending her warning messages. Anything I say, she disagrees with and then accuses me of not understanding or not believing her. I don't know how he puts up with this stuff.* She picked up the phone and dialed Rosalie's home number. Rosalie answered.

"Hi, *ciucci*," she said, using her favorite term of endearment for her daughter.

"Hi, Mom. How are you?"

"Fine, honey. I just had a visit from your *nonno* and thought I'd touch bases with you."

"How is Grandpa?"

"Oh, he says everything is fine. How are you?"

"Things are fine here. The boys aren't home yet. Everything okay?"

"Oh, yeah. Everything is fine. I just wanted to let you know that I invited Grandpa and Grandma over for dinner on Sunday." She heard her daughter exhale on the other end. "Don't worry; I'm sure Grandma will say no."

"I hope so," said Rosalie. "I don't know if any of us could take her for a whole afternoon. What's happened to that woman?"

"I don't know, hon. You remember, she never used to be this way, only these last few years. Grandpa's been trying to get her to see a doctor, but she won't go. Anyway, I thought I'd give you a heads-up just in case. But I'm sure nothing will come of it."

"Well, let me know if she's coming over, all right? Then at least I can let the boys know to bring their Gameboys with them, and Denise and I can have something scheduled afterward so that we don't have to stay too long."

"I know, *ciucci.* I have problems with her myself, and she's my mother. But we all have to try to have some patience with her."

"Okay, Mom. We'll try. But let me know, all right?"

"I will. I'll call you. Hugs all around."

"You too."

Nina hung up the phone and stared out the window at the skyline. *What a cloudy, miserable rainy day,* she thought. It was in such contrast to those beautifully, crisp, clear blue September days when her parents took her on family picnics. She remembered the baskets of food: Italian bread, chicken cutlets, fried eggplant, salads, fruit, cheeses, homemade desserts. *God, I just had lunch, and all I can think of is food.* She remembered her mother from those years—young, an attractive brunette, always so well dressed. Nina remembered teasing her mother that she only owned shoes with high heels. Even her slippers or sandals had heels. Somebody had once bought Tessie a pair of sneakers, and they remained in a box in the bottom of a closet, unused. *She was a good mother then,* Nina recalled. She remembered all of the times Mom had come to school performances and parents' visiting days in elementary school. Pop was always working, it seemed. Nina remembered feeling proud and lucky that her mother was there. Some kids didn't have either of their parents show up.

Nina thought of the day when Joseph died under that car in the garage where he worked. She remembered getting the phone call at home. The first thing she'd done was to call her mother, who came right over. Together they had gone to the hospital where the emergency squad had taken him, even though he'd already died. Her mother had been a great comfort to her then and a big help with the kids. She came through for her, big time. *I have to find a way to have more patience with her,* she told herself. She decided she would make another effort to reach out to her mother . . . *But not now,* she thought, swinging her chair back to her desk and resuming her work.

CHAPTER VI

GRADY

Grady asked Sal to drop him off at a warehouse on Washington Avenue where he often volunteered to help distribute food to shelters and soup kitchens in the city. He could take home some of the food for himself, and he didn't have to show up if he didn't want to. Today it would help keep him occupied and distracted from the memories stirred up by his conversation with Gennero.

He spent the next couple of hours lifting and stacking boxes of canned food, boxes of powdered milk, and other surplus and donated food. It was good physical work, and Grady liked focusing his mind on it and keeping everything else out. Still, there was a nagging idea that kept pressing against the edge of his consciousness. *What was the story with that girl, Tracy?* When he was done, the manager thanked him for coming in and gave him two bags full of food to take home. Grady walked the few blocks back to his small apartment and cleared a space on the counter to make room for the groceries. After going to the bathroom, he went into the bedroom and flopped down on his bed.

He wanted to get in touch with Donny and Tommy, both of whom had played with him and Richie in Onfire. He knew Tommy was still playing sax around town, but he'd completely lost touch with Donny, their drummer. Once he'd made the decision to contact Tommy, he let go and fell into a light doze.

When Grady woke up, he was sitting at his kitchen table, a mess of papers spread out before him and the ashtray filled with butts. *Oh shit*, he thought. *It happened again.*

This was not the first time that Grady had woken up somewhere without having any idea of how he'd gotten there. It was disconcerting, to say the least, and sometimes embarrassing. There had been times when he'd apparently "awoken"—he didn't know what other word to use—in the middle of a conversation with somebody, with no idea at all as to what they had been talking about. Sometimes it was with people who seemed to know him, but who he didn't know. These gaps in his memory scared him. It was as if someone else had control over his life, and he was powerless to deal with it. It was embarrassing as well as frightening, and he carried a strange feeling of shame about it with him, as if he had shit in his pants. He couldn't tell anybody. It was just too weird and too humiliating.

Grady hadn't had a blackout that he'd been aware of for quite some time, and so this incident was particularly upsetting because it was unexpected. He lit a cigarette and looked over the papers on the table in front of him—some names, telephone numbers, addresses. He saw Tommy's name with a telephone number under it, but there was also another number he recognized as an address. It was circled. It occurred to him that he might have called Tommy, had a conversation, and Tommy had given him this address. But was it Tommy's, Tracy's, or somebody else's?

How the hell can I call Tommy back and ask him? He'll think I'm completely off my nut. It was too upsetting to contemplate exposing himself as being so out of control. He couldn't even remember a simple phone conversation that had just taken place. Grady looked at the clock. Four thirty. He'd gotten home around three, so this had all taken place sometime within the past hour and a half. He shook his head and slammed his temples with his fists. *Fuck!* he thought. *Goddamn it.*

Suddenly, he got up from the table, grabbed his cigarettes and the paper with Tommy's number and the circled address, and left the apartment. The address was in the residential section of Fitler Square, so Grady took a bus north and then transferred to the #40 going west on Lombard Street to Twenty-Fourth, where he got off. He thought that first he would see what kind of building the address was and then decide from there what to do. To his surprise, it was a coffee shop. Grady ordered a coffee and then sat down and waited for something to happen. A few minutes later, Tommy entered and came right over to the table. Grady was surprised but relieved.

"Hey, how the fuck are ya?" asked Tommy. "You look fit, man. You working out again?"

"Hey, good to see you. You're looking prosperous."

"Yeah, well, like I told you, I was at work all afternoon. Sorry if I'm late. I had trouble getting out."

Grady nodded, and a hint of an amused smile showed itself. "No. No problem. I just got here myself. What kind of work did you say you did again?"

"Electronic appliances. You know, sound systems, microwaves, shit like that. Gotta get dressed for the part, you know? Not like playing a gig. Different costume."

"Yeah. So now you're part of the system, huh?"

"Hey, you know, can't quit the day job. Got to pay the bills, feed the baby chicks."

"You got kids?"

"Shit, yeah. We have a little girl. I swear, Grady, it's a gas. She is just so goddamned cute. I could eat her up."

"Hey, better be careful," Grady joked, waving his finger at Tommy as if he were a naughty boy.

"Hey, don't even joke about it. No, I'm serious. She is just too scrumptious. I couldn't be happier. How 'bout you? You with anybody?"

Grady gave a little shrug of his shoulders. "Yeah, there's somebody I've been seeing for a while, but I don't know if it's going anywhere."

"You meet her in the program?"

Grady looked at him. *So,* he thought, *I must have told him I stopped using and am in the program.* He just nodded an affirmative.

"Hey, you've got to be careful, man. Don't take the big step with just any chick. Marriage is a hard gig, man. I'm really lucky that Dolores is such a stand-up broad. I really stepped in shit with that woman, I'm telling you. A good partner is a real asset. I hope it works out for you."

"Thanks," said Grady. "I'm glad to hear that you and your wife are doing so well. That's really great." Grady was racking his brain to try to remember if he knew this girl, Dolores, or not. "Did I know Dolores?" he finally asked.

Tommy thought. "I'm not sure if you ever met. We went out a couple of times with Richie and his girl, but I don't remember if you ever met her. She was from Jersey, went to school here in Philly, and worked as a dancer until we started the family. Short, petite, dark hair. Here, wait, I have pictures," he said as he reached into his back pocket for his wallet.

"I might have known," said Grady, laughing. "A proud daddy can't go around without pictures of the family."

"Better believe it," said Tommy, pulling out a portrait shot of the two women in his life. "Here, that's Dolores and Kristen, the baby."

"Good Italian name," joked Grady.

"Hey, you know, Dolores really liked the name, and I don't need to shout to the world that I'm Italian. 'Hey, world, I'm Tomaso Massimo, and this is my girl, Gina Lolabrigida!'" They both laughed.

The waitress came over, and Tommy ordered a coffee.

"So what're you doing with yourself, man?"

"Nothing much," answered Grady. "I help out here and there. Some warehouse stuff, stores in the neighborhood, stuff for my uncle sometimes. I don't have the tolerance to do anything regular. I can't make any commitment ahead of time. I never know when I'm going to explode," he said, laughing. He didn't mention that he received SSI, disability insurance from Social Security because of his mental condition. He was definitely glad to get it but also recognized the stigma in being labeled a wacko, so he never mentioned it to anyone, not even his Uncle G.

Tommy looked at him and became serious. *Fine,* thought Grady, *so he knows about that too.* "So," Grady said, "did I mention on the phone why I called?"

"Are you kidding me, man? You were all secrets. CIA stuff, hush-hush. Can't talk about it on the phone. It really got my curiosity up, I'll tell you that."

Grady took this in. It was reassuring that even in one of these blackout spells or whatever they were, he could maintain some self-discipline. "No, it's nothing like that. No big deal. It's just that I was talking to my uncle—you know, Mr. G. We were talking over old times at breakfast, and Richie's name came up, and I remembered he was pretty serious about a girl named Tracy. Do you remember her?"

Tommy recalled that he and Dolores had double-dated with Richie and the girl, whose name was Tracy Malatesta. He then told Grady that after Richie died, Tracy started dating another guy who worked as a VP for a bank over on Market Street. "Funny guy, walks with a slight limp and has a little speech impediment from some accident or something." Tommy then remembered that Tracy and the VP got married and moved out to the Main Line, the ritzy suburbs west of Philadelphia.

"Do you remember their last name?" asked Grady.

Tommy thought. Then he shook his head no. "I think . . . it's on the tip of my tongue, but I can't . . . I don't know. Maybe Dolores might know. I think she might have had some contact with Tracy after she got married. You know women; they have memories like elephants. She probably remembers everything Tracy ever wore when we went out together." Grady nodded hopefully. Tommy continued, "Yeah, let me check with Dolores, and I'll get back to you."

"You have my number?" asked Grady.

"Probably, but you better give it to me again," he said, taking out a business card from his wallet. Grady gave him the number, and Tommy wrote it down and put the card back into his wallet.

"Wait," Grady said, "give me one of those cards."

"Sure, here," handing one to Grady.

"Thanks, man," said Grady. "I appreciate this."

"So what do you want with Tracy? You already have a girl," Tommy joked.

Grady smiled. "Just a couple of loose ends I have to tie up. Put the house in order, you know?" he said, pointing to his head. "Too much messed up that I need to straighten out."

"Hey, when you finish up, you can start on mine." They both laughed.

Chapter VII

Gennero

Dominic was sitting at the bar, talking to Mickey the bartender, when he saw Gennero coming through the front door. "Hey, look who's here. What a surprise." Dom gave Gennero a big hug. "Oh, it's good to see you," he said, giving his younger cousin a kiss on the cheek.

"It's good to see you too," said Gennero, returning the embrace. "I happened to be in the neighborhood and thought I'd come in out of the rain and get a free cup of espresso."

"Of course. *Mi casa es tu casa.* Come on. Let's go sit in the back."

When Sal came in from parking the car, he saw his boss sitting at a table in the back with the owner, Dominic Giantonio. Sal remembered hearing the stories about Dominic's father, Dominic Sr., who had been a reputed hit man for the Mafia. It was the only hint of violence that Sal had ever heard that had any connection at all with Mr. G. Still, the potential for some sort of physical danger always seemed to be there, a watchfulness, an alertness that kept you on your toes. That was why Mr. G. insisted that he wear a lightweight armored vest and carry the gun, which he was licensed to use. Sal went over to the bar to say hi to Mickey and ordered a cup of coffee to take the chill off.

"So," Dom said, "to what do I owe this pleasure? You never 'just happen' to do anything. I know you. You always have a purpose in mind."

Gennero smiled broadly. "Dominic, you must learn to be patient." He laughed. "How do you expect to grow old and fat if you can't wait for anything, eh?"

"Hey, seventy-eight isn't old? At my age, I can't afford to spend too much time waiting for something to develop; otherwise I might not get to enjoy it." The two cousins laughed. They had known each other for seventy years, since they were little boys when their parents had brought them on family visits to their grandparents' house. They enjoyed busting each other.

"Is Rosalie here?" asked Gennero.

Dom shook his head. "No, she only comes in four days a week. She'll be in tomorrow. Why? Did you want to see her?"

"No. Actually, I'm glad she's not here. I'd rather we keep this between ourselves."

"Hey, now you've got me curious. What's up?"

"No, nothing like that. This is a personal thing."

Dominic waited. A waiter came over and asked if he could get them anything. Dom ordered a pot of espresso and then looked at Gennero. "You want something to put in the coffee?"

"Some Amaretto would be nice."

Dom nodded to the waiter, who then left. "So something personal? What, you want to use my apartment for a matinee, eh?"

Gennero smiled and shook his head. "No, I'm way past that kind of thing. Don't forget, I'm almost as old as you."

"Speak up," said Dom, leaning across the table and cupping his hand to his ear. "I can't hear so good." Both of them laughed.

"I can't," said Gennero. "I forgot what I was saying."

The waiter came with the coffee and a bottle of Amaretto. They settled back and relaxed. "So, Gennero, what can I do for you?"

"You remember when my grandson, Richie, died a couple of years ago?"

"Yeah, they found him dead in his apartment from an overdose of heroin, as I recall."

"Yes. It was very sad. A tragedy. It came as a shock. We had no idea that he used drugs other than some occasional pot, you know? I've always had some questions about it, what really happened. Was it some kind of setup? Suicide? An accident?" He paused and, looking at Dominic, leaned forward and lowered his voice. "Do you remember when he was born?"

Dom pushed himself back from the table and frowned, thinking. "Yeah, there was something about his birth. I'm not quite sure . . . it was a big surprise. Nobody had known that Nina had been pregnant . . . I'm not sure. What about it?"

"This is between us, of course," Gennero said.

"Of course."

"Richie was Maria's kid."

Dominic's eyes nearly popped out of his head. "No shit!" he said.

Gennero continued. "My father, Umberto, was still alive then, and he knew. We thought it was better if Nina raised the baby. She was still married to that idiot, Joey, then. Naturally, Maria always carried Richie close to her heart, you know? She's never been able to come to terms with his death. It just doesn't make sense to her. If he was so addicted to drugs, how come we never saw it? How could the whole family be so blind that none of us picks up on it?"

"That makes sense," Dom agreed. "Granted, he was in the music business, and those guys have a reputation for using. Still, you're right. I never picked up that he was an addict. I knew he drank his share. Maybe whatever I saw, I just attributed to booze. I don't know."

"Right. Maybe that's what we all did. But right now I need to find out." Gennero paused, reached over, and poured a cup of espresso. Deliberately, he spooned in some sugar and then added a little bit of Amaretto. When he finished, Dom did the same, and they sat back and sipped their coffees.

Gennero continued. "Maria went to the doctor's last week for a yearly checkup, and it looks like she needs to have surgery."

"No!" Dom exclaimed. "What kind? What's wrong?"

"Breast cancer," said Gennero somberly. "Looks like she's going to need a mastectomy."

"Oh, Gennero, I'm so sorry to hear this. Does anybody else know?"

Gennero shook his head. "No. She doesn't want anyone else to know yet. She's scared to death, of course, and feels she's got to put this whole thing to rest before she goes under the knife."

"Of course. What can I do?"

"Dom, all of this is very awkward for me. You know me. I pride myself on being able to let go of things. Not everything works out the way we want, but we have to accept reality and move on."

Dom nodded.

"So," Gennero continued, "I don't feel comfortable rummaging around in the past like this, looking into people's private lives. I mean, it's not like it's a business thing, you know? This is strictly a personal thing. But with Maria having cancer, I . . . you know, I just have to do this thing for her. If anything needs to be put right, then I need to find out about it."

"Of course, Gennero. Hey, if she wasn't my cousin, I would have married Maria myself. I always loved that woman. What can I do?"

"Apparently, Richie was mixed up with some woman named Tracy. Her last name might have been Malatesta. And, she probably had a problem with drugs. She could be married now, with a different name. That's all I know."

Dom made some notes on the back of a business card and stuck it in his wallet. "Don't worry, Gennero. I have friends. I'll have her checked out. Do you want me to call you?"

"Yeah, I'd appreciate that, whenever it is."

"Done," he said.

Gennero looked across the table at his cousin and saw the affection in his eyes. "I didn't want to do this myself. I don't want it coming back to me. People asking questions. Maria doesn't need any extra grief right now, and there's no reason for Nina or Rosalie or Andrea to have to hear anything."

"I understand, Gennero. Don't worry about it. I'll take care of it."

"Thank you. You know, I always thought you had a little bit of a thing for my sister."

Dominic smiled. "Yeah, I really did. Aside from being a real looker, one of the things I always admired about her was her strength, the way she took over that store and ran it. And on top of that, she kept your father's affairs in order and took care of him. She could always be trusted, a strong woman." The two men slipped into a little bit of reverie, recalling the old days.

"So," Gennero asked suddenly, "how is your family? How are you doing?"

"Eh." Dom shrugged. "What's to complain? The kids are all doing well, all healthy. The grandchildren are growing. Nicky is doing a fabulous job running this place. He lets me hang out and play supervisor. What the hell, it keeps me off the streets."

"And how are you doing physically?"

"You know, Gennero, the usual. My prostate keeps me running to the bathroom all the time, and I'm more creaky and cranky than I'd like to be, but, all in all, I'm lucky to be alive, never mind doing well. How about you—aside from this other stuff, I mean?"

"Pretty much the same as you. No major complaints. Tessie . . . she's having a hard time with life."

"Yeah, I hear from Rosalie. Tessie is depressed and always complaining about something. Maybe a little paranoid?"

"Yeah," Gennero admitted. "It's always something. But she refuses to go for any kind of help and won't see a doctor, not even a priest. She doesn't trust anybody. Actually," Gennero confided, "it's very difficult. That's the main reason I'm still involved in the business. I need to get out of the house. Dom, this is just between us. I hate to go home."

"How long has she been this way? 'Cause the Tessie I remember was never like this. She was always very outgoing and fun to be around."

"I know," agreed Gennero. "But these last five or six years, it's been gradually getting worse. I talked to some doctors, but they don't have any answers. Maybe this, maybe that. Who knows? But what the hell; that's life, you know. We had almost fifty good years together before this nonsense started, so I can't complain. Besides, what good would it do? And like I said, it gets me out of the house."

"You're a marvel, Gennero. You always manage to put a positive spin on things."

"Well, maybe, but I like to think that I can smell shit as well as anybody. I just don't complain and demand that it smell like something else. Shit is shit, but it's part of life."

Dom shook his head in mock disbelief. "Gennero, you're incorrigible."

Gennero reached for his coat, and Dom pushed himself away from the table.

"Gennero, I want to thank you for putting me on to Rosalie. She's perfect for this place. I don't know what Nicky and I would do without her. It's wonderful to have somebody who's not only competent, but who's also a member of the family, someone who can be trusted."

Gennero tilted his head to one side. "Eh, I'm glad that it worked out for you—and for her. But that's what families are for, right?"

Dominic helped Gennero with his coat and walked him to the front door. Sal saw them coming and left a tip for Mickey and put on his own coat. By the time Gennero reached the front door, Sal was waiting for him with the umbrella. Dominic and Gennero embraced again.

"I'll call you," Dom said. Gennero nodded, gave Dom's arm a squeeze, and then walked out into the rain with Sal.

CHAPTER VIII

GENNERO

Riding home, Gennero watched the rain streaming against the windows and thought about the conversation he just had with his cousin, Dominic. He remembered a time when they were visiting his grandparents in Philadelphia, before his father moved their whole family down from New York. All of the women were gathered in Nonna's kitchen, preparing a meal. Some of the older cousins were outside, and Maria and the other little girls were either helping in the kitchen or running around the large Victorian house.

Dominic must have been eight or nine years old, so Gennero would have been four or five, and nobody was paying attention to them. Dom took him into the bathroom off of the kitchen and offered to show Gennero how the plumbing worked. The two of them made repeated trips through the kitchen to reach the cellar stairs where they went up and down carrying rags to wipe up water and pipe wrenches that were almost as big as they were. Dom showed him how to turn off the water to the toilet and to the sink. Then they proceeded to dismantle everything they could—pipes to the sink, faucets, everything. They were in the process of trying to disconnect the toilet from the floor when one of their uncles, Uncle Tony, walked in on them.

Christ, thought Gennero, a big smile on his face, *was there hell to pay over that.* "Who's supposed to be watching these kids, for Christ's sake? What the hell are you women doing anyway? Can't you see what's going on?" And so on. Gennero chuckled to himself remembering that episode. He always looked up to

Dominic after that, revering him as some kind of genius because he knew how to do that stuff.

He remembered, too, a time when he and Dom had gone down the cellar steps and seen their grandfather using the toilet down there to take a crap, his pants and underwear around his ankles. They could smell his farts, and they held their noses at the stink. But Nonno was sitting there, oblivious, playing his mandolin—just sitting there, picking out some folk melodies from the old country. The two boys were fascinated, sitting on the steps in the shadows, holding their noses and listening to their grandpa playing. *It was wonderful*, thought Gennero. *Those were such happy times*. After they moved to Philadelphia, the four years separating Dom and him seemed to make a difference. Suddenly, he was too young for Dom to spend time with him. But they retained affection and respect for each other. He knew that Dom would find out whatever he could concerning Tracy. Then he'd have to decide what to do next.

It seemed as if no time had passed at all when Gennero noticed that Sal was turning onto his little street. Almost home. Sal pulled up in front of his boss's house and got out to open the back door for him. As Gennero lifted himself out of the car, he noticed that it had stopped raining. Well, the rain was good for the bushes and the grass. He looked approvingly at the modest landscaping in front of his little, two-story brick house. He liked it here. He liked feeling at home, the sense of belonging, the connection he had with some of his neighbors. "Thank you, Sal," he said after getting out of the car. "No need to walk me in. Tomorrow . . ." Gennero took a moment to think over his schedule. "Tomorrow, come by about nine o'clock, all right?"

"Sure thing, Mr. G. Of course, I'll be out here waiting for you as usual."

"I know, Sal. You're very dependable." Gennero tilted his head and gave an approving look to Salvatore. "Yes, you are a great comfort to me, Sal. Your parents would be very proud of you, the man you grew into."

Sal blushed at this comment. "Thank you, Mr. G. I try to do my best."

"I know you do," he said, and he turned to walk into his house. Gennero paused at his front door, took a deep breath, and used his key to open the door.

He heard Tessie in the kitchen, and after taking off his coat and hanging it up in the front closet, he walked through the small hallway into the kitchen. "Ciao," he said, approaching her from behind as she stood at the sink, rinsing dishes. Even as he anticipated an unpleasant interaction, Gennero still appreciated the view from behind Theresa's petite and shapely build. Her hair, once a glorious, soft, dark brown, was now gray and frizzy (he couldn't remember the last time Theresa had been to a beauty parlor), but she still had a good figure.

"How was your day?"

"I really don't want to talk about it," she said, shrugging off his tentative embrace. "You wouldn't believe me anyway."

Gennero removed his hands from her shoulders and sat at the kitchen table. "Tessie, let's not start right off with a goddamned argument as soon as I walk into the house. I'm interested in how you are and in how your day went. It would be nice if you'd share that with me. If you don't want to, then don't. It's up to you." He got up and took a glass from the cabinet and went to the refrigerator where he got a carafe of wine. Gennero poured himself a glass of wine, and after returning the bottle to the refrigerator, he sat down at the kitchen table again and tried to relax.

Tessie continued to fuss at the sink and stove, preparing the supper. He'd wait for her to begin the conversation. He knew that she would be unable to stop herself from complaining about whatever it was that had gone wrong during the day.

Tessie came over with dishes and utensils and began setting the table. Gennero caught her eye and smiled but didn't say anything. Neither did she. Finally, she brought the food—some broiled fish, spinach, spaghetti, and a salad. "Ah," he sighed, realizing he was giving in by making the first sound, "this looks wonderful. Would you like some wine?"

Tessie shook her head no and sighed heavily as she sat down. "I got another hang-up on the phone today," she said.

Gennero looked at her. "A hang-up?"

"Yes, Gennero, a hang-up. The phone rang, and when I answered it, the person on the other end hung up. I think whoever called was just checking to see if someone was here. I'm telling you, Gennero, I don't feel safe here anymore. I know that we're being watched."

Gennero knew better than to respond in any way that was not in agreement with her. However, he did want to be helpful and reassuring if it was possible. Although, he thought, he had been remarkably unsuccessful at that over these past few years.

"Tessie, who do you think would be watching us?"

"Who? Who wouldn't be watching us? The neighbors, the FBI, the CIA, people who have it in for us. Gennero, I keep telling you, and you don't want to face up to reality. Somebody wants us dead. I didn't tell you, but last night when I got up to go to the bathroom, I noticed there was a plane in the sky shining its light right in the bathroom window, trying to look at me. I had to pull the shade down. I didn't wake you because I wanted you to get your sleep, but it frightened me so that I couldn't get back to sleep for over an hour."

Gennero took a deep breath and tried to think. This was beyond him. He felt completely powerless and had no idea of what to do. "Tessie," he said soothingly, "you've been afraid a lot these past few years. So many things frighten you—hang-ups, airplanes, neighbors raising or lowering their shades or blowing their horns. And every time, I've tried to tell you that I think everything is going to be all right, that we are safe. Even so, we put in the security system, and you know that Sal is with me all the time to protect me if I need him. And in all this time, nothing has happened, has it?"

"No, not yet. They're trying to drive me crazy first, and then they'll kill us or Nina or the girls or the great-grandchildren.

They're just playing with us. Why can't you see that?" He saw that she was getting agitated again, and, abruptly, she pushed her plate away from her.

"I don't know how you can be so calm and go on eating when I'm being harassed like this every day. I thought you loved me, Gennero, but you don't love me. If you loved me, you wouldn't let all of this go on. You'd do something to stop it."

"Tessie, what do you want me to do other than what I've already done?"

"I've told you. We have to move. We can't stay here, Gennero. If we stay here, either I'll go mad or I'll have to kill myself before they kill me."

"Tessie, please, be reasonable. I told you, we can't move now. My business, the kids, everything. Besides, what makes you think you wouldn't feel the same way if we lived somewhere else? If somebody wanted to make trouble for you or for us that badly, why would they stop if we moved?"

Gennero was losing his appetite. *Jesus Christ, is there nothing I can do or say that will calm her down?* "Tessie, let me say this again, for the millionth time. If these things—if everything is so upsetting to you—why don't you take something for your nerves to help you calm down a little so that you can deal with everything more easily. Maybe you'd feel safer."

"Gennero, how can you be so stupid, hmmm? It's not me who needs tranquilizers. It's not me who's crazy. It's *them!*" she screamed. Her lips trembled. "They're the ones who need help, those crazy bastards. Why are they doing this to us, Gennero? Why?" She got up from the table, scraping the remains of her dish into the sink. She was crying.

"Tessie," he said gently, "I just want you to be less upset. I thought . . . I think if you'll take something to help calm yourself down, you'll be less upset. Maybe you'll be able to sleep better, eat better. Look at you, for Christ's sake. You have trouble eating you're so upset. You're losing weight. I'm concerned about you. That's all. I want to see you happy again. I wish, Tessie, I wish

I could make you happy again. That's all." Gennero shook his head. He didn't know what else to say.

"I saw Nina today. I was downtown and decided to drop in on her at her office. She wants us to come over for dinner, maybe this Sunday. She said the kids want to see us. I told her I'd check with you."

Tessie continued to fuss with things, keeping her back to him, not answering.

Gennero continued, making an effort to sound natural and to draw her into a more normal conversation. "I think that would be nice, don't you? We haven't been over to Nina's in a long time."

"I told you, Gennero. I don't feel safe going out. Even to Nina's. I don't want to put them in danger."

"I tell you what then. Let's have them over here for dinner."

Tessie turned around to face him. "Have all of them over here? Nina, the girls, the boys, everybody?"

"As many as we can get. Andrea would probably have to be at the hospital. Apparently, they have her working all the time."

"Gennero, use your head. How am I supposed to make dinner for everybody, do the shopping, clean the house? I'm afraid to even go out to the supermarket."

"Tessie, for Christ's sake . . . I'm just trying to say it would be nice if we could have a visit with our daughter and granddaughter and great-grandsons. I don't care how we do it. How would you like to do it? We can go there. They can come here. We can go out someplace. What would you be most comfortable with?"

Tessie leaned against the sink. "I don't know." She sighed. "Let me think about it."

"That would be good, Tessie. Think about it. Whatever I can do to make you more comfortable with it, I will do it if it's humanly possible. If you want Sal to be there—"

"No," she interrupted. "You know I don't like that man. I don't like the way he looks at me. It's not right. I don't know how you can keep him around when he looks at your wife like that. Sometimes, Gennero, I don't understand you."

Gennero bit his lip. Finally, he spoke. "Well, if I ever see him looking at you disrespectfully, I will kill him myself. But until then, I need him . . . and I keep him away from you. I was just trying to say that if it made you feel safer, I could have someone else there. It wouldn't have to be Sal. In fact, if you wanted, I could have somebody stay with you during the day if it would make you feel better."

"Gennero. *Stupido.* How can I have somebody else here? Spying on me? Going through my things? Stealing things? We tried that, remember? I can't trust anybody. No, I don't want anybody here in the house. Definitely not."

Gennero heaved a sigh of submission. "Okay," he agreed. "Anyway, you think about Sunday. It would be nice if we could work something out. And by the way, the supper, it was very good, delicious." He got up and started toward their living room. "I'm going to watch some news. Would you make some espresso?"

Tessie nodded.

As Gennero walked to his favorite chair in the living room and sat down with a sigh, he knew from past experience that Tessie was exasperated with him. She believed that her complaints of harassment rolled off his back, that he didn't care what happened to her. But whatever he did only made matters worse. He didn't know what else he could do to make things better. And he was sure that she believed that all he thought about was his own comfort and his goddamned espresso.

CHAPTER IX

GRADY

Grady and Tommy shook hands and gave each other a brief hug before saying good-bye outside of the coffee shop and going their separate ways. Grady started walking toward the bus stop to go back home and looked at his watch. It was after five thirty, time to get something to eat before going to his seven o'clock NA meeting where he'd meet up with Karen. He walked over to South Street where he took the bus back down Fourth Street to Jimmy's, for one of their infamous cheesesteak sandwiches. Afterward, he took the bus north on Third Street into Old City to his meeting. It was about a quarter to seven when Grady walked into the meeting room in the church annex. A couple of his buddies were there, setting up for coffee, and Grady decided to lend a hand. Just before seven, Karen came in and spotted him right away.

"Hi, honey," she said, a little out of breath from rushing. They embraced, and she gave him a big kiss. "So how're you doing?" she asked.

"I'm good," he answered, "how 'bout you?"

"Great." Karen laughed. "It was a good day. The rain got a lot of people in off of the street, so tips were better than usual."

Karen worked as a waitress in a pub in Center City. They had often argued about her putting herself in harm's way, working in a place that served alcohol, but she always reassured him that booze was not her thing and she had no temptations along that line. He still thought she was in denial about that but wasn't going to lock horns with her over it. Her sobriety wasn't his business, after all. His only responsibility to her was to love her as best he could. Still, her job gave him cause to hesitate in trusting her, and it resulted in his holding back even more than usual on his feelings. For her part, Karen often accused him of being distant, but she made it clear that she saw his emotional distance as strictly a defect that he had, and nothing that she had any responsibility for.

"Good for you. Then you can treat for eats later on."

"Go on," she said in mock anger. "Since when am I your mommy and have to feed you din-din?"

But Grady didn't see the humor in it and glared at her before turning away to continue setting out the preparations for coffee.

Karen rubbed his back. "Hey, I was joking, that's all."

"Yeah, I know. So was I," he said without turning back to her. "Don't mind me. I'm just having another one of those days."

"Okay," she said. "Listen, I'm going to go to the john. We'll hook up later?"

Grady nodded assent but kept at his task.

Karen went to the restroom, and soon their twelve-step Narcotics Anonymous meeting was called to order. Afterward, they sought each other out.

"Hey," he said, "I'm sorry about before."

"That's all right," said Karen, giving his hand a soothing and reassuring rub. He nodded, indicating that he thanked her for accepting his apology and for accepting him in all his fucked-up glory.

"So pizza or Chinese?" he asked.

"Chinese," she answered, and they began their walk toward Chinatown.

Later, in the restaurant, Karen said, "So are you going to tell me what went down today to get you so jumbled up?"

Grady looked at her as if to say, "Who, me?"

"You said so yourself, that you were having a bad hair day. Something must have set you off. Look, Grady, I'm not being nosy. It's just that I see you're preoccupied and touchy, and I thought you might feel better if you talk about it, whatever the hell *it* is."

Grady looked away. "Yeah, I know I'm out of it, but it's nothing I can talk about." He paused. "I don't mean that it's secret and that I don't want to share it; I only mean that I can't put it into words."

Karen waited, questioning him with her eyes.

"It's just that some old shit got stirred up about an old friend of mine, and it's like there's somebody up here," he said, pointing to his head, "who's having a bowling contest. Stuff, shit, is careening around up there and it's . . . I don't know, like a distraction. I can't concentrate. There's this shit going on that's getting me all jammed up. Like there's somebody in here with a jackhammer, making it impossible to carry on a normal conversation."

Karen nodded. "What old friend?" she asked.

"You didn't know him. A guy I used to play with. We grew up together. He died about two years ago—from an overdose of H."

"So," she continued, "what brought all this up today?"

"Just stuff, you know. Something reminded me, and I've been thinking about it. I can't shake it."

"You want to talk about it?"

"Look, if I wanted to talk about it, I would. I'd have brought it up in the meeting. It's too upsetting. I don't want to talk about it, and I want you to shut up about it, okay?"

Karen sat back, stunned, staring at him her mouth open. "Well, excuse me. I was just trying to be helpful. You know, like friends and lovers are supposed to be to each other. Supportive? You know the concept? People showing an interest in another person? Caring."

Both of them sat in silence, Karen staring at Grady, and Grady sitting back, fixated on his empty plate.

"Fine," she said and began to rummage in her purse for her wallet. Grady reacted to this by going for his own wallet. "Don't bother," she said. "It's my treat, remember?"

"What are you talking about? That was a joke. I don't expect you to treat me."

"Yeah, sure."

"Listen," he said, reaching across the table and grabbing hold of her arm in an iron grip. "Don't go getting bitchy on me. I don't have to talk about something if I don't want to. You don't have any fucking right to push me on that. So don't go getting huffy and sarcastic just because I don't want to talk."

"You never want to talk." They glared at each other.

"That's not true," Grady said, more calmly, letting go of her arm and sitting back. He got money from his wallet to cover his share of the bill and put it on the table. "It's not true that I never want to talk. In fact, you may have more shit secreted away than I do. So don't go laying that trip on me. Look to yourself first."

"What the fuck are you talking about?"

"What am I talking about? I'll tell you what I'm talking about. For starters, what about how long you've been clean? Huh?"

Karen gave him a puzzled look and sat back. "What about how long I've been clean?"

Grady looked at her with a cynical smile on his face. "Well, how long have you been clean and sober?"

"You know. I just got my eighteen months' pin two weeks ago."

"Yeah, I know you just got the pin. I know what you've been telling everybody about being straight for eighteen months. But what I asked you was how long you've been clean and sober? Hmmm?"

Karen averted her eyes as the realization came over her. Grady waited for her to come to terms with her lapse. She looked at him and threw up her hands. "Okay, I know. You're thinking about that time when I used the pain medication from the dentist, right?"

Grady leaned in. "Now why would I be thinking of that?"

"All right, technically, that's a slip . . ."

"Technically?"

"Yeah. Look, I know the program frowns on medication, but that was for a fucking root canal. I took it. I stopped. I've been clean ever since. I don't consider that a slip, the legitimate use of medication for pain. I don't think I've been dishonest about that."

"Oh, no? So if you were so honest, did you ever mention it in any of the meetings? Did you ever tell me that you had a prescription for the whole week and that you finished the whole prescription—not only finished the whole prescription, but finished it in two fucking days?"

"I was in pain, you fucker. If you'd ever gone to the dentist to have oral surgery, you'd know what the fuck I'm talking about."

"Don't give me that crap. I've had more goddamn pain than you can even conceive of. Look, Karen, you're not talking to your parents. I'm a fucking junkie too, remember? Don't try to shit me. I've been there. I know the score. You're a junkie! Don't try to make believe you're just some poor, innocent, normal girl who won't say shit if she has a mouthful and can't take some itty-bitty pain from the bad, old dentist. You can't do drugs. I can't do drugs. Not ever. You fucking know that. It doesn't mean a thing whether it's prescribed or not. We're addicted, you and I. We're not like 'normal' people. We don't have the luxury of doing what normal people can do. You never told the dentist that you were a junkie and couldn't take painkillers—"

"But I—"

"Don't fucking interrupt me!" Grady was leaning across the table and talking to her through his teeth, the cords in his neck bulging, his face red. Saliva foamed at the corner of his mouth. "You didn't tell him because you wanted to get your hands on his shit. And you couldn't wait to gobble them up and get high. You never said a fucking word to anybody because you knew you had fucked up, and you wanted to get away with it. You didn't want anybody to know . . . anybody, including me, because you didn't want to face what you did."

Karen slumped in her seat, unable to meet his gaze.

Grady was trembling from rage. "I never said anything to you about it because it wasn't my business. But don't come on like you never hold anything back and somehow I'm obligated to talk about stuff that I'm not ready to deal with. Do you fucking understand?"

Karen nodded. There were tears in her eyes as she looked up at him. "Okay," she said quietly. "Okay."

WEDNESDAY

MARCH 3, 2004

CHAPTER X

GRADY: RECURRENT DREAMS

When Grady opened his eyes and sat up in bed, he had no idea where he was. His heart was pounding. He was having trouble catching his breath. He felt terrified and totally confused, as if in the midst of some disaster, but not knowing at all what the danger was. Then he realized that he was in bed, Karen's bed. He looked down and saw the shape of her beside him. He continued to sit there, propping himself up on his elbows but letting his eyes close. Almost immediately, he found himself recalling a dream. Or was it a dream? It seemed more like a memory, but not a memory of anything he actually recalled having experienced. *This is fucked up,* he thought. But even so, he found himself returning to the dream and reexperiencing it.

He is little, a baby maybe, but standing up . . . in a crib? He's watching a woman, a young woman with long, blonde hair. She's walking back and forth, talking, but he doesn't understand what she's saying. He can see her in another room—a kitchen with linoleum on the floor, an old white stove, a sink with a curtain hanging down in front of it. He's crying. The woman comes over. She feels like his mother. He wants her. She is soothing him; her hand is cool, caressing his face and head, laying him down. There's a man behind her talking. She turns to the man, caresses his face, and kisses him. Grady is confused. She turns out the light. It's dark, and she closes the door. He feels angry and frightened, but he doesn't cry. He falls asleep.

Karen gently pushed against his shoulder. "Grady," she whispered. "Grady, wake up."

Slowly, Grady opened his eyes. He seemed confused and dazed as he looked at her and then around the room. "Grady, you were having a bad dream."

Once again, Grady looked at her blankly, his furrowed eyebrows reflecting his confusion, as if he didn't know who she was or where he was.

"Grady, are you all right?"

He was having trouble getting his mouth to work. Finally, he asked, "What day is this?"

"It's Wednesday morning, honey. We're at my place. Remember? We came here after we went for Chinese last night. We came home. We made great love. Is it coming back to you?"

"Yeah. It's coming back to me now. Christ, I feel like I was in never-never land." Then he looked at her as if seeing her for the first time. "What was I doing? I mean talking or what?"

"Just a lot of moaning, actually more like whimpering, almost crying. I thought I should wake you." Karen looked at him with concern.

Grady reached up and pulled her close, kissing her forehead. "Thanks."

"Do you remember what you were dreaming about?"

"A little bit," he said. "It was . . . like I was a baby, but with a different mother, a young mother, and we're in a small apartment, and . . . there's a guy there, but I don't think he's my father. And she shuts the door on me, and I'm feeling," Grady searched for the right words, "I'm feeling . . . abandoned and frightened. Weird, just weird."

"What's weird about it? It sounds like a pretty realistic kind of dream."

"Yeah, that's part of it. It felt totally realistic, like it really happened. Like I really lived that, you know? Like it really happened to me."

Karen continued to lie there, her head on his chest, his arm around her.

"I've had other dreams like this, now that I think about it. One dream—something about being in a car. I can see the dashboard, like on one of those older cars, chrome on the dashboard. I think I'm with her, and there's this guy—a different guy, I think—who's driving, and I'm on the front seat between them, like a bench seat, not bucket seats." He stopped, lost in thought, trying to remember.

"Is that a frightening dream too?" she asked quietly.

He nodded. "But I'm not sure why."

They lay in silence for a long time after that, and eventually they fell asleep. Later, when they had awakened, Karen offered to make breakfast: cereal, juice, and coffee.

"I'm going in to work lunch today," she said when they finished eating. "You want to come over tonight? Go to the meeting together?"

Grady thought for a moment as he finished his coffee. "Yeah," he said. "I'll be over about five if that's all right?"

"Yeah, five is good."

They cleaned up and then left the apartment together. Grady waited for her bus with her, gave her a kiss, and then started walking toward the river. Even though it was a considerable walk, he enjoyed sitting on a bench and watching the Delaware. Something about it was soothing and helped him to calm down.

Grady thought as he walked, recalling the disturbing dreams he'd had since he'd been a young boy. They were always quite realistic—and yet alien—as if he were dreaming about someone else's life or memories. His mother, Catherine, had given birth to a son. His name was Terry, and he died before he was two. Grady always believed that he was meant to be a replacement for Terry, that he was supposed to be a reincarnation of him, and he had always felt that his mother hated him because he wasn't a bit like Terry. At least that's what she said. *Why can't you be more this way or that way? Terry would have liked it this way. Why can't you be more loving like Terry was?* This belief led Grady to think he had been adopted when he was a baby.

The dream he had last night was one he'd had before. For some reason, he hadn't been prepared to tell Karen everything. But in the past, this dream along with several others (all of which seemed more like remembering or reliving rather than dreaming), led him to consider the possibility that his young mother and father had been killed in an automobile crash and that he'd been adopted. He saw, in his mind's eye, the flashing red of the lights on police cars and a fire truck, felt the cool wet of grass under him, and pain through all of his body. He felt unable to move. He heard vague voices yelling back and forth, giving orders, sounding harried, worried, frustrated. He also had an image of white—white walls and ceilings, bright lights, white uniforms—hushed whispers, some older people crying. Another building with cribs, beds, a lot of other kids, young girls, toys. It was like a puzzle with lots of pieces missing. He wasn't sure if any of it was real, but these dreams and feelings haunted him.

There had been times when he tried to broach the subject with his parents, but they never let on to anything that would have confirmed his suspicion. Still, the dream was partly responsible for his feeling of alienation within the family. It didn't feel like his family. He never felt like he belonged. He felt more at home in Richie's house than his own. Nina felt like more of a mother to him than his own mother had. His own mother? Who did he mean? Catherine or the young blonde in his dreams whom he had come to think of as Kelly?

When he reached Penn's Landing, Grady bought a pretzel and coffee from a vendor and sat on a bench, smoking, watching the river, and letting scenes from his life float by. Grady finished the coffee and looked down at his watch. It was one thirty. One thirty! How the hell . . . ? He couldn't believe that he'd been there for over three hours. He didn't know if he'd had another blackout or had only been lost in thought. He got up and found his body stiff and a little wobbly. Grady stretched and decided to find a phone booth so he could call Tommy and find out if he'd learned anything more about Tracy.

Grady found a phone booth down by the ferry that crossed the river to Camden and dialed the work number on the business card Tommy had given him. A voice answered the phone, and Grady asked for Tommy Massimo. "Just a minute, I'll get him for you," said the voice. A short wait, and Tommy was on the phone.

"Tommy Massimo," he said.

"Yo, Tommy, it's me, Grady Powers."

"Grady. Hey, I'm glad you called. I was going to call you later on."

"Yeah, no problem. I was just hanging out, thought I'd call to see if you had any luck with Dolores."

"Yeah, I talked with her last night. She used to know Tracy pretty good. They went to the same high school up in the northeast, although Dolores was a grade ahead of her. Anyway, Dolores said that Tracy hung out with a pretty fast crowd in high school but that she ended up going to Temple, where she got her degree and then went into teaching." Grady tried to write as much down as he could, not trusting his memory.

Tommy continued, "So let's see, oh yeah, her father is some administrator for the city, the streets department or something, and she has an older brother, Gino, who's a cop—a detective, I think. Oh, and she married this guy, Brian Hoffman, a little over a year ago. He works for some bank downtown. And she's working . . . let's see . . . she's teaching grammar school out in Haverford, I think, and they've got a house out there now."

"Dolores say anything about either her or Brian doing drugs? Hard stuff?"

"Yeah, Dolores said that both of them were into getting high. She don't know just what they did, but they joked a lot about getting high, and Dee got the impression that they had tried just about everything. You know, cocaine, heroin, the whole enchilada."

"Anything else?" asked Grady.

"No, not really. Except that Dolores said she didn't like Tracy all that much. She thought she was a little bit of a showboat, you know? Always trying to impress with how much she's done, what famous cock she'd sucked, stuff like that. Dee can't believe she's teaching in a grammar school. Least likely candidate, you know?"

"Yeah, I hear you. Listen, your wife really sounds nice. Maybe we can get together and do a double some time."

"That'd be great. Listen, this weekend, I'm playing at Christy's place, over on Girard."

"I know it," Grady quickly volunteered.

"Of course you know it; you've played it often enough yourself. So Dee is going to be there. Why don't you and your girl come over, about eleven? I'll get you a good table. We'll have a blast."

"Tommy, it sounds great. I'm looking forward to it. See ya then." And he hung up.

Grady walked along the landing and found a vendor where he bought a soda and a bagel. He then sat down where he could watch the river while he tried to sort things out: Richie saying that he and Tracy were serious; Tracy cheating on Richie with a guy she ended up marrying less than a year later; Tracy and her husband, Brian, both openly getting high; the fact that Richie was doing a lot of drugs, including heroin and coke, but also all kinds of pills, speed, pot, booze, and whatever came his way. And finally, after Richie broke up with Tracy and went into a nosedive from which he never pulled out.

With some frustration, Grady realized that none of these facts answered the question as to whether Richie overdosed on purpose or by accident. From Grady's point of view, that question might never be answered. And, he thought, he didn't have to have a definitive answer. As far as he was concerned, Richie had the right to off himself if he felt that life wasn't worth living. *God knows, I've felt that way often enough. Who am I to judge?* Still, he thought that for what it was worth, he would let Zio G. know what he'd found out. *Just one more thing and then I'll call him tomorrow.*

Chapter XI

Gennero: Business

It was almost nine o'clock on Wednesday morning when Gennero stepped out his front door and looked up at the clear blue March sky. He breathed in deeply. *There's the smell of spring, or at least of grass, in the air,* he thought. He smiled as he remembered one February morning many years ago when he went to put something away in the tool shed and smelled all the stored-up smells of summer: dirt, manure, old mowed grass. Somehow, he always associated that pleasant experience with Nina when she was still a preschooler. Then he noticed Sal waiting by the car, the rear door open. *The sun is shining. No more rain. A beautiful morning,* he thought. *Soon, there'll be bird songs, forsythia, and spring. Maybe this year I'll plant a vegetable garden. Who knows?*

"Good morning, Salvatore. A beautiful morning."

"That it is, Mr. G. It'll be a beautiful day to be out."

Gennero thought, *Almost any day is a good day to be out.* He lowered himself into the spacious backseat. "Today, Sal, we'll do some business. First, we'll go to Fred's Brewery."

"The Brewery, it is, Mr. G."

Gennero was looking forward to hearing from Dominic, but he didn't want to appear too anxious, so he decided not to call Dom until later in the afternoon, maybe not until tomorrow. He thought about the business at hand. Gennero had an important interest in a number of businesses. The Brewery was a microbrewery that sold locally and was making a very nice profit for its owners. Gennero went in about once every month or so to meet with those who were responsible for day-to-day operations and overall planning for marketing, sales, future production, and so forth. As the administrative officer of a privately held holding company, Gennero represented others as well as himself. He was the public face of this corporation and was the funnel through which information and opinions flowed, both ways. Gennero represented the needs of the business and the workers to the other investors and, of course, conveyed the needs and wishes of the investors to the other owners and the managers involved in running the business. Gennero played the same role in a number of other enterprises, including real estate, restaurants, construction companies, and travel agencies, although that list was not at all exhaustive. In each of these operations, Gennero was trusted and respected by all concerned. He was perceived as treating everyone fairly, including himself. This would be a busy day, but Gennero enjoyed these meetings. He liked the challenge of solving problems and finding solutions that were win-win, where everybody involved agreed that this was the best and fairest solution obtainable. All of the businesses were reasonably profitable, and everyone seemed sufficiently satisfied and content.

After his morning meeting at the Brewery, Gennero went to the Penrose Diner, which was where he met with the owners and managers of a string of small restaurants and pizza joints in the Philadelphia area. Sal enjoyed a leisurely lunch at the counter, courtesy of the owners, while Gennero had his meeting at a large table in the back.

During the meeting, Gennero received a call from Dominic, and so when the meeting was over, Gennero told Sal, "We're going to go back to Villa Contursi after this."

Sal brought the car around to the front, and when Gennero finished up his discussions with everyone, he came out and got into the car. While Sal drove, Gennero was on his cell phone rescheduling the rest of his afternoon's appointments. Soon, they were back in Center City, pulling up in front of Dominic's restaurant.

When Gennero lifted himself out of the car, he turned to his driver and said, "Sal, I may be here awhile. This might be a good time for you to run some of these errands for me," and he handed Sal a piece of paper containing a shopping list.

Sal looked at it and then at Gennero. "I'll be back here as soon as I can. You take your time, Mr. G."

Gennero nodded, turned, and went into the restaurant.

Dominic was sitting at the bar at the front of the restaurant when Gennero came in. His son, Nick, was there also, and Gennero knew that Rosalie would be in the office upstairs. Dominic embraced Gennero. "Ciao, Gennero."

Nick came over to give him a big hug. "Ciao, Zio," he said. "How are you?"

"Fine, Nicholas. You are looking good. Success seems to agree with you." Nick smiled self-consciously. "Let's say that when things are going well, it's more fun."

"Very true," he said. "So young to be so wise."

Dominic took his cousin by the arm. "Let's go sit down. Can I get you something to eat? To drink?"

"No, no thank you, Dom. I just had lunch. Maybe just a glass of water."

Dominic caught Nick's eye, and Nick nodded. Gennero had removed his coat and sat down when a waiter appeared with two glasses and a pitcher of water for the two men.

"So," Gennero said, "what have you found out for me?"

Dominic took a piece of paper out of his jacket pocket and gave it to Gennero to read. "Tracy Malatesta got married a little over a year ago to Brian Hoffman. Her driver's license shows her living in Haverford out on the Main Line. It's there on the paper. By the way, I have the only other copy of that." Gennero nodded as he read, and Dom continued, "She works as a third-grade teacher in a charter school there. That address is also listed. Her husband, Brian, works for Philadelphia First City Bank, in the mortgage department; been there about six years or so."

Dominic paused, took a sip of water, and gave Gennero a moment to absorb all of this before he went on. When Gennero looked up from the paper, Dom continued. "This Brian is an interesting fellow," he said.

Gennero's eyebrows went up. "In what way?"

"He has a sheet, it seems; been arrested once for DUI, and once for possession of coke with intent to sell. That got dismissed. Then two years ago, he was badly beaten up down in Old City. No charges were ever brought against anyone. The cops who investigated it thought it might have been a drug thing gone bad, but it was chalked up as a mugging. The cops thought it might have been something to do with drugs because of the location and because Brian had some rep as a small time dealer, although no one ever caught him in the act."

"Hmmm, interesting." He thought for a moment. "What else?"

Dom smiled. "Saved the best for last," he said. "You were right about Tracy. Tracy Hoffman also has a sheet."

"The same girl?"

"Yep. She was caught with a couple of grams of heroin three years ago. That was also dismissed."

"We don't know why?" Gennero inquired.

"No. It would seem that Brian or Tracy knows someone who can do them some favors, but my source couldn't get any information about who that was. Who knows? Could be a friend of his old man or an uncle, a neighbor. Could be anybody. It's not that difficult to make something relatively minor to go away. You know that."

Gennero nodded knowingly. "So both Tracy and her husband, Brian, have a history of drug usage. Maybe even dealing at some small level?"

"On the surface, they look like a nice, young, successful, middle-class couple of kids with a nice house on the Main Line. She's a teacher. He has a nice midlevel job in the banking industry. Maybe that's who they are, with just a couple of minor mistakes in their background. But who knows? Maybe there's more there than meets the eye."

"Thank you, Dom," he said, folding the paper and putting it into his breast pocket. "I'm not sure where this will lead, but I promise I will let you know what I can when I come to that point."

Dom put up his hand in protest. "Gennero, you said this was personal. There's no need. I'm glad to be helpful to you in any way."

"I know. But, you know, when it comes to personal matters, there aren't that many people I can talk to. You and I, we always had a special closeness, you know? Most of the time, we keep things in. That's the way we were trained. Not like nowadays, this openness. But I tell you, Dom, sometimes, it's not so easy." Gennero paused, his eyes averted, absentmindedly twirling his glass on the table. "It used to be different. When Tessie was herself, I could share almost anything with her—except business, of course." He laughed. Both men smiled at recalling Tessie's aversion to hearing anything about the family's business dealings.

"Of course, when it came to business, I relied a great deal on Maria. But now I can't talk to Tessie about anything, and with Maria's cancer, I don't want to burden her . . . and I don't feel free to complain to Nina about her mother. I tell you, Dom, lately I've been feeling older and more alone than I ever have in my whole life. Sometimes I feel like it's only the corporation that keeps me going. And then on other days, I'm ready to give it all up."

"I know what you mean, Gennero. I remember when Mattie died." Gennero grimaced slightly. "We had just had our forty-fourth anniversary. We had no idea she had a heart problem. She went like that," he said, snapping his fingers.

"I remember," Gennero murmured. "We were all shocked."

"She's been gone almost eight years now, and I still count almost every day. She was, like you said about both Tessie and Maria, a great friend. When she died, I didn't know what I was going to do. Thank God for this restaurant and for my kids.

That's what pulled me through. But I'd lost my best friend, my confidante, my partner—not just my lover. It was . . . it was like half my history, half of me, was wiped out, like I wasn't the same anymore. It took quite a while before I felt alive again."

"I remember. We all missed Mattie. And we knew what a terrible loss it was for you and your children. Mattie was very special to all of us."

Dom sat back to get his handkerchief from his pocket to wipe his eyes. "This doesn't happen often, but whenever I talk about her, I feel it all rising up again, like it was just yesterday."

"I know. That's kind of how I'm feeling about Tessie. Almost like she's died. The woman I used to know isn't there anymore. I don't know who this one is or how she got into my life. She has the same name and the same appearance. And I feel like I'm supposed to have the same feelings about her. But, Dom, she's a stranger, this woman. I have to send Sal out to buy groceries, for Christ's sake, because she's afraid to go out of the house."

"Have you taken her to see a doctor?" Dom asked.

"She won't see anyone. Whenever I bring it up, we get into an argument. No matter how I suggest it, she won't have anything to do with it. She says there's nothing wrong with her. It's our enemies who are trying to harm us that are sick and need help, not her." He paused, shaking his head in frustration, and then leaned across the table and lowered his voice. "I've talked to a few doctors on my own—specialists, psychiatrists, neurologists. They don't agree on what might be wrong—some underlying psychological problem, something neurological or chemical. Without examining her, there's no way to know for sure and nothing they can do. One asshole suggested putting antipsychotic medication in her food. That's all I'd have to do. If she caught on to that, she'd never trust me. Dom, as it is, I have to tell you, there have been times when I've gone to bed at night afraid of what she might do."

Dom frowned. "Like what?"

"I mean I don't know if she might be capable of trying to kill me while I'm sleeping."

"Jesus Christ, Gennero. You think she would?"

"No, I don't really think so, but I've thought of the possibility. It's like I sleep with one eye open, you know?"

"So what are you going to do? It's got to be hell living like that."

Gennero shook his head. "I don't know, Dom. I don't know. She wants us to move, but that's not going to do any good."

"I was just going to say that," said Dom. "If she's paranoid here, she's just going to take it with her wherever she goes."

"Yes, exactly. And I don't want to move. I'm seventy-four fucking years old. What am I going to do someplace new? Without the kids, my sister, friends, you, everybody? And I can't leave anybody with her during the day because she won't have anybody in the house." Gennero shook his head. "I don't know, Dom. I just don't know what to do."

Dom studied his cousin. "Gennero, have you thought about talking to a psychiatrist or somebody for yourself?"

Gennero looked at him questioningly. "What do you mean?"

"It sounds like you're living in a loony bin. I don't know how you do it. You need some help in dealing with all this . . . all of this stress. Like you said, you need someone to talk to, not just to unload on, but to get some advice, some feedback. Somebody who knows what your options are."

"Maybe you're right," Gennero acknowledged. "I hadn't thought about it that way, but you're right."

"Do you know of someone?"

"Yeah, I do. One of the psychiatrists I consulted with before. I liked him. He seemed knowledgeable and trustworthy. Yeah. Dom, that's a great idea."

Dom leaned back and smiled.

"Listen, Dom, before I go, would it be all right if I peeked in on Rosalie and said hello?"

"Of course. You know how to get upstairs?" Both men got up from the table.

"Yes, the elevator is back through here, isn't it?" he asked, pointing down a hallway that led past the kitchen.

"Yeah, down the hall, through the door, and the elevator is on the right. You can't miss it."

"Thank you, Dom, for everything. I'll see you on my way out."

Gennero went down the hallway to the elevator and pushed the button for the second floor where Rosalie worked. When he came out of the elevator, he saw a series of small offices and found Rosalie hunched over her desk in one of them. "Hello, sweetheart," he said in his worst Humphrey Bogart accent.

"What?" Startled, Rosalie jumped. "Grandpa! What a surprise! What are you doing here?"

"I just stopped in to talk to Cousin Dom, and how could I leave without seeing my granddaughter?"

Rosalie got up and came around to give him a hug. "What a nice surprise. Oh, you gave me a start. I didn't hear the elevator. So," she said, clearing a chair for him to sit on, "how have you been? Mom said that you and Nonna might come over for dinner this weekend."

"I don't know, *ciucci*. I'd love to come, but your *nonna*, I don't think she's up to it. Going out, visiting, everything seems to take such a toll on her. I miss seeing all of you, but I don't feel right coming by myself and leaving her at home. That wouldn't be right."

Rosalie leaned over and gave him a hug. "I know. We understand, but we miss you . . . both of you. Just the other day, the boys were saying how long it's been since they've seen you. I think they're angling for a ride in your limo."

Gennero appreciated her attempt at humor, but he responded only with a weak smile. "Rosalie," he said, "I know it's difficult. Believe me, I know. But if you could find your way to give Nonna a call once in a while, just let her know that you're thinking of her. Remind her that she's loved and missed."

"Sure. I will. But you need to know that most of the time when I've called, she doesn't answer the phone, and if she does, she tries to start an argument. No matter what I say, she finds something wrong with it, and I end up feeling attacked." Rosalie's exasperation was obvious as she raised her hands in a gesture of futility.

"I know. But even so, it's helpful for her to know that you cared enough to call, even to just say hello and ask how she is."

Rosalie sighed. "Sure, Nonno. I'll try."

"Thank you," he said. "So how are you and the boys and your friend, Denise?"

Rosalie smiled. "Thanks for asking, Nonno. I appreciate that. Everybody is fine. The boys are fine. Bobby is getting so big, and Brian is such a Mr. Personality. I'm so proud of them both. And Denise, she's a dream. I know that it's got to be hard on you and Nonna, but Denise is just so good for me. I've never been so happy."

"Well, that's what's important, isn't it? Sure," he admitted, "it was a surprise, naturally. And it's taken some getting used to, but times are different now. People talk much more about gays and lesbians, not like the old days. And the two of you have handled it well with us. You've been patient with us too, you know. You gave us time to get used to it. Of course, Nonna doesn't get out, doesn't mingle as much as she used to, so she's taking more time. But she'll come around too. You'll see. Maybe," he continued, "I can find a time to stop by the house and get a chance to say hello to the boys and meet this Denise of yours. You know, just a quick visit."

"Of course. Whatever works for you, Nonno. I understand. Almost any evening. Early is good, around suppertime. We're usually all there."

Gennero got up and gave her a hug and a kiss. "You're a sweetheart," he said, "an angel. I have to go, but I'll try to stop by sometime soon."

"Good. And I'll try to call Nonna sometime soon too."

Gennero waved as he turned and went into the elevator.

Chapter XII

Gennero: A Crisis at Home

When Gennero came back down to the restaurant after visiting Rosalie, he saw Dominic and Nick at the front, talking with some patrons. As he approached, Nick came over to help him with his coat. Gennero saw Sal out front with the car, so he said his good-byes and went out into the cold, clear air. After settling himself into the backseat, he got out his cell phone and called his sister. He was concerned about how she was doing and wanted to see if her appointment with the surgeon was still set for the next morning. After a couple of rings, Maria answered the phone. Gennero asked her how she was feeling, whether she was feeling less pain, whether she'd been resting, and finally, about the doctor's appointment.

"All right then, Maria, I'll be there about nine thirty tomorrow morning to pick you up, and we'll go together. No, it's no bother. Don't be silly. I'll see you then. It's settled, so don't give it another thought." After another few minutes, he said good-bye and hung up.

Looking at his watch, he noticed that it was almost four thirty. "Sal," he said, leaning forward, "it's getting to be that time of day. Why don't you take me home now."

On the way home, Gennero reflected on the day: on all of the conflicts and problems inherent in his business, Theresa's unreasonable and angry suspiciousness, Maria's breast cancer and looming surgery, Nina's concern about Rosalie's lesbian relationship, the unanswered questions about Richie's death. He let out a deep sigh. *I could use a stiff drink. And I'm not looking forward to going home.* Gennero tried to think about what options he had. *Dom had a good idea. Tomorrow I'll give Dr. Sacerdote a call and set up an appointment. It'll be good to have someone to confide in.*

As Gennero's car approached the neighborhood where he lived, he took pleasure in seeing the tree-lined streets, noticing that buds were appearing already on the maples and locusts. It would take another month or so before the leaves started to come out. Gennero thought about spring, about puttering around his yard with his azaleas and rhododendra. He wasn't a garden enthusiast by any means, but he liked having a reason to walk around the house, having the feeling that he was doing something constructive—aerating the soil and doing a little pruning, a little fertilizing, or a little weeding. He also realized that for these past couple of years, he had been looking forward more and more to almost anything that gave him a reason to be out of the house. When Sal pulled up in front of his home, Gennero took a couple of deep breaths, as if gearing up for a great expenditure of effort. Sal opened the door and lent Gennero a hand getting up and out. Then Sal opened the trunk, revealing a large cooler from which he retrieved the groceries he'd shopped for.

"Here, Sal, let me take them." Gennero knew that Theresa would blow a gasket if he let Sal carry the groceries into the house. Sal handed the two bags to Gennero.

"Thank you, Sal. Tomorrow, we're taking Maria to the doctor's. So pick me up about ten after nine. Then we'll go pick her up."

"Nine-ten it is, Mr. G. I'm sure everything is going to be all right."

Gennero managed a brief smile. "I'm sure you're right, Sal. I'll see you in the morning then," he said and turned up the walkway to the house. Again, he paused and breathed deeply before turning the key.

Entering the house, Gennero immediately sensed the stillness. He stood quietly for a moment, his eyes and ears scanning for a sign as to what might be happening. Nothing. Gennero looked into the living room to his right. Nothing looked out of place. No notes left in any obvious spots indicating that Theresa had stepped out, was next door, or at the store. No note either on the small table in the entry hall.

Gennero removed his coat and hung it up in the closet. Then, picking up the groceries, he went into the kitchen. There were no signs of any preparation for dinner. No notes were on the fridge or on the table or counter. "Theresa," he called. "Theresa? Are you here?" There was no answer. *Hopefully she's gone shopping or visiting or to get her hair done. Maybe she's been having one of her rare good days.* Gennero emptied the bags onto the counter and then put the things needing refrigeration into the fridge.

Feeling his fatigue, Gennero slowly climbed the stairs to the bedrooms and bathroom on the second floor. "Theresa? Are you up here?" Again, there was no answer. Gennero was now convinced that no one else was in the house, and he allowed himself to relax a little bit, thinking, *Maybe I'll lie down before supper.* He glanced into the spare bedroom, which was used by Theresa for her sewing and quilting projects. Nothing. Then he moved down the hall into their bedroom. As he pushed open the bathroom door so he could go in to relieve himself, he saw her body on the bathroom floor.

Oh, Jesus! "Theresa, are you all right?" Tessie was lying on her side, her head resting on her right hand, like a pillow, her legs pulled up toward her belly. She was fully dressed and looked like she had lain down to take a nap. Then he noticed the empty bottle of Tylenol on the sink. The cap was off, and the bottle was empty. "Tessie. Tessie. Wake up. Can you hear me?" Gennero reached down, pulling at her left arm and shoulder. Her body was completely limp, but his shaking elicited a soft moan. She was alive but unconscious.

Shit, he thought as he patted his jacket pockets. Quickly he straightened up and hurried back down the stairs to the front hall closet, retrieving his cell phone from his coat pocket. He hurriedly dialed 911 and asked for an ambulance, telling the operator that it looked like his wife had taken an overdose of Tylenol and was unconscious. He gave her the rest of the information, and within a few minutes, he saw the flashing lights outside as the ambulance pulled into his driveway. It was beginning to get dark when he opened the front door and turned on the lights for the paramedics. They rushed upstairs and took Tessie's vital signs. Before he knew it, they had her on a stretcher and were taking her down the stairs. They told him they were going to take her to Methodist Hospital, which was the closest, but that he couldn't ride with them in the ambulance. Gennero nodded and quickly dialed Sal's number.

"Sal, it's me, Gennero. I hate to do this to you. They're taking Theresa to the hospital, and I need you to take me there as quickly as possible." Of course, Sal said he'd be there right away. Gennero went back inside. Mrs. Carlucci, his next-door neighbor, was rushing across his little patch of lawn to find out what had happened. "I'm sorry, Antoinette. I don't have time to talk. You must excuse me. Yes, they took Theresa to the hospital. I don't know what happened. I found her unconscious. Please, I have to go." And he turned from her and went inside, closing the door behind him. He thought for a moment and then went into the basement where he found a small suitcase that he took upstairs. By the time he got to the second floor, he had to sit down on the edge of the bed and catch his breath. He rummaged through Theresa's dresser drawers and found some items— underwear, a couple of bras, a couple of nightgowns. Then he collected some things from the bathroom—a robe and slippers, a comb and brush, deodorant, toothbrush, and toothpaste. He couldn't think what else she might need. By the time he closed the small suitcase, he heard the familiar beep of the limo horn. *Sal made good time. God bless him.* Gennero carried the suitcase downstairs, got his coat from the closet, and went out, locking the door behind him.

"Thank you, Sal, I really appreciate this."

"Don't worry about it, Mr. G. Now, which hospital?"

Gennero told him, and Sal practically laid rubber pulling away from the house. Gennero appreciated that Sal knew not to ask any personal questions, though he was probably wondering what happened. Gennero would tell him what he wanted him to know, and he would do it when he was ready. When they arrived at the emergency room, Sal got out and helped Gennero from the backseat.

"Sal, I expect I'll be here for quite a few hours. God knows when I'll be leaving, so I'll grab a cab to go back home." Sal started to protest, but Gennero held up a hand. "Don't worry, I'll be fine. Unless you hear from me, I still want you to pick me up tomorrow morning at ten after nine. But who knows. I'll call you in the morning if there's a change in plans."

"Right, if I don't hear from you before then, I'll see you at the house at 9:10."

Gennero nodded and then headed for the ER entrance. As he entered the hospital, he glanced at his watch. It was only ten after six. He approached the woman at the admissions desk and told her that he was Mr. Giantonio. "They just brought my wife here in the ambulance," he told her.

She handed him a clipboard full of forms. "If you'll fill these out for me first, sir." Gennero had enough experiences with hospitals to know the routine. So he took the clipboard with its attached ballpoint pen and found a seat. He took off his coat, checking to see that he had his cell phone and keys in his suit jacket. Then he set about filling out the insurance forms, waiver forms, permission forms, medical history forms, medication forms, forms asking for everything except the names of pets. Finally, Gennero finished and returned the clipboard to the woman.

"Thank you," she said, without looking up. "Someone will come and get you when your wife is ready to be seen."

Gennero motioned to where he'd been sitting and asked, "I should wait here?" She looked up and nodded and then returned to her work. Gennero frowned and reluctantly went and sat down. A TV was suspended from a corner of the room, loudly playing a rerun of a soap opera that was bad the first time it played and had not improved with repetition. The magazines were either out of date or totally uninteresting, geared to a thirteen-year-old mentality. *I wonder how many adolescents wait out here,* he thought, settling back and closing his eyes.

When he opened them again to see who else was there, he saw a young Latino couple, an elderly black woman, and eight empty aluminum chairs. His thoughts turned to Maria. *She'll be getting the word tomorrow from the surgeon as to whether he thinks she does or doesn't need surgery. But from what she told me about the size of her tumor, there's no question she's going to need surgery—and quickly too. They won't mess around with her.*

Then Gennero let himself think about his wife. There was no doubt in his mind that she had taken an overdose of Tylenol in a deliberate attempt to end her life. *It was a lucky thing I came home earlier than usual. God knows how long she was laying there and how much longer would she have had before she died.* Gennero realized that he was angry at her. If only she would have been open to getting help, to admitting that she needed help. Dr. Sacerdote had told him that there was nothing anyone could do to force her to receive treatment unless she was judged to be a danger to herself or others. This suicide attempt would demonstrate that she was a danger to herself. Maybe now they could force her to receive treatment. He wondered if he should give Dr. Sacerdote a call but decided it would be better to wait and see what the doctors here had to say. He was sure they would call in a psychiatrist to examine her.

Gennero realized that he was making an assumption that she would recover from this overdose and that she would be discharged and coming home fairly soon. *Then what? I don't know if I can go back to the way things were.* He felt his stomach tightening. *Butterflies. I'm not sure if I'm hungry or nervous. Probably both.* He looked around. There was no food anywhere around. He thought of looking for candy or soda machines and then discarded the idea. He came back to the question of what he could do, what he wanted to do. He didn't think he had much choice. *I can't abandon her. I'll just have to find some way to live with her. But how do I do that?*

It wasn't until twenty after eight that a nurse came to get him and led him through the double doors and down a corridor into the ER. He was glad to get away from the TV and to find out what was happening with Theresa. The nurse walked him toward a cubicle, and pulling aside the green curtain that hid the bed, revealed Theresa lying there in a polka-dot hospital gown, with oxygen tubes running into her nose and an IV in her arm.

"We had to pump her stomach. We're running some blood tests and liver function tests now. We'll be admitting her upstairs soon. Right now, we're just waiting for a bed. Dr. Levy is her doctor and will be coordinating everything here. We've called for a psych eval, but we're still waiting for the psychiatrist on call to come in. You can stay with her for now. Dr. Levy will be looking in on her later on. If you need anything, just push this button here," she said, indicating a button wired to the wall behind the bed. Then she gave him a brief, little smile and pulled the curtain shut, leaving Gennero there with Theresa. He looked at her. Her eyes were closed, but she seemed to be breathing normally.

"Tessie," he called softly. "Are you awake? Can you hear me?" He saw her stir, but she seemed to be having trouble opening her eyes. "Tessie, it's me, Gennero. You're going to be all right. Just rest." He took her hand and gave it a squeeze. She responded weakly but continued to lie there with her eyes closed. Gennero noticed the clip on her finger, which measured either her pulse or her temperature; he couldn't remember which. Then he saw the oscilloscope, or whatever it was called, with its waves of spikes floating across the screen. He assumed that that was her heart rate. There were some other numbers indicated, but he didn't know what they represented. He sat in silence, holding Theresa's hand, and waited for the doctor to come.

After about a half hour, Dr. Levy came. He was young, either an intern or a resident, obviously not someone with a whole lot of experience under his belt. He looked like he hadn't even begun to shave yet.

"Mr. Giantonio, I'm Dr. Levy. I wonder if you could step out here and answer some questions for me?" Gennero got up and accompanied the doctor a few feet away. "Can you tell me what happened tonight?"

Gennero was stunned. *She's been here for four fucking hours, and I've filled out a ream of forms, and you don't fucking know what happened?* Gennero paused, took a breath, and said, "Well, Doctor, it seems that she took an overdose of Tylenol and tried to kill herself. But I assume you already knew that."

Catching the tone of voice, Dr. Levy looked at Gennero. "I'm sorry, Mr. Giantonio. Of course I knew that. What I meant to ask was whether you had any idea of how many Tylenol she might have taken."

"It was a regular bottle, not extra large and not extra small. The bottle was empty when I found it. I have no idea how many pills might have been in the bottle."

"I see. And do you have any idea as to whether she might have taken anything in addition to the Tylenol?"

"No," Gennero answered. "I didn't see anything else out on the sink. I don't know."

Levy was writing brief notes into her chart. "Can you tell me if Mrs. Giantonio was taking any other medication or over-the-counter products?"

Gennero recounted as best he could what Theresa regularly ingested—occasional ibuprofen or Tylenol for arthritis and general aches and pains, vitamins and calcium, but no prescriptions. "Theresa hasn't been to a doctor of any kind in about four years or so. She won't take any prescriptions, as I indicated on one of the forms I filled out. My wife is a very suspicious woman and doesn't trust anyone. She thinks everybody is trying to harm her."

Levy wrote some more notes. "Has your wife ever threatened or attempted suicide before?" he asked.

"Yes, I have to admit. These past few months, she's been after me to move. She says she can't stay here with everybody trying to hurt us and that if we don't move, then either they'll end up killing us or she'll have to kill herself."

Dr. Levy raised his eyes and looked at Gennero over his clipboard. "And what did you tell her?"

"I told her that we couldn't do it. Where are we supposed to go at our age? Move? It's crazy. We have all of our family here. I told her, you think you're going to feel safer somewhere else? But I never thought she would actually do anything to hurt herself. I thought that part was just as crazy as the rest of it. To tell you the truth, I didn't pay that much attention to it."

Levy asked a few more questions about her family and medical history, and Gennero patiently repeated all that he had already put down on the forms. *Do these people ever talk to each other?* But he bit his lip and made no comment, knowing it was the quickest way to get to the next step.

When Levy finished getting all of the information he needed, he told Gennero, "We'll be admitting her upstairs tonight. We're waiting for them to clear a bed."

Gennero had an image of them dumping a current patient down a laundry chute and putting clean sheets on the bed.

Levy continued, "We'll have a psychiatrist come in tomorrow morning to do a consultation. She won't be fully responsive until then. Mr. Giantonio, I want you to realize that your wife is in very serious condition. An overdose of Tylenol can be very dangerous. We'll have to keep her here for three or four days at least. Sometimes it takes that long for damage to the liver to show up. We don't want to risk discharging her before we know for sure that she's going to be all right."

"You're saying that she's going to live. She's not going to die?"

Levy shook his head. "I wish I could promise that. No, what I'm saying is that we won't know for a while whether she'll make it through this crisis or not. Her vital signs aren't good. They're weak and unstable, and, to be truthful, she might not make it. But we've pumped her stomach, and we're filling her with the appropriate medications and antidotes. We're hopeful. We're doing everything that we can do for now, until we know more.

Now, assuming that she makes it and gets stronger, then our plan is to keep her and continue to monitor her liver functioning and everything else and make sure she gets whatever she needs to get well."

"What do you suggest I do, Doctor? Do you recommend my staying or should I go home and come back in the morning?"

Levy looked at his watch. "To be honest, Mr. Giantonio, there won't be a lot that you can do for her tonight. I'd suggest you stay with her until they move her upstairs, which should be within an hour or so. That way, you can see where she is. I noticed you brought a suitcase with some of her things. Anyway, you'll get an idea if she'll need anything else. Maybe she'll start to come around a little as the medication begins to take effect. I'm sure it will be a comfort to her to be able to see you there. Tomorrow, visiting hours start at ten in the morning. She'll be in intensive care, so you'll be able to come anytime during the day after that. The psychiatrist will probably be coming in earlier, so we may have more information for you by then."

"Will you be her doctor up there too?" Gennero asked.

"No, I'm only down here in the ER. She'll have another doctor in intensive care. If there's a particular doctor you'd like to be treating her, then let the staff know tomorrow morning, and we'll do what we can to accommodate him or her, depending on whether he or she already has staff privileges here or not."

"I understand, Doctor. Thank you."

"Just let me look in on her and see how she's doing, and then I'll leave you with her. The nurses will come to transfer her upstairs as soon as they're ready." After a few moments, Dr. Levy left, and Gennero went back through the green curtain to take up his vigil.

Chapter XIII

Grady

Grady got back to Karen's apartment about a quarter to five and let himself in with his key. He put her mail on the kitchen table and opened the refrigerator. Surveying the options, Grady took the half gallon of milk out and poured himself a glass. Then he took off his jacket and sat down at the table. He was only halfway through the glass when Karen came in with a bag of groceries.

"Hi. I thought I'd beat you here," she said, coming over to the table and leaning over to give him a kiss.

"I just got here a few minutes ago. How was work?"

"Good," she answered, taking off her coat and emptying the bag: juice, apples, bread, some other stuff. Nothing that would go with the remainder of the milk in his glass. "Lunch is usually busy. I made out well." Karen continued to put things away, a flurry of activity.

"You're still at work," Grady noted. "Slow down, take a load off."

"You're right. It was like this all afternoon. I didn't even have time to pee. Which reminds me, I have to go. Be right back."

Grady smiled as she disappeared into the tiny bathroom down the hall.

"You want to eat something now?" she called. "Or you want to go out for something after?"

"I'm hungry now," he answered, "but I'll be okay with an apple to tide me over, and then we can go for something later."

Karen came back into the kitchen. "Good. Let's do that then."

Later, when they arrived at the meeting, they split up and gravitated to different parts of the room. They had decided that it would be better if they didn't flaunt their relationship at the meetings; better to play it cool and not emphasize it. They found that there were fewer jealousies and other problems this way. After a while, the meeting started, and they had a speaker who told his story. Afterward, there was a discussion, and Grady was surprised to see Karen stand up and announce herself.

"Hello," she said. "My name is Karen, and I'm a heroin addict." After getting the usual acknowledgment, she continued, "A couple of weeks ago, in my home group, I received my eighteen months' pin." A murmur of applause and congratulations. "Thank you," she continued, "but I need to . . ." She paused, searching for the right words. "I need to say something about that. Last night, my friend, my very best friend, called me on something, something that I had not wanted to face before. So I need to, I want to thank him for that, and I want to apologize to all of you." Everyone was silent and watching her, waiting for what seemed to be some sort of admission.

"About six months ago, six months and thirteen days, to be exact, I had some root canal surgery. When the dentist went to give me a prescription for pain medication that contained codeine, I never said a thing to him. I told myself that it was a legitimate use of medication, but I knew . . . I really did know . . . what I was doing. I didn't want to admit it to myself, so I lied to myself, and I lied to everyone else by not saying anything about it. If no one knew, then no one would confront me, and then I wouldn't have to know." No one said anything. Karen took a deep breath and continued. "But my friend knew, and he waited and let me deal with it. Finally, when the time was right, he made me face the truth. He made me realize that I've been lying . . . to you, to him, and to myself. And I realize that a life of sobriety built on a lie is no good. It's a shaky foundation at best, and sooner or later it's going to come crumbling down. Nothing lasting can be built on a lie. Thanks to my friend, I realized that sometimes it's very difficult to tell where the line is between what's acceptable and what's not. Sometimes, for me at least, it's only by crossing over that line that I find out where it is. It's only by having to experience the consequences of crossing over that line that you . . . that I . . . find out why it's there in the first place. So," she said, taking another deep breath, "I wanted to share all of this with you and to say that the good news is that I've been clean, I mean really clean, for six months and ten days." And she sat down.

Karen got a positive response from the group, including a lot of hugs and clapping, and Grady had tears in his eyes. *What a courageous thing to do. What a ballsy broad she is.* He found himself clapping along with the others and whistling too.

When the meeting was over, Grady waited outside for her, letting her enjoy and take in all of the individual responses he knew she'd be getting from the other NA members. He was aware that he was feeling good about himself, knowing that he'd had a helpful and positive impact on her struggle with her addiction. He was also aware that her action was a statement to him as well as to herself about their relationship, and he felt his capacity for trust expanding a little bit.

Karen came out of the door looking for him, and he went over to her, his arms open wide. "Let me chime in with my congratulations," he said, wrapping his arms around her. "And let me buy you the biggest bacon cheeseburger we can find." He gave her a big kiss and looked into her eyes. "I am very proud of you," he said. "I is very proud that you is my woman." They both laughed and started to walk toward their favorite burger joint.

"Wow," she said, "am I ever glad that that's over. I wasn't sure I could do it."

"You've got balls, kid," he said, giving her a squeeze. Karen looked at him and smiled, snuggling in closer.

Then Grady took her by the shoulders. "Wait here a minute, will you? There's something I want to talk to Andy about."

"Sure," she agreed. "I'll wait for you up ahead," she said, pointing to a cluster of women from the meeting.

Grady walked back toward the door to the church basement where the meeting had been held. There were two men standing in its light, lighting their cigarettes and talking. "Andy," Grady called, "can I talk to you a minute?"

"Sure." Then turning to the other guy, he said, "Why don't I meet up with you at the diner?" The other guy turned out to be another friend of Grady's, a Latino named Alex.

"Hey, Alex, I didn't recognize you in the dark. Stick around. I just wanted to ask you guys something." They both looked at him curiously and waited. "Both of you used to score down in Old City, right?" Andy and Alex looked at each other and smiled self-consciously.

"Don't tell me you're looking for a buy," joked Andy.

"Listen," Grady said, putting his finger on Andy's chest, "if that's what I was thinking, I wouldn't be asking you for directions. I know my own way back to hell." They laughed, keeping it light. "No, what I was wondering was if either of you knew a fellow named Brian Hoffman."

Andy paused to think, but Alex spoke right up. "Brian Hoffman? Works as a mortgage broker or something in Center City, blond guy, about average height, thirtyish?"

"That's the guy. What can you tell me about him?"

Alex snuck a quick look at Andy, and Andy gave an imperceptible nod. Alex returned his attention to Grady. "Well, when I was using, I bought from him a few times. He used to hang out in that Irish place on Second Street, The Harp." Grady knew from previous meetings that Alex had also been addicted to heroin and coke, so he surmised that this was what Brian had been dealing. Then it occurred to him that The Harp was the name of the club that he and Richie had followed Tracy to that night.

"What else?" asked Grady, taking out a cigarette and lighting it up.

"I don't know." Alex shrugged his shoulders. "He seemed all right. Seemed to have a lot of money, dressed nice, had nice wheels. I never had no trouble with him. His stuff was cut, of course, but no worse than anybody else's."

"When was the last time you scored from him?"

"I don't know. I been clean almost a year now." He paused and thought. "Maybe a little over a year ago, around the holidays. That would be, let's see, around Christmas of 2002. Yeah, it was after the anniversary of 9/11. I remember. It was down at The Harp. He was with this blonde chick that he was almost always with. I think they might have been married. I'm not sure."

"Thanks," Grady said. "I really appreciate your sharing." They chuckled at his ironic use of one of their pet phrases from the meeting. "Seriously," Grady added.

"It's cool, man," Alex said, shaking the hand that Grady extended. "No problem. I'm glad I could help you out."

Then Grady turned to Andy. "Listen, I talked to Tommy Massimo today, and he's playing over at Christy's place on Girard Avenue this weekend. Karen and I are going to drop in around eleven Saturday night. You want to join us?"

"I'd like to, Grady, but I can't. I don't trust myself in those places yet. I'd be glad to hook up with you guys later, at a diner or something, but I'm not back into the club scene yet."

Grady put his hand on Andy's shoulder. "I understand. Don't worry about it. I'll be in touch." Again, he shook their hands and then turned to catch up to Karen.

Thursday

March 4, 2004

Chapter XIV

GRADY: GETTING STARTED

When Grady woke up, it took him a minute to figure out where he was. This bouncing back and forth between his place and Karen's was sometimes disorienting. He opened his eyes and recognized his bedroom. He reached behind him and felt Karen's body. At least he hoped it was Karen's. *I better take a look just to make sure*, he thought, turning his head and looking over his shoulder. Relieved, he sank back down into the bed and looked at the clock. It was not yet seven o'clock. Waking up was always something of a challenge because he was never sure if he'd had a blackout or had simply been asleep.

He thought he'd wait until at least eight thirty before calling Gennero with what he found out about Tracy and her husband. He wasn't that upset about the possibility of Richie having committed suicide, if that's what happened. But he also knew of lots of situations where people had either shot up too much or shot up with dope that was a lot stronger than they had been used to. And he knew there were those times when the dope was bad, cut with rat poison or even worse, which all added up to plenty of opportunities for an accident. He still couldn't think how any of what he'd discovered about Tracy and her dealer husband, Brian, would shed any light on what had actually occurred. Still, he could understand why Gennero would want to know as much as possible about what happened to his only grandson.

Karen must have felt him shifting around in bed. She reached over, put an arm around him, and snuggled closer. It felt good. He was surprised at how comfortable he was feeling with her show of affection. For so many years, he had kept his relationships unemotional and purely physical. He knew why. He'd been through enough counseling and self-examination. He was afraid of abandonment. He had never felt that he could trust his mother, Catherine. He could never tell where he stood with her, never knew when she would lash out at him, verbally or physically, or when she would be relatively solicitous and unexpectedly kind. It was like she'd been two different people.

In fact, he remembered one incident when he was about three. He'd gone outside to play in their yard and couldn't get back in. The screen door to the kitchen apparently had been locked. He'd called for her and she hadn't come. He called louder. Finally she came, opened the door, and yanked him into the kitchen, shouting at him to stop yelling. Then she slapped him hard across the face with a wet dishrag. It stung like hell. "Stop that crying," she screamed, "and don't you dare move." Then she went down the hall and into a room. He was terrified.

Sometime later, she came back out. He was still sobbing, trying to catch his breath. But he hadn't moved. She bent down and looked into his face, wiping his nose and his eyes with her handkerchief. "What's the matter, honey? Why are you crying? Here, let Mommy give you a big hug. That's my boy." He was scared to death. He was sure there were two mommies: a good one and a bad one. And they switched places in a secret room down the hall. In fact, he spent hours examining the back of the linen closet and the walls in his parents' bedroom, looking for a secret panel, but he never found it.

He never told anyone. It was that kind of fear and mistrust that had lurked in the background of every relationship he'd ever had with a woman. *But this feels different. I'm feeling a degree of safety lately with Karen that's new. I feel like I know where I stand with her.* He found himself holding her hand and pressing it close to his body, letting her know that this closeness felt good. It felt comforting.

They fell back asleep, and when they awoke, they made love. Afterward, they were lying in bed, resting, enjoying relaxing with each other. "I'm going to take my shower," Karen announced. "When I'm done, how would you like some French toast for breakfast?"

Grady smiled a goofy smile. "Does a wooden hobbyhorse have a hickory dick?"

"Oh, you," she said, tickling him.

Grady squirmed away from her, laughing, and said, "Don't you dare. Just go on and take your shower and make that French toast. Make the French toast, and I will forgive you everything." They kissed for a little bit, and then Karen got up and went into the bathroom. Grady looked at the clock. It was a quarter to nine. He reached over for the phone and dialed Zio Gennero's cell phone.

Gennero answered, "Hello."

"Zio, it's me, Grady."

"Good morning, Grady. How are you?"

"Oh, I'm good, Zio. I'm just calling because, well, after our last conversation, about Richie? I got to thinking about it, and I thought I'd check with some old friends to see if I could come up with any, you know, details that you might be interested in knowing about. Anyway, I found out some stuff about this girl, Tracy, and the guy she ended up marrying—the guy Richie beat up. I wondered if you wanted to get together so I could tell you what I learned."

"Listen, Grady, I appreciate what you've done. Things are"— he paused—"extremely busy for me today, and I'm not sure what tomorrow will bring. Let me think a minute." He took a deep breath. "Listen," he continued, "is there any place I can get back to you, maybe later this morning, maybe close to noontime?"

"Zio, I don't have any schedule. I can hang out at home all day if you want me to, and you get back to me whenever you can."

"Thank you, Grady. I'll try to get back to you by noon, but if I can't, don't feel that you have to wait for me. Feel free to go about your business. We'll get in touch with each other one way or another. Listen, on this matter, I found out some things too. So when we get together, we'll pool our information and see what we have."

"Great. I'm sure I'll be here, so don't worry about it. Call me whenever it's convenient for you. I just wanted to let you know what I found out, that's all."

"I know, Grady. I understand. I'm looking forward to finding out what you have. I'll talk to you soon."

"Okay, Zio, talk to you later."

When Karen came out of the shower, he looked admiringly at her naked body. "Christ," he said, "all this and French toast too."

"Only if you're good."

"Oh, I'm good," he answered. "In fact, I've been told I'm great."

"Oh, yeah?" Karen smiled, putting her hands on her hips. "Somebody was trying to make you feel good."

"If I'm not mistaken, it was you."

Karen smiled. "So I lied." And that's when he threw the pillow at her.

Chapter XV

Gennero: First Things First

At ten minutes after nine, Gennero stepped out of his house and smiled gratefully at the familiar sight of Sal waiting by the car. As soon as Sal saw him, he opened the back door to the limo. When Sal got into the driver's seat, Gennero told him to drive to Maria's house. *First things first. First Maria's appointment with the surgeon, then to the Methodist Hospital to see about Theresa.* Gennero didn't know what to expect regarding Theresa. Everything there would be new: the doctors, their diagnosis, her condition, everything. With Maria, he was sure that she was going to need surgery and that it would be very soon.

In the back of his mind, he was also developing an awareness that all of this might impact his work. He thought about the fact that he had not scheduled any appointments to look in on any of the corporation's businesses. For the first time, he was beginning to think about the possibility of retiring or maybe cutting back . . . if the board would go along with that. He'd have to be in touch with Paolo this afternoon, after he knew more.

Sal pulled up in front of Maria's brownstone. "We should just be a few minutes," Gennero was saying, when he heard the front door to the house open. Apparently Maria had been ready and had watched for them through her front window. "Well, all ready for us, I see," he called to her.

Maria held the railing as she came down her steps. She was dressed in her finest coat and carried one of her better purses. Going to the doctor's was still an occasion to get dressed up for.

Maria reached the car, and Gennero gave her a kiss on the cheek, helped her into the backseat, and then got in next to her.

"How are you feeling?" he asked softly, taking hold of her hand.

She withdrew her hand brusquely from his. "I'm fine," she said irritably. "There's nothing to be worried about. It is what it is. What will be, will be."

"Yes, that's true," he said quietly, "but this is not going to the Acme to buy a can of tomatoes. This is about your health, your life. It's natural to be concerned."

"I'm not concerned, I told you," she snapped. "You, you're concerned, but I'm not. At my age, who needs these things anyway?" she asked, indicating her breasts with her eyes. "Gennero, you know as well as I do that I'm going to have to have surgery. They're going to want to remove both of my breasts and all of the lymph nodes, a total radical mastectomy. A double or whatever they call it. Then I'll probably have chemotherapy and maybe some radiation too. Then my hair, such as it is, will probably fall out, and I'll feel nauseous and weak for a while, and then, before you know it, I'll be back to normal, just a few pounds lighter and making breakfast for your secret meetings again." When she finished talking to him as if he were a little boy, she sat back in her seat, her hands folded across the purse in her lap.

Gennero looked at his older sister with raised eyebrows. On the one hand, he had admiration for her courage and for the homework she had obviously done to prepare herself for the coming ordeal. He was also amused at her apparent need to deny having any concern or anxiety for the potential dangers involved. Then it dawned on him that part of her need to take control of the events was not only her characteristic way of dealing with stress, but was also her way of protecting him, just as she had always done since they were children. She was the little mother surrogate taking care of him even when her life was on the line. Rarely did she give him the opportunity to be the protective brother.

"So you've got it all figured out, I see. I wouldn't be surprised if you've already printed out and signed all of the insurance and waiver forms he's going to ask you to fill out."

Maria looked at him sideways. "No," she answered, "I didn't have time. But I would have if I could."

"I know you would." Gennero laughed. Then he took her hand again and gave it a quick squeeze before letting go. "I have no doubt, Maria," he continued, "that we both will be able to cope with whatever happens. I know you're going to come through this all right. And I know that you know that I'll be here for you to help in any way possible."

Maria smiled and then took his hand and gave it a squeeze. "I know, Gennero. We'll both be fine. I know."

Soon, Sal pulled in front of the doctor's office and went quickly around to the back of the car to help Gennero and his sister out. He stood by the car as they entered the building.

In the doctor's office, it was almost exactly as Maria had predicted. The surgeon manually examined her breast, looked at her chart, and concluded that the size of the tumor and the apparent speed with which it had grown were not good signs. In all likelihood, it would prove to be malignant. Of course, they wouldn't be able to tell for certain until they did a biopsy, but in any case, the tumor had to be removed. They would do a biopsy while they had her open in the OR and would then do whatever seemed most prudent. In the worst-case scenario, they would do a double radical mastectomy, but if the tumor was benign— which the odds were against—then they would just remove it, and that would be that.

On the other hand, worst-case scenario, the surgery might have to be followed up with further treatments, possibly radiation and/or chemotherapy, depending on what they found. Before they left the office, they scheduled her admission to the hospital for the following morning and the surgery for Saturday morning. Both Maria and Gennero nodded gravely at all of the doctor's pronouncements, asked a few clarifying questions, shook his hand, and were out of the office within an hour. Sal had the door open by the time they reached the car. They both got in, looking drained and tired.

"Home?" Gennero asked her. Maria nodded and then looked out of the window.

Gennero leaned forward slightly. "Back to Maria's house, please, Sal." Sal caught his eye in the rearview mirror and then slowly rolled away and entered the flow of traffic.

"Maria," Gennero began, "of course, I'll be here tomorrow morning to take you to the hospital, and I'll be back later in the day to see if you need anything. But I was wondering if you will be all right alone today or if you would like me to drop by later."

Maria took his hand. "I'm going to be fine. I have lots to do to get ready for tomorrow: stop the mail for a while, a little cleaning, pack, you know. And then there are some of my friends I need to call so I can let them know what's going on. No, I'll be all right. But I'll appreciate your being here in the morning."

"Good. Then I'll see you in the morning, about eight o'clock?"

Maria thought for a moment. "Yes, that will work out fine." Then they settled into their own thoughts and were silent for the rest of the short trip back to her house. After dropping her off, Gennero told Sal to take him to Methodist Hospital and spent the remainder of the ride thinking about Theresa.

In the hospital, Gennero went to the bank of elevators he had used the night before to go up to Theresa's room in intensive care. Once on the floor, he went to the nurse's desk and asked if it was possible to speak to the doctor in charge of her case. They said that they would let the doctor know that he was here. Then Gennero walked down the hall until he came to her room. Theresa was in bed, still with an IV inserted in the back of her hand. She was propped up and surprisingly alert, given her condition the night before.

"Well," he said cheerfully, a big smile on his face, "you're looking much better this morning. Got your beauty rest, I see." He leaned over and gave her a kiss, noticing her restrained response. "So how are you feeling?"

Theresa gave a little shrug. "Good as can be expected, I guess. A little tired."

"Of course, your body has been through a lot. You're a lucky girl, you know, to be here at all."

"If you say so."

Gennero took a deep breath and struggled to keep a calm composure. Finally, he asked, "What do you mean by that, 'if I say so'?"

"Just what I said. If you think I'm lucky to be here, then I must be lucky to be here. After all, whatever you say goes, right?"

"Tessie, what are you talking about?"

"Nothing. Forget it."

Gennero stared at her for a moment and then decided to take his coat off. He looked for a place to put it down. He took one of the chairs and brought it over to the side of the bed and sat down. It was a long silence. Gennero sat back and looked at Theresa. "Tessie, why are you so belligerent this morning?"

Theresa glared at him. "Because they don't want to let me go home. They'll listen to you. If you tell them to let me come home, then they'll let me go. But I know you. You don't want me to come home. You're glad that I'm here. You wish I had killed myself yesterday. You want me out of your life, you bastard."

Gennero had not been ready for such a vicious onslaught. It was true, he didn't want her home, not in this condition, but it wasn't true, not really, that he wished her dead . . . although he remembered wishing that he could be free of all this craziness. And he had experienced a feeling of relief at the time. He shook his head in disbelief.

"Theresa, listen to me. You tried to commit suicide. You tried to kill yourself. That's not normal. Normal people don't go around trying to kill themselves. You obviously have a serious problem, and you need help for it. So you're right, I don't want you to come home right now. I want to make sure that you get the help that you need. I don't want you to come home and then have both of us go through this again."

"You won't have to worry, Gennero," she said. "The next time, I'll make sure to finish the job so that you won't have to be inconvenienced."

"Is that what you think this is? An inconvenience?"

"What else? All you care about is your coffee. As long as you get what you want, you don't care about anything else."

"Theresa, what in God's name are you talking about?"

"How many times, Gennero, have I told you that people are trying to hurt us—you, me, our daughter, our granddaughters? How many times have I asked you to get us away from here to someplace safe?"

They held each other's gaze. Finally, Gennero spoke. "Tessie, moving is not the solution to your fears. Your fears are exaggerations; they're not real."

"See! You don't believe me. You don't listen. You dismiss what I have to say as unimportant. You don't care if somebody is trying to kill me . . . or you. I'm trying to protect you. You'd think you would have the decency to do the same. Some husband you are. Some man! A real man who loved his wife would protect her, not wave her off like some housefly."

Gennero didn't know what to say. He was damned if he was going to make believe that he agreed with this nonsense about their lives being in danger. In fact, he wondered if he had been coddling her too much as it was, not being confrontational enough.

Theresa continued, "Tell me, Gennero, my dear husband, how long has it been since we made love?"

Gennero looked up from his hands, which he'd been holding in his lap. His gaze wandered out the window, to the blue sky, a tree, still bare but with noticeable buds beginning to appear. "I don't know," he said. "It's been a long time. I've lost track. A few years, I guess. Why?"

"Why? Is it normal for a husband who supposedly loves his wife to not want to have sex with her for over three years? Huh? Why is that, Gennero? Could it be you have a girlfriend on the side that's getting all of your attention now that you're getting rid of me?"

"Theresa! What are you talking about? We haven't made love in three years, if that's what you say it is, because you kept refusing me until I gave up. It wasn't me who lost interest. It was you who rejected me. But I didn't complain. Maybe I should have, but I figured if you weren't up to it, I didn't want to force you. After all, it's not like I'm still forty or fifty years old. Sex doesn't have the same urgency for me now that it did then. But that doesn't mean that I don't miss making love to you. I do. And a girlfriend? That's preposterous, Tessie. All I need in my life, on top of everything else, is another woman in my life. A girlfriend. Ridiculous."

It was during the tense silence that followed that Dr. Sung entered the room. "Good morning. I'm Doctor Sung, Mrs. Giantonio, Mr. Giantonio."

Gennero got up to shake his hand, and then Doctor Sung went over to Theresa's bedside and put out his hand. She looked away and refused to take it. He hesitated and then turned his attention back to Gennero, although he clearly was speaking to both of them.

"As we explained to Mrs. Giantonio this morning, and as they told you last night, Mr. Giantonio, we are quite concerned about the possibility of severe liver damage as a result of the Tylenol overdose, and it will be at least another three or four days before we can be sure of the results of the testing. In the meantime, it is vital that we frequently monitor Mrs. Giantonio's condition. So, for that reason, alone, it is imperative that Mrs. Giantonio stay with us for the next few days."

Gennero understood. Of course, medically, this made sense. He was aware, however, of Theresa giving out a loud exasperated sigh, making her disagreement and displeasure quite obvious. Gennero guessed that Dr. Sung and perhaps other staff had already gone over this territory with her earlier this morning.

"In addition," Dr. Sung continued, turning occasionally from one to the other, "we also had a psychiatric consultation earlier this morning, and Dr. Weinstadt thinks that Mrs. Giantonio still constitutes a danger to herself. That is, there is a strong possibility that there could be another suicidal attempt. It is his suggestion that we transfer Mrs. Giantonio to the psychiatric department where she can begin to get some treatment for her depressive condition and where we can still monitor her liver functions."

Theresa loudly interrupted, "There is no way I'm going into a nut house. No way. Gennero, don't you dare let them do this to me. I'm warning you."

Gennero, who had sat back down in his chair, lowered his chin and looked up at his wife. "Theresa, listen to me. The doctor is being reasonable. You nearly killed yourself. In spite of what you think, nobody wants you dead—not me, not our daughter, not our grandchildren, nobody. You have to get the medical care that you now need because of what you did. You damaged your liver, and you can't come home until they're sure you're well enough. I want you home, but I want you home well. I don't want you to come home to die. You understand? Now, maybe this is not the best hospital for you to be in, but maybe it is. I'll look into that, and I'll talk to the doctors. I promise you, Tessie, that you will come home as soon as it's reasonable for you to come home. But not before. *Basta*! *Finito*!"

Again, Dr. Sung stepped into the silence. "That's essentially what we've already told you this morning, Mrs. Giantonio. Now, it's time for us to take some blood." He nodded at a technician who had been waiting at the door. "Mr. Giantonio, if I may speak to you for a moment?" he said, motioning to Gennero to follow him out of the room. "You'll be able to come back and visit more in a few minutes. Mrs. Giantonio, I'll look in on you later."

Once in the hallway, the doctor led Gennero away from the room where they could talk privately. "Mr. Giantonio, your wife is a very sick lady, both medically and psychiatrically. This morning, we had quite a difficult time with her. She wanted to leave the hospital and was refusing treatment. She tried to rip the IV out of her arm and refused to take any medication, including the antidote for Tylenol poisoning." Doctor Sung paused to make sure Gennero understood the import of his words. "We had to physically restrain her," he added.

Gennero said he understood how serious this was.

"Dr. Weinstadt believes that we should start her on an antidepressant and an antipsychotic medication as soon as possible, but so far she's refusing to cooperate, other than agreeing to let us take the blood samples. If she continues to insist on being discharged from the hospital, we will do that only if she signs papers indicating that she's leaving AMA, against medical advice."

"Is there any way to force her to stay and receive treatment?" Gennero asked. "I mean, now that she's demonstrated that she's a danger to herself, can't you institute involuntary commitment proceedings against her?"

Dr. Sung looked at Gennero approvingly and smiled for the first time. "Yes, exactly. That is what we would like to do. I wasn't aware that you knew of the proceedings. Yes, we'll have to go to court. If we can do it by tomorrow morning, that would be best; otherwise, it would have to wait until Monday morning, and I don't know if we can hold her that long if we can convince her to stay."

"Is there anything you need me to do to facilitate this proceeding?"

"Yes, Mr. Giantonio, there is. First, it might be helpful if you were to tell your wife that we—and you—are prepared to do this. If she believes there's a good chance that you're going to cooperate in an involuntary commitment proceeding, she may stop lobbying for you to take her home. Also, if you'll remind her that if she signs herself in, what we call a voluntary commitment, then after forty-eight hours, she'd be able to sign herself out, so she would retain a measure of control.

"We would prefer that course for a couple of reasons. One is, as a matter of policy, the hospital doesn't like to get involved in involuntary commitment proceedings. Second, we believe that within a couple of days of starting the antipsychotic medication, we'll begin to see signs of more rational behavior, and there will be less danger of her acting out. The other thing you can do is to fill out some forms that we have here at the nurses' station. This would help us document that your wife has been disturbed for a while and will help us make the argument that she needs to be protected from herself."

Gennero asked a few additional questions and then shook hands with Dr. Sung and headed back into Theresa's room. As soon as he entered, she glared at him.

"Well, did the two of you have a good time talking about me?" Her voice was as dark and as bitter as the wild look on her face. With her uncombed hair in disarray and her face distorted by her anger, she looked like a witch.

Gennero took a deep breath and sat down in the chair. After some silence, he looked up at her. "Tessie, of course we spoke about you. Dr. Sung is responsible for your care while you're here, and I'm responsible for you financially, as well as for everything else. You think I don't care what kind of treatment they plan for you? Of course I talked to him about what their plans are. I care about what happens to you."

Theresa let out a loud harrumph and turned her head away, as if she couldn't bear to listen to such nonsense. "You say that you care, but you don't care. You don't give a damn what happens to me. Did you see how he looked at me? Of course you saw. How could you miss it, that leer."

"What are you talking about?"

"That doctor. He practically undressed me with his eyes, right here, right in front of you, and you did nothing. Nothing! And this morning," she quickly added, "he tried to feel my breast."

"Theresa, he's a doctor. I'm sure he was only—"

"Don't do that! Don't go dismissing me all the time. You weren't here. You didn't see. He tried to feel me up. And before, he winked at me. I know he's going to come back and try something. Gennero. I can't stay here. I'm not safe. This doctor is evil."

"*Cara*, I'm not dismissing you. I'm just trying to point out that maybe you're mistaken, maybe there's another explanation—"

"No, damn it! Listen to me for once. You think I'm a fool. I know how men look at women. You think because he's a doctor he's different? You're all the same. Pigs."

"Theresa, listen to me. Look at me," he commanded.

Theresa slowly turned her face back toward his.

Gennero decided he had to change the subject. "You did . . . you possibly did great damage to your liver. There is absolutely no question that you must stay in the hospital for at least another three or four days while they do their tests. And," he continued forcefully, "during that time, you must take the medication that they ask you to take. It will save your life and help you to recover from this damned fool thing you did." He looked at her and tried to stare her down. "Now there's no question of your coming home until we know that you're healthy, so if you don't take their medicine, you won't get well, and you won't come home. Is that clear, Theresa?"

She shrugged her shoulders and looked away again.

"In order to make sure that you get this treatment, the hospital is prepared to go to court tomorrow morning and have you committed. Do you understand?"

"They can't do that. They have no right."

"No, *cara*, you're wrong. They not only have every right, they have a legal obligation. If they let you go home now, and you end up dying of liver damage or being crippled by it, or making another suicide attempt, you or I or even Nina could sue them. We could sue all of them—the doctors, the hospital—for negligence. It's their duty to see you get treated."

"Not if I sign myself out of the hospital. Then they aren't responsible." Theresa had a smirk on her face, as if she had just played her ace of trump.

"Tessie, they aren't going to let you do that, and neither am I. If necessary, I'll go to court tomorrow morning and help them.

I want you to get well. I want you to be who you used to be. Theresa, I need you to get well. I can't have you home like this."

Theresa looked confused, shaking her head, not knowing where to look or where to focus. "Gennero, you would do that? You would sign papers committing me to a hospital, to a loony bin?" She shook her head in disbelief. "I should have known. I did know. I didn't want to believe that you were really against me, but I knew it. In my heart and in my soul, I knew it. You've had enough of me, and now you want a younger woman. Throwing me away, after all these years." There were tears in her eyes. Then abruptly she was angry. "You bastard. How could you do this to me?"

"Tessie, I'm willing to do this, if you make it necessary, because I want you to get well. When you calm down, you'll see this is the best way. It's what we have to do."

Again, Theresa turned away from him, looking out of the window.

"Tessie, I'm sure they told you. There's another much easier, much simpler way to do this. All you have to do is to agree to stay in the hospital. Sign the papers yourself. Do it voluntarily. Then, after a few days, if you still want to come home, and your liver is healthy, you can sign yourself out. Do you understand?"

She ignored him.

"Theresa, look at me. Do you understand what I'm saying about this voluntary business?"

"Commitment," she said, "voluntary commitment. You needn't be afraid of the word, Gennero. You were quite willing to use it before. Remember? You were willing to help them commit me. Don't you remember?"

"Yes, Theresa, I remember. It's something that I'm prepared to do to make sure you get the treatment that you need—if you make me do it. But you can do this yourself and have more control over things. I'd think that would appeal to you, to be more in control of what happens to you."

Each of them remained silent, she avoiding his eyes by looking out of the window, and he, trying to gauge her state by scrutinizing her.

"Theresa, I don't like to argue with you. I'm going to go now, but I'll be back later this afternoon. In the meantime, I want you to think about this. I want you to take all of the medications that they bring to you. I want you to cooperate with them in every way so that you'll get well faster and come home sooner. Understand?"

Theresa kept her face stiffly away from his.

"One other thing. As I said earlier when Dr. Sung was here, I'll talk to some people I know. If I find that it would be better for you to be in another hospital to get the treatment you need, then I'll arrange for a transfer. But, Theresa, one way or another, you're not coming home until we're sure you're well again." Gennero got up, leaned over, and kissed her cheek. Then he turned, picked up his coat from the foot of the bed, and walked to the doorway.

"I'll be back sometime this afternoon. Let me know if there's anything you want me to bring."

He watched as she kept herself rigidly turned away from him, and then he turned and walked down the hall to the nurses' station, where he wrote out a note for Dr. Sung, informing him of what had happened. Then he picked up the forms he needed to fill out for the commitment proceedings, if they needed to use them, and walked toward the elevators.

Chapter XVI

Maria

Maria knew that Gennero would keep the car there until she was safely into her house. Without turning, she heard the soft murmur of the motor as she opened her door and went inside. Once in, she leaned back against the door and took a deep breath. Pulling herself up straight, she put her purse on the table and hung her hat and coat on the old oak coatrack that had belonged to her parents. Going into the kitchen, she put a pot of water on for some espresso, and, taking the telephone from its receiver on the wall, sat down at the old Formica table and called her friend Mona next door.

"Mona, it's me, Maria. Are you busy right now? No? Good. Listen, can you come over for a little while? About ten minutes? Good. I just put water on for espresso. Sure, I've got tea. About ten minutes then? Good, just come on in; the door's unlocked."

Maria went to the bathroom and washed up a bit. She was coming down the stairs into the foyer when Mona opened the front door. Maria gave her a hug, which Mona returned, although somewhat tentatively.

"What's happening?" she asked, holding Maria at arm's length and looking intently into her face. "What's wrong, Maria? You seem upset."

Maria grimaced and lowered her eyes. "That's what I love about you, Mona, that x-ray vision you have." She took her friend by the arm. "Come, let's go in the kitchen. The water should be done."

Mona followed her friend into the kitchen and sat at the table while Maria poured the water into a cup for tea and the rest into the espresso pot, before sitting down herself.

"Well, I just wanted to let you know that I went to the doctor's this morning. Gennero brought me back about ten minutes ago. It looks like tomorrow I'm going into the hospital."

Mona appeared too stunned to say anything. She reached across the table and took Maria's hands into her own.

"I've got a tumor, Mona, a breast tumor. I go into the hospital tomorrow morning and have the surgery on Saturday."

"Maria, I don't know what to say. Do they know if it's cancer or not, if it's benign?"

"Not really. They'll do a biopsy when they remove it, but the surgeon is pretty sure that it's not benign. Mona, it's a big tumor, almost the size of a lemon."

Mona's dark eyes, which usually appeared to be squinting, a combination of her Asian heritage and her round, plump face, grew large with amazement and shock. "Oh my God!" she exclaimed, raising her hand to her mouth. "That big?"

Maria nodded as she poured her coffee and spooned in some sugar. Mona took the opportunity to prepare her tea and took a tentative sip.

"So," Maria continued, "assuming that it's cancer, there's a good chance that it has already metastasized, given its size. I know I'm jumping the gun, Mona, but I want to be prepared for the worst." She paused and caught Mona's eyes. "Worst-case scenario is they do a double mastectomy and then chemotherapy and radiation and . . ." She lowered her eyes. "Then in maybe a year, I'll die of it anyway."

"Maria, don't talk that way. People recover from cancer all the time. You know that. My god, look at the women we know who have had mastectomies and now are perfectly healthy: Sarah across the street and Josie down the block, for example."

"I know, Mona," Maria quickly replied. "I know. I've done all my homework. I even went to the library and had the librarian help me get on the Internet. I know most women survive. But,

Mona . . ." Maria paused, her eyes filling up as she reached over and plucked a tissue from the box on the radiator next to the table. "I don't have a good feeling about this at all. Look, I'm seventy-six years old. Most women who survive are much younger; their bodies can take the treatment better."

"Yeah, but you're strong, Maria."

"Not that strong," she countered. "Mona, you know what these treatments do to the body. Never mind the cancer; you can die from all the poisons they pour into you. Besides, I'm not sure I want to go through all of that."

"What are you saying? That you'd rather give up and die than lose your hair? Maria, at our age, no one gives a hoot whether we have our hair or not, and I'm ten years younger than you. You think my Glenn would care if I were bald for a while? As long as he's getting some nooky, he's happy."

"I know, Mona. Glenn loves you very much, and of course he would prefer to keep you with him as long as possible. But our situations are different. I'm older. I'm tired," she said, raising her hand to stifle Mona's attempted reassurance. "The tiredness may be partly from the cancer itself. I know. Still, I don't have the same reasons to squeeze out another year of life, not if it's going to be a year of pain and discomfort. I don't have the same reasons to push on that you have."

"Oh, Maria, aren't you getting ahead of yourself? You just came from the doctor's with some horrible news. Of course you're upset. But you're ready to jump into the grave and cover yourself up. Why don't we just take it one step at a time? Tomorrow you go in. Saturday you have surgery. Then they'll do the biopsy, and we'll see where that leaves us."

"Us?" Maria chuckled.

"Listen, honey, I'm with you every step of the way. I'm right next door. I've got plenty of time. Listen," Mona's eyes filled with tears that streamed down her puffy cheeks, "we're like sisters, you and me. With what you did for our son and his wife, selling them your store, and all that we've been through together, you can't keep me out of this. Don't you worry about anything. While you're in the hospital, I'll collect your mail and keep these plants watered and happy. And when you come home—"

"*Basta*, Mona. I'm not your grandchild. I have no intention of being an invalid."

"No, no, no, Maria. I didn't mean that. I just meant that you're going to be a little weak, and I'll be here to do whatever you would like me to do. No, I know you too well. I have no intention of trying to take over your life. I don't need to be your mother, but I am your friend, and I do intend to help out. And," she said, reaching across the table to take Maria's hand, "you're not going to be able to stop me."

Chapter XVII

THERESA

Theresa refused to look to see if Gennero was still there. Part of her wanted him to be standing in the doorway, reluctant to go, sad and concerned, even frightened. But she wouldn't risk giving him the satisfaction of looking. She kept clenching and unclenching her fist and looking out the window, seeing nothing, until finally she couldn't stand it any longer, and she stole a glance. The noises that she had been hearing, that had fueled her hope that Gennero would still be there, looking hopefully to her for some sign that she forgave him, turned out to be just unexplained hospital noises. The doorway was empty, and her heart sank. *I knew it, the bastard. He doesn't love me. He doesn't give a shit about me.*

In the relative silence of her room, she couldn't help but replay the conversation with Gennero. She knew he was right. They weren't going to let her go home if they thought she'd make another suicide attempt. And she knew that they weren't going to let her go home if there was a chance that she'd die from liver damage. She was furious about it, but smart enough to recognize that they—the hospital doctors and Gennero—held all the cards. If she wanted to go home, she'd have to appear to cooperate with them. Theresa had just resigned herself to this idea when an African American nurse's aide came into the room.

"Mrs. Giantonio?"

Theresa looked up at her. "Who are you?"

"My name is Latoya. I'm going to be here keeping you company for the rest of the day."

"Company? What are you talking about? I don't need you to keep me company."

"Well, I have my orders. The doctor doesn't want you to be alone."

"Oh, you mean you're here to keep an eye on me, to spy on me."

"Whatever. I'm supposed to stay in here with you so that you're not alone. So if there's anything I can do for you while I'm here, you just let me know."

"With all I hear about hospitals being short-staffed, you're going to sit in here, babysitting me, reading or watching TV or whatever? What a waste. Listen, what did you say your name was?"

"Latoya," the aide answered from the chair in the corner of the room near the window where, apparently, she was planning on taking up residence. She took a book out of her cloth bag, which also contained knitting needles.

"Latoya, don't expect me to keep you entertained. And it has nothing to do with your color. It's only because I have no intention of talking to anybody here. So you just go ahead with your reading and knitting and leave me alone. And I don't want that TV on."

"That's fine, Mrs. Giantonio. I'll be over here, keeping myself occupied, and like I said, if there's anything I can do for you, just let me know."

Theresa didn't bother answering. She had no intention of being polite or easy or pleasant to anybody. She was still too angry. She went back to the conversation with Gennero. She couldn't get over the sense of betrayal, that he would conspire with the doctors and the court to have her imprisoned here against her will. He, of all people, to go to court to get her locked up. She felt a deep and hollow sadness, as if her stomach had been ripped out.

What am I going to do? she asked herself. *I have nobody. Everybody is against me. The one person I counted on to save us, to protect me, has joined them and become my enemy. How do I* know they won't try to kill me here? That's why they don't want me to go home. They want to keep me here where they can feed me with poison. This woman here, this Latoya, she's not here to protect me. She's here to see that I don't escape. And she's a big, strong, young woman. There's no way I can fight her. Maybe if she gets bored enough, she'll fall asleep. Oh, what am I going to do?

Can I eat the food? Are they going to drug me? Maybe give me some kind of truth serum and ask me questions? Maybe Gennero is trying to see if I'll say anything against him. But I don't know anything, Gennero. You never told me anything. How could I hurt you? I'd never turn against you, you bastard. I took care of you. I always stood up for you. I tried to protect you. And what do you do? You turn your back on me. You walk away from me. You threaten me. Just you wait until I get home. I'll get even with you for this. Married for over fifty years, fifty-four years this June, and this is what happens. Just because I'm old, not as old as him—I won't even be seventy-three for another six months—he throws me away. He doesn't care about sex anymore, probably has some young chippie on the side.

They all do nowadays. Poppa didn't. He would never have treated Mama this way. They stuck together, not like this one. Poppa was strong. Strict but strong. He would never have let people hound me, harass me, threaten me the way Gennero has, let them get away with murder. That's what he's doing. He's going to let them get away with murder!

Theresa's eyes opened wide at this insight. Of course, that was it. He was behind it all. Of course, how could she have been so blind? He wanted her out of the way so he could be with his mistress and so he wouldn't have to give her any money. *He's afraid I'll tell everybody about him if he asks for a divorce. So he'll just eliminate me, wipe me out, erase me. I've got to get a lawyer, a good one, who'll protect me.*

From time to time, a nurse came in to monitor Theresa's vital signs, to give her medication—which she took—and to take blood samples for the liver tests they were doing. At one point, Dr. Sung came in, and Theresa made a real effort to appear more agreeable and cooperative. "I've been thinking about what you said this morning about signing myself in," she said, putting her best smile on her face. "Maybe you could explain to me again how that works?"

Dr. Sung had been looking at her chart, noting with some relief that she had been more cooperative in taking the medications, which included antipsychotics and antidepressants as well as the antidote for the Tylenol poisoning. "Well, Mrs. Giantonio, I'm delighted to see that you're cooperating with our attempts to treat you. By signing the voluntary admission form, it simply means that you're acknowledging that you're here voluntarily, that you recognize your need for treatment, and that you plan to continue to cooperate with us in making you well. However, if you change your mind at any point, you can give us a forty-eight-hour notice. Then, if you still wish to, you can sign yourself out of the hospital."

"I thought that's what you said this morning. Of course, I was pretty upset then. I imagine you would have been too, if you found yourself in the hospital, being threatened with psychiatric commitment."

"Well, Mrs. Giantonio—"

"I know, I know," she interrupted him. "I have only myself to blame. I know. I guess I was more upset than I knew. Anyway, I think I could sign those papers. I just want to talk it over again with my husband and make sure that's what he wants. You know how it is. Would that be all right?"

Dr. Sung hesitated, but after a pause, he finally agreed. "Of course. Are we expecting him to visit again this afternoon or evening?"

Theresa smiled again. "Oh yes, he said he'd be back this afternoon. So I'll talk about it with him then."

"Good."

CHAPTER XVIII

GRADY

Grady was sitting in a kitchen chair, looking out of the window and playing his guitar when the phone rang. It was Zio Gennero, and he suggested that he come by and pick Grady up for lunch. Grady said sure and looked at his kitchen clock: twelve thirty. Grady washed up, put on a clean T-shirt and sweatshirt, his leather jacket, and went downstairs to wait. It wasn't long before he saw the familiar Lincoln Town Car coming down the street. Grady stepped out into the street and opened the back door to get in. "How you doing, Zio? I didn't expect to see you today. I thought we'd just talk on the phone."

"Yes, I thought so too, but to tell you the truth, Grady, I need a break. It's been a tough morning. I thought we'd grab a quiet lunch someplace and see where we are with this other business." Grady picked up that Gennero was playing it very close to the vest. Maybe he didn't even want Sal to know what was going on.

"Great," Grady agreed, "I'm like you, always ready to eat." They both laughed, and in a few minutes, Sal pulled up in front of small Italian restaurant on Eighth Street. It was close enough that Grady could have walked to it from his place.

When they stopped, Gennero told Sal to go take a leisurely lunch and then come back for him. Once inside, they sat down at a small table and chatted until after the waiter had taken their order and left. "So, Grady, tell me what you found out."

"Well, first, this Tracy, Tracy Malatesta, went to high school with the wife of a friend of mine. She was a little on the fast side in high school. After that, she went to Temple, got a degree, and is now a grade-school teacher somewhere on the Main Line. Looks like she hung out a lot with Brian Hoffman—the jerk Richie and I beat up—who works in a bank or something downtown, a mortgage broker maybe. They got married about a year ago, and now they live out on the Main Line. Now the really interesting thing is that both Tracy and Brian were into the drug scene, and Brian used to deal drugs. Maybe he still does. I know a guy who used to score heroin from him at a club down in Old City called The Harp. My friend is clean now and last bought from Brian back at the end of 2002." Grady sat back in his chair. "That's about it. I'm not sure what it means, but I thought you'd want to know."

"Good work, Grady. You'd make a good private detective. It confirms everything I heard, plus." Gennero leaned forward. "The bank Brian Hoffman works at is Philadelphia First City Bank. He's been arrested twice, once for DUI and once for possession of cocaine. Both cases were dismissed, which probably means that he's got a friend somewhere. Now Tracy, she's also been arrested for possession of heroin. Interestingly, that case, which was only three years ago, was also dismissed. Maybe the same friend."

Grady perked up. "That reminds me. I almost forgot. My friend told me that Tracy's father works for the city, an administrator of some kind, with the City Water Department, I think. And," he added, leaning forward for emphasis, "she has an older brother, Gino, who's on the force, maybe a detective."

Grady sat back in his chair again, just as the waiter arrived with their lunch. Grady had ordered veal Parmigiana with a side of linguini, and Gennero had ordered the lobster ravioli and a salad. Gennero had a glass of red wine with his lunch, but Grady stuck with his glass of water.

Gennero thought for a few moments while he tasted his first ravioli and savored it in his mouth. "God," he said, "I love these ravioli. Like heaven."

Grady smiled, but with his mouth full, didn't say anything.

Shifting back to the original topic, Gennero continued, "So it's possible that Tracy's father or her brother might be able to pull some strings for them."

"That's what I was just thinking, Zio, although we don't know anything yet about his family, do we?"

"No, not yet. But I'm not sure that it's important to know who their friends and protectors are. Not yet, anyway. I agree with what you said before, Grady, that maybe none of this adds anything to our understanding of why Richie overdosed. One thing I know for sure that I didn't know before we spoke a couple of days ago is that Richie was into drugs a lot more heavily than I had thought. You told me that. And all of these other things, Tracy being arrested for heroin possession and her husband dealing heroin, confirm that was the circle Richie traveled in. Even you, his best friend, were a heroin addict, which I didn't know until you told me. So now when I look back, it seems obvious. I mean, drug addicts die from overdoses all the time. I'm sure my granddaughter, Andrea, often runs into it in the hospital."

Gennero paused and took a sip of his wine. Grady continued to eat while he listened.

Gennero seemed to be thinking out loud. "It's funny, I suppose—human nature, the way it works. You love somebody, and it literally makes you blind. I remember hearing once, 'There are none so blind as those who will not see.' We in the family—me, his mother, his Zia Maria, all of us—didn't want to see Richie as an addict. We didn't want to know how much trouble he was in. Of course, he did his best to keep it from us, but we did our part too. We looked away. We used kinder words, more positive words to describe him: how much life and vitality he had, how it was good that he had music as an outlet for his emotions, what a crazy wild culture this rock-and-roll stuff was. Not even when he was found dead in his apartment with a needle in his hand did we admit what had been going on."

Gennero took another ravioli and savored it while gazing absently into the distance. Then he sighed heavily. "This is the first chance that I've had to reflect on all of this." He looked at Grady. "You've been very helpful, Grady. Talking about this with you has helped me see the truth. My grandson was an addict. He hung out with addicts. He was in love with an addict. His best friend," he said, pointing his chin toward Grady, "was an addict. We loved him for his beautiful personality, his energy, his talent, his good nature. We didn't love him because we thought he was an angel or because we thought he didn't do any drugs at all. That was sad, that he did drugs, but it was irrelevant to why we loved him. Accepting that he was an addict is only accepting the truth. It doesn't change anything. And accepting that he died of a drug overdose is also the truth . . . and I guess . . . I guess I've finally come to accept it."

Grady wanted to say that he found himself agreeing with what Gennero said, but it seemed disrespectful to give approval to Gennero's thought process. He wanted to let Gennero know that he was with him. Simpatico was the word that came to mind. "It sounds like you've found a sense of peace with this."

Gennero looked up from his plate. "Yes, that's a good word. Peace, acceptance. You know, Grady, I've lived most of my life admiring people who were able to accept the reality of their situation. But it's not easy to be able to do that, to be able to accept things as they really are instead of how one might wish things were or thinks things should be. We get caught up in our desires, what we see as our best interest, and we get attached to those outcomes. That's the word the Buddhists use, 'attached.' You young people, you use the term, 'go with the flow.' It means the same thing: accept reality and go with it. Even embrace it.

"Did you know the Navajos use the phrase 'he who walks in beauty' to indicate a special person, a revered person, who is able to find beauty in whatever reality he's in? But, Grady, sometimes, it's so damned hard to do that, to accept a reality that's the opposite of what I thought it was and wanted it to be." Gennero pushed back from the table. "Grady, I have to tell you, there are a couple of other things on my mind right now."

Grady looked up at Gennero and waited for his uncle to continue.

Gennero leaned forward again. "My sister, Maria, has cancer, breast cancer."

"No."

"Yes. She'll be going into the hospital tomorrow morning and will have surgery on Saturday morning."

"How does it look?" Grady asked.

"Well, we're putting a brave face on it, but in the long haul, I have to admit I'm not optimistic. She's handling it well, and the short term looks pretty good, although in these matters, sometimes the treatment is as bad as the disease. This chemotherapy and radiation can make you as sick as a dog, so that sometimes you wish you were dead, you know? But the reality is that the tumor is pretty large, and there's a good chance the cancer has already spread. So in the long run . . . I don't think . . ." Gennero slumped back into his chair and shook his head sadly.

"Jesus, Zio, I don't know what to say. I had no idea. Listen, if there's anything I can do, just let me know. What hospital will she be in? Will I be able to visit her?"

"Sure, she's going to be in Pennsylvania Hospital, down here on Eighth Street. I'm sure she would love to see you. That would be wonderful. But that's not all. My wife, Theresa, is having a mental breakdown, and she's also in the hospital, as of last night."

"Oh my God," Grady exclaimed. "Holy shit! What the hell's been happening in your life?"

Gennero put a hand up to calm Grady down. "I know, it sounds crazy. It is crazy," he said, smiling to himself at the unintended pun. "But as my sister said, 'It is what it is.' Anyway, Grady, because of all of this, I'm going to have my hands full the next few days. I have no idea what's going to happen or what I'm going to be doing. Everything's upside down. So, with this Richie business, as far as I'm concerned, we can drop it. But if you—out of your own curiosity—want to follow up for any reason, then feel free to do that. And if you do, then let me know if I can be helpful to you. But as you can see, I'm going to be pretty occupied for a while." Then he took the paper that Dom had given him and handed it over to Grady. "I won't need this anymore. You take it."

Grady took the paper, glanced at it, put it in his pocket, and sat back and scratched his head. He looked across the table at Gennero. The waiter came and cleared the dishes. Gennero ordered espresso for both of them, "A big pot."

"I'm truly sorry to hear about both Maria and Theresa. I don't know what to say. Would it be all right to visit Theresa too?"

Gennero shook his head no. "That wouldn't be a good idea, Grady, but thank you for your concern. This is, of course, all confidential." Grady nodded, and then Gennero raised his hands. "What am I thinking, that I should say that to you? Forgive me. I know that you recognize what's private without having to be told. I wasn't thinking."

"No, Zio, that's okay. I understand. Jesus, this has got to be rough. Listen, anything I can do to be helpful, just let me know— run errands, anything."

"Thank you, Grady. I appreciate your thoughtfulness."

They lingered over the coffee. Gennero seemed to be in no hurry to go. When they finally got outside, they decided to walk around the block. Grady needed a cigarette, and Gennero indulged himself with one of his small cigars. When they got back, Sal was waiting for them with the car.

"Grady, you want a ride someplace?"

"No thanks, Zio. It's nice out, and it's only a few blocks. I'll walk. I'll talk to you soon."

"Thank you, Grady, for helping me to see the reality. Now, if only I can find a way to see the beauty in it." They smiled and waved, and Grady turned toward home.

Grady started walking toward his apartment, but as he walked, he realized that Karen was working both lunch and dinner today and wouldn't be home until very late. He slowed his steps as he thought and then stopped, lit up a cigarette and turned, looking north, back toward center city, toward Market Street where Brian's bank was located. In spite of what Gennero said about accepting the truth, Grady thought he'd be doing his uncle a favor if he pursued this a little further.

Philadelphia First City Bank had its headquarters in a tall, modern, glass building on Market Street. Grady went in and walked around but didn't see any sign of Brian Hoffman or the Mortgage Department. It was almost three o'clock, and he assumed everything would be shutting down soon, so he went outside and spotted a low stone retaining wall that acted as a container for some small shrubs. He picked a spot where the retainer met the wall of the building, sat down, and lit up. Grady was in no hurry. The weather was pleasant, and he had a good view of the main entrance.

It was almost four fifteen when Grady spotted Brian coming out of the door with another man. Grady recognized him from that night, the blond hair and the fair, fleshy face. Only now, Brian had a slight limp. He was nicely dressed in an expensive topcoat, was hatless, and his longish hair was being blown about by the brisk breeze. He and the other man were talking animatedly as they walked past him. Grady slowly put out his cigarette and fell in behind them at a comfortable distance.

The two men parted company at the corner, and Brian hurried across the street toward the train station as Grady kept him in sight. Brian entered the train station, and Grady watched from a distance as Brian headed for the platform that would take him out to the Main Line. Watching from behind the glass partition on the second level, Grady waited until Brian boarded the train. He then went to buy a roundtrip ticket to Haverford, the town where the Hoffmans lived. *Let's see where this dude hangs out*, he thought.

He checked the paper that Gennero had given to him, thinking that he would be able to find the street once he was out there. He wanted to see where these people lived. While he was waiting for the train and then riding it out to Haverford, Grady found himself thinking back to his earlier life with Richie.

From the time they first met until Richie died, they were evenly matched, remarkably similar in so many ways. Growing up, they were always testing their physical skills against each other: wrestling, boxing, stick ball, baseball, basketball, football, even swimming and diving on those occasions when they could get to one of the city pools or when he would go on a day trip with Richie and his parents to someplace that had a pool.

When both of them became interested in music, they complemented each other rather than competing. Richie took up piano and then keyboard while Grady played lead guitar. Of course, each one dabbled at the other's instrument while recognizing that the other was significantly more accomplished. Their rivalry was an affectionate one and served only to bond them more tightly. They shared everything. They were like identical twins. Nothing came between them.

That's why Grady remembered feeling a little hurt when Richie told him that he was serious about Tracy. He remembered wondering how Richie could get so serious about somebody he'd hardly known about. He remembered feeling left out, excluded, and couldn't understand why. *Now, I wonder what else he might have kept from me. He certainly didn't tell me that he was suicidal.* Then he realized with a guilty twinge that he'd never shared his blackouts with Richie, those losses of memory he was so ashamed of. Of course, eventually Richie had introduced him to Tracy, and he had seen her and Richie once or twice, and heard Richie on the phone with her. But he still had trouble imagining the two of them getting married.

And another thing, how come Richie was doing so much heroin? Sure, we did H when it was available, but Richie wasn't into it as his very favorite thing. Zio was wrong when he said that I was a heroin addict. I used it, but no more than—in fact a lot less than—a lot of other stuff. We both preferred coke and speed and even booze, for that matter. So when did smack become his dope of choice? Grady frowned as he thought about this for the first time. *On the other hand, it could be precisely because heroin wasn't his usual thing that an accidental overdose was possible. Yes, it was true that after Brian's beating, Richie was upset and had trouble forgiving himself for such murderous violence. But why would that result in his apparent turn to heroin? Why not more coke or speed, an upper to combat the guilt?* More and more, Grady found himself wondering whether Tracy and Brian might have had anything to do with Richie's overdosing on heroin.

When the train pulled into Haverford, Grady got off and asked a couple of the people who got off with him where he could find the street he was looking for. Twenty minutes later, he was walking down their block. He passed their house once, slowly, noticing what he could: a nicely landscaped, old-fashioned, two-story home with a big front porch on a picturesque tree-lined street. *It was very nice*, he thought. The Hoffmans had a two-car garage with a white SUV sitting in the wide driveway. Nobody was outside, on the entire block. *Nobody goes outside anymore, unless it's to get into a car. I bet kids never play on this grass.* He remembered how he and Richie and the other kids were always outside, playing in their narrow street or in the city park a couple of blocks away. They would have died for yards like this to play in.

Grady walked down to the corner and then turned around, and checking that no one was watching him, he retraced his steps. He noticed the lights in the houses this time, especially the lights on the first floor of the Hoffmans' house. He imagined a living room and dining room in the front, a kitchen and maybe a TV room facing the back, a stairway leading upstairs to three or four bedrooms, maybe a couple of bathrooms. Then he walked back to the train station. When he got back to Philly, he grabbed a cheeseburger and coffee and then took a bus home. It had been a long day.

Chapter XIX

GENNERO: PAOLO

Gennero almost didn't know who to call first, Dr. Sacerdote, Nina, or Paolo. He decided on Sacerdote and got his answering machine. "Dr. Sacerdote, this is Gennero Giantonio. I saw you about six or seven months ago about a family matter. Things have taken a dramatic turn for the worse, and I'd like to talk to you as soon as possible." He left his cell phone number and hung up. Next would be Paolo. He tapped in the number of the president of the board and got Paolo's voicemail. "Paolo, this is Gennero. I haven't talked with you in a while, but a family matter has come up, and I may need to take some time off. I'd appreciate it if you would give me a call so we can set up a time to sit down and talk privately." He left his cell number although he knew that Paolo would have it handy. Lastly, he gave Nina a call. *Finally, a live person*, he thought, when Nina's receptionist answered the phone. "Hello," he said, "this is Mr. Giantonio. May I speak with Nina please?" In a moment, Nina was on the phone.

"Hi, Pop, how are you?"

"I'm fine Nina, but Mama isn't doing too well."

"What happened? Is she all right?"

"Well, we had to take her to the hospital last night."

"What?" she exclaimed. "What happened?"

"To tell you the truth, Nina, she took an overdose of Tylenol. She tried to kill herself."

"No! Son of a bitch! How is she?"

"Well, she's alive, but apparently the Tylenol is like a poison and can damage the liver. So they have to monitor her for three or four days before they'll know whether her liver is okay or not. The complication is that she's insisting on coming home and doesn't want to cooperate with the doctors. You know, take the medication they want to give her, the antidote for the liver."

"Geez," said Nina. "Holy shit."

"If she doesn't agree to cooperate, the hospital is going to commit her to make sure she gets the treatment she needs."

"Commit her? You mean like to a psychiatric facility?"

"Yes. We could go to court tomorrow morning. They want me to be a witness."

"Does Ma know about this?"

"Yes. I just told her that that's what we're going to do if she doesn't cooperate."

"Oh boy, I bet she's royally pissed."

"You might say that," Gennero responded dryly. "So listen, I thought I might stop over this evening and fill you in on that and some other things that are happening."

"Sure, Pop. You want to come for dinner?"

"Maybe, *ciucci*, but I'm not sure where I'll be. I'll be going back to the hospital, and then there are some other people I have to talk to. So don't hold anything up for me. I'll get there when I can, and if I can't make it at all, I'll give you a call, all right?"

"Of course. Listen, Pop, if there's anything that I can do to help out, let me know, okay? But I'll see you later."

"All right, *ciucci*, I'll talk to you later."

Gennero had just hung up with Nina when his phone rang. It was Paolo. They talked for a minute, and Gennero hung up and then leaned forward slightly. "Sal, let's go to the Penrose. I'm going to meet Paolo there, but come inside and have something at the counter while we meet."

Sal nodded into the rearview mirror and headed to the diner in southwest Philly.

Gennero was sitting at a booth when he saw Paolo walk in. He got up to greet his old friend, and they embraced. "Thanks for meeting me so promptly," Gennero said quietly as they sat down.

"Eh." Paolo shrugged it off. "You're having a personal problem. That takes precedence. So, Gennero, what's going on?" Paolo was not quite yet sixty. He was small-boned and thin but clean-shaven, and his hair was still mostly dark and wavy. Paolo's father had been a close friend of Gennero's father, and the families had known each other for decades. Paolo had been one of the founders of the corporation, as they called it, their holding company. Gennero was an original member of the board and their main troubleshooter for the last fifteen years. He had tremendous respect for Paolo's unfailing business sense. Everything they did—well, almost everything—was fairly legitimate and legal. They were at least as clean as 90 percent of most businesses, thanks to Paolo's good judgment and good sense and his ability to convince the others on the board not to take unnecessary risks.

"Paolo, everything is going well with the businesses, so let me put your mind at ease there. All is well. Profits are good. Everybody's doing what they should be doing, and we'll have a very good quarter. But in my own life, the shit is hitting the fan." Gennero let out a big sigh and sat back. "My older sister, Maria, you know her, she's got breast cancer. Well, she's got a tumor in her breast that's as big as a lemon. She goes into the hospital tomorrow morning to have it removed. They'll do a biopsy, of course, but the likelihood is that it's cancer, and they'll probably do a double mastectomy and then some more treatment. I tell you, Paolo, I'm not usually a pessimist, but I'm not optimistic about this. My guess is she's going to be quite sick for quite a while, and then it's going to get worse, and then she'll die." Tears welled up in his eyes.

"So that would be enough, you know, to fuck me up. Maria and I have always been very close." He knew Paolo understood. Everyone who knew Maria admired her strength and good sense. She had filled in admirably for her father and had always been a strong silent partner for Gennero, giving him good advice.

"Gennero, I'm sorry to hear that about your sister. My mother passed away from breast cancer that had metastasized, so I know something about what you and Maria might be facing."

Paolo would have continued, but Gennero interrupted him. "But," Gennero added, "there's even more."

Paolo tilted his head to the side and waited for Gennero to continue.

"My wife, Theresa . . ." Gennero paused, gathering himself before pushing ahead. "She's been going through a tough time these past four years, a mental thing."

Paolo was concentrating intently on Gennero.

"Bottom line," Gennero said, "she tried to commit suicide last night."

Paolo fell back in his seat as if he'd been shot in the chest. Just then the waitress came over, offered her honeys and dearies, and took their order for ice cream and coffee.

When the waitress left, Paolo leaned forward again. "Theresa, she tried to kill herself?"

Gennero nodded.

"How? How is she?"

"Paolo, Tessie's grown more and more suspicious these past four years or so. She thinks people are trying to kill her or me or our grandchildren. She trusts nobody. She hardly goes out of the house. I haven't been able to get her to a doctor or take any medication. All she wants to do is argue about everything. If you don't agree with her, then you're the enemy. She's wanted us to move. Of course I told her no. So I think that's why she did it. She took an overdose of Tylenol, and I found her when I came home yesterday. She's in Methodist Hospital now. She wants to come home, and the hospital wants to commit her since she's a danger to herself."

"Jesus Christ," Paolo whispered. "So Theresa's flipping out on you, and Maria is fighting cancer. You've got a full plate, Gennero." He sat back, shaking his head in disbelief. "Have you thought about what you want to do, what you need?"

"Paolo, I'll be frank with you. I'm flying by the seat of my pants. I don't know from one minute to the next what I'm going to have to contend with. Maria, I think I know what's going to happen there. If I know Maria, she's not going to let me do too much for her other than maybe take her for doctor visits. But there's a good chance that there will be plenty of those, what with chemo or radiation or both. But the big unknown is Tessie. I don't know what's going to be involved there. I can't plan anything."

Paolo nodded and sat thinking. He turned away and looked out the window and then back at Gennero, who was absentmindedly toying with the ice cream in front of him. "I'm sorry to hear that you've got these things going on in your family. I can see how it's affecting you. Jesus, Gennero, you were always the epitome of competence and confidence. You always conveyed such strength and stability to the rest of us. You inspired us. Now, shit, it makes me feel so sad for you, to see you going through this trouble with Maria and your wife. Of course, Gennero, it's obvious you're going to need time to figure things out and to get back your energy. But I have to ask you—what about our business interests? Nobody is more on top of these matters than you are. What do you want to do?"

"I'm not sure, Paolo. I think I need to take at least a couple of weeks off before I'll have an idea as to what's happening. If I were sure that in two weeks everything would be back to normal, then I'd say I'm taking a little vacation. But I don't know what the story is going to be in two weeks or three weeks. I can't commit to being able to stay on top of things.

"How about this? Why don't you start grooming somebody to take over for me? Let him fill in for me for these two weeks. If he has any questions, then he can call me, and I can offer him my advice. If within a couple of weeks, things look like I'll be available, then he can continue to assist me, and I'll fade into the background. And after six months or a year, he can take over, and I'll retire. On the other hand, if things stay fucked up, then I'll continue to be the voice behind the scenes, and he'll end up taking over a lot sooner." Gennero looked at Paolo questioningly, as if to ask, "What do you think?"

Paolo pursed his lips. "Could work." He nodded. "Did you have anybody special in mind?"

Gerard R. D'Alessio

Gennero sat back and opened his hands, "Paolo, you have a much better view of the big picture than I do. As president of the board, I know that you meet with some of our friends with other enterprises. You have a better idea as to who's on the way up, who needs an opportunity to shine or do somebody a favor. No, I don't have anybody in mind, and I'm sure that whoever you choose would be capable and competent to do the job. Whoever it is, I'd be able to work with him and make sure that it'd be a smooth transition."

Paolo smiled. "As a matter of fact, Gennero, there are a couple of such people who come to mind. I'll think about it and let you know within a couple of days. It sounds like a good plan. But tell me, Gennero, you sound like you're feeling some relief at giving up this job, which, by the way, you have done a hell of a job at for these last fifteen years or so. Is that true?"

Gennero remained thoughtful for a few moments and finished his coffee before he answered. "Paolo, I love what I'm doing. I take pride in being able to go into a business where somebody has grown it and nurtured it like it was their child, a member of the family. Where they've identified with the business as if it were an extension of themselves. Their whole ego is tied up with their being The Owner. And then, because they fucked up and got into serious debt with us, here we come, uninvited, to become not only a silent partner, but the partner with the ultimate say-so. They're pissed at themselves and at us. They're frightened of what we might do to them and their families, as well as their business.

"And then I show up, the face on all they have ever learned—right or wrong—about Italians. The Mafia. Organized crime. And here I am, just this little, old Italian guy in a limo and a nice suit. And I put all those fears to sleep. I treat them better than they feared. Not only that, they see that we really want to increase their profits. We want to grow their business and really see it succeed. Sometimes we even infuse money into it to make it more efficient or more marketable. In the end, they're grateful. They love to see me come, like I was an angel.

"Of course, part of it is that respect, that fear that's just dozing under the surface, and every so often I have to nudge it awake with a little reminder of what their reality is. But, Paolo, I've loved every minute of it, and I've taken great pride not only in making us as profitable as we've been, but in doing it in a way that has kept all risks as low as possible. We've made remarkably few enemies over the years."

"Gennero, all of us are indebted to you and to the influence you've had on the board, keeping us from making some mistakes that others, more headstrong perhaps, would have made. Which reminds me, we're going to have to talk about compensation. Of course you will continue on the board. There's no discussion there," he said, pointing a finger at Gennero. "We need you there. You'll attend meetings, no matter what else happens. And as a major shareholder, you'll continue to get your share of the profits each month, same as always. But if we are going to be putting somebody else in place as our troubleshooter, we'll have to make some adjustments there."

"Of course," Gennero readily agreed. "That would only be fair. Suppose we keep things as they are for two weeks. That will give me time to find out what the hell the story is going to be with Tessie, and it'll give you time to decide on who my successor is going to be."

Paolo extended his hand across the table. "Agreed. You'll keep me informed?"

"Of course," Gennero replied. "I'll give you a call next week and give you an update."

Both men got up, and Gennero picked up the check, leaving a tip next to his cup. Sal and Paolo's driver, Gus, were sitting at the counter and, seeing their bosses getting up, put some money down and hurried to the front door. Gennero and Paolo shook hands and went to their cars. Gennero looked at his watch. It was after four o'clock. Time to get back to Methodist and look in on Theresa.

Chapter XX

Gennero: Tessie

It was close to five o'clock by the time Gennero got to Theresa's room. He had received a call from Dr. Sacerdote and had made an appointment for the following afternoon. Then he had stopped at the nurses' station and had a talk with the social worker who brought him up to date on the commitment proceeding. On one hand, he was glad to hear that Tessie was being cooperative and had indicated a willingness to sign herself into the hospital. On the other hand, he was uncomfortable with her having some degree of control over when she could be discharged. He was concerned that if she came home too soon, she might make another suicide attempt, and he wasn't confident that he'd be able to do anything to stop it. He walked into her room, his coat over his arm, and all of his antennae on full alert. He had no idea what he would be walking into. The first thing he noticed was the young Philippine woman sitting by the window. Then he remembered the nurse telling him that Dr. Sung ordered twenty-four-hour observation, which meant someone being with Tessie all the time. Gennero nodded in her direction and glanced at the bed where Tessie was resting, an untouched food tray on the bed stand.

"How you doing?" he asked as he leaned over to kiss her on the cheek. She opened her eyes at the sound of his voice.

"Hi, Gennero," she said, reaching up, indicating she wanted a kiss on her lips. "I'm all right, just a little tired and bored. How about you?"

He was surprised by this relatively normal response and a little taken back. "I'm fine," he said. "It's been a long day, but I'm good. I see you haven't eaten yet. What's the matter, not hungry?"

She smiled sheepishly. "I don't know. Hospital food. You know what they say. I'm not sure it's okay to eat, you know?"

"Tessie, I know it's not a five-star restaurant, but hospital food isn't that bad. You should eat. You need your strength. Let's see, what do you have?" he asked as he leaned over and took the lid off of a plate. "What's this? Looks like roast beef, mashed potatoes, carrots. Tessie, it looks pretty good."

"Oh, I don't know, Gennero. You taste it for me and see if it's all right."

Gennero caught her eye. He knew that she was concerned about her safety and knew if he didn't hesitate to dig into her food, it would soothe her fears. "I was hoping you'd invite me to share your supper. I haven't eaten for hours, and I'm starved." He made sure to take significant portions of everything on her tray, including her apple juice, applesauce, and her roll and butter. "Thanks," he said, wiping his mouth on her napkin. "It's really not bad. Not like you cook, but not that bad. At least it should hold me for a while. I'm going to stop by over at Nina's after I leave here. I'm sure she'll have some leftovers that she'll offer me." He saw that she was reassured. As he moved the tray closer to her, she boosted herself up in bed and began to eat. He surmised that this was the first she'd eaten all day.

"You know," he offered, "tomorrow, if they bring meals, and I'm not here, maybe Miss Whatshername over here," indicating the aid in the corner, "can taste the food for you, to make sure it tastes all right."

"Oh, Gennero, I forgot. Let me introduce you. This is Joy, my evening babysitter. During the day today, I had another one. Her name was Latoya." Gennero turned to say hello to the aide. Theresa continued, "They have someone with me all the time, like I'm a two-year-old, but that's all right. It's kind of nice to have company."

"Well, I'm glad to see that you're accepting everything so well. That's quite a change from this morning."

Theresa made a dismissive gesture. "This morning, I was upset. But I had a chance to think over what you said. You were right. That was a stupid thing I did. There's no excuse. I guess I didn't realize what would happen. I wasn't thinking right." Gennero was sitting on the side of the bed, holding her hand and looking at her. He nodded, and she smiled.

"So you're taking your medication?"

"Oh yes. They're in here all day long with their little cups of pills. And I've still got this," she said, indicating with a toss of her head the IV bottle draining into her wrist.

"It seems they're taking good care of you."

"Oh, they are, Gennero. Everybody is real nice. I talked with that Chinese doctor this morning, and he explained to me again about signing the papers, which would mean that I'm here voluntarily . . ."

Gennero waited for her to finish; there was no need to let her know that he had already been informed. She might interpret that as everybody talking about her behind her back, which of course they were.

Theresa continued, "I told him that it sounded like a good thing, but that I wanted to wait and talk to you before I actually went ahead and did anything about it."

"I'm really pleased to you hear say that, Tessie. I need to know that you're going to be well, medically and in every way— that your liver is going to be all right and that you're going to be okay and not make any more suicide attempts when you get home."

"I know, *caro*," she said, holding his hand more tightly. "I'm so ashamed about that. I'm sorry. I must have caused you a lot of embarrassment. I just wasn't thinking right."

"To tell you the truth, Tessie, I'm really glad to hear that you feel that way. It shows me that your thinking is more realistic." Gennero was wondering, *Can the medications, the tranquilizers and everything, be kicking in already? Is that possible?* "So what have they told you about your condition? Have the tests shown anything?"

"No, they say it's too early to tell for sure whether my liver is damaged or not. So they'll still keep taking those tests. And they started me on some antidepressants and tranquilizers for my depression. That's what they say I have. Dr. Sung and the psychiatrist, what's his name?"

"Weinstadt," Gennero interjected. "Dr. Weinstadt."

"Right," she agreed. "Anyway, he, Dr. Weinstadt, said I was depressed. Normally, he would have me receiving some group therapy while I'm here, but that would be in a psychiatric ward, and I'm here in intensive care, so . . ." She raised her hands, indicating that she was stuck with the realty of receiving only medication.

"From the smile on your face, *cara*, I see that you're not especially upset by that, having to do without group therapy."

"Please, Gennero, washing our dirty clothes in public? No, that's not for me."

Maybe for the first time during the visit, Gennero's smile was genuine and came easily. The idea of Theresa being in group therapy, talking about herself to strangers, was ridiculous and impossible to conceive of under any circumstances. "No, Tessie, I have trouble seeing you in group therapy, or me for that matter." And both of them laughed. The release of tension felt good. *It felt almost normal*, he thought. *Christ, I can't remember the last time it felt this good.*

They squeezed hands and took a moment to relish the moment of intimacy. "So," Gennero continued, "you're going to go ahead and sign the voluntary admission papers?" He had deliberately not used the word "commitment."

"You think I should?"

"Yes, I think it's best. Do you want me to tell them at the desk?"

"Yes, if you would. I might as well get it over with."

"Is there anything I can bring you, anything you want or need?"

Theresa gave him a list of some personal things, including some clothes and some reading material. They talked for a little while longer, and when Gennero looked at his watch, Theresa suggested that he go on to Nina's and have enough time to visit with all of them. They embraced. Gennero picked up his coat, waved good-bye to Joy, and left.

Gennero stopped at the desk to tell the nurse that Tessie was willing to sign the voluntary commitment papers and that she seemed much better than she had in the morning. As he stood waiting for the elevator, he smiled to himself. *Maybe this was the best thing that could have happened. Now she knows that she needs help. She seems better, more realistic. Maybe it's going to work out. Thank God, I hope so.*

Once outside, Gennero checked his watch. It was close to six o'clock and fully dark already. He saw Sal standing by the car a little way from the entrance and started toward him. As Sal opened the door for Gennero, he asked, "How's Mrs. Giantonio?"

"Much better, Sal. I'm very pleased. Thanks for asking."

"I'm glad to hear that she's doing well. That must be a big relief."

"It is, Sal. Big time." When Sal got in, Gennero told him, "Sal, take me to Nina's house and then you can go home. Getting home from Nina's won't be a problem. Now, tomorrow morning, we're going to take Maria to the hospital. So pick me up about twenty to eight, and then we'll swing by and pick her up."

"Sure thing, Mr. G., tomorrow morning at seven forty at your house."

When they arrived at Nina's home, a three-story brick home on a narrow, tree-lined street, Sal helped Gennero out of the backseat. Only when Nina opened the door and embraced her father did he get into the limo and drive away.

"Pop, I'm so glad that you could come. Come on in. Look, everybody, look who's here."

There seemed, all at once, to be a huge crowd of people emerging from the dining room to crowd around the front entrance: Rosalie, with her friend, Denise, hanging in the background, and the two boys, Bobby and Brian. All Gennero could see was a blur of smiling faces. Everyone got a hug, even Denise when he worked his way to her.

"You too, Denise, come on, give me a hug. I'm delighted finally to get a chance to meet you."

Denise, a tall, thin, pretty brunette, with short hair, a wide shy smile, and twinkling dark eyes, mumbled something about being glad to meet him too. Nina and Rosalie led him through the living room into the dining room where they had been seated around Nina's long table. Bobby brought over a chair from its place against the wall and urged his grandpa to sit between him and Brian. Nina went into the kitchen to get a place setting for him. Everyone was talking at once, asking questions about Theresa, Maria, him. Finally, he was seated, a dish and silverware in front of him and a glass of red wine in his hand.

"*Salud,*" he said, holding up his glass. "Bon appetite." The others, including Bobby, clinked glasses and returned the toast. Brian joined in with his glass of water.

"Well, let me say first," Gennero started, "that I'm delighted to be here. I've missed seeing all of you." He gestured toward Denise, who sat opposite him next to Rosalie. "And I'm delighted to finally meet this charming young woman who I've heard so much about. And I'm really happy to have this seat of honor between my two most favorite great-grandsons."

"Your only great-grandsons," chimed in Brian.

"Even so, it's still a seat of honor, and I appreciate it, especially after such a long, hard day."

"Here, Pop," Nina interrupted. "Let me give you some chicken cutlets."

Immediately, everyone started passing food to Gennero: salad, string beans in tomato sauce, spaghetti. When Gennero had filled his plate, he sat back and looked around the table. What a happy, contagious energy was flowing around the table, such warmth. His eyes moistened to think of how long he had been depriving himself of this kind of experience because of Theresa's fearful suspicions and his catering to them. *No more.*

No matter what happens, no more do I let her craziness dictate my life—especially staying away from this, from my family. He found himself picking up his glass again and announcing, "I want all of you to know how special it is for me to be here. It's wonderful, and I love you all, each of you, with all my heart."

Brian nuzzled up against him. "I love you, Nonno."

"Thank you, Brian. I love you too," he said, throwing his arm around Brian's shoulder and squeezing him.

During the course of the dinner, Gennero brought them up to date on both their Zia Maria and their Nonna Theresa. "My older sister," Gennero said, with a nod toward Denise, explaining who Maria was, "will be going into the hospital tomorrow morning, and they'll be performing the surgery on Saturday morning. They'll do a biopsy then and do whatever they have to do. Anyway, she'll be at Pennsylvania Hospital, and I know she'd enjoy having a visit from each of you. We'll just have to wait until Saturday before we know how that's all going to turn out."

Rosalie asked, "Are they going to do a mastectomy or just a lumpectomy or what?"

"Who knows, *ciucci*? They'll do as little as they can get away with and as much as they have to. Your zia is concerned that they'll likely perform a double mastectomy, and there's a good chance they will. But we won't know for sure until they do the biopsy and see whether it's malignant or not and whether they think it's already spread." Everyone at the table received this news with sadness.

"How about Great-Grandma?" asked Bobby.

Gennero pondered how much detail to go into. Bobby was a sensitive, thoughtful, and very bright sixteen-year-old—almost seventeen, as Nina had reminded him—but Brian was still young. And there was Denise. How much of family business to let her in on? "Nonna seems to be doing much better. I just came from the hospital, and she just had a nice dinner of roast beef. She's taking her medications and is fully cooperating with the doctors. So I'm hopeful."

"But what happened? Why did she have to go into the hospital?" Brian wanted to know.

"Well, seems that she has been very unhappy, depressed, and sometimes when people are depressed, they get discouraged and want to give up. So your Nonna took an overdose of pills, and we had to put her into the hospital until she gets better."

"I don't understand, Grandpa," Rosalie chimed in. "What has she got to be so unhappy about? I seem to remember her as always being a lot of fun and enjoying life. Remember all of those holiday dinners at your house? I remember, as a little girl, cooking in the kitchen with her and going shopping with her. She never seemed depressed to me."

"Ah, Rosalie, you're so right. This business is all new, not the way she used to be at all. That's part of why it's so confusing. I don't understand it myself." He grew thoughtful while everyone ate in silence and waited for him to continue. "I can tell you this: before we got married in 1950—and she was only eighteen then—but before that, when she was living at home with her family, she had some tough times. I don't want to go into her private business. But maybe those old demons are haunting her now. I don't know. I'm just as surprised and confused as any of you. But I can say that I'm hopeful that the medication they put her on will bring her back to being her old self."

"I'll drink to that!" Nina exclaimed, raising her wineglass.

Everyone joined in, "To Nonna!"

Gennero turned the conversation away from himself and asked the boys about their activities. Brian, a freshman, was enjoying school. He had been on the freshman wrestling team and was hoping to be on the varsity team next year when he would be a sophomore. Brian was the more aggressive and outgoing of the two, more impulsive and more given to taking risks. "I'm looking forward very much to seeing you wrestle, Brian. I hope I'll be able to make some of your matches."

Bobby, a junior, was in the midst of taking SATs and thinking about which colleges he wanted to apply to next year. "I'm thinking about Penn," he said, "but if I don't get in, I've got to come up with some other schools. I'm hoping to get some kind of scholarship, but if I don't, I guess I'll take out a loan."

Gennero looked over at Nina and raised his eyebrows.

"I've told the boys," Nina said defensively, "that you and Nonna would take care of all the school expenses, but our young man here is very proud and very independent and wants to do as much of it himself as he can."

Bobby straightened up in his chair and stuck his jaw out, ready for an argument from his great-grandfather.

Gennero put his arm around him, hugging him. "Now I wonder where he would ever get an attitude like that."

He laughed, and Bobby relaxed and smiled.

Gennero continued, "I'm very proud of you, Bob. You make me proud to be your great-grandfather. What a fine young man. Let me just say this: I'm a firm believer in reality. If your plan turns out to be realistic, then fine, I wish you every success. If, however, your plan turns out to be somewhat unrealistic, then I stand ready to help in any way possible. Whatever you may want me to do, I'll do. And that goes for you too," he said, turning to Brian and embracing him with his other arm.

"And you, Denise," Gennero said, "what's going on in your life, other than making my granddaughter happy?"

Denise mumbled something.

Rosalie turned to encourage her. "Go on, hon. Tell my grandfather about what you do, where you work."

"Well, I'm a securities analyst for Merrill Lynch. I do research on companies, mostly small companies in developing countries. Right now, I'm working on some new start-ups in South Africa, and Mexico and Eastern Europe." Denise smiled shyly and glanced at Rosalie to see if what she said was sufficient.

"Tell him about your promotion," Rosalie said, egging her on.

"Well, I just got a promotion, to a senior analyst . . ."

"And?" Rosalie questioned.

"And they made me the head of my section, and I'll have four people working under me that I'll be responsible for." She sat back in her chair and wiped her mouth with her napkin as if to say, "That's all, folks. No more from me."

Gennero looked at Rosalie and winked. "I see why you're proud of this young woman." And turning back to Denise, he said, "It's good to be modest and not take yourself too seriously. You maintain a better perspective of reality that way. But it's also good to have a realistic view of your strengths. Obviously, you're very bright and very conscientious and have good social skills, including the skills necessary to manage four people.

"Just as you obviously don't want to overestimate what that means, you also don't want to underestimate it either. You have a right to be proud of what you've accomplished. So congratulations on your promotion and to your continued success," he toasted, raising his wineglass. Again, everyone joined in, and Brian wheedled a sip from his *nonno*'s glass.

After dinner, Nina made espresso for her and Gennero, while Rosalie and Denise had tea. The boys went off, ostensibly to do their homework.

"So, Pop, what do you really think is going on with Mama?" Nina asked.

Gennero carefully put his cup down. "*Ciucci*, it's like I said earlier. I can only guess, but I really haven't a clue as to what's happening. I don't know if it's senility or if it's a brain tumor . . ." He leaned forward. "You know, her mother had a brain tumor."

"No, get out!"

"I'm serious, Nina. You wouldn't remember her, of course. She died when your mother was sixteen. I forget what she died of, but they did an autopsy and found that she had a brain tumor. So who knows, maybe your mother has one too. But I really don't know."

Denise mustered the courage to join in. "I had an uncle who attempted suicide twice. He hung himself. One time in the basement and once in the garage. The first time, my cousins found him. They were still little, so they called my aunt, and she had to come to cut him down. The second time, she found him. He finally died about ten years ago of cancer. But my cousins were all ashamed of him. They never wanted to talk about it. Nobody knows why he did it. I mean, obviously he was depressed, but otherwise, everything seemed to be going good as far as we could tell. Of course, I was only a little girl then, so I probably wouldn't have understood anyway."

"Shit," said Rosalie, "I'm embarrassed, and I'm not little, and she's not even my mother. It's embarrassing having a wacko for a grandmother."

"Rosalie," Gennero blurted out. "Please, some respect."

"I'm sorry, Nonno, but Nonna's been really strange for a long time now. I have trouble remembering when she was different. It seems like ages ago, like it was a different woman altogether."

"Rosalie's right, Pop," Nina came in to defend her daughter. "You can't say that this is anything recent. And I don't buy that it's just depression, either. She's paranoid as a . . . a . . . I don't know what, with her suspicions and fears. I mean, it would be funny if it weren't so sad."

"There's nothing funny about what your mother is going through. She's terrified. She lives in a panic almost all the time. She can't sleep, can't eat. She worries all the time that somebody is going to try to hurt you, or you," he said, gesturing toward Rosalie, "or the boys, as well as fearing for her own life and mine.

"I'll admit, she is difficult . . . almost impossible to live with. You have no idea. I've never wanted to complain to you. She's your mother. But believe me, you have no idea what it's like." Gennero crumpled his napkin in his fist, and his eyes were brimming with tears. "But she's no joke. She's a problem, a serious problem that has to be solved. She's difficult, like I said, really impossible. But she's my wife, and she's your mother, and your grandmother," he said, again gesturing to Rosalie, "and we have to try to deal with it as best we can." Gennero's outburst was met with a chagrined silence.

"You're right, of course, Pop," Nina said soothingly. "Mama has been frustrating for all of us to deal with. I can't even begin to imagine what it's been like for you to live with her day in and day out. We'd love to be able to do something constructive, but none of us knows what to do anymore."

Rosalie turned to Denise and asked, "Denise, what did your aunt do after your uncle tried twice to kill himself?"

Denise bit her lip and then shrugged her shoulders and blurted out, "She left him. He wouldn't be serious about getting any psychiatric help. He went a couple of times after each hospitalization, 'cause they took him to the ER each time and admitted him for a day or two. She finally left him and got a divorce."

All three women looked at Gennero to see how he would accept this news.

Gennero shook his head at them. "You don't understand. That's not an option for me. We've been married for over fifty years. Theresa has only us, her family, no one else. She hasn't worked for fifty years. How would she survive on her own? She has no friends left. Who would be a resource for her? No, it would be cruel to do that. It's not an option. Maybe, Denise, it was the right and logical thing for your aunt to do, but the circumstances were different. I have responsibilities here that I can't ignore."

Gennero's statement was met with silence. "Well, Pop," Nina finally ventured, "we certainly hope Ma gets better and that somehow this hospitalization will turn things around so everything is more like it used to be. If there's anything that we can do to help, you have to let us know. We'll each do whatever we can. But she's got to make an effort too. If Ma attacks us for everything that we say, well . . ." She left the thought hanging in the silence that had settled on the table.

"Of course. None of us are magicians. If your mother doesn't cooperate, then there's very little, if anything, that any of us can do." He shook his head. "Let's hope it doesn't come down to that."

With that, Gennero looked at his watch, and everyone took it as a signal that dinner was over and began to get up, the women gathering up the plates and clearing off the table.

"Nina, it was good to be here tonight, to see you and everyone again. It was good for me to be with all of you." They gave each other a hug.

"I know," she whispered into his ear. "It was good for us too, to finally be able to talk about all of this. I know we'll all do whatever we can to help."

"I know you will. I'll keep you informed of how things go, and I'll tell her that all of you were asking for her. If it looks like visiting her will be helpful, I'll let you know."

Nina walked him to the front door, where Rosalie and Denise and the boys came to say good night. Rosalie volunteered to walk with him to the corner, where he was expecting to catch a cab, and the two of them quietly walked there arm in arm. A cab, its roof light on, came almost immediately.

"Thanks, Nonno," she said, giving him a hug and kissing his cheek. "I really appreciate your being so nice to Denise. She was scared to death of meeting you."

"Rosalie, she's a charming and beautiful young woman. If I was your age, I'd be after her myself." They both laughed as he opened the door to the taxi. "Seriously, I meant everything I said to her."

Rosalie smiled her thank-you and blew him a kiss as he got in and closed the door.

Chapter XXI

Gennero

When he arrived home from Nina's, Gennero made himself comfortable and poured himself a glass of wine. Then he went into the living room and, after putting on a favorite CD, sat on the sofa. With the music playing in the background, Gennero looked around the room. It was the first time that he had sat alone in this room in a long time, and he smiled as he admired the comfortable contemporary furniture, the Persian carpets, and original artworks on the walls done by local artists. He sipped his wine and savored the solitude. A delicious feeling of freedom came over him and made him feel lighter and, for a moment, almost giddy.

It was the first time that he had been in the house alone without Theresa in years. He felt relieved at not having to take her suspicions and fears into account, not having to be on guard to avoid a senseless argument. Gennero wondered what was going to happen. What would his life be like if Theresa succeeded in killing herself? What would he do if she didn't kill herself but remained as obstinate and persistent in her crazy beliefs as before? For the first time in almost fifty years, he found himself thinking of a life without Theresa. New possibilities opened up to him. He hadn't been a single man in fifty-four years and hadn't acted like one for almost as long, since his brief affair with Francesca.

He and Theresa had been married less than five years. Nina was only three years old, and Theresa was proving to be difficult regarding sex. Always an excuse. "The baby will wake up. The baby will come into the room. What if the baby hears us?" *Jesus Christ, could she come up with excuses to avoid having sex!* He thought that was all he was looking for, more sex.

In those early days, before joining the corporation, he held a number of different positions working for and with various uncles and cousins. His Uncle Paolo was the grandfather of the Paolo who was now president of the corporation. Then, of course, there were his cousins: Frank, Giancarlo, and Dom, who now owned the Villa Contursi, named after the town in Italy where his father and his entire family had been born.

After World War II, things changed, and all of the family operations became more businesslike. He and his cousins were encouraged to go to college and night school to learn more about business skills and practices. It was while he was taking a night course at Temple that he met Fran. He was twenty-five, and she was twenty-three and recently married. Her husband was working for the phone company. All he could talk about, apparently, was that damned phone company—switches and relays and whatnot. He'd come home, get drunk, talk about wiring telephone systems, verbally abuse her, and then fall asleep.

She was miserable but didn't feel entitled to separate and get a divorce. Like Gennero, Fran was a Catholic, but their rules and guilt and hierarchies of sin didn't stop them from becoming attracted to each other and starting an affair. Gennero felt grown-up having an affair, as if it were a rite of passage. Most of the other men he knew had someone on the side. He was fortunate in having freedom and the time to meet Fran whenever she was available. They often went to a motel in Jersey and sometimes, during the summer, stayed at the shore for a day or two. He could always make an excuse of "business" to justify being away. Theresa never wanted to hear any details about what his work consisted of.

Gennero allowed himself to reminisce about Francesca— the wonderful sex they had, his introducing her to oral sex and her initial embarrassment at having him go down on her. What moments of delight they shared. How exciting it was to sneak around and have to tell lies about where he was going. He remembered how surprised he'd been by how attentive Fran was, how she remembered things he had said and would later ask him, "What ever happened with . . ." He realized that he felt taken for granted by Theresa and that he was resentful—not just about the lack of sex, but also about not being loved enough.

After about a year and a half, Fran couldn't take the guilt anymore. Her husband was worse than ever, and she was resigned to getting a divorce, but the idea of an affair had lost its glamour. The sneaking around and the lying had taken its toll. He had been very clear that he would not get a divorce, that he was in his marriage for the long haul, come hell or high water. So she finally decided to call it quits. They both cried a lot. They met for lunch and were standing outside of a restaurant when she told him it was over and done. Thinking back now, he imagined tears streaming down from her eyes—only on the inside of her body— and being secreted away, forming a kind of emotional pearl.

He felt miserable, not sure if he wanted to continue to live without her. How could he go on without feeling her body, her small and slender waist, her beautiful ass, her wonderful lips and mouth? He was depressed and irritable for almost six months afterward. The worst part was not being able to tell anyone, not being able to express his grief. But finally, he was able to move on. Having learned all that he did in the course of being with Fran, he let Theresa know that he required more attention from her, and in the final analysis, their marriage benefited from their improved communication and his being more assertive with her. *God, I haven't thought about all of this in years,* Gennero thought as he finished his wine. Then he slowly got up, turned off the CD player, put out all the lights, and climbed up the stairs to his bed.

That night, he was suddenly awakened by Theresa standing over him. It was dark, except for the glow from the streetlight down the street, but he knew it was her. "Hurry, Gennero," she said, "they're coming. Hurry. There's a lot of blood. It's everywhere, all over. Hurry, come on, get up." She practically pulled him out of the bed.

What's she talking about? Did he ask her that or did he just think it to himself? Her voice sounded hollow, disembodied, and far-off, like in a scary movie, as if she were a ghost. He allowed her to lead him downstairs to the kitchen.

"Come on, Gennero, you have to do something. You have to help me."

He saw her face more clearly now. Her eyes were wide, and he could see white encircling the irises of her eyes. He had the sense that she was sleepwalking, that she was having a bad dream. He tried to wake her. "Wake up, Theresa," he said. He tried to shake her by the shoulders, but she resisted him.

"No, Gennero, we don't have time. We have to clean up all of this blood." She opened the refrigerator, and he saw her reach into a bowl of red Jell-O. She reached into the bowl, scooping out the Jell-O with both of her claw-like hands. Pieces of red Jell-O dropped onto the shelves and onto the floor.

Ah, he thought, *she thinks the Jell-O is blood*. "Okay," he said, "we can do that. We can clean all of this up right now. Don't worry about it," he said soothingly, hoping that this would allay her fears. Then he woke up with a start.

FRIDAY

MARCH 5, 2004

Chapter XXII

GRADY

It was still dark outside when Grady became aware of Karen's body snuggled against his, her arm over his waist. Quietly, he eased himself out of bed and went to the bathroom. When he returned, she had turned over, and he folded himself against her. He smiled to himself, enjoying how good she felt. He enjoyed her fine, clean, scentless hair. He hated the smell of hair spray and its sweet, sticky stiffness. Karen did not go to great lengths to create a false impression; at least this was how Grady saw it. He was grateful that she did not do the things he couldn't stand in other women, like use excessive makeup, especially bright red, smeary lipstick. He hated the taste of it when he kissed them. She wasn't into shopping and accumulating all kinds of crap. He admired her simplicity, her smarts, her toughness. He hugged her closer and felt her body respond, nestling into his. He fell back asleep with a contented smile on his face.

He is a little boy, feeling cozy and comfortable. He can see Kelly, his mother, through the doorway. She is singing. She is beautiful with her long, straight, blonde hair. She is talking to him, laughing and happy. He's smiling. He feels so good. Now he's sitting in the car, in the front seat between her and him. Who is he? Another one of her friends? So many of these men friends. He doesn't like them. She shuts the door when they come to visit. Sometimes they yell and shout. They come and go. Sometimes she cries afterward. He's now spinning, flying. Crashing squealing sounds . . . wet grass, flashing lights, pain . . . whole body hurts. Where is she? Where did she go? His whole body hurts so much . . .

Grady opened his eyes, and the first thing he saw in the early morning sunlight was Karen's short brown hair. At first he was startled and confused, but then he remembered where he was, who he was with. Then he remembered the dream and the feeling that came with it: the pain, the physical pain, but also the emotional pain of loneliness and abandonment, the deep pain of longing.

He was both sad and angry. There was a part of him that expected his relationship with Karen to end up with sudden loss and abandonment, like the one with Kelly. But he also realized that Karen was different. Yes, there were similarities, but there were differences too. He kept telling himself that Karen was different. This time when he hugged her close, she turned over and pressed herself into him. Still half-asleep, he pulled her close and found her neck. He loved kissing her neck, the soft, silky smoothness of it, the smell and the taste of her, her responsiveness. Sleepily, they loved each other and slowly aroused each other until, in a leisurely way, they found their passion and began more hungry and urgent and energetic lovemaking.

Later, during breakfast, Grady lit up a cigarette and, leaning on the table, decided to tell Karen what he had been thinking. "Remember the other night you asked me what I was wound up about, and I got all huffy?"

Karen looked up from her plate where she had been mopping up the yellow yolk of her eggs with a piece of toast. "Sure," she answered, "how could I forget?"

"Well, I'd like to tell you about it."

"Wonderful," she said.

"When I was a kid, I had this best friend, Richie Batiste. I knew him from when I was four years old, when my folks and I moved to Philly from Jersey. Richie and his parents and his older sister, Rosalie, lived downstairs in a basement apartment. We started kindergarten together and went all through school together. We were in each other's houses all the time, although more in his than in mine. We were like brothers, and his mother was like a second mother to me. We were this close," he said, curling his middle finger around his index finger. "When we were about thirteen, we started a band, Onfire. Richie played keyboard, and I played guitar. We had a couple of other guys, Tommy, Donny, but Richie and me, we were what it was all about. We were the nucleus. Without us, there wouldn't have been any band. We shared everything, told each other everything . . . well, almost everything. There were a couple of things I never told him, and apparently there were some things he never told me. But we were very, very tight with each other. Anyway, about two years ago, Richie was found dead in his apartment up in Northern Liberties."

"Oh, how awful. What happened?"

"Obviously, he had been shooting up H. He overdosed." He said it almost nonchalantly, as if to say, "Of course that's how he died. How else would he die?"

"The question, at least in my mind," Grady went on, "is whether it was an accident or deliberate." He paused to let this sink in. Let her come up with the word suicide. He wasn't ready to say it. He was surprised to discover how reluctant he was to say the word out loud. "And if it was an accident, then how the hell did that happen? I mean, both of us used smack, but we were using almost everything so that we weren't especially addicted to any one thing. We were just addicted to getting high."

They looked at each other, each thinking of how this difference between them had been an ongoing issue. Grady couldn't believe that she wasn't tempted by alcohol and that working in the pub was not a danger for her. For him, everything was a temptation, and in that sense, his recovery was much more difficult. To hear Karen tell it, only the sweet oblivion of heroin was appealing, and nothing else constituted any temptation whatsoever.

"So how could it have been an accident? On the other hand, I thought at the time that he might have had a reason to . . . off himself."

Karen still didn't say anything. Grady put his cigarette out in the ashtray and poured himself another cup of coffee. Then he continued.

"Richie had been dating a girl, Tracy. He told me that they might get married. But when Uncle G., Gennero, Richie's grandfather, talked to Richie's mother recently, she didn't think that Richie would have married Tracy. I don't know if she was right or not. The truth is I only met her a couple of times—which, when I look back on it, is strange in itself. I mean, I used to think I knew everything that Richie did, but it seems that I hardly knew anything at all about his relationship with her. But anyway, Richie found out that Tracy was seeing somebody else, and one night Richie—actually, both of us kind of, I mean, I was there—Richie beat the shit out of the dude. Almost killed him."

Grady paused to sip from his mug. He took a deep breath and looked around the room as if to get a reprieve from this position he had put himself in. Karen waited, intent, totally focused on him. Finally he brought his gaze back to her.

"I think what was really significant was that Richie meant to kill this bastard. He tried to kill him. The guy just didn't die."

Grady caught the question in her eyes.

"I didn't actually do anything except for keeping a couple of guys from interfering and stopping him. But that situation, the fact that Richie could so lose it, go so totally ballistic, woke me up to what these drugs were doing to us. I mean, of course we were high at the time, who knows on what. But, I figured, time to straighten up and fly right. I've been sober ever since." He paused, drinking his coffee, more as an excuse to get some relief from the telling of it than anything else.

"Richie, he was real upset afterward. He withdrew into himself. From what he said, I always assumed it was a combination of his girlfriend, who was his fiancée, cheating on him; you know that sense of betrayal, when the floor just drops out from under everything you've always believed, and now you don't know if you can believe anything anymore? A combination of that plus his guilt at wanting to kill somebody and almost doing it. I mean, it wasn't any fault of his that the bastard lived. If Richie had anything to say about it, that asshole would have died right then and there."

Grady took a drink from his mug and looked at Karen over the rim. What he saw was a pretty, young woman with tears in her eyes, half of her breakfast still uneaten and forgotten on her plate, her mug of coffee getting cold. He smiled weakly at her. "I was really afraid to tell you that."

Karen pressed her lips together and returned a sad, knowing smile.

"I was afraid that, you know, you wouldn't want to be with me anymore." He paused to look up at her, hoping for some kind of confirmation that his fear had been unfounded. He saw her roll her eyes and shake her head.

"Anyway, all of this came up recently when my Uncle G. wanted to know how it was that Richie came to die with a syringe in his hand. Funny thing with him, with Gennero, just when he gets up the nerve to ask about why his grandson died from a heroin overdose, his sister gets cancer, and his wife freaks out on him and tries to commit suicide."

"What?"

"Yeah, I just found out yesterday when I had lunch with him. Anyway, I've kind of been following up on all of this for him, and it turns out that Tracy, the girl Richie said he might marry, ended up marrying the guy she was cheating with, a guy named Brian. I found out from Andy and Alex that Brian was dealing smack in a bar downtown called The Harp, the place where Richie . . . and I beat him up. The thing is, I want to talk to her, see what she knows, tie up some loose ends. You understand?"

"Sure," she answered immediately. "Of course, I understand."

Grady studied her intently.

"What?" she asked.

"I was wondering if you would go with me when I go to talk to her."

Karen was taken aback. "Oh my god! Are you sure? I mean, of course I'll go with you. I'll help in any way I can. I'm just surprised that you want me to. I mean, it seems so personal for you, and you usually don't . . ."

"I know. I haven't been the most trusting dude. But I really want you with me."

"Of course. It's only a question of timing, because of work. When would you want to do this?"

Grady felt a huge sense of relief. All of the tension in his face and upper body melted away.

"I hadn't really thought it through. Both Brian and Tracy work during the week, so maybe Sunday during the day might be good. I could call and try to set something up for then." He looked at her questioningly.

"Sunday afternoon would be perfect for me. I'm working tonight and then all day tomorrow, eleven to eleven, but Sunday I'm off."

"Good. I'll call her later on, when she should be home from work. She teaches elementary school. Can you believe it? Oh, and don't forget, after you get off tomorrow, we're going over to hear Tommy play."

"I won't forget," she said, and then she got up and came around the table to Grady and sat down on his lap. Karen was slim but not petite. She was tall and solidly built. She sat on his lap anyway and put her arms around his neck and looked him in the eye. "Grady, I know that for you the hardest thing in the world is to trust. I just can't tell you how happy I am—for me—that you trust me enough to tell me all of this. But I'm also so proud of you for having the balls to take this risk. Grady, look at me." He had lowered his eyes, and she pulled his face back up so that he was looking at her. "I won't ever let you down, babe. Never. Not ever."

Afterward, they cleaned up the kitchen and took their showers and got dressed. Karen was going to a women's meeting before going to work, and Grady decided to put in a couple of hours at the food shelter before going to a meeting later that afternoon. He also thought he would try to visit Maria in the hospital if he could. Sometime later in the afternoon, he'd try to get in a phone call to Tracy. *That will be interesting. I wonder how that will go.*

Chapter XXIII

Maria

Maria stood in her living room, looking through the lacy white curtains, waiting for her brother to arrive. He was always so punctual that she knew he wouldn't arrive until eight o'clock, but she had been standing at the window since twenty of eight, just in case he did come early. She didn't want to keep him waiting. She noticed the floral patterns of the lace on the curtains, hers this past half century since her mother died. *When I get back home from the hospital, I'll have to clean them. It's been too long. And do the windows too. My God, if Mama could only see how lax I've become regarding these things, she'd roll over in her grave.* Maria looked down at her feet. She had her overnight bag and purse. She checked her fingers and ears once again to make sure she had remembered to remove her jewelry. Her hand went to her throat to make sure her gold chain and cross were removed also, safe upstairs in their special little box in her dresser drawer. She felt an urge to go to the bathroom again, but she had already peed three times, and she didn't want to have to climb the stairs another time. She pictured once again giving the key to her house to Mona, who would see to the mail and the plants and any other emergencies that might crop up. She had Mona's phone number in her coat pocket, ready to give to Gennero, just in case he needed it. She had already given Mona his number. *Thank God for each of them.*

At eight o'clock, she saw the familiar black Lincoln coming down the street. There was no place to park. Sal got out and was leaving the car double-parked. Quickly, she picked up her bag and purse and opened the front door. Sal was almost there, ready to take the small suitcase from her and help her down the front steps. She saw Gennero in the backseat waiting for her. Sal opened the door and helped her in, putting the suitcase on the floor in the front.

"Ciao, *sorella*, how are you holding up?

Maria waited until she had lowered herself into the seat before she answered. "I'm fine," she said testily, gathering herself together, holding her purse firmly on her lap as if someone was going to try to snatch it from her there in the backseat of Gennero's limousine.

"Good," he said. "I'm glad to hear it. Sleep well?"

"Fine, like a log."

"No bad dreams?"

She bristled and was ready to challenge him on why all these stupid questions when she saw the smile on his face and the twinkle in his eye. "You," she said, scolding. "You never grow up. Always the tease." Then, after letting out a big sigh, she turned to him. "Yes, if you must know the truth, I'm nervous as hell. On the one hand, it all makes perfect sense, and I'm really quite accepting of the fact that I need surgery. But on the other hand, whenever I picture a scalpel slicing through the skin of my breast, and I see my blood oozing out, and I imagine what they're going to be doing next—slicing through layers of fat and muscle and tissues, sticking pieces of gauze into me to sop up the blood, like big pieces of Italian bread soaking up tomato gravy, I get all shivery inside like some scared little girl. And no, the truth is I slept rotten. I kept waking up. I must have gone to the bathroom at least once an hour."

"Me too. I have the same anxiety for you, and I'm not even the one getting the surgery. Of course, we have all the confidence in the world that everything will go smoothly. Still, we hear those horror stories like when doctors cut off the wrong leg or whatever. So of course we're going to worry. But we know," he looked at her and leaned in close to get her full attention, "we know that we'll get through this. Right?"

"I know." Then reaching into her coat pocket, she said, "Here's Mona's phone number just in case you need it for anything. She'll be picking up the mail and whatever."

Gennero took the piece of paper from her. "Maria, I've had Mona's number for years. Relax. Everything will turn out for the best. You'll see."

Before they knew it, Sal was parking the car in front of the main entrance of the hospital and helping them out of the car. Gennero said that he would stay with her until she was settled safely into her room.

When Gennero left her, Maria was resting comfortably in her bed, waiting for a day of scheduled tests. She had a book and a magazine, and the TV and was all set to enjoy a relaxing day. She lay back on her bed propped up on doubled pillows and looked out of the window. It was a cloudy, overcast day, although later on, the sun would probably come out. For some reason, she thought of high school, her freshman year—the anxiety she felt at anticipating switching schools that coming September and going to a more academically competitive school. She liked biology and science and had dreamed of becoming a physician. She hadn't been sure whether she wanted to be a pediatrician or a general practitioner. She smiled to herself remembering how influenced she was in this decision by her crush on their family physician, Dr. Panbianchi. She recalled his coming to the house when she was a little girl when she had pneumonia. She laughed to herself to recall how proud she had felt to have such a serious illness.

But Poppa had needed her in the store, and an education for a girl wasn't deemed all that important. Even Gennero didn't get to go until he took those evening courses at Temple. Of course, Gennero, being male, was expected to take on responsibilities in the various family enterprises that she wasn't supposed to know about. Except, Gennero always confided in her anyway, and she had always felt like his secret partner. In some ways, she was more logical in her decisions than he was, less influenced by emotions. She was more like her father in that respect. Gennero had always thought that Papa was a cold bastard, while he was more emotionally sensitive and sentimental like their mother. She thought of it as discipline and plain logic. It wasn't logical to be carried away by emotions, which could be so easily swayed and manipulated. Still, there were times, like today, when she was grateful for his empathy and emotional support.

A nurse came in and interrupted her reverie, informing her that they would soon be taking her downstairs for tests in preparation for tomorrow morning's surgery. Maria picked up her book, which lay closed on her belly, and put it on the nightstand. "Sure," she said, "whenever you want."

Chapter XXIV

Gennero

On his way from Pennsylvania Hospital where Maria was going through the preparations for tomorrow's surgery, to Methodist Hospital where Theresa was, Gennero found himself thinking of some housekeeping chores: shopping for food, cooking meals, laundry, dry cleaning, cleaning the house. Up to now, these were things that Theresa had assumed responsibility for, even if he ended up taking on some of it, like with the food shopping. He never bothered to think of these things on his own, assuming that they would be taken care of by her. Now part of him was hopeful that her good mood of last night would become permanent just so that she could come back home and take care of these things and let him get back to his own work . . . a world in which he felt much more competent and comfortable. He shook his head in disgust with himself. *Christ, if a crazy woman can do it, I certainly should be able to do it.* He started compiling a to-do list in his head: ask Theresa for the name and number of the cleaning lady, learn how to use the washing machine and dryer, see if there was any gravy in the freezer.

Sal rolled up in front of the hospital and helped Gennero out. Gennero pulled some money out of his wallet. "Sal, we're going to be running around a lot today. Why don't you pick us up a couple of hoagies or cheesesteaks and something cold to drink? I expect that I'll be here about an hour or so, and then I might want to run home to take care of some things before I go to a doctor's appointment around two. Then we'll come back to both hospitals."

Sal took the money and asked Gennero if he had any preferences. Once Gennero was inside the hospital, Sal got in and drove away.

No one was available at the nurses' station, so Gennero went directly to Theresa's room. He found himself holding his breath walking down the corridor and approaching her doorway. She had proven to be so completely unpredictable these past few years that he had no idea what to expect from her: the more pliant, apologetic, and cooperative woman of last night or the hostile, attacking, crazy woman she'd been in the past. Upon entering the room, he saw her in bed, propped up and watching TV. "Ciao, *cara*," he said, smiling. "How are you feeling this morning?"

"Ah, Gennero, finally. I've been waiting for you," she said, holding her arms up ready to embrace him. He leaned over and gave her a kiss.

"You seem to be feeling a little better," he said.

"Oh, I'm feeling much better. The doctor says that the blood tests are coming back much more positive—or is it negative? Anyway, they're much better, and he says if they keep on going in that direction for two more days, I'll have nothing to worry about." She gave him a big smile, like a proud little girl who had just earned an award at school for doing something special.

"Well!" Gennero was somewhat taken by surprise. "That's wonderful news. So you are actually getting better, recovering from the poisoning."

"Yes," she agreed enthusiastically, "and whatever medicines they're giving me are making me feel so much better. I just can't understand what would have ever made me even think of killing myself. I feel like that was some other woman, someone I don't even know, not me at all."

Gennero took off his coat and laid it on one of the two chairs in the room. It was then that he noticed they were alone. "Where's Miss Whatshername?" he asked, indicating with a turn of his head the chair where the aide had sat.

"Well, that's what I'm telling you, Gennero. You have to listen to me." A familiar tone of sharpness had entered her voice, and he turned to her more attentively. But she still wore her big, proud schoolgirl smile. "I'm doing so well that the doctor said that I don't need to have a babysitter anymore. In fact . . ."

She paused to make him wait, drawing out the silence until Gennero was forced to raise his hands and ask, "Yes? In fact . . . what?"

"I'm sure you will be quite relieved to hear that I'll be coming home Monday morning."

Gennero's eyes grew wide. "So soon?" This was unbelievable. Already she would be coming home? A day ago, they were planning on committing her, and that would have meant at least two weeks of treatment in the hospital. Yesterday morning, the doctor told him that it might take two weeks for some of the tranquilizers or antidepressants to have their effect. And now, just a day later, she was telling him she's coming home Monday morning?

"Are you sure? Is that what the doctor said?"

"Yes, of course the doctor said it. He said it would be all right. But he wants me to continue to take the medication, and he wants me to see someone. I told him I would. No clinic and no group, but somebody private, a woman. I agreed that I would do that, and he said fine."

"Dr. Weinstadt, the psychiatrist, or Dr. Sung?"

"Both of them. Aren't you happy? Aren't you glad I'll be home? I can't wait until I'm home again. I want to cook you a good dinner."

Gennero looked at her big, happy smile, so full of enthusiasm. He hadn't seen her smile like this in years. Inside, he was full of misgivings and doubt. It all seemed too goddamned quick to him, not well thought out at all. He couldn't believe they were letting her go home so quickly. Yet here she was, waiting to be praised for her wonderful achievement.

"Of course I'm happy. I'm delighted. Nothing could be better. I hadn't even dared think of such a possibility," he said. "Funny, you mention cooking dinner. I was going to ask you if you had any gravy in the freezer so I could cook up some pasta. But now

I'm going to have my wife home again. This is wonderful news. And," he added, "I'm really very glad to hear that you agreed to see someone to talk to and to continue to take the medications." He took her hands in his. "I've been very worried about you. I didn't know what was going to happen to us. This makes me very happy. I'm really very relieved to hear this. Wonderful." He gave her another kiss. "Did either of the doctors have anyone in particular in mind for you to see?"

"No, but Dr. Weinstadt said he'd look into it and come up with a referral for me before Monday morning."

"I'll check around too, see if I can come up with someone you might feel comfortable with. This is good news, Tessie. You've made me a happy man."

They talked some more. Gennero told her that he would be taking a couple of weeks off from work and after that might cut back considerably. Maybe they could do some traveling. She should start thinking of someplace she'd like to visit. He told her of the kids, his dinner at Nina's, and of Rosalie's pretty friend, Denise. For some reason he couldn't quite articulate to himself, he deliberately didn't mention Maria's hospitalization. He wanted to and was in a talkative frame of mind, but something inside made him hold back, so he never brought it up. Finally, he told her that he'd be back later in the afternoon. Theresa asked him to bring her some clothes since she was now permitted to get out of her bed, given the good laboratory results, although they were still monitoring her and didn't want her to overexert herself. Finally, they embraced, and Gennero waved as he left, a satisfied smile on his face.

On the way out, Gennero passed Dr. Sung at the desk. "Dr. Sung, do you have a minute?"

"Oh, Mr. Giantonio, what can I do for you?"

"My wife just told me that she's coming home Monday morning. I was really surprised. Is it true?"

Dr. Sung put down the chart that he had been writing on and looked around to make sure they had sufficient privacy. "Yes,

Mr. Giantonio, she's telling you the truth. We are planning on discharging her Monday morning as she requested."

"As she requested? She said that both you and Dr. Weinstadt said she could go home."

"Well, yes, we did. But there wasn't much else we could do. Last night after you left, she gave her forty-eight-hour notice that she was exercising her right to be discharged. That would put it at Saturday night. We finally got her to agree to Monday morning when we have a full staff to take care of all the paperwork and everything. We figured that would give us an additional twenty-four hours to see how she's progressing. But the truth is the lab results are improving each day so far, and the likelihood is that they're going to continue that way. And, in addition, there's been a total reversal in her mood and attitude. I don't know exactly what to attribute that to, possibly the medication, but more likely the attention and the seriousness of the hospitalization itself have given her a different outlook on reality. In any case, we really don't have much choice at this point. Of course, Dr. Weinstadt insists that she continue the psychotropic and antidepressant medication and that she begin seeing someone in therapy after she's discharged."

Gennero took all of this in. This put a different twist on things. Yes, she was better, more cooperative, but her coming home had been her doing, her decision, not theirs. In fact, she had pulled the fast one that he'd been afraid she would pull. She had agreed to sign herself in, the voluntary commitment, only to turn right around and give her forty-eight-hour notice. *I never used to think of Theresa as devious, but either she's developed a new skill or I've been blind to it in the past.*

As Gennero left the hospital, looking up the street for his car, he felt like a man in a whirlpool: frightened, confused, out of control, and unsure of what was going to happen next. *God, I'm glad I'm going to see Sacerdote later.*

Chapter XXV

Maria: Nina's Visit

Maria had just finished her lunch of soup and Jell-O when Nina entered her room. Immediately she perked up and pulled herself into an upright position. "Nina, what a wonderful surprise."

"Hi, Zia, how are you feeling?" Nina leaned in over the bed to give her aunt a kiss on the cheek.

"Me? Oh, I'm fine. They haven't done any damage yet." She laughed. "Ask me again tomorrow." She cleared a place on the bed. "Here, come sit next to me," she urged. Nina, who had been looking for a place to put her coat, laid it on the chair and sat next to Maria. "You're looking good," she said to her niece.

"Thank you. So are you, actually. I wasn't sure what to expect. My father only told me yesterday that you were sick."

"Eh, I'm not sick, really, just this thing they have to take out. No big deal."

"Well, let's hope that's how it turns out. Get you out of here in no time, back making manicotti where you belong." They both laughed at the memory of Nina helping Maria stuff the long pasta shells with ricotta cheese for family dinners that were sometimes held at her house. "Seriously, Zia, we're all hoping that everything goes well. The girls send their love."

"Thank you. You here on your lunch hour? Did you have anything to eat?"

"I had a cup of yogurt at my desk. I'm fine. Tell you the truth," she said, patting her belly, "I'm trying to lose a few pounds. Oh, before I forget, I was talking to your cousin Dom this morning. He sent his best wishes and said he'll try to come by and visit."

Maria called up an image of her cousin. She hadn't seen Dom for a while, not since his wife, Mattie, died. She had always liked Dom. He had been a real wild one when he was younger—dark hair, handsome, a real lady's man, and smart as a whip. Two years older than Maria, she had looked up to him and had had a crush on him. She remembered feeling a little jealous of Mattie when he married her. "You'll have to give him my very best," she said to Nina. "It's been too long since I saw that handsome face of his. How are his children?"

"Well, you know Nick is managing the restaurant. I think he's married to his job. He loves it. And Joe, you remember he's three years older than Nick, he got divorced from his wife, but he's doing well also, working over in Atlantic City. And then little Rena, who just turned fifty, she and Mike have these two adorable little girls."

Maria's mind raced over a collection of images of these relatives, an assortment of cousins of varying degrees—first, second, and third. One of the chains of associations led her back to Nina and her consulting firm. "Your business, you like it? I mean, dealing with the corporation."

Nina chuckled. "I know what you mean, Zia." She looked around to reassure herself that they were alone. "Being responsible for making these businesses more profitable, especially for the corporation, but also for them." She laughed. "At first it was a little scary, being in on all the little secrets, knowing what could happen if I screwed up. But hey, it's what all businesses do anyway. We're no different. And I feel good knowing that I'm helping the family. And I really enjoy working with everybody. It's a real challenge to analyze all of these different businesses and to come up with suggestions that will help them make more money and also help create more business for our other clients."

"I remember your mother was very upset when Gennero suggested that you start your firm. She didn't want you involved in any way in any of the family businesses. She was really pissed at your father over that."

Nina registered a look of surprise. "I didn't know she didn't approve. She never said anything to me about it. Are you sure?"

"Am I sure? Think about it, Nina. Did she ever ask you about your work? Ever encourage you to talk about it?"

"No, I guess she never really did."

"Your mother is a little too delicate for my tastes," she said, making a face. "She never approved of the family, of our businesses, the work your father did to earn his money."

Nina shook her head. "I don't think I recall their having a disagreement in front of me. I always saw Ma as devoted to him, looking up to him. I don't think she ever criticized him."

"Maybe not in front of anybody. She has too much sense for that. But she doesn't give your father the support he needs either. He works hard, and he's no spring chicken, you know."

Nina cocked her head quizzically, "Are you sure, Zia? The way she always waited on him and catered to him, I'm surprised to hear you say that she didn't support him emotionally in his work too."

"Well, your father hardly ever complains, so I don't know if he'd tell you if you asked him. Just take it from me. By the way, how is she doing, your mother?"

"Well, Pop came over last night for dinner after visiting her, and he thought she was doing a little better."

"What? What are you saying?"

"Zia, you mean you didn't know?"

"Know what?" asked Maria, a little more aggressively.

"Why, that Ma is in the hospital. Not this one, of course; I mean, she's in another hospital. She made a suicide attempt. Let's see . . . Wednesday night. She took an overdose of Tylenol. You mean you didn't know?"

Maria sank back against her pillows, and her hand covered her mouth. It took a few moments for the news to register. "That son of a bitch, he never said a word to me. All the time he's carting me back and forth to the doctors and here, and he never let on that anything was wrong."

"I guess he didn't want to worry you. Maybe Pop figured you had enough on your mind without having to worry about this too."

"That's just like your father, taking on responsibility for everybody else. If I let him, he'd be telling me when to brush my teeth. So, anyway, tell me about your mother. How is she? What happened?"

"Pop said that Wednesday night when he came home, he found her on the bathroom floor. She had taken a whole bottle of Tylenol. She was unconscious, and he had to call 911. The doctor said that she could have died and that she might have liver damage. That's really all I know. Pop said that it wouldn't be a good idea to visit her just yet."

"My God. I had no idea it had gotten this bad. Your father, he doesn't like to complain, but little things he said, I gathered that she's been quite unreasonable and difficult." They both fell into a silence. Maria thought back to 1950 when her twenty-year-old brother married Tessie Villari, not yet nineteen and just a year out of high school. Gennero was working for his uncles then, her father's younger brothers, Tony and Dominic. They both ran a trucking company, and it was there that Gennero began to learn about labor relations from the ground up. Gennero hinted that he had also done some small jobs for Uncle Dom, but he never went into the details. She didn't want to think about that and turned her thoughts back to Tessie. Such a pretty girl, but too stuck on herself, thought Maria. She always complained whenever she was asked to do anything or if she wasn't the center of attention. Maria wondered if all of this craziness was just an old lady's bid for more attention.

"I didn't mean to upset you, Zia," Nina said softly, reluctantly interrupting her aunt's thoughts. "I thought you knew, that Pop would have told you."

"Oh, honey, don't worry. Your father was just trying to take care of me. He meant well. No, I'm glad that you told me. Now, he and I can talk about it instead of his having to keep it all bottled up inside. These men! When will they learn?"

"I know. Joe was even worse. He would never talk about anything except when he was drunk, and then all he wanted to do was yell and give orders."

"Yes, I remember. He was a real loser, that one. It's a shame that he died the way he did, a car falling on him. And so young. But we were all glad that you were free of him."

"Yeah, we were married twelve years—do you believe it? Twelve lousy years with that jerk. I don't know if I ever would have divorced him. It wasn't something we did so easily back then. Now, it would be a different story. I'd never let a man treat me that way again."

Maria patted her hand. "Good for you. You finally came to your senses. I hope you passed that on to your girls."

"You bet. Of course, Rosalie had to go and marry that louse, Rob Negroni. At least she had the good sense to hold out longer than I did. I was only seventeen when I married Joe Batiste. Of course, I was pregnant at the time. But Rosalie waited until she was eighteen and at least out of school before she married that bastard. And she only waited four years before she kicked him out and got divorced."

"Well, I think he knew what was in store for him if he didn't go," Maria said quietly. The two women smiled and nodded at each other. "I think Gennero put him wise," Maria continued. "I think he told Rob what was up, what the consequences might be if he caused any trouble for Rosalie."

"Did he? Here I thought it was because my daughter was so tough, telling him to get out after we heard that while she was at the shore with the kids, he had the nerve to bring one of his girlfriends back to their house and have a party in his own backyard with his friends and their girlfriends. All the neighbors saw them getting drunk and carrying on. That bastard must have had a death wish. He's lucky I didn't kill him on the spot when I heard. Rosalie was furious. She told him, 'Pack your bags and get the hell out right now and don't ever let me see your fuck-ugly face again.' Pardon my French, Zia."

"Gennero heard about it that very night while Ro was still in Ocean City. He got a hold of Rob the next morning and quietly told him how things were. Gennero told him that he had to straighten out or else, and that when Rosalie found out, and she would, that if she wanted him to go, there would be no sense in arguing with her about it, because one way or another he would be gone."

"Wow, I had no idea. I guess Rosalie thinks it was all her doing too. I certainly did. Wow, Pop really has a way of working behind the scenes, doesn't he?"

Maria smiled proudly. She really did love her brother. Her eyes filled with tears. *I hope I'm not going to die. I will miss him so.*

Nina looked at her watch. "It's getting late, Zia. I have to get back. There's so much to do." She leaned over to give her aunt a hug and a kiss.

"Of course, I understand. Thank you so much for coming and for telling me about your mother. I hope she gets better real soon."

"Thanks. We have our fingers crossed, and last night Pop said he was a little more hopeful."

"Good. Give everybody big hugs for me."

"I will. Ciao, Zia."

"Ciao, baby."

Chapter XXVI

Gennero: Dr. Sacerdote

Gennero had Sal drive him up Kelly Drive, where Sal parked in a parking lot, and the two of them walked across the grass of Fairmont Park until they found a bench facing the Schuylkill River. They ate their lunch, enjoying the warmth of the sun, but with their collars up against the chilly weather. It may have smelled of spring, but it still felt too much like winter. After eating his sandwich, Gennero decided to telephone Paolo and find out if he had found someone to fill in for him.

Sal got up, stretched, and walked over to the river's edge. It was a bright March day, breezy, but not bitter cold. The ground was still hard, but everything was beginning to turn green. There were few people using the park, although the next day, Saturday, it would be more crowded.

Gennero got through to Paolo, and they talked about business, and then Paolo asked how the family was doing. Gennero told him that it looked like Theresa would be coming home on Monday but that he wasn't sure yet what that would mean and that he was glad that he had his days cleared so that he could deal with whatever came up. Gennero asked Paolo if he'd given any thought as to who would be filling in, and Paolo told him that one of the people he was considering was Joe Giantonio, Dom's oldest son, who had been managing some other operations in Atlantic City up to now. Gennero looked out across the grass to where Sal stood at the water's edge, watching some ducks in the river. He remembered Joey, who was forty-seven now. He was mature, experienced, and free of entanglements. He had divorced his wife, an angry, hysterical lush, ten or twelve years before.

"Paolo, I think he would be an excellent choice from what I know. His father, of course, has been very proud of what he's done out in Jersey. I know he has a good character and, I think, a good temperament for this kind of work."

"I'm glad to hear your opinion, Gennero. It confirms what I've been thinking. All right, then. You take care now, and I'll let Joey know the good news. I'm sure he'll be in touch with you."

"Oh, I'm sure he will be. Okay, Paolo, thanks. Ciao." When he hung up, he thought of his cousin Dom. *He's going to be so proud of Joey. I'd love to tell him, but I'll let Paolo handle it. Still, maybe I'll go over there for dinner tonight and help them celebrate.* Gennero looked at his watch: one thirty, a half hour until his appointment, time to get going. He gave a whistle to get Sal's attention, and when Sal looked up, Gennero waved him over. Then he got up and stretched, working out the stiffness in his body and enjoying the sun and breeze on his face. *It's a good day. Whatever happens, it's a good day.*

Gennero arrived at Dr. Sacerdote's office a few minutes before his appointment. The three-story building was set back a short distance from the worn brick sidewalk, behind a wrought-iron fence and gate and small ivy-covered front yard. Gennero looked up into the small camera that hung above the front door and rang the bell. Shortly, a soft buzz let him know that the door was unlocked, and he went in to the small foyer where he hung up his coat before entering the waiting room, formerly a front parlor. It was only two or three minutes before the connecting door opened, and Dr. Sacerdote came out of his office. "Good afternoon, Gennero, please come in."

Once in the office, Gennero took a seat in a leather chair that he had used on his previous visit. Dr. Sacerdote took a chair opposite him, across from a low, round table that lay between them, rather than taking the chair behind his desk, which was positioned by the window, overlooking the enclosed backyard.

"You mentioned that the problems with your wife have come to a head," he began.

"One might say that," Gennero said, sighing. Then, gathering himself up, he sat forward in his chair. "I had decided to call you on Wednesday, after talking to my cousin Dom. But then when I got home from work that evening, I found Tessie on the floor, unconscious from an overdose of Tylenol. I had to call 911, and the ambulance came, and they took her to Methodist Hospital. On Thursday morning when I visited, she was being totally uncooperative and wanted to come home right then and there. I put my foot down and said she had to get treatment, the medical treatment they said she needed in case of liver damage, and the mental treatment that she needed. I wasn't going to bring her home only to go through all this again. So, at that time, I figured I'd call you and get your ideas on how I should handle this crisis and also whether she should stay at Methodist. Dr. Weinstadt is her psychiatrist there. Or whether she should be transferred to Pennsylvania Hospital or some other place.

"The doctors were planning on going to court to have her committed to make her get the treatment she needed. I was all in agreement with that. But by Thursday night, she had changed her mind and was full of apologies, saying that she saw the light, so to speak. She agreed to sign herself into the hospital and cooperate with the treatment—take the medications, let them do their blood tests, all of that. So I was a little encouraged, you know? This was the most rational she'd sounded in a long time.

"But"—he paused and shook his head in disbelief—"this morning when I went to visit her, she told me that the doctors agreed to let her go home on Monday. On Monday! At first, I couldn't believe it, but it was true. Only not the way she said. She led me to believe that she was so much better, physically and mentally, that they decided to discharge her. But after I left her, I ran into her regular doctor, Dr. Sung, and found out that she gave them her forty-eight-hour notice last night after I left. They felt lucky that they were able to talk her into staying through the weekend rather than having to let her go home Saturday night." Gennero sat back and took a deep breath.

Dr. Sacerdote sat across from him in a long-sleeved white shirt and tie, his suit jacket hanging on a coatrack in a corner of the room. Like Gennero, he was shorter than average, five foot four or five. But unlike Gennero, he was thin and small-boned. Although younger than Gennero, Gennero guessed he was around sixty, as his hair and moustache were already quite white. He spoke softly and with a slight trace of Italian accent. "So, at this point, she is expecting to be discharged on Monday morning?"

"Right. Apparently, the laboratory tests for the liver are coming back healthy, no signs of liver damage. So, medically, they're more willing to let her go home. And the truth is she has been totally cooperative with them, and she is very apologetic about what she did. She's taking the antidepressant and the tranquilizer they have her on and says she's feeling less depressed and looking forward to coming home and cooking again."

"Gennero, you don't happen to know which medications they have her on by any chance, do you?

"No, I don't." Gennero thought for a moment. "Dr. Sung might have mentioned their names, but I don't think so."

"That's all right," Sacerdote said. "If it's important, we can find out. Please continue, Gennero."

Gennero concentrated, trying to regain his thoughts. "So she's on medication, and she seems better. She was much more, I guess you might say, affectionate or considerate. This past year, she's been increasingly angry and hostile. No one can talk to her or say anything without her taking it the wrong way. For example, she'll say something crazy, like," he looked up, searching the ceiling for an example, "she'll say, 'I saw this car pass the house this morning, and its license plate was such and such.' And I'll say, 'So?' And she'll say, 'Well, can't you see what that means? Don't you have any brains? How can you be so stupid? Of course you know what that means. You're just in cahoots with them, making believe you don't know. What, are you trying to drive me crazy? Is that how you plan to get rid of me?' Stuff like that."

Sacerdote nodded his head slightly while he sat, one ankle propped up on his knee, one hand supporting his chin.

"But not last night or this morning," Gennero continued. "She was smiling and agreeable, like a penitent little girl trying to get back in her father's good graces."

"And why do you think she might have wanted to do that?"

Gennero gave him a puzzled look.

"If she believes that you are not to be trusted as a source of loving support, if you wish her ill in some way, why would she want to get into your good graces?"

"I don't know. I guess I thought that she figured that we, the doctors and I, had some power; so if she wanted to get out of the hospital, she had to give in and play by our rules."

"So you're suggesting that maybe she was putting on an act?"

"I'm not sure. At the time, I thought she was being sincere, although I was questioning it; how could she change so fast? Dr. Sung said that the antidepressant should take at least a week to begin to have an effect, and here, within a day, she seemed to be more normal than I had seen in over a year or so. So, yes, I wondered if it was a real change or not. But I have to tell you, it felt good to see her smile at me again, to use a normal tone of voice again." Gennero paused, recollecting his experiences of that morning and the night before.

"Then, after I left her and talked to Dr. Sung, I realized how manipulative she had been. I was angry about that. But still, I figured, okay, she's feeling better and wants to come home, and she's just doing what's necessary in order to make it happen. That doesn't mean that she's not better. In fact, her being that realistic might even be some kind of proof that she is better. I don't know, Doctor. I'm all confused about this. I feel like I'm in a whirlpool, just going round and round, not able to get my bearings."

"Let's try to sort it out," Sacerdote said, using his fingers to enumerate his points. "Theresa has been increasingly paranoid over these past five or six years." He looked up and got a nod of agreement from Gennero. "Over this past year or so, she has been increasingly angry with you, accusing you of somehow, one way or another, being against her, unsupportive of her, not protecting her, in a conspiracy with others against her. In general, she accuses you of no longer loving her and of abandoning her. She feels all alone and unsupported, totally vulnerable and without anyone who cares."

"Yes, that's all true."

"Is there anyone," Sacerdote asked, "who she believes still cares about her?" Gennero thought. Sacerdote prodded him, asking, "Your daughter, any of your grandchildren, friends, neighbors, family doctor, priest?"

"No, not really. She has avoided going out, meeting people. She's avoided going to our daughter's house, and whenever anyone calls, she launches into a complaint about how she's being harassed by airplanes, license plates, people looking at her with an evil eye. She turns people off or ends up getting into an argument with them if they aren't sufficiently supportive of her right away. And she complains that none of the kids really care about her. So, no, I don't think there's anyone who she feels is on her side, who she can trust."

"So," Sacerdote continued, "she's feeling completely alone, surrounded by danger and enemies on all sides. She's feeling not only extremely frightened but also outraged that none of you, who supposedly she should be able to count on for your love, none of you come to her aid. None of you pay any attention. You turn your backs on her." Gennero agreed. Sacerdote continued, "In fact, it is obvious to her—and it's true—all of you *do* wish for the relief of not having to deal with her. She's a nuisance, a big pain in the ass to all of you, and she knows that at some level you do want to be rid of her."

Gennero started to protest, to explain and qualify, but then he saw the point. *From Tessie's point of view, all of it is true. She can't see that she's the cause of it all, that it's her behavior that he and Nina and Rosalie are responding to. But, given their behavior, yes, it is true; they all do want to be rid of having to deal with*

185

this argumentative, suspicious, irrational woman. Resignedly, he nodded in agreement. "Yes," he said, "you're perfectly right. We have abandoned her. I've abandoned her."

"Yes, Gennero, from her perspective, you have abandoned her. But it is equally true that from your perspective, she has driven you away. From your point of view, a monster has come into your home, gobbled up your wife, and now threatens to eat you. Of course you want to save yourself. Who in their right mind would sacrifice themselves, would give themselves up to be consumed by such a monster?"

"But what should I do? I mean, if she gets better, if she's once again her old self, there's no problem. But what if she's just putting on an act to get out of the hospital? Or what if she really is better but doesn't continue to take her medicine or follow through with her therapy? Oh, I almost forgot. One of the conditions of their discharging her is that she's to go for private therapy. Dr. Weinstadt was going to come up with a referral by Monday morning, but I was wondering if you might know of someone who Tessie might be able to get along with. She was thinking of a woman, Italian maybe, not too pretty." Gennero looked across the table and saw something on Sacerdote's face that made him add, "Whoever you think might be a good fit."

"What you're asking, Gennero, is if the monster comes back into your home, what options do you have?"

Gennero thought for a moment. "Yes. Exactly. I feel like I have no options. I have a wife of fifty-four years, who is now seventy-two years old. I have a responsibility here. If she's irrational, I can't just leave her to her own devices. She can't even go shopping for food, for Christ's sake. I have to have my driver, Sal, go shopping for me. We keep a goddamned cooler in the trunk so we can buy cheese and eggs. How can I leave her?"

"Is that what you want to do?"

"What I want, Doctor, is to have my Tessie back. Like in *Red Riding Hood*, I want to kill the wolf, open up its belly, and take my Tessie back out."

"And if you do, are you wondering if there was anything about your relationship that might have contributed to her illness?"

"What do you mean?"

"Gennero, aren't you wondering at all if there was something about your relationship with each other—maybe you're not paying enough attention to her, maybe she's too dependent on you, whatever—something that might have contributed to her feeling so hopeless and depressed?"

Gennero made a face and looked down at his feet. He thought. Sacerdote leaned back in his chair and crossed his other leg over his knee. "Yes, I guess I did wonder about that, if I caused it. But up until five or six years ago, everything seemed fine. I thought we were both content. I wasn't aware of any problem. I don't think she ever complained about anything. We never fought or argued. I always thought she was with me on everything we did, which is why I was so surprised when she started to change. I thought, *Where the hell is all this coming from?* You know? But I don't know what we should have done differently. I don't know what we could do differently."

He thought for a moment and then added, "I did talk to . . . my boss, my employer, and I'm taking a couple of weeks off from work. I thought I might pull back, work less. You know, maybe kind of retire." He paused. "I guess I was thinking that if she doesn't get better, I'm going to need more time to handle things, and if she does get better, maybe I should be paying more attention to her, doing more things with her."

"You think that might help?"

"I don't know. I've tried to do some of that all along, suggesting things to do together: go visit our family, go out to dinner, go to a movie. She won't have any of it. She always finds excuses. No, it hasn't helped up to now. Maybe with medication, it might be different."

"Then one option is to stay together and try what you've tried before and hope for the best."

"What else is there? Dumping her somewhere in an apartment? She'd never survive. It would be murder. I couldn't do that to her, my own wife. What would my daughter, my grandchildren think? What kind of example is that?"

"So setting her up in a place of her own seems like an unacceptable option?"

"Of course."

"What would be necessary to make it a workable option?"

"What do you mean?"

"What additional elements would you have to add in order to make it work? For example, Gennero, if you were struck dead right now, let's say by a heart attack, and you were able to look down from heaven and see the aftermath, what would you be directing people to do to help her make it on her own?"

Gennero looked up. "I don't know. I guess I'd want somebody to be with her, some kind of companion, to make sure she had everything she needed, but she won't have anybody."

"She won't have anybody as long as she has you. As long as she has you, she doesn't need anybody else. She doesn't trust you either. Having somebody else she doesn't trust, but upon whom she feels some kind of dependence, might not be all that different." Gennero made a face, conceding that it was a possibility, albeit a remote one.

"At any rate, Gennero, it's something to think about. Listen, we're almost out of time. I'm going to be away for the weekend, but if you need to reach me, my service can get hold of me. Otherwise I'll be back in the office on Monday morning. Let's set an appointment for Tuesday. This will give you a chance to see how she is on her first day home and if there have been any real changes or not.

"Meanwhile think about this. If she doesn't trust you and sees your lack of support or lack of belief in her as reflecting some hostile intent toward her, then she might not necessarily be better off in your company. A different kind of caretaker might even be better. But I agree with you; leaving her all alone without any support is not an option. So think about that. Also, talk to the doctors and see what medications she's on and what dosages. Let Theresa know that you're consulting someone to get help for your own confusion about what's going on. And try to get her permission to allow her psychiatrist to talk to me. If she will give him written permission to talk to me, he can give me all of the medical results I'll need to make sense of this.

"Finally, I do know a woman psychologist. She's in her late fifties, I believe. She's an excellent therapist and works a lot with a senior population. She comes from a partly Italian background, so I think Theresa will see something there that she'll be comfortable with. I'll give her a call and see if she has any openings, and when I see you on Tuesday, I'll give you her name and number."

Gennero thanked him. Sacerdote wrote out a bill for the visit, and Gennero wrote out a check. They made an appointment for two o'clock on Tuesday afternoon and shook hands. As Gennero walked out of the front door, again seeing the bright sun, already seeming to be a little lower in the sky, he felt a sense of relief, a surge of hope. Maybe he did have more options than he thought. Maybe it all would work out after all. He saw Sal standing by the limo up by the corner, and as he walked toward his car, he found himself whistling: *It's a big, wide wonderful world, we live in . . .*

Chapter XXVII

Grady

After leaving the food warehouse, Grady grabbed a hoagie and a coffee on Ninth Street and then walked the nine blocks or so over to Pennsylvania Hospital to visit Maria. On the way, a cabbie went through a crosswalk and nearly hit him. "Watch it, asshole!" he shouted at the driver. The driver stopped his cab, halfway blocking the street, and got out.

"Who you calling asshole?" he yelled back. He was a big guy, as tall as Grady, but much swarthier. Grady, who was halfway across the street, turned and glared at him. "I'm talking to you, wise guy," the cabby yelled again. "You got something to say to me?"

Grady walked back around the rear of the cab and stood toe to toe with the driver. Quietly, through clenched teeth, his jaw extended, his eyes ablaze, Grady looked him in the eye and said slowly and deliberately, "Listen, motherfucker, get back in your fucking piece of shit and get the fuck out of here while you still can." Grady turned to walk away, and the cabbie grabbed him by his left arm. Grady instantly spun to his right, his right forearm slamming into the cabby's upper right arm, knocking him off balance and face-first into his taxi. With his left hand, Grady grabbed and pulled hard on the driver's hair from behind and with his right hand, took hold of the cabby's belt, and lifted sharply upward. Then Grady pulled him backward and tossed him headfirst into the front seat of the cab.

By then, horns were honking. Grady walked across the street and continued toward the hospital, half hoping the driver would follow him so that he'd have an excuse to kill him. Of course, that didn't happen. But Grady's adrenaline was way up. His heart was pumping so hard that he swore he could hear it. He knew he had to calm down or somebody was going to get hurt, and he didn't really want that to happen.

Even though he was short on cash, he decided to get a cup of coffee from one of the venders outside of the hospital. He took it across the street and sat on the steps of an office building trying to breathe slowly and calm down. On the one hand, he was angry with himself for having walked back to the cabby and allowing himself to get drawn into a confrontation. On the other hand, he kept thinking of much more violent things he could have done, half wishing that he'd done them. Each time he thought of them, he'd get angry again and then had to make a conscious effort to cool off and calm down. Even so, by the time he finished the coffee and headed inside, he was still agitated.

Fortunately, the blue-haired old lady at the information desk was reasonably friendly and helpful. Before heading upstairs, Grady found the men's room where he relieved himself and took his time washing his hands and face and combing his hair. He was taking all the time he needed to cool off. Upstairs, he found Maria's room and peeked in. She was watching television, but when she saw him, she smiled and motioned for him to come in. "Grady, it does an old lady good to see that handsome face of yours." She turned off the TV and motioned for him to pull the chair closer to the bed.

"How are you feeling?" he asked. "I was shocked yesterday when . . ." He stammered a little, unsure of how to refer to Gennero. "Zio G. told me you needed surgery. I had no idea that there was anything wrong."

"Eh, what can you do? All machinery runs down eventually. So they need to do a checkup."

"Well, I hope they don't find anything," Grady said. "I hope everything turns out all right. When are they going to operate?"

"Early tomorrow morning. They'll probably be waking me up about five thirty, assuming I can sleep, that is. So I guess I won't be able to go out dancing tonight."

"Damn," Grady said, "that means I'll have to find another date."

"You won't have any trouble with that, a good-looking brute like you."

"Actually, I've got a girl."

"You do?" Maria said, raising her eyebrows and struggling to sit up straighter. "I didn't know. You have to tell me all about her. What's her name? How did you meet? What does she do? Everything."

Grady was not used to talking about himself like this, but he realized that, in bringing up the subject, he was looking to tell her. Maria was like an aunt to him. He wasn't as close to her as he was to Gennero, but she had always occupied a special place in his life, even if she didn't always approve of what he did. "You'd like her, Maria. Her name is Karen Rooney. She's twenty-nine and works as a waitress. We met in NA a couple of years ago. She's also a recovering addict, like me, and she's doing very well. She's what a friend of mine would call 'a stand-up broad.'"

"You mean she's tough?"

"Very tough. We help keep each other straight. It's good. We're good."

"I'm glad to hear that, Grady. It's about time you found somebody who's good for you. You know, you haven't always showed a lot of wisdom in your choices for girlfriends." She gave him a wink, indicating that although she spoke the truth, she didn't want him to take offense at it.

"No, you're right, Maria. I went with some real skuzzballs. I guess," he said. "I figured no woman could really be trusted anyway, so why pretend? I picked broads I knew were no good to begin with." He paused and then, looking at Maria, smiled and said, "I didn't even know women like Karen existed."

"You trust her?"

"Let me say that I believe 90 percent that she's trustworthy, and I'm working on learning how to take the risk of trusting. I've got a ways to go, and the reality is that we're both still recovering. There's always a chance that one of us could relapse. I'm not the most stable person going, either." He shook his head and then went ahead and told Maria about his run-in with the cab driver. "It's been a long time since I've really hurt somebody, but that potential, it's always there just beneath the surface. It doesn't seem to get any easier, no matter how hard I try."

"Grady, some things just don't ever get any easier. You have to accept that, for whatever reason, you have a violent nature. Many men do. Some women too. You'd be surprised. So this is something you may always have to struggle with. And just maybe your being so aware and so afraid of this part of your nature will help keep you a good person. Maybe it's even a good thing. Who knows?"

"Maybe," he said, "but it sure isn't comfortable."

"Eh, comfort. Aside from feeling good, it may not be so good for us."

Grady smiled. "You may have a point there. Listen," he said, changing the subject, "is there anything I can do for you? Anything I can get for you or bring to you?"

"Thank you, Grady. That's very kind of you, but no, I have everything I need, and Gennero will be bringing me some things later on. Just your visit, taking the time to come and visit, this was good. You really perked me up. I hope I'll see you again soon."

"Count on it, Maria." He got up from his chair and leaned over to give her a kiss. They hugged briefly, and then he straightened up. "Lots of luck tomorrow," he said. "I'll be thinking of you."

"Thank you, Grady."

He waved as he left the room. Downstairs, he saw from a wall clock that it was after three o'clock. *I'll wait until four before I call Tracy. She'll be home by then.* Then Grady started the mile walk home.

Chapter XXVIII

Grady: Making the Call

On his way back to his apartment, Grady passed through the Italian market and picked up some vegetables and fruit. He felt a connection to the store that had once been Maria's, and before that, her father's, so he usually did his shopping there when he was in the market. But walking along Ninth Street was always a challenge for him. The loud, gruff voices of the men hawking their produce turned him off. And the crowded sidewalks, like the two fat women walking side by side, blocking the path and taking their own sweet time, tended to infuriate him. He'd find himself clenching his teeth and his fists, holding his breath like a smoldering volcano ready to explode. Sometimes he'd "wake up" up at home, sitting at his kitchen table with a bag of vegetables in front of him and have no memory of where he'd been or how they got there. He knew that this kind of minor frustration with the lack of civility in people was often a trigger for his blackouts.

This time, already feeling revved up, he bought some things that seemed to be inexpensive and then took one of the smaller side streets out of the market in order to avoid going through the next couple of blocks of stalls and people. Grady tried directing his attention to more positive things—nice cars, interesting jackets people might be wearing, little kids, attractive women. Mostly though, what he saw was garbage in the gutters, fat slobs, disrespect and disregard, ugliness in many forms. *Christ*, he said to himself, *it's like I'm looking at the world through ugly-colored lenses. Is it me, or is it really this way?*

When Grady got home, he took off his leather jacket and stuffed the plastic bag of vegetables into the fridge. Standing there, looking into the refrigerator, looking for something to put into his mouth and his belly, to squelch the fire a little, the thought occurred to him, *I wish I had a beer right now.* The image stayed with him for a few moments, the feel of the cold can in his hand, the pop of the tab, the little fizz and slight rising of foam, imagining the dark yellow liquid, the smell from the can, the cold liquid in his mouth and throat. He found himself searching the inside of the fridge, looking for the cans that surely must be there. Then he took a deep breath and took out the container of orange juice. He poured himself a big glass before sitting down and thinking about his call to Tracy. He took the paper Gennero had given him out of his pocket and reviewed it all again. It was after four o'clock, time to call.

Tracy picked up the phone on the third ring. Her voice, though breathless, was lower than he remembered, almost musical, low and soothing. "Hello?"

"Tracy?"

"Yes, who is this?"

"Tracy, this is Grady Powers. I don't know if you remember me?"

"Grady Powers?"

"I was a good friend of Richie Batiste. We played in Onfire together. We met a few times."

"Oh, Grady, of course. The last name didn't ring a bell with me. Sure, I remember you. The big guy with the droopy moustache. Sure."

"Listen, Tracy, a couple of days ago, I was talking to Richie's grandfather. Obviously, he's an old guy, in his seventies . . ."

"Uh-huh."

"And we were talking about stuff, you know, and Richie's name came up. Anyway, the grandfather has a lot of questions about how Richie died and what all was going on in his life. He's trying to understand what it all means, Richie being his only grandson. You understand."

"Yeah?" She said it long and drawn out, more like a question.

"So, afterward, I remembered how tight you two were, and I thought if we could get together, talk a little bit, you might be able to fill me in on some stuff; you know, help the grandfather have a more complete picture of his grandson."

"You want to get together with me and talk about Richie?"

"Yeah. I . . ." Grady paused, catching himself almost giving away the fact that he knew as much as he did about her. "I figured you probably work during the week, Monday through Friday like most people, so I was hoping you might be free for a little while on Sunday. I thought maybe we could meet somewhere Sunday afternoon and, you know, just talk a little."

Tracy was silent.

"What do you say? Is Sunday good for you?"

"Gee, I don't know, Grady. Sunday? I, we might have something planned for then. I'd have to check with my husband, see if we're free . . ." She trailed off.

Grady never thought it would be easy and that she would be eager for a meet, but he figured he'd have to give that possibility a shot. Now he could see that she was looking for an excuse, a way out. Hubby would have other plans, and gee, even though she wanted to be helpful, she just couldn't. He could see it coming. His voice took on a stronger, firmer tone.

"Tracy, listen. This is important to me, and it's probably not going to take more than twenty minutes out of your life. If Sunday isn't good for you, then you tell me when is good. And you decide where we meet. If you want to meet someplace in the city, or at your place, or someplace after you're done with school, just let me know, and I'll be there. I want to make it as easy for you as I can." He deliberately let her know that he knew something about her.

Tracy, he knew, was beginning to understand that this was not a cold call from some charity asking her to buy a subscription to a magazine that she could blow off or even just hang up on. He knew that she realized she would probably have to meet him. Now the question was where and when.

"Gee, Grady," she crooned into the telephone.

God, what a beautiful, sexy voice she has.

"I really want to be helpful. But our schedule is so crazy this time of year. Couldn't we just do it over the phone? Just ask me whatever questions you have? Can't we do it now?"

"Tracy, I know this is an inconvenience. I realize I'm asking you to do something that you didn't ask for, and it's an imposition. I realize you hadn't planned for this, even though it's not really a big deal. We could meet over a cup of coffee or something, whatever. But you have to realize, we're talking about a guy who was like a brother to me. A guy who's dead. It's not like I have a list of questions I have to ask you like I'm doing a goddamned report. I need to be face to face with you to understand what you're saying."

He felt himself getting riled up. He took a sip of orange juice and a deep breath. She was silent on the phone. He softened his voice somewhat. "Tracy, you'll be doing me an awfully big favor. Just tell me when would be good for you . . . but this is something we have to do." There, he'd said it out loud; no way for her to avoid it anymore. Either outright refuse, try to delay, or agree. "You hear me, Tracy?"

"I hear you, Grady." Obviously, she would have in her mind images of the last time she had seen him, the night of Brian's beating. There would be the implication of the possibility of some kind of force, if not violence. "Listen . . . let me think a minute . . ." She was silent, figuring out her options.

He waited.

"All right," she continued, her low voice sounding calm and assured. "Tomorrow morning, I've got some time. We're going to be away the rest of the day, but early tomorrow morning could work. Is that possible for you?"

"How early would you like, Tracy?" he asked, knowing that she couldn't make it too early for him. He'd sleep on her doorstep if that's what it took.

"How about eight o'clock? There's a diner out here on Route 30, the Starlite Diner, in Wynnewood. Do you know it?"

Grady didn't know it. He never went out toward the Main Line. His trip to their house was his only time out there. But he did know that Wynnewood was two towns over from Haverford. *So she's picking a spot away from home. And she hasn't mentioned Brian once, although there were a couple of "we" mentions, letting me know there's a husband in the picture.* He could take a train out, and it might be early enough so that Karen could still come with him. He also realized that it was still possible that Tracy might end up bringing Brian with her. *No problem there. It might even be better to have his input.* Grady had no way of knowing which way would yield more information. *No sense in trying to control that aspect; just let come what comes.*

"The Starlite Diner, Route 30, Wynnewood, eight o'clock tomorrow morning. I'll see you there." He paused a beat and then added, "I'm sure we'll recognize each other."

"Oh, I'm sure of that," she said softly, almost as if to herself.

"Thanks, Tracy. I really appreciate this. I'm sure it'll be a big help to the grandfather. I'll see you in the morning then."

"Uh-huh," she muttered before hanging up.

Grady sat back from the table after hanging up the phone. His eyeballs slowly rotated upward, and his eyelids fluttered downward, almost closing.

Chapter XXIX

Gennero: Negotiating with Tessie

It was a little before three o'clock when Gennero settled into the backseat of his Town Car, feeling more relaxed and relieved than he had in some time. He saw Sal's eyes in the rearview mirror, waiting patiently for him to make up his mind where to go next: to visit Maria or Theresa? Gennero felt annoyed with Theresa because of her manipulating, so he was not eager to go back there. On the other hand, keeping her waiting would only make her more upset and could worsen her condition. Maybe it was better to pay attention to that problem first. And, he thought, *it would be more relaxing to end the afternoon in Maria's company.* "We'll go first to visit Theresa," he announced, "and then we'll go to see Maria."

Sal silently eased the car away from the curb and into the stream of traffic. Gennero reminded himself that before going to see Theresa, he'd have to stop by the house to pick up the clothes that she wanted. He leaned forward, catching Sal's attention. "Sal, I almost forgot, I'll have to stop home first to pick up some things for Theresa." Sal nodded. Gennero wondered how Maria was doing, a whole day of waiting around in bed with nothing to think about except the surgery to come. He knew he would have a tough time in those circumstances unless he had something to distract him and divert his attention.

It was a beautiful, sunny day, the sky a brilliant blue. It made Gennero feel good to see the brightness of the sunshine reflected off windows of buildings they passed. He noticed the buds popping out on the still-bare branches of trees and bushes and found himself looking forward to spring and possibly having more time for himself, being able to putter around the yard. *Maybe this partial retirement thing will work. Who knows?* When they got to his house, Sal opened the car door for him. "Thank you, Sal. Listen, I won't be too long, just getting a few clothes for Theresa. But if you want to, come in—use the bathroom while you're waiting." He left the invitation hanging in air.

"Sure, Mr. G., that's very kind. Thank you." The two men went into the house, and Gennero pointed up the stairs to the bathroom. Then he realized that the suitcase was still at the hospital, so he went into the kitchen and started looking for something he could use. He found Theresa's store of brown paper bags in a cabinet under the sink and took a couple of them with him upstairs. Sal was coming down as he was going up.

"Make yourself comfortable, Sal. I'll just be a few minutes." Upstairs in their bedroom, Gennero opened her closet, and, after standing there for a few minutes, unsure what to pick out, he finally chose a couple of pairs of slacks, a couple of tops, and a sweater. Then he retrieved more underwear and some socks— *Oh, and shoes.* With everything stuffed into the bags, he went downstairs. At first, he didn't see Sal, but then he noticed that he was out on the front lawn, taking some sun.

When Gennero went outside, Sal immediately offered to help with the bags.

"Thank you, Sal." Back in the car, Gennero told Sal to go to Theresa's hospital first.

Going into the hospital, it occurred to Gennero that it would be nice to bring some flowers. He had a little tinge of guilt that he hadn't thought of it until now, but then he remembered that he already had his arms full with the two bags of clothes. *Maybe tomorrow.*

When he got to the nurses' station, he leaned over and spoke to one of the women there. There was no way of knowing whether they were doctors, nurses, aides, or housekeeping staff. They all dressed alike, but he took a chance. "Hello," he said, "I'm

Mr. Giantonio. My wife is in 213. I just came from my doctor's, and he was asking about her medication. I was wondering if you could write down the names of her medications and the dosages so I can give it to him for his records?" He noticed that her nametag said her name was Roberta Brown. "I can give you his name and phone number if that will help, Roberta."

"No, that's all right, Mr. Giantonio. Would it be all right if I have it ready for you after you visit Mrs. Giantonio?"

"Certainly," he said. "I know you have a lot of work to do. When I come out will be fine. Thank you. I really appreciate it."

"No problem, Mr. Giantonio. You stop by, and I'll have it for you in an envelope." He smiled another thank-you and then proceeded to Theresa's room. He was glad that it had been that easy. He had been concerned that they wouldn't give him the information without Theresa signing a release. *But if Theresa doesn't have to know, that's even better. One less thing for her to be suspicious about.*

Entering the room, Gennero was surprised to find Theresa out of bed, sitting in one of the chairs with a thin hospital robe over her nightgown and those silly, little rubberized hospital socks on her feet. "Well, look at you," he said cheerily, "up and about." He put the bags down on her bed and leaned over to kiss her.

"Well, up anyway. Not so much about. As a matter of fact, I was just thinking about going back to bed. I'm getting kind of woozy."

"Here," he offered, "let me help you." Gennero extended his arm and helped her out of the chair. Then he moved the bags of clothes out of the way and helped her to sit on the edge of the bed. She removed her robe and then slid in under the sheet and light blanket.

"That's better," she whispered. "I was hoping you'd be coming soon. I was waiting and wondering where you were, what you were doing."

"There was somebody I wanted to talk to, to check out some people. I may have the name of a nice woman psychologist you can see. It's just a question of whether she has time, but I'm sure we can work something out."

"Is she Italian?" Theresa looked worried, like this was really very important.

"To tell you the truth, I don't remember if she's Italian or not . . ."

"Well, what's her name?"

"Theresa, calm down. I don't know her name. The doctor I talked to didn't want to give me her name until he had talked to her first. That's the way they do things. Don't worry, it'll be fine. I'm sure it will work out."

"I don't want to talk to just anybody, you know." Then she gave him a conspiratorial look. "I'm sure that you don't want me talking to just anybody either."

Gennero nodded, letting her know that he understood her implication—that in therapy, she would be talking about him as well as other things, and that she had some things of interest to say. "Theresa," he said gently, "the only thing I'm concerned about is that you have somebody to talk to who you can trust and feel comfortable with. If the first doctor isn't the right one, then we'll keep looking until we find the right one. We'll work together on this." He reached over and grasped her hand, squeezing it reassuringly. "We'll fight this together, you and me, all right?"

Theresa squeezed back. "So what else have you been doing with all your free time?"

"What are you talking about? I was here this morning. I had lunch. I went to talk to the doctor to get a name for a therapist for you. I went back to the house to pick up your clothes, which are in the bags, by the way. So what free time are you talking about?"

"Well, with me not home, you must have a lot more free time on your hands. You said that you were taking some time off, so you're not working. I was just wondering, that's all."

"Theresa," Gennero said with some exasperation, "I don't have a girlfriend. I'm not seeing other women. I'm seventy-four years old. If I have any free time, I'll take a nap."

"Who said anything about a girlfriend? I never said anything about a girlfriend. Is that your guilty conscience talking?"

"No, you didn't mention girlfriend just now, but you've mentioned it enough in the past for me to know that's what you're thinking. Don't go playing games with me, Tessie. This, all of this," he said, opening up his arms to encompass the whole room, "is much too serious to be making jokes."

"I'm not making any jokes, Gennero. I only asked a simple question. I don't know what you're getting defensive about."

Theresa sounded serious, but there was a little hint of a smile playing about her face. Gennero couldn't tell if she was teasing him or if the amused look on her face was the secret, superior smile of someone whose enemy fell into her trap. Was he Tessie's enemy? He felt angry and frustrated and uneasy. Was Tessie still really suspicious of his having a girlfriend? Could she really be thinking and believing that? If so, it was disappointing, and it pointed out that he had allowed himself to be too hopeful too early. *Maybe things will work out eventually, but not by Monday.*

Gennero smiled at his wife. "Tessie, it's wonderful that you still think I've got what it takes to be a hit with the ladies. That's very flattering. But you see how tired I get. You see that I spend all my free time at home. What would ever make you think I would be interested in another woman? You are all the woman I need. I just want you back, Tessie. I just want you back the way you were . . . the way we were. That's all."

"Oh, Gennero, you think I don't know? I see the way the women on our street look at you. I know how women are. You can't trust them," she said, shaking her finger at him. "You have to watch out. They're sneaky, like snakes. I know they're after you, and I wouldn't blame you if you gave into them. After all, they're younger than I am, thinner, and more beautiful. I know."

"Theresa. This is nonsense. You're going to make yourself upset talking like this. Please. Let's change the subject."

"Fine. What is Mister Giantonio willing to talk about?"

Gennero felt himself getting angry. He hated it when she deliberately baited him and tried to provoke him. He felt like she was winning something if he let himself get angry, as if she were proving a point—that he was an authoritarian, dictatorial man, interested only in dominating her. So although that's what he felt like doing, ordering her to be reasonable and pleasant, he swallowed it down. "Well, we could talk about the grandchildren and great-grandchildren," he suggested. "They're asking about you. Would you like to see them, maybe have a visit when you get home?"

Tessie pursed her lips and thought for a minute. "What did you tell them about why I'm in here?"

"I told them the truth. I told them that I came home and found you after you had taken an overdose of pills and that I called 911, and the ambulance came, and they brought you here. They asked if they could visit, and I said, no, not yet, but that I'd let them know when would be a good time."

Theresa remained silent, thinking. She looked up at the television, which was playing without any sound, and then looked sadly back to Gennero. "I'm sorry that I'm so much trouble to you. You must hate me."

"No, Tessie, no. I don't hate you. Nobody hates you."

Theresa smiled to herself, as if she knew better and was not going to be taken in by his kind and supportive words. "Sure, Gennero, if that's what you want. They can come visit when I'm home. But, please, not the first day."

He ignored the dig, "if that's what you want," once again making herself the victim of his dominance. "I know that they're looking forward to seeing you. Suppose I ask them to come over on Wednesday? How would that be?"

Theresa gave a little shrug of helplessness. "Sure, why not? Wednesday is perfect."

"You want them to come over in the evening, maybe after dinner? Maybe for coffee and dessert? I could get something at the bakery."

Theresa was silent. She pursed her lips and looked disinterestedly down at her hands, which played aimlessly with the fringe of the blanket.

Gennero persisted, "Would you prefer it if they came over in the afternoon sometime?"

"No, it sounds like you prefer the evening. That's fine. We'll do dessert and coffee, like you said." Theresa's voice was lackluster, as if she were resigned to having to do something she didn't want to do.

"Theresa, I know you aren't exactly excited about this, but I think it'll be good for you to see the kids. It's been a long time since you've seen them, and they miss you. They don't have to stay long. It'll be all right, you'll see." He patted her lifeless hand reassuringly.

Theresa managed a weak smile. "Don't mind me, Gennero. I'm still tired from all of this."

"Of course, I understand. Your body has been through quite a shock, and then there's the medicine that you're taking, still getting used to. I understand." He looked at his watch. "Listen, why don't I let you get some rest? I'll come visit you in the morning, eh?"

She agreed and stretched up her mouth for him to kiss.

"You rest, and I'll see you in the morning."

Theresa nodded and smiled wanly as he left the room, giving her his best effort at a cheery wave.

Chapter XXX

GENNERO

On the way to the elevator, Gennero stopped by the nurses' station. Roberta Brown was still there. Smiling, she handed him an envelope with his name on it.

"Thank you so much, Roberta. I really appreciate this."

"No problem, Mr. Giantonio. Have a nice evening, now."

"Thank you, and you too," he said, giving a little wave as he tucked the envelope into the inside pocket of his suit jacket. In the elevator, Gennero reviewed his visit with Theresa. It was disconcerting. More than that, infuriating how she could upset him. Did she take pleasure in upsetting him? He suspected that she did, and for the first time, he began to think that her apparent anger at him, her crazy jealousy, was not just a result of her becoming unhinged, but was also the product of some real grievances. She wasn't angry with him only because of her craziness, but she was really angry at him. God knows for what, but he was more sure of it the more he thought about it. Gennero gradually began to form the idea that maybe she hadn't been as happy in the marriage as he thought she'd been. Maybe there were secret grievances she had, perceived hurts or slights that she had harbored. This line of thinking put things in a different perspective. If she hadn't been as happy as he'd thought, if she had only been pretending to be happy, then maybe it wasn't such a good idea to stay together after all. Gennero shook his head. *All of this is too confusing, all supposition. Who knows what's real?* He felt hurt, angry, and betrayed.

When he emerged from the building, he looked for Sal and spotted the black Lincoln sedan. Sal saw him coming and had the back door open by the time he reached the car.

"Thank you, Sal. Let's go see Maria now," he said as he lowered himself onto the backseat. He let out a sigh and only then realized he had been stiff with tension. *She's going to drive me crazy, that woman.* He shook his head and, taking off his glasses, massaged his face with both hands. It felt good to feel the blood come tingling to the surface. He sighed again and took a deep breath. *It'll be good to see Maria.* He thought of getting some relief and comfort from her company. He had a fleeting association of the comfort he had gotten from his mother in times of stress when he was a little boy. He smiled to himself at realizing that Maria still was something of a mother figure to him. He hadn't thought of that since he was nine or ten. He recalled how his big sister used to take care of him and comfort him. Well, he felt that he could use some of that now.

When they arrived at the Pennsylvania Hospital, Gennero turned to Sal. "Sal, it's getting late, and I don't know how long I'll stay here. Why don't you go on home. I'll take a cab from here."

"Are you sure, Mr. G.? It's no problem for me to wait."

"No, no. You go on. And tomorrow, I'll just be visiting at the hospitals. You take the day off. Have a long weekend," he joked. "But Monday morning, we'll be bringing Theresa home, so I'll need you around nine o'clock. I'll give you a call and let you know for sure. God knows when Maria will be coming home. These days, they kick everybody out as soon as possible. But if I need you, I'll call you."

"Sure, Mr. G. Thanks. Don't hesitate to call me anytime."

Gennero smiled and then turned to enter the hospital. Sal was a good man. He didn't know a lot about Sal's home life. He had been married but got divorced back when he worked for the police department. *Seems like most cops get divorced.* He remembered that Sal had a couple of kids from that marriage, but he didn't know anything about them. He knew that Sal had a lady friend who stayed over some times, but he didn't know anything about her either. *Well,* he thought to himself, *it's better to keep a little distance. Familiarity breeds contempt,* he remembered his father saying once.

Walking into Maria's room, Gennero was surprised to see Artie Palucci sitting by the side of Maria's bed, the two of them laughing loudly. "Artie," he said, stopping dead in his tracks, "what a surprise! How are you?"

Artie got up from his chair. "I'm fine, Gennero. Apparently a lot better than your sister, here. How 'bout you? How're you doin'?"

Gennero walked closer and gave Artie a big hug. "I'm doing fine, Artie, just fine. I see you haven't yet shrunk with age," he said, looking up at the considerably taller man. "What is this? Am I the only one here who's getting shorter?"

"Actually, Gennero, I'm two inches shorter than I was when I graduated from high school. It's just that from down in that rut of yours, I still look taller."

Gennero looked at Maria. The big smile on her face made her look beautiful. "This salami here, he's still into busting chops. I hope he hasn't been giving you a hard time," he said to her, "or I'll have to teach him a lesson."

"He's incorrigible, Gennero. He'll never grow up. Just give him a kick in the pants for me."

"Here, sit, Artie," Gennero said, urging Artie to take his seat again. Gennero walked to the other side of the bed, leaned over to give his sister a kiss, and then sat on the edge of the bed.

"Maybe I should get goin'," Artie said, still standing. "Give you two a chance to visit?"

"No, Artie, don't go yet," Maria pleaded. "It seems like you just got here, and it's been so long since I've seen you."

"You sure?" Artie asked, looking at both of them.

"Hey, this is my room. I'm the queen here. I say you stay," she declared pompously.

"You heard her, Artie," Gennero said. "If you go, I'll have to have you whacked."

"Well, in that case," he said, taking his seat, "I'll have another round and some of those hot hors d'oeuvres you been holdin' out on."

"What?" Gennero said, frowning. "You think we have room service in this hotel?"

"Well, Gennero," Artie countered, "I don't know what kind a guy would put his only sister in a cheap place with no booze and no room service. I guess those rumors I heard about you bein' a cheapskate are true after all. And to think of all those guys whose ass I had to kick, defendin' your good name."

"For which you shall always have my deepest thanks," Maria chimed in.

"Really, Artie, how have you been?" Gennero asked, more seriously now.

Artie shrugged his big, broad shoulders, his whole chest heaving in the process. "You know, the tailpipe is rusted out, I'm burning oil and need a ring job. The battery is wearing out, and the shocks are bad, but I still get to church and back on Sunday mornings."

Gennero chuckled. "Hey, for that, you only have to walk around the corner. You're still right off Christian Street, right?"

"Same time, same station. I been there my whole life. I'll die there, I'm sure. But," he added, wagging a finger, "not till I reach a hundred."

"I'll drink to that," Maria said, raising her empty right hand.

"I was just telling Maria," Artie said to Gennero, "that I happened to be in the shop when Mona comes in to get some veal chops, and I'm passin' the time with her, you know, and she tells me Maria is in the hospital. You coulda knocked me over with a feather, I was so shocked. Maria? In the hospital? No way. She's too strong and stubborn to ever go in a hospital. I had to see for myself. Now I can go back to the neighborhood and spread some real rumors."

"You do and you'll answer to me," Maria threatened.

"So," Gennero asked, "what's going on in your life? You still collecting wives for a hobby?"

Artie smiled. "What? You think I'm stupid or somethin'? I got married twice. That was enough. No, I've been takin' it easy. You know, take in some games, sometimes, visit with my brothers or my cousins and their families, help out in the shop once in a blue moon. Actually, my knees ain't so good, so I end up sittin' down a lot. I'm gettin' real good at sittin' down."

"Actually," Gennero said, "I'm kind of looking forward to doing some of that myself."

Maria looked surprised. "Oh? What's this?"

Gennero looked at her, indicating in the briefest of moments when their eyes met, a warning of sorts: *I'll tell you later.* "Just that I've been thinking of cutting back a little, maybe spend more time around the house; you know, a little gardening, a little fixing up. Maybe even get one of my great-grandsons to teach me about the computer and go on the Internet."

"All, I can say, Gennero," Artie said with assurance, "is that having some extra time, some free time is like gettin' a great gift. Bein' able to do things at your leisure, at your own comfortable pace, without rushin' around all the time, it's just wonderful. You'll love it. You can spend more time with your sister," he suggested.

"I'd love that," Maria said. "But if I see much more of him than I have, he'll have to start paying me rent."

"And you, Maria? How are you feeling this afternoon?" Gennero asked.

"You know, this may sound crazy, what with me having surgery tomorrow morning and maybe finding out I have cancer, but this has been a wonderful day. I had a surprise visit from Nina, and then earlier this afternoon, I had another surprise— Cousin Dom came by for a visit."

"Dom Giantonio, from what, the Villa Contursi?" Artie asked.

"No kidding?" Gennero said. "Well, he said he would try to stop by, but he sure didn't waste any time getting here. So you're a popular lady."

Maria smiled, but her eyes indicated there was something else, something he'd have to wait until later to find out. He'd wait until Artie left.

"So what did Cousin Dom have to say? Anything special?"

"No, he just came to visit and wish me well. We talked about his children and his grandchildren, his daughter Rena's two little girls. He said you had stopped by this week and told him that I'd be in the hospital today."

Gennero nodded without elaborating on his visit to Dom.

Artie looked at his watch. "Well, listen, Maria, I'm goin' to let the two of you have a little privacy. But I will be back. Not tomorrow," he said. "You'll be feelin' like shit tomorrow, but on Sunday. Assumin' that you're still here, I'll come by then."

Maria reached out to pull him closer. "It's wonderful to see you, Artie, to see that you haven't changed. I'll look forward to seeing you then."

They gave each other a kiss and looked into each other's eyes.

"*Bona fortuna, cara.*"

"*Mille grazi,*" she said.

"See you Sunday."

Maria squeezed his hand. "Don't forget."

"I won't forget. I'll tie a string around my sausage to remind me."

"Artie!" she cried. "You're terrible."

"Yeah," he said, smiling, "I know. But I'll see you Sunday." Then, turning to Gennero, he said, "G., it's good to see you again."

"Same here, Artie. I really enjoyed seeing you after all these years. Take good care of yourself."

"You too," said Artie, retrieving a jacket from the back of his chair.

Maria and Gennero watched as Artie left the room and then looked at each other.

"Did you have anything to do with this?" she asked.

Gennero smiled broadly. "To be totally truthful with you, the answer is no. Mona beat me to it. I was going to wait until after the surgery, when we knew more. But it looks like it was a good idea. You really brightened up. You look like you lost twenty years at least."

"Yes. It was very good to see Artie again." She smiled, shaking her head. "He always made me feel good. He really embraces life. So much energy."

"I don't know how he does it," Gennero said admiringly. "Everything's a joke to him. I don't know if he takes anything seriously."

"Maybe you take everything too seriously," she chided.

"Maybe you're right. I've been thinking recently, aside from enjoying my work and enjoying our conversations, or my infrequent visits to Nina's, I haven't been enjoying myself very much."

"Not having enough fun?"

"No, I don't think I have. It's funny. You'd think I'd be aware of that, like not having enough water to drink or oxygen to breathe. But fun isn't like that. A person can be without it for a long time without even noticing it. Then all of a sudden, one day he realizes that all of the color has slowly drained out of the picture, and it's all just kind of washed-out, you know?"

Maria nodded. "I think fun hasn't been an important part of our life in the way that work and responsibility have. When we're young, it's mostly about having fun. But once we've grown up, it's like it's not supposed to be important anymore. But for Artie, he's still a kid. Having fun is still the most important thing to him. Responsibility always was toward the bottom of his to-do list."

"Well, he may have something there." Gennero paused, reflectively. "Anyway, I think we both, you and I, need to make a point of putting some more fun into our lives."

Maria grimaced. "Gennero, you think we still know how to do that? It's been a long time for either of us."

"Maria, if we don't start to have a little fun now, then when are we going to do it? Neither one of us has forever."

Maria made another face. "Don't remind me."

Gennero rolled his eyes. "Sorry." There was a short silence, and then Gennero changed the topic. "Was there something else about Dom's visit you wanted to tell me?"

Maria thought back. "No," she said, "not about Dom. I wanted to tell you that Grady Powers stopped by. I didn't want to mention it because I didn't know if it would lead to the whole business about Richie. No, I just wanted to let you know that he stopped by. Actually, Dom came soon after Grady left. So it's been a busy afternoon, with all of these wonderful people coming in. It really made me feel . . . I don't know, special. You know?"

"Sure. That's good. That's the way you're supposed to feel."

"That reminds me, Gennero Giantonio . . ."

"Oh-oh, what did I do now?"

"Why didn't you tell me about Theresa?"

Gennero grimaced. "Ouch!" he said. Then smiling, he asked her, "Who told you? Nina?"

"Of course Nina told me. The question is, why didn't you tell me?"

"What can I say? You know why I didn't tell you. You had enough to think about without worrying about what I'm going through with Tessie. I figured I'd wait until after the surgery and see how you're doing and what's happening with her, and then I'd bring you up to date."

"So bring me up to date now. Where is she? How is she?"

Gennero sighed. He got up from the bed and walked around to the chair that Artie had vacated and sat down. "Well, *sorella*, I'm really not too sure how she is. Physically, she seems to be better. At first, they were quite concerned about the possibility of liver damage, which could have been fatal. But now, they think she's going to be all right as far as that's concerned. But mentally, I don't know. It turns out she's going to be discharged and is coming home on Monday."

"Monday? Why that's only . . ." Maria started counting on her fingers.

"Yes. Really only four days. In fact, last night, she agreed to sign herself in voluntarily, and then she turned around and immediately gave her forty-eight-hour notice. But rather than discharging her tomorrow night, they persuaded her to stay until Monday morning. The only good news is that she's agreed to continue to take her medication and has agreed to see someone in therapy."

"Gennero, just how bad is she?"

"Maria, I don't know if she's any better than she was or not. At first, I thought that the medicine was like a miracle. We seemed to have a moment of normalcy last night that I haven't had with her in years. But today, I find that she's manipulative and deceitful in ways that, frankly, surprise me. I didn't think she had it in her. And then just now, before I came here, I had the impression that she's been a lot more unhappy in the marriage than I'd ever thought. I'm feeling like," he stammered, searching for the words, "not only don't I know who she is anymore, but maybe I never knew who she was."

"So what are you going to do?"

Gennero pursed his lips. "What can I do? I'll take her home on Monday morning. We'll see how things go with her medication and with her therapy. Maybe things will get better. If not . . ." His voice trailed off. "I went to see a psychiatrist earlier this afternoon. If Tessie reverts to her crazy ideas and this jealousy of hers, accusing me of having a girlfriend, then maybe I have some other options. But," he sighed, "I can't go on like this. Maria, I never wanted to burden you, and I never felt comfortable talking about Tessie behind her back, but you have no idea what I've been putting up with these past few years. I just can't do it anymore. I feel like I've just been battered, relentlessly battered."

Maria looked at him. Her eyes were glistening. "Oh, Gennero. You should have told me. Maybe there's something you could have done sooner, maybe seen this psychiatrist sooner. Something."

"Yeah, well . . . I thought I could reason with her. But I couldn't. It just kept getting worse. Maybe this suicide attempt is the best thing that could have happened."

"Yes, I think so." They were both silent for some moments. "Gennero, I'm so sorry that this happened to the two of you. I'm sorry for Tessie. She must be going through hell. And I'm sorry for you and Nina, but especially you, living with it day in and day out." Maria suddenly started to cry. At first the tears just filled up her eyes and spilled out onto her cheeks where they ran silently down to her neck. But almost immediately, she began to sob and was reaching for the box of tissues on the bedside table.

"Maria, what's the matter?"

"Oh, Gennero. I'm just thinking, what if I'm not able to be here to help you?"

Gennero got up and went to her, leaning over awkwardly to embrace her. They hugged each other this way, consoling each other, until Maria had to push him back so she could blow her nose. Gennero sat back in his chair and, taking the handkerchief from his pocket, wiped his eyes and blew his nose too.

"Maria, we're strong people. I know I can get through this craziness alone if I have to. But I get tremendous strength from you too. Earlier, on the way here, I was thinking of how you used to be like a little mother to me when I was a boy. I was thinking of you and Mama and how you've always been a source of strength and support for me. I hope I've been that to you too."

"Oh, you have, Gennero. You have."

"Maria, whatever happens, we'll always be there for each other."

Maria looked at him, cocking her head to one side, a sad smile on her tear-streaked face, her eyes wet and shiny. "I know. I know."

Gennero took a deep breath. "So what time are they getting you up tomorrow?"

"Five thirty. The surgery should start sometime around seven. Then, depending on how much they have to do . . . and then there's the recovery room. I should be back here by noontime or so."

"All right, then. I'll go visit Tessie first, and then I'll come over here. I'll probably be here before noon."

"Gennero, there's no rush. I'm going to be out of it anyway. I may not even remember that you were here at all."

"I know, but that's all right. I won't mind. I'll bring something to read to pass the time."

It was at that point that an aide came in with Maria's food tray.

"Well, maybe time to go," Gennero said. "Oh, I almost forgot to tell you . . ." He waited until the aide left. "I told Paolo that I needed to take a couple of weeks off and then see what happened at home. I suggested that he might want to get somebody to fill in for me. And afterward, if I go back full-time, this person could be my assistant and eventually be groomed to take over. On the other hand, if things are too chaotic for me to come back full-time, then this person could take over, and I'd be available as a consultant as long as necessary."

"That sounds good. So that's what you meant about sitting down some more and taking it easy."

"Yes. I talked to Paolo today on the phone. Guess who he's going to pick?"

Maria made a face and shrugged her shoulders. "How should I know? I have no idea."

"Joey Giantonio. Dom's oldest son."

Maria's face lit up. "Joey? Oh, that's wonderful. Oh, Dom is going to bust his buttons. Does he know yet?"

"I don't think so. Dom would have said something this afternoon when he visited if he had heard anything. But I was thinking of going over there, maybe having a drink before dinner. If they do hear, I want to be able to congratulate them."

"Well, if they've heard, then give them my very best wishes too."

"I will." Gennero got up and leaned over to give her a kiss good-bye. "*A domani.*"

"Until tomorrow."

Chapter XXXI

Grady: Blackout

The first thing Grady was aware of was the bright flash in front of his eyes. The second thing was the odd cold but burning sensation he seemed to be sucking down into his throat, making him cough. A man's loud voice above him said, "Jesus Christ, man, is this the first fucking time you ever inhaled?"

Grady stood up from his bent-over position, where he had just lit a cigarette from the man's lighter. Grady looked at him, a beefy guy about his age, but with wild black hair and a scraggly beard. He didn't know him. The man laughed as he put his lighter away, and Grady looked at the cigarette between his fingers. Kools? He hadn't smoked that shit in years. Only then did Grady hear the loud music and the incomprehensible babble of people all talking at the same time. He looked around and discovered he was in a bar. A basketball game was playing silently on a TV above the bar. Grady had no idea where he was or how he had gotten there. He looked back at the man who had lit his cigarette. He had turned his back to Grady and was now talking to two other guys on the other side of him. Grady looked at his watch, 10:30 p.m. The female bartender came toward him and leaned into the bar. He had trouble lifting his eyes from her cleavage to her face as she asked him what he wanted. At first, he felt confused, like her words didn't make sense. She repeated herself, louder. "What do you want?" she shouted.

Grady shook his head. His mouth felt numb, and he was having trouble making his lips move. His face felt like rubber. He shook his head again, turned away from the bar, and headed outside, staggering through the crowd of young men and women who stood in his way, holding their beers and talking animatedly. His legs felt like rubber, and he had trouble maintaining his balance. Outside, he leaned against the cold brick. The street looked familiar, but he couldn't place it. He shook his head again, more vigorously. He began to feel cold and realized he had no jacket, just his sweatshirt on over his T-shirt. He leaned over and rubbed his thighs, bringing some circulation back into them. Then he stepped out onto the sidewalk and looked up at the sign over the front: Charlie's Pub. That struck a bell. That was down on Third Street in Old City. How the hell had he gotten down here? He checked his pockets. He had his wallet, twelve dollars, some change, a subway token, his keys, and a new pack of Kools.

He leaned against a car and tried to figure it out. The last he remembered—a fight with a taxi driver, a visit to a hospital, Maria Giantonio, walking home, the Italian market. Oh yeah, the phone call to Tracy, sitting in the kitchen and talking to Tracy. He took a drag on his cigarette and looked around. Ten thirty. Karen would be getting off around eleven. He decided he'd go over to the pub where she worked and go home with her. He started to walk south toward Market Street. At first, he felt wobbly and was embarrassed, thinking that he looked like he must be drunk. But as he walked, his normal sense of control and the normal feelings in his body slowly returned to him. *That's what it's like*, he thought, *like my body has been somewhere else, as if somebody else was in control of it, and I'm only now getting it back.*

On Market Street, Grady waited for a bus to take him closer to where Karen was working. Normally he was a good walker, but now he didn't feel up to it; he was too exhausted. Additionally, he was frightened by the prospect of a blackout that had lasted over six hours and where he had come perilously close to having some alcohol. He had no idea what he had been doing for these past six hours or so. He ran his tongue over his teeth, seeking a clue as to whether he'd had anything to eat or drink, but he couldn't detect anything. He tried to remember how much money had been in his wallet but couldn't recall, so he couldn't figure out if he had spent money drinking or not.

Grady glanced around to see if anyone was looking at him strangely, but no one seemed to notice him. Finally, the bus came, and he took a seat in the back, rode it to his stop, and then got off and made his way over to Karen's pub. He went in, ordered a Coke, and sat at the end of the bar until she noticed him. Karen looked shocked.

"My God," she mouthed silently, as she made her way toward him. "What are you doing here? Are you okay? You look like you were run over by a bus. What's the matter?"

"It's a long story. I'm all right. I just thought maybe we could go home together."

"Of course we can go home together. But I'm working until midnight tonight. They need an extra hand. Can you wait around?"

Grady nodded.

"Are you sure you're all right with hanging here for another hour?"

"Yeah, I'll be fine. I'll just wait here until you're done."

"Great. I'll get off sooner if I can." Karen looked at him questioningly.

Grady forced a smile. "I'll be fine. You go. Do your thing."

Karen nodded and squeezed his arm, surprised as always to feel how hard and muscular he was. Then she melted back into the crowd. Grady sat at the bar and nursed his Coke and smoked his Kools. *Kools,* he puzzled. *Why the hell would I buy this shit*?

Close to midnight, Karen came toward him, her jacket on and carrying her purse. She took him by the arm, said good night to the bartender, and they headed for the door. Once outside, she asked seductively, "Your place or mine?"

"Yours is closer," he said, "but I don't have a jacket, so maybe we should stay at my place."

"What happened to your jacket? Don't tell me somebody ripped it off."

"No. Nobody ripped it off. I think I came out without it."

Karen stopped and looked at him, frowning. "You think you came out without it? Don't you know?"

Grady made a face and looked away for a moment.

"Don't you know, Grady?" she repeated.

"No, I don't know," he answered, his voice sharp and edgy. "I don't know if I went out with or without my jacket, and I don't know . . . I don't know what the hell I've been doing or where the hell I've been between four thirty and ten thirty today."

"Grady, what are you talking about? Have you been drinking or something?"

He shook his head and looked away. "No. I honestly don't think so. But I'm not certain. I don't think so, but I don't know for sure."

"All right," she said, taking his arm and leading him toward the bus stop where they would catch the bus to his place. "You just take your time. You tell me what you want to tell me. Go at your own pace."

He nodded, and they walked in silence to the bus stop. No one else was there. Slowly, he began to tell her about the blackout and his long history of them, how embarrassed and frightened he was of them. He told her how helpless he felt, that there was nothing he could do to prevent them and how sometimes he felt as if somebody or something else took over. He told her how tonight he had only one thought—to seek her out, to get her help.

"I'm really fucked up, Karen. I'm really very, very damaged. You have a right to know what you're getting into with me. I'm really a nutcase."

"You may be a fucked-up nutcase, but you're my fucked-up nutcase." She reached up and kissed him on the lips. "Grady, both of us are whackos. You think I thought you were normal?"

Grady laughed at that. It was good to release some of the tension.

On the bus, on their way to his apartment, Grady remembered his phone call to Tracy. "I meant to tell you," he said quietly, "I called Tracy this afternoon. She wants to meet tomorrow morning at a diner in Wynnewood, at eight o'clock."

Karen's eyes opened in mock horror. "Eight o'clock? In the morning?"

"Yeah. I thought we could catch a train out if we get to the train station by seven."

Karen looked at her watch and rolled her eyes. Then she gave a shrug of her shoulders and smiled weakly at him. "Well, if that's what we have to do, then that's what we'll do."

CHAPTER XXXII

GENNERO: OLD TIMES

It was approaching dusk when Gennero exited Pennsylvania Hospital onto Spruce Street. Increasing cloudiness made it seem even darker and cooler, and Gennero found himself wishing that he had worn his coat after all instead of trying to rush spring by going out only in his suit jacket. He soon spotted an empty cab, hailed it down, and found himself hurtling over Center City's bumpy streets on the way to Dom's restaurant. He hung onto the strap for stability but found himself, much like he had when he was a kid, enjoying the sensation of recklessness, like an amusement park ride. Arriving at Villa Contursi, he paid the driver, complimented him on his driving skills, and laboriously extracted himself from the backseat of the taxi.

Entering the intimately lit atmosphere of the restaurant, Gennero noticed that Dom was at the far end of the crowded bar, schmoozing with one of the patrons, an old friend that Gennero had also known for years. As he walked over, Dom looked up and spotted him. "Hey, Gennero." Dom opened his arms in greeting. The man he had been talking to, Vincent Carbone, a former lawyer and now a judge, turned around.

"Well, I'll be," he said in his low, raspy voice. "Gennero Giantonio. I haven't seen you in years." Gennero shook his hand enthusiastically.

"Vincenzo, how are you? It's good to see you too. It's been way too long."

"Gennero," Dom cut in, "I was just telling our good friend, the judge, about our good news."

222

Gennero smiled in anticipation but struggled to appear as if he didn't know what Dom was going to say. "Good news?" He looked sideways at Vincent and saw him smiling gleefully in anticipation of Gennero's reaction.

"Gennero, you wily son of a bitch, don't go pretending that you don't know. I'm talking about Joey. I just got a call today from him. Paolo Romano drove all the way out to Atlantic City, walked into his office, just like that, just to tell him the good news in person."

Gennero smiled broadly, "Which is . . . ?"

Dom, happy but also somewhat embarrassed, hesitated. Gennero prompted him again. "Come on, Dominic, I want to hear it said out loud."

"He's making Joey your stand-in. He's going to be the new executive officer for the corporation, until you're up and running again." Dom embraced Gennero. "G., I don't know how to thank you for putting in the good word for Joey. I know Paolo wouldn't have gone ahead and chosen him without your approval. I owe you one, cousin. Anything you need, you let me know."

Gennero was almost giddy with happiness. He was delighted to his core to be able to bring such joy to his friend and cousin.

"Dom," he said, "I'm thrilled to have been in a position to have helped, but the truth is Joey's earned it. And if I didn't think he was the right person, in spite of my love for you and for him, I wouldn't have recommended him. But like I said, he's earned it. You did a magnificent job with him, with both your boys. You should be very proud, both you and your Mattie, God rest her soul."

"Here," Vincent interrupted, "I'm buying. Gennero, what'll you have? We have to have a celebration drink."

"Well," Gennero mused, "the occasion calls for champagne, but I'll settle for a nice glass of Cabernet."

"Done," said Dom, who stepped behind the bar to get a glass and open a fresh bottle of wine. While he was busy, Vincent and Gennero put their arms around each other, glad to be feeling their old friendship and camaraderie.

"So how do you like being a judge?" Gennero asked.

"I like it," Vincent answered thoughtfully. "It's busy but not like the crazy pace of private practice. I've got a little more time to myself, which my wife, Connie, is grateful for. And I still have time to play some squash at the gym so I can keep in shape."

"It looks it," said Gennero approvingly. "You look fit. Old as Methuselah, but fit."

"Fuck you too," Vincent joked, giving Gennero a mock punch in the arm.

"One glass of Cabernet for a very dear friend," Dom chimed in. "Hey," he said to Vincent, "no rough stuff here. We don't need the cops here, giving the place a bad name."

"So," Gennero said, turning to Dom, "it sounds like Joey is happy about the news?"

"Happy?" Dom exclaimed. "He couldn't be happier. This is a big step up in responsibility, not to mention the money. And he's thrilled to be working more closely with the board. If he does well, he's got it made for the rest of his life. He's happy as a clam."

"I'm glad." Gennero beamed.

"Listen," Dom said, "I just decided. I'm going to have a celebration party. Christ, this is all so new and overwhelming I haven't had time to think straight about all of it yet. Yeah, I'm going to have a party here tomorrow night. You two are invited. Vinnie, bring the lovely Lady Carbone with you. No excuses are accepted. G., tell Nina and her kids. Everybody, bring everybody. Nick!" he hollered. He turned back to the two men. "Excuse me. I have to tell Nick to start making arrangements, call people."

"Go," Vincent said. "Go make the arrangements." Dom smiled boyishly at them both and then went off to find Nick.

Vincent hugged his old friend. "So, Gennero, what's with this 'stand-in' stuff? And until you get 'up and running again'?"

"Eh, just some personal family matters. Theresa had a bad reaction to some medication a couple of days ago and had to go to the hospital."

"Anything serious?"

"At first they thought it might be pretty serious, but apparently all of the tests are coming back negative, so that's good news. In fact, it looks like she's going to be coming home on Monday."

"Ah, that is good news," Vincent said. "These medications, they can be tricky once we get to be our age. Some of these doctors don't know what the hell they're doing. They don't realize that we don't metabolize as quickly as a younger person. That happened with Connie's sister. The doctor ended up overmedicating her. She was in the hospital for a week before they figured out what the problem was."

"Anyway, we're hoping that everything will get back to normal now. But in the meantime, I'm taking some time off until I see how much Tessie needs me at home."

Vincent made a face. "Me, I'm afraid to stay home. I'm afraid I'll turn into a lump, bore myself to tears, and end up drinking and eating too much."

"You don't want to retire?"

"Not me," he said huskily, shaking his head. "The only way I leave the bench is feetfirst."

"That can be arranged," Gennero joked and received another punch on the arm.

Dom came back to join them. "Nick's on top of it. You'll probably get a call, but it'll be seven o'clock here for drinks and then dinner at eight. Nick will have Dolpho prepare something real special. It'll be a gala. Gennero, I was wondering, do you think you can ask your driver, Sal, to come? Maybe provide a little extra security, you know? Just in case?"

"I just gave him the weekend off, but I'm sure he wouldn't mind. He may have a lady friend in tow, though." He raised his eyebrows, indicating that he was really asking for permission.

"No problem. Tell him to bring her along. Paolo's driver is pitching in too. What the hell? The more the merrier," he said, extending his arms. Gennero couldn't remember having ever seen Dominic so expansive.

"Dom," he said, "I don't think you were this excited when Joey was born."

"You may be right. This is definitely one of the happiest moments of my life." He reflected for a moment and then, poking Gennero in the chest, asked, "G., do you remember when Rena was born?"

"Of course."

Dom turned to Vincent to tell him the story. "Vinnie, it was our first. Mattie started getting pains about eleven o'clock at night, and then around midnight, her water broke. She's nervous as hell. Of course, me, I'm Mr. Cool, right? So we called the doctor, and he said it's time to get to the hospital. So, me, what do I know about babies, right? Only what I saw in the movies. So we get in the car. Mattie is so nervous she can hardly walk. She's shaking so much. So we're in the car, and I'm fucking racing through the streets. I figured it's time; I've got to get to the hospital as quickly as possible, just like in the movies. I have visions of nurses wheeling her down the hall on a stretcher, her crying out in pain, me holding her hand and telling her not to worry. You get the picture?"

Vincent nodded, smiling at the scene of a nervous daddy's first experience with his wife giving birth, as if it were the first time in the history of the world.

"So I'm going through red lights, speeding like crazy. We get to the hospital in, like sixty seconds flat or something. I screech to a stop in front of the emergency room and run to get a wheelchair from inside and bring it back out. Then I wheel her in. I leave the fucking keys in the car, the motor running, the doors open, everything; I figure there's not a moment to lose, right?

"Now, I get her inside, and I'm calling out, 'Help! My wife is having a baby! Come quick. Help me!' A couple of nurses come out, an orderly, whatever, and they take the chair and tell me they'll take her up to the maternity ward, but—I've got to go to admissions.

"So I'm in the admissions office, and this woman—about 160 years old—you know, blue hair, every hair in place. It's

Midnight, for Christ's sake, and she looks like she just came out of a fucking beauty parlor. And she has these glasses on a rope hanging around her neck, and even with the glasses, like Coke bottles, she still can't see what she's typing. Talk about slow! I'm there practically pissing in my pants, thinking my wife's upstairs having a baby, and this old fart is taking her own sweet time asking me my name and my address and where I was born and when I was born. And in those days, remember, they didn't have computers. It was all with a typewriter—original and three carbons. You make a mistake, you have to correct each page separately. I swear, Vince, it felt like a fucking eternity.

"Finally, she's done, and I race to the elevator, and I'm waiting," he demonstrated, tapping his foot, wringing his hands. "I can't wait. I run up the stairs and find my way to the maternity section, and a nurse tells me my wife is inside, and she's dialing or dilating or whatever it is they do, and they'll notify me when she delivers. It's not like now when the father is in the delivery room with the mother and sees the whole thing happen. In those days, you had this waiting room for fathers. Remember?" Both Vincent and Gennero recalled their own times in the fathers' waiting room.

"To make a long story short, Vince, I was in that goddamned waiting room for twelve fucking hours."

Vincent sucked in his breath. "Twelve hours in labor?"

"Yeah! Twelve fucking hours! After all that rushing and racing through the streets, I could have gotten us killed. Twelve hours!

"But then at twelve thirty the next afternoon, a nurse comes out and says my wife just had a little baby girl and would I like to see her? Would I? She leads me to the nursery, and there she is, in her little pink beanie, all wrapped up in a pink blanket, with a little sign on her basket—whatever you call it—saying Baby Girl Giantonio. I was so proud. So happy. Right away, the first person I call, even before my mother or father or Mattie's parents, the first person I call is this guy right here," he said, pointing to Gennero.

"I used the pay phone in the hall, and I called Gennero, and I said—I swear to god, Vince, this is the truth—I say, 'Gennero, you won't believe this. I'm not being biased or prejudiced or nothing, but Mattie just had the most beautiful baby girl in the whole world.'"

Both Vincent and Gennero smiled broadly, knowing exactly how Dom felt.

"I swear, Vince, I thought I was being totally objective. It wasn't until after Rena was all grown-up that I looked at those baby pictures of her and saw what a wrinkly little monkey she looked like."

Vincent patted his friend on the shoulder. "Dom, if only all fathers and mothers would feel that way about their children. All too often, I see in my court people who never got that feeling from their parents, that they were the most beautiful or the most talented, or most loveable, or charming, or whatever. There are too many kids out there feeling like garbage, unwanted and disposable. This was a beautiful story." Vincent looked at his watch. "Well, paisanos, it's time for me to be heading home. Dom, congratulations again. Connie and I will be honored to be your guests tomorrow evening. We'll be looking forward to it."

Dom and Gennero said good-bye to him. Gennero looked at his cousin. "I have no need to hurry home. I think I'll have something simple to eat here."

"Good," Dom said. He called a waiter over and asked him to seat Mr. Giantonio. "Let me wrap up some details, and then I'll come over and talk."

"Take your time. Do what you have to do. I understand. This is a very happy occasion for you. Enjoy it."

Dom grasped Gennero's hand in both of his. "*Multi grazi*, Gennero."

Chapter XXXIII

Gennero: End of the Day

Gennero sat back and enjoyed sipping his espresso. It was nice and hot, the way he liked it, and the little sliver of lemon peel and a little Amaretto made it that much more enjoyable. Dominic was busy greeting and schmoozing, and the restaurant was almost filled to capacity with most of its tables filled and Mickey busy behind the bar. Nick, of course, was back and forth between the kitchen and the front, keeping everything flowing smoothly. Gennero enjoyed the soft tinkle of glasses and the low, intimate murmur of the melding of everyone's voices, the soft lighting, and the background Neapolitan music. He was relaxed and still glowing from the wine and his happiness for his cousin.

Nick approached the table. "How's everything, Zio? Anything I can get for you?"

"No, no, Nick. I'm fine. I was just thinking to myself what a great place you've made here. It's very comfortable and relaxing."

"Not too relaxing, I hope," Nick joked. "We don't want anybody falling asleep on us."

Gennero smiled. "No fear of that, Nicky. Not with such good food. No, it's a quietly stimulating atmosphere, very romantic."

Now it was Nick's turn to smile. Nick was slender and wiry, like his father, and also like his father, his smile was wide and boyish. "Thank you, Zio. That's nice to hear."

"You're going to have your hands full, preparing for tomorrow night."

"You have a capacity for understatement." Nick laughed. "It would have been nice to have a week, nevermind less than twenty-four hours. But we'll do it. I've already spoken to our chef, Dolpho, and he's thinking about the menu. I'm sure it'll be something special."

"I'm looking forward to seeing everybody here."

"Yeah, I'm looking forward to that too, having all the friends and family, all the big shots. For some of them, this might be their first time here. I feel like I'm getting a chance to show off the place and let everybody see what a good job we can do."

"Nicky, I have no doubt whatsoever that everybody will be impressed with the place, the food, and what a great job of organizing you did on such short notice."

"I hope so, Gennero. I hope so." Nick paused to look around, taking a glance toward the bar and the front door. "All right then, I'll see you tomorrow night."

"Ciao," said Gennero, raising his demitasse in salute.

When Gennero finished his coffee, he left enough money on the table to cover the bill and the tip and walked toward the front.

Dominic broke away from a young couple and came over to say good-bye. "I hope everything was all right," he said, putting his hand on Gennero's shoulder.

"Everything was wonderful, Dom. I had a nice relaxing and delicious meal. Now, I'm ready to call it a day."

"We'll see you and Nina and everyone tomorrow night?"

"Are you kidding? I wouldn't miss it for the world. But I still have to let Nina and the kids know. Hopefully they'll be able to make it on such short notice."

"I hope so. Until tomorrow, then."

"*A domani*," said Gennero.

On the way home, slouched down into the backseat of a cab, Gennero called Nina on his cell phone. His sixteen-year-old great-grandson Bobby answered the phone.

"Hello," Gennero said. "Who is this? Bobby?"

Immediately, Bobby's voice lifted from a bored monotone and became more lively and animated. "Nonno?"

"Yes, Bobby, it's me. How are you?"

"Oh, I'm fine, Nonno. We're just getting ready to leave to go home. How's Nonna?"

Gennero was a little taken aback. "How nice of you to ask, Bobby. Actually, Nonna is doing much better. It looks like she'll be home from the hospital on Monday. As a matter of fact, we were just talking today about having all of you over for dessert on Wednesday evening, after supper."

"Cool," Bobby said. "I haven't been over to your house in ages."

"I know," Gennero acknowledged sadly. "It's been much too long." Then, changing the subject, Gennero asked, "Is your grandma there?"

"Sure, Nonno, she's standing right here."

Nina got on the phone. "What's up, Pop?"

"No bad news. Only good news," Gennero said. "I just called to let you know that there's a big party tomorrow night at the Villa Contursi. Your cousin Joey got a promotion, and Dominic is celebrating by throwing a big dinner party. Everyone is invited."

"Tomorrow night?"

"Yes. Cocktail hour is at seven, and dinner at eight o'clock."

"Let me ask Rosalie if she and Denise can make it—"

"And the boys too," Gennero interrupted.

"Okay. Hold on for a minute."

Gennero heard Nina calling Rosalie in the background and a discussion taking place. Finally, Nina got back on the phone.

"Rosalie and Denise had planned to go to a movie tomorrow night, but they can change those plans easily enough. They just want to be sure that you think it's a good idea for them to show up together."

"Nina, you are all my family. Rosalie is my granddaughter. Anything she does, short of deliberately offending someone there, is going to be perfectly fine. Denise is an attractive, bright, and respectful young woman. Believe me, there won't be any problem. I guarantee they'll be made to feel welcome."

"All right then," Nina answered, still not quite at ease with the prospect of showing up with her lesbian daughter and her lover in such a gathering. It wasn't a group of people noted for their progressive and liberal views.

"And the boys?" asked Gennero.

"Rosalie says that if you think it's okay for them to be there, then it's fine with her. They were going to stay home and watch a video and have pizza anyway."

"I have no idea as to whether there will be any other teenagers there. Maybe not. But it'll be a good opportunity for them to meet a lot of their relatives they haven't seen in a while. And it won't do them any harm to learn a little about the family businesses either."

"All right, then," Nina agreed. "Should we meet there at between seven and eight or do you want to go together or what?"

"No, there are too many to fit comfortably in one car. I'll meet you there. And don't forget to tell Andrea. Maybe she can get off work and come, even for a little bit."

"I'll tell her, Pop. Oh, and what about Mama? How is she doing?"

"I just told Bobby. Ask him. You're all invited over for dessert on Wednesday evening after supper."

"You're kidding," Nina exclaimed.

Gennero smiled to himself. "I know. It's hard to believe, but it's true. But we'll talk more about it tomorrow night."

"Good. We'll see you then. Good night, Pop."

"Good night, *ciucci*." Gennero shut his cell phone. He was just about to reopen it to call Sal when the taxi pulled up in front of his house.

After paying the cabby, Gennero lingered for a while in front of his house, enjoying the smell of grass that was just starting to grow. He heard his name being called and looked around. It was Antoinette Carlucci, his next-door neighbor. "Gennero," she called again, as she started walking toward him, her little dachshund, Frankie, trailing behind her on his leash. "I haven't seen you to ask you about Tessie. How is she? Did they find out what was wrong?"

"Good evening, Antoinette. Yes, thank you. Tessie is feeling much better. In fact, we're expecting her home on Monday if all goes well."

"Ah, that's good news. So what happened?" she persisted. "We were all so worried about her. Did she have a heart attack or a stroke?"

"No," Gennero said. "It seems she had a bad reaction to some medication. They were quite concerned at first, but it looks much better now, with no major complications."

"Oh, how terrible. You both must have been so frightened. I know we were."

"Well, yes," he allowed, "we were quite concerned. But like they say, all's well that ends well."

"Tell me, Gennero, has Tessie been very ill? We used to be so friendly, and then, it seems, she just dropped out of sight. She stopped coming outside, didn't answer the door if I knocked, never returned my calls. I wondered if she was too tired or if it was something from some major illness."

Gennero had to acknowledge the truth of these observations. Antoinette was a good woman, and she and Tessie had indeed been fairly close friends. "I know, Antoinette. Tessie hasn't been herself these past few years. She hasn't felt up to socializing. Even visits with our family have been cut back. Please don't take it personally."

"Oh, no . . ."

"It's been too much for her. Nothing definite medically that we can pin down. But maybe now we'll get some new doctors taking a look, and hopefully we'll be able to get her back to feeling like her old self."

"Well, I hope so, Gennero. Anyway, please tell her that I was asking about her."

"I will, Antoinette. I'll tell her tomorrow when I see her." Gennero turned to go into his house. "Good night, Antoinette. Thanks for asking about Tessie."

"Good night, Gennero. Lots of luck with this."

"Thank you." Once inside, Gennero turned on some lights, pulled the shades, and then took off his jacket, his shoes, and his tie and plopped into his favorite chair. Taking out his cell phone, he called Sal.

"Hello, Sal," he said when Sal picked up, "it's me, Gennero."

"Hi, Mr. G. Anything wrong?"

Gennero smiled to himself. After the events of the past couple of days, how could Sal have any other reaction? "No, Sal, nothing wrong, except I will need you tomorrow night, after all." Gennero pictured Sal taking in a deep breath. Maybe he had made other plans and was now quickly considering how he could change them. "I'm sorry, Sal, if this presents an inconvenience for you . . ."

"Oh, no, Mr. G.—"

Gennero cut him off. "There's an important family function that's come up for tomorrow evening. My cousin Dominic is throwing a party tomorrow night for all the family and our friends. He specifically asked if you could come just in case they need any extra security. It will be all right if you want to bring someone with you as your guest."

There was only a slight hesitation before Sal responded. "Of course, Mr. G. What time would you like me to pick you up?"

"Oh, seven o'clock would be fine."

"Fine, Mr. G., seven o'clock tomorrow night it is." Sal paused for a moment. "I was just wondering, would you prefer that I drop you off and then come back for my lady friend?"

"No, Sal. That won't be necessary. Why don't you pick her up first, and she can ride in the back with me. I'd enjoy having a chance to meet her."

"Thanks, Mr. G. I'll see you tomorrow night then at seven."

"Thank you, Sal. Again, I'm sorry if this put a crimp in your plans."

"No problem, sir. See you then."

"Good night, Sal." After hanging up, Gennero shuffled into the kitchen, took a cursory look around, and then opened the refrigerator without seeing anything of interest. Then he turned out the lights and climbed upstairs to bed.

He hadn't been asleep long when Theresa came into the room and shook him by the shoulders. "Get up, Gennero," she said urgently. "I've just had a terrible accident with the car. You have to come help me."

It was dark in the room, and Tessie was mostly indistinct, except that he could see quite clearly that there were streaks of red henna dye in her long, dark, brunette hair. He was about to ask her about her hair when she once again intruded into his thoughts. "Come on, Gennero, hurry. The car is out front. I need you to come look." She had taken hold of his arm and was trying to pull him out of bed.

What car is that? he wondered. *Did we buy a car? Did she go out shopping and buy a car without telling me?* He put on his slippers and robe and let her lead him through the open bedroom door. He took a couple of steps down into a sunken living room. *This all seems so new,* Gennero thought. *We must have just moved here. I guess I don't know where everything is in this new house yet.* Tessie was hurrying away from him across the slate floor of what actually seemed like a large solarium. It had a very high ceiling, and he noticed that it was raining, and the roof was leaking.

"Hurry!" Tessie called. "You have to help me."

"Wait a minute," Gennero told her irritably. "First I have to move these little plants so that they'll catch the water where the roof is leaking."

Tessie stood in the open doorway, the wind and rain behind her. He felt the cold draft . . .

He woke up feeling chilly from the open bedroom window and realized he had to take a leak.

SATURDAY

MARCH 6, 2004

CHAPTER XXXIV

GRADY: BREAKFAST AT
THE STARLITE

Grady and Karen emerged from his apartment at 6:40 Saturday morning. It was chilly and rainy, and despite their umbrella, repeated buffeting by gusts of wind got both of them wet from the waist down. Fortunately, the bus came on time, and it was warm and dry inside. They still felt half-asleep and were quiet on the ride into Center City where they would catch their train to Wynnewood on Philadelphia's wealthy Main Line. Grady noted that the other people on the bus, who were probably going to work at such an early hour on a Saturday, were mostly blacks, Mexicans, and Asians. He felt like one of them and imagined that he shared many of their hardships and that many of their daily problems were similar to his own.

Grady and Karen were greeted by more blustery wind and driving rain when they got off of the bus, but luckily they had only a half block to go, hugging the side of the building before they got to the doorway leading into the station. Once inside, they went downstairs to the windows of the Regional Rail Lines where they bought their two roundtrip tickets to Wynnewood. They'd be arriving there at 7:40, which would give them time to find the Starlite Diner.

Sitting in the station, waiting for their train, Grady realized that he was avoiding thinking about the upcoming meeting with Tracy. He was anxious and apprehensive, although he wasn't sure why. For some reason, he felt that it would be important, and he didn't want to screw it up. But his old insecurities were bubbling up inside him, and he wasn't sure he was up to the job of getting from Tracy whatever information she might have about Richie that could prove to be helpful. He wanted very much to be able to give Gennero some unexpected morsel of information that would be helpful to the old man. Somehow, it felt like he would be making things right, but he wasn't sure he understood how.

Karen tugged at his arm, and he looked at her. "You seem preoccupied," she said.

"Yeah, I guess so," he muttered.

"What was he like?" she asked.

"Who?"

"Your friend, Richie. What was he like? You never really told me that much about him."

"Well, like I *did* tell you," he said sharply, "we were very tight. We knew each other since we were about four years old. We went all through school together. He was . . ." Grady paused, looking up and around the station, searching for the right words. "He was generally a good guy, easygoing, and with a good sense of humor. You know, fun to be around. He was a very good musician. I mean, really good.

"The women loved him. He was always juggling a couple of girlfriends, which is why I was so surprised when he said that he and Tracy were probably going to get married. Up to then, neither one of us had any interest in settling down. Playing music was everything. Playing, writing, jamming with other guys. Then, of course we were doing all kinds of dope, getting high, getting laid. It's not only that we were having fun; we were doing exactly what we wanted to do. This is who we were. We felt free, you know? Nobody was telling us what we had to do or couldn't do. No parents, no wives, no debts. We had no constraints. We could practically dictate our jobs. We played where and when and how we wanted.

"Richie wasn't as angry as I was back then. I'd get royally pissed at people, big time. Richie was more easygoing. He'd cool me down, tell me to blow it off. 'Consider the source,' he'd say. 'Don't sweat it. Let it go.' I rarely saw him angry. I've seen him, you know, like with hecklers? Somebody would be trying to bust his balls, and he'd keep blowing it off, laughing at the guy and just ignoring him, deflecting it, you know, like a bull fighter. Me, I'd be ready to kill. Richie always calmed me down. He'd give me a wink, you know, like he was saying, 'You catching this asshole? Is this guy for real or what?' and I'd end up laughing at what a clown the jerk was making of himself." Grady shook his head. "But I was never able to do that on my own. I never learned how to let that shit roll off my back."

"He sounds like he was a neat guy. I'm sure I would have liked him."

"You would have loved him. And he would have loved you."

The train came. Most of the people who were coming into the city for work were well dressed and white. But Grady noticed it was again the minorities, blacks and Mexicans, who were taking the train out of the city to low-paying jobs in the suburbs. Once past Thirtieth Street, the train remained above ground, and everything looked gray and dirty in the rain. The garbage and debris discarded along the tracks upset him, and he felt himself getting increasingly edgy. At 7:40 on the nose, the train pulled into the Wynnewood station, and Grady asked the ticket seller if he knew where the diner was. He gave Grady and Karen directions, a little less than a mile away. Normally they'd walk it, but the wind-driven sheets of rain convinced them to splurge on a taxi, and by ten of eight they were inside the diner.

Grady looked around but didn't see any sign of Tracy. They waited a few minutes for a booth to open up and then went and sat down. Grady took the seat facing the door so he could see her when she came in.

"I don't know about you," Karen said, "but I'm starved."

"I guess I'm too hyped up about this," he acknowledged. "I really don't have that much of an appetite."

A waitress came and asked if they wanted coffee, which they did. They were still waiting for her to come back with their coffee when Grady saw Tracy get out of her SUV in front of the diner and rush toward the entrance. *So she did come alone after all.* "Here she comes," he said to Karen. "Tracy. She's just coming in."

Grady saw Tracy looking around, and he half stood up and waved, catching her eye. She started walking over, opening her raincoat in the process. Grady noted that she was not smiling, her face set in stone. *Of course*, he thought, *she'll be wondering what Karen is doing here.*

Grady got up as Tracy reached their booth. "Hi, Tracy. Thanks for coming."

"You picked a rotten morning to do this," she said with some annoyance, apparently forgetting that she was the one who had done the choosing. It was hard to tell if she was joking or really complaining. Again, Grady noted her low, sexy voice, which always took him by surprise, given her petite stature. Grady was also surprised to be reminded of how beautiful she was. With her long, straight, blonde hair, creamy complexion, and big eyes, she looked like an All-American cheerleader, a real wholesome Miss America. It was an effort to remember what Tommy had told him about her.

"Here, have a seat," he said, indicating the bench across from him and Karen. "Tracy, this is my girlfriend, Karen." The two women smiled briefly at each other as Tracy slid into the booth and removed her raincoat.

The waitress arrived with the two cups of coffee, and they ordered, Tracy opting for a cup of tea and an English muffin. Both Karen and Grady ordered an omelet and toast.

"So," Tracy said, all business, "what was it about Richie that you thought I could help you with?"

"Well," Grady began, trying to smile his most disarming smile, "to start with, Tracy, I'm curious about what your reaction was to Richie's dying."

Tracy looked at him blankly, as if waiting for him to continue.

"You know, were you surprised or what? What did you think happened?"

Tracy looked away briefly, through the window to the parking lot, where she probably saw her car. "I don't know, Grady. It was so long ago. I guess I was surprised. I wasn't shocked, though. I knew Richie used heroin. So I wasn't shocked. But, yeah, I guess I was surprised to hear that he died of an overdose."

"How do you account for that, Tracy? I mean, what do you think happened?"

"I don't know. How am I supposed to know what happened? I mean, people do heroin and sometimes they OD. It's just something that happens."

"So you think it was just an accident? That he somehow made a mistake and just took too much?"

"I guess," she agreed. "What else could it be?"

Grady studied her, taking all of her in—her seductive beauty, her coldness, her expensive clothes, her scent. Suddenly, he realized he was having one of those moments when everything seemed to be in slow motion. He remembered being younger, playing baseball and swearing he could see every stitch on a baseball as it came toward him, either in the batter's box or in the field. He felt totally on top of his game. Now, with Tracy, he felt that way, suddenly totally confident and hyper alert. He knew she was avoiding something, certainly avoiding the truth.

"Well," Grady suggested, "had you two broken up?" He was thinking of the possibility of Richie being depressed over a breakup, leading to his committing suicide.

"What do you mean, 'broken up'?"

Grady sat back and opened his hands. "Come on, Tracy. You don't know what it means to break up?"

At that moment, the waitress came with their orders, and they were silent as she laid the plates on the table. Grady kept his eyes on Tracy. He didn't trust her at all. She was the enemy, and all of his senses seemed heightened. The waitress left, and still Grady waited for Tracy to respond. He was aware that Karen, sitting beside him, was taking everything in as well.

After spending time immersing her teabag in her cup of hot water, Tracy looked up, speaking in her low, almost soothing voice, "Of course I know what it means to break up. I just didn't think to associate it with me and Richie, that's all. It's not like we were going together or anything."

"What?" Grady exclaimed. "'Not going together or anything'? Richie was under the impression that the two of you were going to get married."

"Married?" Now it was Tracy's turn to be surprised. "Whatever gave you the idea that Richie and I were going to get married?"

"Because that's what he told me."

"Richie told you that we, he and I, were going to get married?"

"That's exactly what he said. Now why would he say that? What would have given him the idea that the two of you were going to get married?"

"How the hell should I know?" she said, her voice rising. "I'm not responsible for what went on in his head."

"You were banging each other," he said quietly, holding her gaze. He saw her Adam's apple bob as she gulped in response.

"So we were having sex. So what? That doesn't mean we were going to get married. Jesus, give me a break." Then, with a slight nod of her head toward Karen, she continued, "Don't tell me the two of you aren't having sex. Does that mean I hear wedding bells in your future? Come on!"

"No, I agree with you, Tracy. Just getting laid wouldn't be enough to make Richie, of all people, think of getting married. There had to be more between you than that. And you know what, Tracy? I'm beginning to wonder what the hell it is that you're trying to hide. What is there to hide . . . Tracy?" Grady was conscious of almost stumbling over her name, wanting to call her Kelly. For a moment, he wasn't even sure where the hell that name came from, and then he remembered his dreams and realized that in some way he was merging or confusing the two of them in his mind. *Stay cool, Grady,* he said to himself. *Stay cool.*

Tracy took some time to compose herself. She sipped her tea. She took a bite of her English muffin, all the time keeping her eyes fixed on Grady's. "Grady," she said more sweetly, "I swear I'm not hiding anything. It's just that Richie and I weren't all that serious. So we had sex. Maybe he was in love with me. Maybe he fantasized about our getting married. I don't know, or if I did, I don't remember. He was just another guy I was dating."

"You were pregnant." It was Karen, leaning in from Grady's left. Up to now, she had been silent. Her voice was strong and straight, and when she spoke, she caught Tracy off guard.

Tracy looked at her, her eyes wide, as if to say, "How the hell did you know?" Her reaction was a dead giveaway. Tracy lowered her head and made a face. Then she looked up, at Karen rather than Grady. The two women's eyes met, and for the first time Tracy paid attention to Karen. There was a measure of respect in her voice now as she answered Karen.

"You're right," Tracy acknowledged. "I was pregnant. Richie found out. I don't remember how. Either he found the test indicator in my wastebasket or he just figured it out. I really don't remember. Anyway, he was sure it was his, and he was thrilled."

"And he wanted to get married," Grady interjected.

Again, Tracy acknowledged the truth of that.

"But," Karen cut in, "he didn't know the baby wasn't his, did he?"

Tracy could only smile in admiration at Karen. Then she said, "You've been there yourself, haven't you?"

"Yeah. I'm a heroin addict too. I know what it's like. Yeah, I've been there. I'm assuming you wanted to abort the baby."

"Of course. What woman in her right mind, who's been shooting up, is going to risk going to full term with a baby and risk all the complications, the birth defects? I didn't want to give birth to an addicted baby, for Christ's sake."

"So what did you tell Richie?" Grady asked. He had taken advantage of the dialogue between the two women to dig into his own breakfast and coffee.

Tracy turned to him. "You mean about the baby?"

Grady nodded as he sipped his coffee.

"I told him that he was being silly, that neither one of us really wanted to get married and that I was going to get an abortion."

Grady kept looking at her and simply raised his eyebrows as he shoveled a forkful of omelet into his mouth.

Tracy returned his stare. "What?" she finally asked.

"What do you mean 'what'? What was his reaction when you told him that you didn't want to get married and were going to get an abortion? And don't fucking tell me he was cool with it."

Tracy took a deep breath. "No," she admitted slowly. He wasn't 'cool' with it. He told me that I was being the silly one and that this was a great chance for us. It was what he needed. I told him . . . I told him I couldn't have the baby, that I'd been doing too much H and that I wasn't into raising a deformed kid. He said it wasn't a problem, that we weren't doing that much shit and that I could stop, that we'd both stop. It was still early enough. It would work out."

Karen put her fork down and sat back, looking at Tracy. "Richie didn't know you were shooting up on your own?"

Tracy looked at her and then averted her eyes and shook her head no.

Karen ran her hand through her hair and thought for a moment before continuing. "So you were scoring on your own?"

Tracy nodded.

Grady watched the two of them as he finished his eggs and picked up his coffee. It seemed clear to him not only that Karen had a better understanding of Tracy than he did, but that Tracy felt more comfortable with her than with him. He was content to let Karen run with this while he let everything sink in. But one question occurred to him, and in a pause in the conversation, he dove in. "You were getting the smack from your source for you and Richie?"

Tracy looked at him, as if trying to decide what to tell him: the truth, a part of the truth, or some story. "Yeah. Sometimes Richie would score, but mostly he would show up with other stuff that I wasn't really into all that much—you know, pot, pills, some coke. So I got my own supply. Sometimes, if Richie didn't have anything, I'd bring out some H, and we'd share it."

Grady asked, "Did Richie know who your dealer was?"

Tracy didn't immediately reply. Grady thought she was stalling and was about to get in her face about it when she startled him by throwing up her hands. "It wasn't like that, Grady. It wasn't like I had a dealer. I had a friend, a friend who would share it with me. I didn't have a dealer. It wasn't that way at all. It was much more . . . informal."

"More personal?" Karen suggested.

"Yeah," Tracy agreed, "more personal."

Karen sat back and smiled.

Tracy looked at her and then lowered her eyes, sipped at her tea and looked away, out the window, into the rain. Tracy looked at her watch. "I have to go. I'm already late." She started to slip her raincoat on.

"Just one more question," Karen said, leaning in toward Tracy. "Did Richie know him?"

Tracy looked at her and then took a long, hard look at Grady, which took him by surprise. "Of course Richie knew him," she said bitterly, staring at Grady with eyes full of hatred. "Now I have to go."

Grady and Karen looked at each other for the first time. They read in each other's eyes the same message: no sense in pushing it any further. Let her go. Grady got up and stood in the aisle.

"Listen, Tracy," he said gently. "I want to thank you for doing this. It's been a major help to us, to his family. I'm sorry if it was upsetting to you."

Tracy grimaced and muttered something under her breath. When Grady shook her hand, hers was cold and lifeless. She left without saying anything more and without turning around. Grady sat down again next to Karen, and they watched through the rain-blurred window as Tracy got into her vehicle and drove away. The waitress came over, and they ordered more coffee. Then Grady swung around to the other side of the booth so he and Karen could look at each other.

Karen smiled. "Did you get what I got?" she asked.

"I think so," he said. "She was banging Brian for the dope, and Brian was the father of her baby."

"And Richie knew it," she said.

"Yeah," he agreed. "I think you might be right. Maybe he did know it."

Then Grady sat back and stared at Karen. It was a minute before Karen realized that he wasn't really looking at her, that his eyes seemed blank and far away. She was just about to say something when she noticed his eyelids fluttering.

"Grady?" He didn't respond. She called him again, a little louder, "Grady, are you okay?" Still, Grady didn't respond. His eyes closed, but his position didn't change. Not a muscle moved. His fingers continued to nestle the cup in its saucer. He seemed to be in a trance of some kind.

Karen got up and slid onto the seat next to him. "Grady," she whispered urgently into his ear. "Grady, it's me, Karen. Come back to me, hon. Come back to me. It's Karen, honey. Listen to me. Pay attention to me, Grady. I need you to come back, now." She grasped his hand and held it tightly, squeezing it as hard as she could. "Listen to me, Grady, it's Karen. Hold onto my hand, hon. It's all right. Everything is all right. Everything is going to be fine. I'm here for you, hon. I'm not going anywhere. Hold onto me, baby. Hold onto me." With her other hand, she kept stroking his hair, his neck, his shoulder. After a few minutes, she felt him returning the squeeze of her hand. She looked into his face. Slowly his eyes opened, and he turned to look at her, his face screwed up in puzzlement.

"It's okay, hon, I'm here. It's me, Karen. I'm here. Hold onto me, baby. Everything is going to be all right."

Grady, still looking confused, tried working his mouth, as if he were just discovering how to form words. Finally his body seemed to let go, to relax, and he slouched back against the back of the booth. He looked around and finally seemed to recognize where they were. Then he looked back at Karen. "How long was I out? What happened?" he asked huskily.

Karen continued to stroke his hair. "Just a few minutes. We were talking after Tracy left, and all of a sudden you went into a kind of trance. You had this faraway look in your eyes, like you were absorbed in thinking about something. Then your eyelids began to flicker, and that's when I tried to get you back. It was only a couple of minutes. You didn't do anything, nothing at all. Everything's cool."

"We were talking, I think, about Tracy?" He looked at her for confirmation.

"Yeah, her and Brian and his being her dealer boyfriend . . ."

"And maybe Richie knowing about it . . ."

"Yeah. Which, I suppose," she offered, "would explain why he went into a rage that night."

Grady was silent. He took a sip from his coffee. It was still hot, and he was surprised at what immense satisfaction it gave him, real experiential proof that he really hadn't been blacked out that long. He looked at Karen again and kissed her.

"You know," he said, obviously uncomfortable and still trying to regain his bearings, "when she was here, there was a moment when I felt like she was Kelly, the woman I've dreamt about—if it was dreaming—as being my mother, my real mother. And I was filled with rage. And I realized that on one hand I've always had this longing for her, as if going back to her would be going back to something good, a paradise. But it wasn't a paradise. Kelly wasn't a good mother. I don't know if I've dreamed her up as a kind of better choice than what I had or what, but either way, real or imagined, she was not a good mother. It seemed she was always out of reach. And then, there were all these men coming and going, in and out of the apartment. In my dreams, or my fantasy, or memory, whatever—these were just her friends. It's the way a young kid would understand it, I guess.

"But this morning, looking at Tracy sitting across from me, with her hair just so, and her expensive clothes and that car," he said, pointing his head toward the parking lot out front, "I realized what a fucking phony she is. It all came to me clear as day. It's as though I could see right into her. I know I'm right about this. She's all pretense. I don't care what kind of degree she has; she's pretending to be a school teacher, pretending to be Miss Main Line Suburbia, pretending to be a normal, educated, middle-class woman. And she's not. She's a piece of fucking shit. She's a fucking whore dope addict. She's got no fucking clue what reality is or who she really is. She's incapable of being honest, with herself or with anyone else. With her, everything is an act. Her whole performance here this morning was a fucking act. And her whole relationship with Richie was an act. My guess is that Brian, who's a piece of shit himself and probably deserved the beating he got, has no idea that her relationship with him is one big fucking act as well."

Karen listened, taking in what he was saying. "What you're saying, Grady, it's probably true. I remember my own scams and cons when I was using, the way I manipulated people in order to get money or dope, the constant lying. It's one of the things about recovery that's so fucking difficult—not only coming to terms with the fact that I was addicted, but owning up to what a shitty, dishonest, deceitful bitch I'd been—especially to those who cared most about me."

Grady went on. "I wanted to kill her. At one point, I wanted to reach across the table and smash her," he said, suddenly slamming his fist into his hand. "I guess I was able to hold on until she left."

Then he turned once again to Karen. "I'm glad you were here. I heard you calling and telling me to hold onto you, that you were here for me. I can't tell you what it meant. I felt safe. I felt like I was far away or out in space or something, and I didn't know where your voice was coming from, and then I felt your hand in mine and my head being stroked, and I felt . . . safe. I really felt safe. I don't know if I have ever felt that before."

Karen saw his eyes glistening with moisture and she pulled him close and hugged him. They stayed that way for a while. Then Grady pulled back.

"I think I figured some of it out, about Richie."

Karen looked at him curiously, waiting.

"Tracy said very clearly that Richie knew who she got her dope from, and there's no doubt that it was Brian. But up until that night when he spotted her out clubbing with someone, after she had told Richie she was staying home, I don't think Richie thought about him. If Richie knew that she was banging Brian for her stash, he wouldn't have been so eager to marry her. She said that Richie believed the baby was his. That's why he wanted to get married, and she wasn't straight with him when she told him she'd consider not getting an abortion."

"No, Grady, that's not what she said. What she said was that *Richie* said they could go ahead and have the baby if she stopped using. She never said how she responded to that. But I agree with you that she probably would have led him to believe that she'd consider stopping and would think about having the baby."

"Right, she would have led him to believe that she'd consider stopping smack and keeping the baby and, by implication, get married."

"Yeah," Karen agreed. "That seems to be what she would have done."

"So Richie wasn't angry about anything—not about her using, not about other supposed relationships—until that night when he saw her pass the club. You know, I don't think Richie recognized that the guy was Brian, because he never said anything to me, so I don't think he really knew Brian all that well. We were together that whole night in the car, watching Tracy's place, waiting for her to come home. If Richie knew anything or suspected anything, there's no fucking way he'd keep from telling me that night. No way."

"That sounds right," Karen said. "You spend the whole night together in a car, and there's nothing else to do but talk. You're right—no way, especially considering how close, like brothers, the two of you were. Of course he'd tell you."

"So if he didn't say anything, it's because he didn't know anything. Even that morning when she comes home with the guy, Richie doesn't realize who he is. Then that next night, at The Harp, Richie finally gets a good look, and that's when he recognizes Brian and figures it out. And he's thinking—*This bastard isn't only supplying heroin to my pregnant fiancée, but now he's fucking her too!*"

Karen made a face. "It's got to be much more of an emotional shock than simply finding out your girlfriend is stepping out. I mean, that would be bad enough, but having your pregnant girlfriend stepping out is unimaginably worse, and then, in addition, having somebody feeding her dope . . . Richie must have felt like Brian was killing her."

"And the baby," Grady added.

"Yeah." Karen sighed. "And his baby."

The wind had died down outside, and although it was still raining lightly, the sky was brightening. They decided to walk back to the train station, enjoying the coolness of the fresh air. Mostly they walked in silence, but Grady held her hand the whole way, something he usually did not do. Every once in a while, they gave each other a squeeze and looked at each other and smiled.

Inside the station while they were waiting for the return train to Philly, Karen turned to Grady. "I was just thinking: from the way Tracy looked at you there at the end, it seems very clear that she knows that you had something to do with beating up Brian."

Grady considered it for a moment. "Yeah, I think you're right. At the time, I wasn't sure why she suddenly seemed so pissed, but yeah, that makes sense."

"Doesn't that mean that she—both she and Brian—knew that both you and Richie were there?"

Grady pondered this new idea. "You know, I had always assumed that Richie and Brian didn't know each other and that

Brian had no idea who was beating the shit out of him. I guess I also assumed, since nothing ever happened, you know, no police investigation, that Brian had suffered severe concussions and was unable to recall what had happened." Grady smiled. "I guess I've had enough experience with memory loss to be able to imagine it happening to someone else. But now it's a different story. If Richie knew Brian, then Brian knew who Richie was. Brian probably told Tracy what happened, and she was able to ID me."

"I wonder," Karen said, thinking out loud, "how she felt about Richie attempting to kill Brian."

"Well, she wasn't that invested in the baby. She wanted an abortion. They've been married over a year, I think, and they don't have any kids now. So I don't think that was a major issue with her, you know, the father of her soon-to-be-aborted baby getting beat up."

"No," Karen said, "I agree with you . . . and with what you said earlier about her too—that she thinks only of herself, always acting and manipulating, unable to really care about anyone else. You know what, Grady? I think the only thing she would have been really upset about was losing her supplier."

"Yeah, and she still seems pissed about it." He thought a moment. "You think she would have married him, just to keep her supply?"

"Her *free* supply? Sure. Lots of women hook up with their dealers just to insure their continued free supply. Tracy wouldn't be the first. And," she added, "you're right; she is still pissed about it."

"Yeah," Grady said, "big time."

Even though the train ride back into the city was relatively short, they leaned back and closed their eyes, hoping for a little rest to compensate for having had to get up so early. The next stop was Market East, their station, and Karen was rousing herself, getting ready to face a long day on her feet at the pub when Grady startled her by suddenly bolting upright, bringing both palms up to hit himself in the head. "Jesus Christ," he said, "how stupid can I be?"

"Grady, what's the matter? Are you all right?"

He put his hand reassuringly on her arm and started to say something when the conductor called out their station. "Wait," he said. "We get off here. I'll tell you after we get off." People started standing up in the aisles, lining up to exit. Grady and Karen joined the line, and when the train stopped and the doors opened, the mass flowed out onto the platform and up the stairs. There, Grady pulled Karen aside, and they found a place to sit down.

"I was wondering, given that both Tracy and Brian knew that Richie was the one who beat up Brian, why they didn't report that to the police. I mean, it wasn't like he was beat up while he was selling dope or anything. And then I thought, the reason they didn't do anything about it," he stopped to make sure he had her attention, "was because they did do something about it."

Karen's head tilted to one side as she tried to fathom what he was saying.

"Suppose Tracy decided to get even with Richie by getting Brian to give her high-grade heroin? Alex told me that Brian usually cut his stuff, and that's what Richie would have been used to. Remember she said that mostly Richie had other drugs, so most of the time, if they shot up together, she provided the smack she got from Brian."

Karen indicated that she was following him and, so far, in agreement.

"Now, suppose she asks Brian *not* to cut some. It would be . . . probably a third more powerful or maybe even twice as powerful, 50 to 100 percent more powerful. It could have killed Richie, especially if it was a big dose."

Again Karen indicated that she thought it sounded logical.

"We know she's still pissed. Imagine what a fucking rage they must have been in at the time. Tracy couldn't have done it without Brian's help, and he wouldn't have had access to Richie without her help. Somehow, she got to Richie, maybe a pretense of making up or whatever. Who knows? Then she gets him to shoot up—and poof! He's dead to the world. Literally."

Karen lowered her head as she thought about it. "I have to admit, Grady, it makes sense. I don't know if there are other explanations, but this certainly sounds logical to me."

"It's the only thing that makes sense to me. That fucking bitch got even. She got payback by murdering Richie and making it look like an accident or a suicide."

Karen pondered this for a moment and then looked Grady straight in the eye. "Grady, I don't want you to do anything crazy. Let's just sit on this for a while, let it settle. We're both stirred up about this and it's all . . . so new and so . . . speculative. We're coming up with ideas and assumptions. Maybe they're true, and maybe not. Let's just let it simmer on a back burner for a while, okay?"

"Yeah. We'll think about it for a while."

"Listen, I've got to get to work. You going to be all right?"

"I'll be fine." He looked at her and smiled. "Really, I'm fine. I'm going to go home and get some sleep, probably go help at the food distribution place later on for a little while. The physical work will feel good."

"Good. I'll come over tonight after I get off, all right?"

"Don't forget, we're going to hear Tommy play. You want me to meet you at the pub?"

"Oh Christ, Grady, I'm going to be dead on my feet. I won't be done until eleven, and then by the time I cash out . . . can you go without me?"

He made a face and thought a moment. "I'm disappointed, but I understand. I'll be able to grab a nap, probably a nice long one, while you're working twelve hours straight. Sure, either I'll go alone or I'll call him and set another date."

"You're sure you're okay with that?"

"Yeah. I'm sure. Don't worry about it. I understand." They kissed each other, and he watched her head off to work while he headed for the bus to go home.

Chapter XXXV

Gennero

It was a rainy Saturday morning when Gennero opened his eyes and peered out under the slightly raised shade. The window was open a few inches, and the morning air felt damp and raw, which was why he was snuggled under his covers. He heard the splattering of rain on the window and wondered if rain had come in, but the sill looked dry. He stretched, relieving the ache in his hips and shoulders, and thought about the upcoming day. First, he would visit Theresa and then Maria. His stomach sank at the thought of his sister. He took a deep breath and tried to steel himself against the bad news he feared was coming regarding Maria's cancer. A wave of sadness washed over him. He didn't want to get up, and he didn't want to face this day.

Theresa was a different story. He was just as pessimistic about what her future held for him, but he felt more hopeful that one way or another, he would be able to deal with it. Stretching again, Gennero moved the covers aside and sat up on the side of the bed, taking another deep breath before standing up. When he finally went to the window and rubbed his hand along the sill, it was a little damp. He closed the window. *It's going to be a miserable, lousy day*, he thought.

After showering, Gennero got dressed. Nina had bought him a pair of walking shoes that were waterproof. He'd never worn them. But today, he decided to dress casually, not his customary suit and tie. He chose an older pair of slacks and a turtleneck shirt, also a gift from Nina that he had not yet worn. To this, he added a tweed sport jacket. Gennero looked at himself in the mirror and was pleased. He was not a vain man, but he was pleasantly surprised by the relaxed image that reflected back to him. *I can afford to relax a little bit now if I already have one foot in retirement.*

Staying in this more permissive attitude, he decided to call a cab and have breakfast at the diner over on Snyder Avenue. Taking the cab to go for breakfast by himself felt like a major indulgence, and he allowed himself to enjoy every second of it. He bought a copy of the *Philadelphia Inquirer* from the machine outside and brought it inside with him. Breakfast was leisurely. The pancakes were a wonderful extravagance, and the hot coffee satisfying. *Now,* he said to himself, *I'm ready to see Theresa.*

Gennero took another cab from the diner to the hospital, and once inside, he took the elevator upstairs. On the way to Tessie's room, he passed the nurses' station and noticed that Roberta Brown was sitting behind the high counter. He waved to attract her attention and wish her a good morning and received a big warm smile in return. He wasn't sure that he would find as friendly a greeting upon entering Tessie's private room. He was a little surprised to find her fully dressed in slacks and a sweater and sitting, legs crossed, in a chair by the window, reading the morning newspaper.

"Ciao, *cara*," he greeted her. "Look at you, looking fit as a fiddle." Theresa put down her paper and smiled weakly, reaching up to lightly embrace him as he leaned over to kiss her cheek. Gennero sensed, as he was in the process of leaning over, his own ambivalence about kissing her, the angry feeling of betrayal that he had experienced yesterday. He also was aware of a degree of cold reserve on her part. "How are you feeling this morning?"

"Pretty good," she said. "I feel a little stronger, more rested." Then, sighing deeply, she seemed to muster the energy to smile more broadly. "Actually, I'm looking forward to coming home."

"Of course you are," Gennero acknowledged, taking off his coat and laying it on the foot of the bed. "And another couple of days of rest will make you feel even more rested and relaxed, that much stronger."

Theresa tilted her head and smiled, more coyly this time. "Well, I have a wonderful surprise for you, Gennero," she said, drawing out his name.

He arched his eyebrows, looking at her, and then sat down on the edge of the bed, waiting to hear what he feared most.

"I'm coming home tomorrow," she said, eyes all wide and bright. "Aren't you glad?"

"Tomorrow?" Gennero struggled to maintain a look of mere surprise on his face, working to keep his annoyance hidden. "But I thought everything was all set up and agreed upon, that you were going to come home Monday morning . . ."

"Why wait? I'm all better. I'm fine. There's no need for me to stay. Really, I wanted to come home today and thought I'd be able to surprise you by being all ready to go home with you right now. But Dr. Sung and Dr. Weinstadt said the forty-eight hours wouldn't be up until tonight, and they wouldn't be able to release me until tomorrow morning at the earliest. So we'll have to settle for that. But that's good, isn't it, my coming home a day early?"

Gennero managed to brighten his face a little. "Of course, *cara*. Of course, it's good news." Then, after what he hoped was a sufficient pause, he said, "Did Dr. Weinstadt mention the name of the therapist he wanted you to see?"

"Yes," she said, reaching down to one of the brown bags on the floor beside her. She rummaged in it for a moment and then withdrew a piece of paper from Dr. Weinstadt's prescription pad, containing the name and phone number of a woman psychiatrist. "He said she was very nice, that he had already talked with her, and that she would be expecting my call."

"Good," said Gennero, brightening for a moment as he took the paper from her and put it into his wallet. He was pleased by her apparent positive attitude about seeing this psychiatrist. *Maybe she really is feeling better and really is going to cooperate with all of this.* He felt a surge of hopefulness, and he relaxed his shoulders and chest, aware that he had been tense.

"So what have you been doing with yourself?" she asked. "Have you been taking good care of yourself? How have you been eating?"

"Of course I've been taking care of myself," he replied. "This morning, I went to the diner and had pancakes for breakfast."

"You went to the diner? The one on Snyder Avenue? Gennero, that's not a safe area."

"What do you mean, not safe?"

"There are all kinds of riffraff over there," she persisted. "You never know who you'll meet in a place like that. Who knows what could happen? Gennero, you have to be more careful."

"Tessie, you're such a worrywart. Life isn't so dangerous. Actually, it was very pleasant. I enjoyed it. It was good. I should do it more often. So should you. We both should get out more."

"What? With all of the things going on? Rapes, murders, purse snatching? Gennero," she said, shaking her head and lifting her eyes to the ceiling, "are you never going to learn? It's not safe, Gennero. It's just not safe out there." Then, leaning closer to him and lowering her voice, she said, "Why do you think I have to go home early? I have to get out of here because it's not safe, not even here. Only at home."

"What are you talking about, *cara*? You're perfectly safe in here."

"No!" she whispered hoarsely. "There you go again, Gennero. You aren't listening to me. You never listen to me. You never support me. If you were in danger, I'd support you, because I love you. How am I supposed to trust you if you're never on my side and always on theirs? If you truly loved me, the way you said you do, then you would support me."

"Tessie, I am on your side. I want only the best for you. But how aren't you safe here? I don't understand."

Theresa glanced at the doorway to make sure no one was eavesdropping. "Gennero, they're all perverts here. There are all kinds of sexual orgies going on in the other rooms. They want to involve me in it, but I won't let them."

"Sexual orgies? Here in the hospital? Tessie, that's really very difficult to believe."

"Gennero, I'm telling you. It's true. I'll prove it to you."

"You have proof?"

"Look," she said, getting up and retrieving a piece of paper from her night table. "Look at this."

He looked at the paper, the menu for the day's meals that she was supposed to have filled out for today, Saturday. "So? This is a menu. How come you haven't filled it out?"

"Don't you see what it says? Are you blind?"

"What? It lists choices for breakfast, lunch, and supper. What has this got to do with orgies?"

"My god, Gennero, it starts right with the top: *fruit juice.* The juice from fruits? From homosexuals? Juice? Gennero, do I have to spell it out for you? This is their way to say they want me to engage in lesbian things with them, with the nurses."

"Tessie," he said, smiling in spite of himself, "it's a breakfast menu, for god's sake. Fruit juice is just fruit juice: orange juice, prune juice. Lesbians! Jesus, Mary and Joseph, do you have any idea how absurd you sound?"

"There you go . . ."

"No, goddamn it. Don't give me any more of that crap about me not supporting you. I've supported you my whole life. But how can I agree with you on something so ridiculous? Fruit juice. Jesus, Theresa, tell me you were just joking. You can't be serious about this."

"Gennero, you don't know. You don't see how they look at me. The faces they make. Winks. No, don't interrupt me. I know it sounds crazy. But I was hoping you would believe me. Just once, Gennero, just once I need you to believe me." Her eyes teared up, and she turned to look out of the window.

Gennero was unsure what to do. He couldn't agree with her. He couldn't get himself to go along with her crazy assertions. He wanted to break out laughing at the absurdity. Fruit juice. Jesus Christ, who would ever believe him if he told that story? Still, he could understand, from her point of view, that he wasn't being supportive or protective.

"Tessie," he said finally, "I hear you. I understand that you don't feel safe here. It's difficult to believe that they want you to participate in sexual orgies. I mean, after all, *cara*, you're seventy-two years old, not exactly in the prime of your life."

"I know, Gennero. That's what makes it all the more sick. How can they do this to me, an old woman? I can only imagine what they're doing to younger women. And children . . . oh my god, Gennero, what kind of a place is this?"

"Well, whatever is going on, Tessie, it looks like you've done what you needed to do. So you'll be coming home tomorrow. Do you know what time? What time should I pick you up?"

"Come early, Gennero. Come as early as you can. You have to come early and get me out of here."

"I will, *cara*. I will. I'll ask at the desk and find out what's the earliest I can come pick you up and take you home."

"Thank you, *caro*. Thank you. I promise everything will be fine when I get home."

Gennero nodded and smiled sympathetically. "Yes, I'm sure it will be."

They were both silent for a minute. He was thinking about this absurdity, her belief that the nursing staff wanted her to participate in sexual orgies, the complete idiocy of it. How could she be so completely out of touch?

"Tessie," he said, "you're still taking your medication, aren't you?" She turned from where she had been looking out of the window, observing something with great interest, and stared at him. He wasn't sure, but he sensed more than really saw the faint hint of a smile around her mouth. "You're not taking your medicine, are you?"

Theresa shot a glance at the doorway and slowly raised her finger to her lips. Then, leaning toward him, she whispered barely loud enough for him to hear. "They're trying to dope me up. I'm not so stupid. I know what they're trying to do."

"So," Gennero pursued cautiously, "when did you stop taking your medicine?"

"Yesterday," she answered. "Gennero, they're so easy to fool. They think I'm just a stupid, crazy, old Italian woman without a brain in my head. So I let them think that. They don't bother to watch. They think I don't know what's going on." Theresa gave a smile of satisfaction at outwitting the staff and getting away with something. "I know I have to protect myself."

"What do you do with the medicine?"

"It's easy. I make believe I take it. Like I said, they don't even pay attention. Then, later, when I go to the bathroom, I get rid of it. Then I pretend I'm under their control, like they want. I act dopey, you know, sleepy. But I fooled them. I'm getting out of here tomorrow, alive and in control of my own mind. And they can all go to hell."

Gennero behaved as if he agreed with everything she had said. *Well, it's obvious, isn't it? She hasn't gotten one bit better. She's still crazy. This place hasn't been able to do a damn thing for her except keep her alive. When she comes home, things won't be any different at all. She's still going to play games with the doctors, with the medication, and with me. Nothing is going to change—*nienta. Gennero shook his head in sad resignation.

While Theresa went back to watching something outside, Gennero sat and thought. He had no confidence that keeping her in the hospital would accomplish anything. It was clear that she didn't trust any of the staff. She felt unsafe. Everyone here was her enemy. Perhaps the only thing to do was to let her come home. That seemed to be an accomplished fact anyway. Then, when he saw Dr. Sacerdote on Tuesday, he would get his input. Meanwhile, he'd have to try to let her know that there would have to be some changes and that he couldn't go on as he had before.

"Theresa," he said gently, calling her attention from outside, "I know how afraid you feel, how difficult it is to trust anyone, but . . . you realize that this thing you did, the business with the overdose, it has me very worried."

"I know, Gennero. That was a foolish thing to do. It didn't accomplish anything. But I didn't know what else to do."

"I know," he said. "I think I understand how desperate you've been feeling, and I'm sorry if I haven't seemed more supportive."

"Well, you haven't been," she shot at him. "You haven't been supportive of me at all, not believing me, always disagreeing and arguing with me . . ." She gave up in disgust and returned to watching outside.

"Yes," Gennero continued, "I know. But, Theresa, your judgment sometimes has left something to be desired."

"What are you talking about?"

"Well, like the overdose, for example." She didn't bother to answer or even look at him. "Anyway, Tessie, when you come home, I insist that you take your medicine and see a doctor." This time she turned and looked at him. "I mean it," he said.

Theresa looked at him for a moment and then nodded. "Look, Gennero, what they're doing outside."

He got up from the bed and went over to the window. "What?"

"Down there, look. All those people standing by that store. What do you think they're doing?"

"How should I know? Maybe they're waiting for a bus or something."

"No, there's no bus stop there."

"Well, what do you think they're doing there?" Gennero felt a little twinge of pride, like he was finally learning how to deal with her.

"I don't know, Gennero. But they're up to no good." Then she turned to him. "Be careful when you go out there, Gennero. Something is going on. I don't know what it is, but something's going on."

Gennero put his hand on her shoulder, stroking it. *How sad, how terribly sad. She used to be such a good person—thoughtful, kind, considerate, loving. Now she's capable only of seeing danger and evil all around her. There's no beauty in her life at all—none.* "Don't worry, *cara*. I'll take good care of myself . . . and of you too. Everything will be all right, you'll see. We'll beat this thing, you'll see. Trust me."

She reached up and put her hand on his. "I hope so," she said softly. Then she looked up at him. "You'll come for me tomorrow, Gennero? You'll take me home tomorrow?"

He nodded vigorously. "Yes, of course. I'll be here in the morning. I'll check on it now, on my way out."

She smiled sadly and turned to look outside again.

Gennero kissed the top of her head. "*A domani*," he said quietly.

"Ciao," she answered without turning.

Gennero withdrew his hand from her shoulder, giving it a parting squeeze, and left the room. When he looked back, she was still looking out of her window at the gathering of evil outside.

Gennero felt tired and drained as he walked to the nurses' station. He sought out the familiar face of Roberta Brown and caught her eye.

"Yes, Mr. Giantonio, can I help you?"

"Yes, thank you, Roberta. My wife told me she's going to be discharged tomorrow morning. I was wondering what time I should come to pick her up."

"Yes," she said, raising her eyebrows and flashing a knowing smile, "I noticed that we have her scheduled to go home tomorrow morning. I think she's going to be quite happy with that. Anyway, anytime around ten o'clock would be good. That would give us plenty of time to do all of the paperwork."

Gennero nodded. Paperwork. He imagined big laundry baskets full of papers and different colored folders heaped into them, spilling out onto the floor. *What would any business worth its salt be without all of the requisite paperwork?* "I understand," he said flatly. "By the way, is either Dr. Sung or Dr. Weinstadt around?"

Roberta shook her head. "Dr. Weinstadt is usually here only early in the mornings when he makes rounds, and Dr. Sung is off for the rest of the day, but he should be here tomorrow when you come in to pick up your wife."

Gennero accepted this news, as it was not entirely unexpected. He could imagine that neither of the doctors wanted to be around to explain how his frightened, delusional, and crazy wife had outwitted all of them and successfully manipulated them into agreeing to send her home less than four days after she had tried to kill herself. Well, at least he knew that he was going to take a stronger stand with her once she was home, and that gave him some confidence that maybe things would be better.

Out on the street, Gennero hailed a cab to take him to see Maria. His heart felt heavy at the prospect of seeing her and finding out the results of her surgery. The lingering aftereffect of his visit with Tessie didn't make him feel any lighter. It was only then, aware of his slouching into the seat like a lump of self-pity, that he realized what he was doing. He deliberately straightened up and looked around him, trying to make contact with his immediate surroundings in an effort to come out of himself. He made a point of looking at the driver of his cab, appreciating the man's youth and athletic thinness. He looked at the displayed name and picture of the driver: Indian or Pakistani, most likely. He tried to imagine his story. Was he married? Did he have children? Did he have other ambitions? Who was he? He was about to ask some of these questions when he realized they were almost at Pennsylvania Hospital, and he busied himself with getting out his wallet instead.

It was shortly after eleven in the morning when Gennero emerged from the elevator onto Maria's floor. He stopped at the nurses' station and asked when Maria would be expected to be returned to her room and was surprised when they informed him that she was already there. Quickening his pace, Gennero hurried to her room. When he entered, she was resting, but he noticed that her eyelids were partially open and that she was awake. Her face looked gray, lacking her usual warm glow. Obviously, she was exhausted. Maria opened her eyes when she heard him come in and managed a smile.

"Ciao, *mio fratello.*"

"Ciao, *mia sorella.* How're you feeling?"

"Not so good." She struggled to form her thoughts and her words. "Sore . . . dopey . . . tired. And I have a big *mal a testa*, a big headache."

Gennero took her hand. "Have you seen the doctor yet?"

Maria was slow in responding. "I think he was here . . . maybe not here. Maybe before, in the other room . . . the recovery. I'm not sure. It's like a dream. I can't remember it so well."

"That's fine. Don't worry about it. We'll find out all we need to know soon enough. Just rest for now. Do you want to go to sleep?"

Without any further discussion, she closed her eyes and immediately drifted off. Gennero took a seat in the one chair that was provided and waited. He didn't want to think about Maria's future until he had a chance to talk with the doctor and find out what her medical condition was. Similarly, he was reluctant to try to figure out what to do with Theresa until he had a chance to discuss it with Dr. Sacerdote on Tuesday.

His mind skipped over various business problems. They wouldn't be his immediate concern any more, at least for a while. He was happy that Dom's son, Joey, would be filling in for him these next couple of weeks, and he anticipated—as he was sure that Dom and Joey did too—that it would soon become a permanent arrangement.

Thinking about Dom reminded him of the time when he was about eight years old. Dom would have been about twelve. Gennero had come out of his house after lunch and, going around to the alley behind their buildings, saw Dominic up on the roof of a garage that belonged to the old woman who lived on the next street. A couple of other kids were in the empty lot next to the garage, and they had a small fire going. Dom called to him to get a piece of smoldering wood from the fire and bring it up to him on the roof. There were some boxes and barrels piled along the side of the garage, and the idea was for Gennero to climb up and hand the piece of smoking wood up to him.

What for, Gennero wanted to know. Dom and the others couldn't stop laughing. They were going to play a trick on Rocco. Rocco was a really fat kid, a mama's boy who everybody loved to tease. Rocco's mom was constantly afraid that he was going to get kidnapped and would hardly let him out of her sight. She wouldn't let him do anything. Dom filled Gennero in on the plan. They were going to place a piece of smoking wood on Mrs. Priggie's garage roof, and then when Rocco came out, they were going to point to the smoke and make believe that they had accidentally started a fire. "Oh, what are we going to do now? Oh, we're going to be in so much trouble!" The idea was to get fat Rocco all upset.

Sure enough, Rocco soon appeared, probably reluctantly let outside by his mother to play, and right away all of the kids, including Dom, who was now down from the roof, went into their act: moaning and whining about all the trouble they were bound to get into and what were they going to do? Rocco was predictably upset, wanting to be included by all of the other kids, but clearly not wanting to get into trouble, knowing his mother better than anyone did. Behind Rocco's back, everybody was winking at the great joke as Rocco couldn't take his eyes off the smoke coming from Priggie's garage roof. Then he pointed and said, "Holy shit! Look at the size of those flames!" Everyone looked—and, Christ, the roof *was* on fire.

Gennero smiled to himself as he recalled this incident. Somebody called the fire department, and a couple of fire engines came, the firemen dressed in their heavy coats and funny hats, carrying big axes and dragging the hose from the fire hydrant on the corner. They gave all of the kids a lecture on fire safety, pointing out that the garage had been filled with paint and could have caused a major disaster if it had caught fire. The police came, took their names, and all of them had to go to juvenile court with their parents. The judge lectured them and told them that they now had a police record and that their next offense would land them in prison—so they had better watch their step from here on out. Gennero had been quite scared, but at the same time, he had admired Dom's creative and adventurous thinking and was secretly proud to have been part of the escapade.

Pulling Gennero from his reverie, Maria's surgeon came into the room and greeted Gennero, who stood up. The surgeon checked Maria's pulse and chart, during which time she opened her eyes and smiled bravely.

"Well," the surgeon began, full of authority in spite of being covered in green—green slippers over his shoes, green shirt and pants, mask hanging below his chin, and a little green skullcap. "Did your sister give you the news?"

Gennero and Maria looked at each other, and then Gennero spoke. "Maria doesn't have a clear memory of talking to you before, so . . ."

"I'm not surprised. It'll take a while for the anesthesia to wear off. In fact, for the next couple of days, you won't really feel like your old self," he said, directing himself to Maria. "But it's worth repeating. The tumor was malignant, as we suspected, but it was only stage one, which I was surprised at, frankly."

"Stage one?" Gennero interrupted. "That's good news?"

"Yes, Mr. Giantonio. Stage one is the earliest and least advanced stage. That means we, more than likely, removed it before it had a chance to spread or metastasize. Even so, we checked the lymph nodes. They seemed to be in good shape. So, except for the one we took for the biopsy, we didn't remove any of the others. Given that the tumor was encapsulated, we merely did a lumpectomy and didn't have to remove the entire breast."

"And you got it all out, the cancer? It's all gone?" Maria was incredulous.

The surgeon smiled. "I love this, giving good news. Yes, Maria, I think it's safe to say that we got it all out. We have the option of doing some radiation or using some chemotherapy, like Tamoxifen, just to make sure, but we can talk about that later when you're feeling clearer mentally than you are right now."

Gennero was speechless. *She's not going to die,* was all he could think. He impulsively moved to the surgeon, grasping his hand and shaking it vigorously. "Thank you, Doctor. Thank you."

"Mr. Giantonio, believe me, it is entirely my pleasure. Nothing makes me happier than to be able to tell the two of you this kind of news."

Maria kept shaking her head in disbelief and finally broke into a fit of the giggles.

"It's going to take you a few hours before you're feeling completely awake and less groggy. Don't be surprised if you have trouble remembering our conversation. So," he said, turning to Gennero, "make sure that she calls my office for a follow-up appointment for next week. We'll take a look at the stitches and talk about further treatment options. Here's a prescription for some painkillers, just in case she needs them. And that's about it."

"When does she come home?" Gennero asked, still somewhat in a state of shock.

"Tomorrow morning."

"Tomorrow morning?" both Maria and Gennero chorused.

"Sure, figure about ten or eleven o'clock. Of course, you'll want to take it easy for a few days, but by Wednesday or so, you should be feeling pretty good. Make an appointment to see me Thursday or Friday next week. Before you know it, you'll be better than new."

The surgeon shook hands with both of them and, smiling broadly, left them alone.

At first, they just looked at each other and smiled. Then they laughed, and Gennero went to her and gave her a big but gentle hug.

"I can't believe it," she said, still somewhat breathless. "Here I was all ready to die, and now I have a whole new life. I can't believe it."

"I never dared to hope for this. It's a miracle."

Gennero was so happy, thinking of bringing Maria home, he almost forgot about Theresa. "Oh," he said, suddenly shaking his head.

"What's the matter?"

"I just remembered, Theresa is being discharged from the hospital at the same time, about ten o'clock tomorrow morning."

"Tomorrow? I thought you told me that she was coming home on Monday."

"I did. I just found out. Somehow she managed to get them to let her go home a day earlier. I'm supposed to pick her up tomorrow morning."

"So? What's the problem? You go pick her up. I'll call Mona. She and Glenn will come and get me."

"Are you sure? I can send Sal for you . . ."

"No, I don't need Sal. It's Sunday. Mona and Glenn will be glad to do it, and I'm just next door to them. It'll be easy for them, I know."

Gennero agreed. It made sense, although he felt badly for not being the one to take her home. He felt like he was shifting his responsibility onto somebody else.

"Gennero, why don't you call Mona right now for me? Tell her what the situation is and ask her if she and Glenn want to take me home. If it's a problem, then you can call Sal."

Gennero agreed. "Even half knocked out with anesthesia, your brain is still working better than mine." Gennero took out his cell phone and called Mona. Just as Maria had predicted, she was delighted to have the opportunity to be of some real and tangible help to Maria. He told her the details, especially the good news about the results of the surgery, and they made arrangements to come the next morning to take her home.

"Everything is all arranged. You can rest easy now, take the rest of the day to recover from this and sleep the day away. Tomorrow you'll be home in your own bed." He thought for a moment. "I imagine that I'll be busy all day with Theresa." He paused, clenching his jaw. Then he looked up and tried to smile. "But I'll be by to see you sometime on Monday."

"Gennero, you go now. I'm having trouble keeping my eyes open. I just want to go back to sleep."

"Fine, *sorella*. Sleep. I'll see you on Monday. Meanwhile, have wonderful dreams." With that, Maria closed her eyes. Gennero picked up his coat and quietly left the room, pausing only to look back and smile at the sight of his sister lying there, alive, breathing, sleeping, and free of cancer.

CHAPTER XXXVI

GRADY: PASSING IT ON

Emerging from the train station, Grady discovered that both the rain and the wind had kicked up again. Waiting for the bus, he found some protection in a niche alongside the building, but by the time the bus came, he was drenched and chilled to the bone. Once he was home, he undressed and went to bed, burying himself under the covers to get warm. He felt somewhat guilty thinking of Karen having to be at work for the next twelve hours. He was also riled up at the thought—or was it more a revelation—that Tracy and Brian had successfully conspired to murder Richie. But neither train of thought kept him from falling asleep.

When he awoke about an hour later, Grady got dressed in dry clothes and made himself a sandwich for lunch. He sat at his kitchen table, eating and drinking a glass of milk and thinking about the meeting with Tracy. He found himself being curious as to why she seemed to go to such lengths to keep Brian out of it: the choice of the meeting place, her lack of references to him during their breakfast, her coming alone. It could be something quite simple, like Brian being busy with something else. Or it could mean something entirely different. Grady didn't trust her at all. Maybe she was trying to hide the fact that Brian was involved in any way. Maybe she thought that bringing him to the meeting might imply that he knew Richie and therefore might have had a motive for revenge. Grady felt his head spinning. *Karen was right. Just let all of this settle.*

He put on a heavier sweatshirt under his jacket and went back outside, walking the few blocks to the warehouse where he was looking forward to putting in a couple of hours of good physical effort. It was after three thirty when he arrived back home and decided to call Gennero.

Gennero answered after a couple of rings. "Zio, it's me, Grady."

"Ciao, Grady. How are you?"

"I'm fine, Zio. Listen, this morning, Karen, my girlfriend, and I had breakfast with Tracy Malatesta."

"Who?"

"Tracy, the girl that Richie had been going with. Tracy Malatesta. Only she got married to that guy, Brian Hoffman. So now her name is Tracy Hoffman."

"Oh yes, of course. I remember. So you met with her?"

"Yeah. Me and Karen went out to Wynnewood and met her at a diner out there."

"And how did it go?"

"Zio, I don't know how to tell you this, but I think that she and her husband, Brian, set Richie up. I think they killed him." Grady felt overwhelmed with emotion as he spoke these words out loud. He heard the agitation in his voice and felt it in his tightened chest.

"Grady, slow down." Gennero took a deep breath. "Now, slowly, tell me what happened."

"Well, part of it was what she said. Part of it was how she said it, how she acted. But the bottom line is this. Tracy was more into heroin than Richie was. Richie was happy getting stoned or high on almost anything, but Tracy had a real preference for heroin. She said that usually Richie only had other drugs with him and that she had to have her own supply of smack, which she would share with him. And her supplier was Brian Hoffman. Apparently, Richie knew Brian slightly. My guess is he met him a couple of times, and he probably would have known that Brian was Tracy's source of H.

"Now, it also turns out—Tracy admitted this—that she was pregnant. Richie found out and thought that the baby was his. That's why he wanted to get married. But Tracy didn't want to get married or have the baby. Brian was probably the baby's father, although that may not be all that important. Anyway, when Richie found out that Tracy was cheating on him, he was upset because he believed that she was pregnant with his baby, and he thought that she was going to stop using drugs, have the baby, and marry him. Then, I think, it was only when he went into The Harp that he recognized Brian as Tracy's dealer. Richie didn't know that Tracy was trading sex for dope. He just saw a drug dealer feeding poison to his supposed pregnant fiancée and screwing her too. That's when he lost it. He probably had thoughts of this son of a bitch killing his child."

"*Bastardi!*" Gennero muttered. "Now I understand why Richie would be so angry. This bastard was threatening not only Richie's relationship with Tracy, but also the well-being of their child."

"Right. Now for these past two years, I assumed that Brian and Richie didn't know each other. But they did. Not well, but they did know each other. That means that Brian knew it was Richie who attacked him. Tracy was really pissed at Brian getting beat to shit and put out of commission. She's still pissed about it. You should have seen her, really in a rage, Zio. So my guess is this: Tracy got Brian to give her uncut heroin. Then she met with Richie in his room. She couldn't have obtained uncut heroin without Brian's knowledge and cooperation. Then she got Richie to shoot up. Only the dope is two or three times more potent than what he was used to, and he died as a result, leaving it to look like an accident or a possible suicide. And only Tracy and Brian know the truth." Grady stopped talking and waited for Gennero's response. "What do you think?"

"Let me think a minute, Grady."

Grady waited for Gennero to digest what he'd just told him.

"What you're saying, Grady, is that Richie didn't die because he was a heroin addict. And he didn't commit suicide or die because he was reckless and bought contaminated heroin. You're saying that he died because this woman, Tracy, deliberately gave him a lethal dose. He died because she murdered him. It wasn't Richie's fault. That bitch is to blame. Grady, what you say adds up. It makes sense."

"Zio, the more I think about it, it's the only thing that makes sense."

"Yes, I can see how you feel that way. But listen, just because it all hangs together doesn't mean that it's true. There might be other possibilities that could explain things too. Let's not forget that we already accepted the idea that it was an accident. Just because Tracy and Brian might have had thoughts of revenge doesn't mean they acted on them."

"No, you're right. But, given how angry they were, how angry she still is, wouldn't they have told the police that Richie beat him up? I think they didn't have to do that because they had their own plans for payback."

"Yes, that seems reasonable, Grady. But wasn't Brian a small-time dealer? Maybe they were afraid to accuse Richie because they didn't want more of an investigation into their activities and decided they would be better off if they let it drop."

"That's true, Zio, but wouldn't that make it all the more likely that they would look for another way to get even? Remember, Brian was in a coma. He nearly died and was left with permanent injuries."

"You have a point, Grady. Let me think about this. I don't want to go off half-cocked on something so important. Let me digest it for a while."

"Of course. I just wanted to share it with you while it was all fresh in my mind."

"I understand, Grady. I'm very impressed with what you found out. It was you and your girlfriend who met with this Tracy?"

"Yeah. I brought her along for moral support. Good thing I did. She had some amazing insight into Tracy and was the one who was able to get her to admit to things, like being pregnant and wanting the abortion. I mean, Tracy was trying to deny everything, even that she and Richie were going together. Karen saw right through all her bullshit."

"And Karen, she agrees with your suspicions?"

"She agreed that it made sense. But, like you, she said that we should let it settle for a while and not go assuming that it's necessarily the whole truth."

"Karen seemed like a smart woman. She reminds me of Maria. By the way, Grady, I want to thank you for visiting Maria. It meant a lot to her."

"I was going to ask you about her and about your wife. How's everything going?"

"Good news, Grady. Maria's surgery was successful, and the doctor thinks they got all the cancer out. It looks like she's going to be good as new. She'll be coming home tomorrow morning."

"Wonderful!" Grady exclaimed. "Wonderful. And what about Mrs. Giantonio?"

Gennero cleared his throat. "Theresa also will be coming home tomorrow morning," he said.

"That sounds like good news too," Grady said, not actually too sure if it was good news, judging from the more subdued tone of Gennero's voice.

"I hope it is. We'll have to wait and see how that develops. But for now, there's not much point to her staying in the hospital. We'll have to wait and see how she does at home."

"Zio, you know I'm wishing you all the luck in this. I hope everything goes the way you want it to."

"Thanks, Grady. Listen, I've been thinking . . . are you and your girlfriend free tonight, say between seven and eight?"

"I am, but Karen's working. Why?"

"We're having a big family get together at my cousin's restaurant. I thought it would be a good opportunity to meet this girlfriend of yours and to sit down with the two of you to discuss this whole Richie business in person."

"Like I said, Karen's at work. She won't be off until after eleven tonight."

"Another time then. We'll make plans to get together sometime next week maybe for breakfast or lunch."

"That would be great, Zio. I'd love to have you meet her."

"It's settled then. In the meantime, let's let ourselves think about this."

"Right. Have fun tonight at your dinner."

"Thanks, Grady. Take care now."

"You too, Zio."

CHAPTER XXXVII

GENNERO: CELEBRATION PARTY

After his phone conversation with Grady, Gennero went into the kitchen and made himself a pot of espresso. When it was ready, he took it to the kitchen table where he sat down in his usual seat that gave him a view of his brick patio and small garden. He felt he needed the coffee to help shake the grogginess from his nap, but also to calm down. Richie murdered? His own grandson (actually, his nephew) murdered? He had never even considered such an idea. He couldn't have ever imagined such a possibility. It could not be true. Grady had to be mistaken.

He had always assumed Richie's death was due to some kind of accident, maybe a result of some bad drugs cut with poison or something, even though there was no official mention of that in the police report. That document had simply said: *Death as a result of an overdose of heroin.* So maybe it wasn't bad drugs after all. But there was still the possibility of suicide, wasn't there? But if Richie usually got his heroin from Tracy, then he probably would have chosen to commit suicide with an overdose of some other drug, some pills that he was more in the habit of using.

Gennero continued to sip his coffee and contemplate the rain, which was being driven hard against the back door and kitchen windows. *Like a goddamned monsoon*, he thought. He forced himself back to the topic of Richie. Suicide. Grady said that Richie usually had other drugs with him, but it was also likely that if Richie really wanted to buy heroin, he would have been able to do it. It would have been highly unlikely that Richie would have had to rely on Tracy as his only source of heroin. And if he usually had other drugs—and not heroin—it would have been because that's what he chose. So why would he decide to use heroin to kill himself if he wouldn't even bring it to Tracy when he knew very well that that's what she preferred? Heroin was her favorite drug, not his. For Richie to commit suicide using heroin simply didn't make any sense.

Also, given how enraged Richie was at Brian, he would have been enraged at Tracy. At the very least, he would have been angry with her for endangering what he believed to be their child. But Richie had seen her with Brian the previous night. She had been out all night with him. So Richie would also have been angry at her for cheating on him. Gennero shook his head. *This doesn't sound to me like someone who wants to commit suicide. It's not like she was the only woman he ever had, maybe not even the only pregnancy he was responsible for.* The more he thought about it, the more he tended to agree with Grady's conclusions. *If you rule out accident and suicide, then murder is the only explanation left. And these two* bastardi, *they had the reason to kill him. They had the method. And they could have arranged for the opportunity.*

Gennero finished his coffee and carried the pot and cup and saucer to the sink where he rinsed them out. Then he went into his living room where he put on one of his favorite CDs, the opera *Tosca,* and stood looking out of his front windows, thinking, while the dramatic and passionate music filled the room behind him.

At a couple of minutes after seven, Sal pulled into the driveway. He got out with his big umbrella and came up to the front door. He was about to push the bell when Gennero opened the door and greeted him. "Hello, Sal," he said, smiling. "Right on time as usual."

"A couple of minutes late, Mr. G. This rain is playing havoc with the traffic."

"Yes, it's been miserable weather." Sal ushered Gennero to the back door of the limo, and when he opened it, Gennero saw that Sal's lady friend was already sitting in the back. He immediately remembered having suggested this to Sal, but he had forgotten it with all of the other things that were going on.

"Mr. Giantonio, this is my friend, Rose Cohen. Rose, this is Mr. Giantonio." Gennero lowered himself into the seat and turned to offer his hand to her.

"Rose, I'm very pleased to meet you," he said.

"And I'm very happy to meet you at last," she said. "Sal has often mentioned you and how much he enjoys working for you."

Gennero smiled politely and nodded.

She went on. "I want to thank you for inviting us to your party. It's very kind of you."

"Oh, it's my pleasure, Rose, and the least I could do for interrupting your plans for this evening. It should be a wonderful dinner, and I hope that you'll have an enjoyable time. You'll get a chance to meet most of my family and," he added, "some very interesting people."

Gennero and Rose made small talk while Sal drove the Lincoln through the rain to Villa Contursi. During the course of the ride, Gennero discovered that Rosie, as she preferred to be called, was divorced, had a twelve-year-old daughter, and worked as an office manager in a real estate firm. She and Sal had known each other for a long time, having met before he retired from the force.

Soon, they pulled up in front of the restaurant. Valets with umbrellas were escorting people into the restaurant and parking the cars in a nearby garage. Once inside, Gennero introduced Rosie and Sal to Dominic and Nick and to Joey, the man of the hour, who were gathered in front to greet everyone as they entered.

As they embraced, Gennero whispered into Dominic's ear, "Anytime this evening that's convenient for you, I need to speak with you privately." Dominic pulled back so that he could look directly into Gennero's face. Gennero was smiling but mouthed the words, "It's very important."

Dominic nodded and put his greeter's smile back on. "Of course, Gennero," he said. "I won't forget."

Gennero noticed that Nick guided Rosie to a table occupied by wives and girlfriends of others like Sal, who would be helping out in some capacity tonight. Gennero looked around and saw many familiar faces. Then he saw a table with Nina, Rosalie and Denise, and Andrea. His face lit up on seeing his granddaughter, who evidently had been able to get off from work at the hospital. As he was making his way over to them, he spotted Bobby and Brian walking toward their table with tall glasses of soda.

"Ciao, everybody. I'm so happy that all of you were able to come." Gennero went around the table giving everyone a hug and a kiss. "Andrea, I haven't seen you for such a long time," he said, embracing her.

"I know, Grandpa. I feel like I've been living at the hospital. It's wonderful to have a night off and actually have a chance to get dressed up and go out."

Gennero held her by the shoulders and looked at her. She was taller than he was, maybe five foot eight or nine inches. She was slim, maybe even a bit too thin, and a little tired looking, but her athletic build and her attractive face with her wide, toothy smile made her look absolutely wonderful to him. "We're all so proud of you, Andy."

"I know," she said, blushing a little under his gaze.

Gennero turned to his two great-grandsons. "I see you two young men have already found the bar."

They smiled at him, looking a little uncomfortable in their shirts and ties. They weren't quite sure what to make of this affair, although they were certainly ready to be on their best behavior.

Gennero took a seat at the table. There were so many people here that he knew and was close to. Many were related to him in one way or another. Not only Dom's family and children and in-laws were here, but also his cousin Paolo Romano and his wife and children, as well as other members of the board. Gennero surveyed the scene around him. Such a festive atmosphere, like a wedding. Mixed in with his relatives were old friends and longtime business associates. Gennero was amazed that

Nick and Dom were able to garner such a crowd in less than twenty-four hours. He believed it was a tribute to them and to the family, a sign of the esteem and affection in which they were held. Gennero felt a warm, happy feeling spreading through him. *What a wonderful moment. So many good feelings here.*

"Excuse me, everyone," he said to his family at the table, "there are so many people here I must say hello to. So many long-lost cousins to meet. Save my place," he said jokingly as he got up and went to greet his numerous friends and relatives.

Waiters came by the table with platters of hors d'oeuvres and cocktails. Bobby and Brian got permission to have one cocktail they could sip at. Rosalie gave them stern warnings about not trying to take advantage of that leeway. Cousins who Rosalie and Andrea knew came over to say hello. Bobby and Brian knew some of them and were introduced to the others. Some of Gennero's old friends also stopped by to say hello and asked where Gennero was, not having seen him yet in the crowd. Some asked for Maria or Theresa and were simply told they weren't able to make it tonight.

There was a soft buzz in the candlelit restaurant. Music played unobtrusively in the background. The atmosphere was intimate and relaxed. People were already enjoying themselves, simply being among friends and relatives whose company they had not had an opportunity to enjoy for too long. From time to time, Gennero came back to the table with someone in tow, explaining to his family who this particular relative or friend was and showing off to that individual his daughter, granddaughters (and partner), and great-grandsons. No one raised an eyebrow at Denise, and soon she too, was floating along in the warm, happy currents of the room.

At one point, while Gennero was enjoyably engaged in conversation with two old friends, Dominic approached him from behind, putting an arm around Gennero's shoulder. The conversation continued for a couple of minutes, and then Dominic asked them to excuse him while he dragged Gennero off to meet another old friend. Crossing the room, Dominic led

Gennero to the far end of the bar where they were alone and away from the other guests.

"Gennero, what can I do for you?"

Gennero smiled a mischievous smile and, wagging his finger at his cousin, said, "Be careful. You don't know what you might be volunteering for."

"G., you sound like a man of mystery. Like the old Shadow radio shows, remember? 'Who knows what evil lurks in the minds of men . . .'"

"I remember. But I'm serious, Dom. Let me tell you what this is all about." Gennero then went on to explain in detail what he had learned about Richie's death.

When he was finished, Dom looked at him in disbelief. Dom's face expressed a mixture of anger, sadness, disgust, sympathy . . . all jumbled together. "That little cunt bitch," he finally said. "What do you want to do about it?"

Gennero leaned in a little closer and shared his ideas with him. The two men stood that way for a while, huddled close together in quiet conversation. Then they straightened up. They shook hands, patted each other on the back, nodded, smiled, and turned to return to the wonderful party in Joe's honor.

Gennero heard an announcement that dinner would soon be served, and everyone was asked to find a seat. When he got to the table, Dom's son, Joey, was talking to Nina. They had agreed, rightly or wrongly, that they were third cousins to each other, and both Bobby and Brian were trying to comprehend the possibility that, by their calculations, that made Joey their fifth cousin.

Joey embraced Gennero and thanked him for putting in a good word for him regarding the promotion. They exchanged a few words, and Gennero assured him he would be glad to be helpful in any way and would always be accessible by phone. They agreed to get together for lunch on Monday to discuss it further. When Joey left, Gennero sat down and began to catch up on the latest with his family. Nina sat to his right, then Rosalie, Denise, Bobby, and Brian. Andrea sat to his left. Gennero moved over to his left to talk with her and ask her about her internship and her plans for a residency.

"I'm still torn, Grandpa. On the one hand, I really love OB and GYN, but on the other hand, I'm really hoping to get married someday and have kids and raise a family. The idea of working twelve- and fourteen-hour days, being called out to the hospital in the middle of the night . . . I just can't see how that's going to allow me to have any kind of family life."

Gennero didn't have any words of wisdom for her but was reassured to hear that she had some mentors she really respected, with whom she was discussing her options. "I'm sure that you'll use their advice wisely and that you'll make a good decision. But, you know, *ciucci*, most things aren't life-and-death decisions. If the choice you make turns out not to be what you expected, you can always change your mind. Nothing is written in stone. And whatever you choose, whatever happens, you'll learn from it and grow from it. So don't be afraid of making a mistake. You do the best you can, and one way or another, it'll work out for the best."

"I hope so, Grandpa."

"Me too." He laughed.

Waiters came by carrying trays loaded with jumbo shrimp cocktails. Other waiters brought wine or water or other special orders from the open bar. Gennero wondered where Nick had obtained all of the extra wait help on such short notice. The appetizer was followed by an asparagus soup with floating parmesan custards. While they ate, they talked. Gennero informed them that Maria's surgery went much better than expected and that not only would she be coming home tomorrow morning, but that she was expected to recover 100 percent and be totally free of cancer. Everyone at the table raised their glasses to toast Maria. Gennero gave a nudge to Nina to keep an eye on Bobby, who looked like he was beginning to feel the effects of the cocktail he'd been sipping. Rosalie dumped a couple of ice cubes into it to dilute it a little more.

"Watch it, buster," she cautioned him.

Gennero filled them in, as well, on the fact that Theresa would also be coming home tomorrow morning. Everyone registered their surprise. Of course, the plans were still on for a visit to his house on Wednesday night. Gennero tried to present this as good news.

"Pop," Nina said, turning to him, "if there's anything that I can do to be helpful, just let me know. You know that I've got a lot of flexibility, and I can come over almost any time if you need me."

He expressed his appreciation and smiled weakly, unable to muster much bravado. It was true, he was worried. He had no idea what to expect from Theresa. He was caught between the mountains of his hopes and the valleys of his fears. He suspected that his hopes were totally unrealistic, although he was unwilling to let go of them altogether. Like gas-filled balloons, he was afraid they would float away forever if he didn't hold on to them. And regarding his fears, he suspected that they were realistic, although he hoped that they weren't: more absurd paranoid fears and delusions, another suicide attempt, constant arguing. Who knew what was possible?

In the lull before the next course, Vincent Carbone and his wife, Connie, came over to the table. Gennero got up and introduced the judge and Connie to his family. Remarkably, neither of the boys appeared to be bored. In fact, they seemed genuinely interested in the people and conversations, not once complaining at not having their Gameboys with them. Connie engaged the boys in conversation, complimented Rosalie on them, and got involved in a discussion with Andrea about the state of health care in Philadelphia.

Vincent put his arm around Gennero's shoulder and turned him away from the table. "I just had a little talk with Dominic," he said softly. "I wanted you to know."

Gennero looked at his friend and smiled.

"To friendship," he said, raising the wineglass he'd been holding.

"To friendship," said the judge, raising his empty hand as if to clink glasses.

They then heard Dom's voice on the sound system. "Dear friends and family members, I hope all of you are enjoying this wonderful meal, prepared for this special occasion by our fantastic chef, Dolpho, in honor of my son, Joey. We'll have some speeches later on. I know that's the part of the evening that all of you are looking forward to . . . but right now, I only want to say that this next course is in honor of my beloved cousin, Maria, who is unable to be here tonight, although I'm sure she is here in spirit. This morning, she underwent surgery for breast cancer, and I'm informed that the cancer was totally removed and her prognosis is excellent. In any event, Maria is to manicotti as the pope is to the Catholic Church, and this next course is in her honor. Thank you."

Gennero exchanged glances with Vincent as the judge and his wife returned to their table and Gennero sat down. Soon, the waiters were circulating with trays of manicotti. Gennero looked at his plate, the two tubes of pasta filled with ricotta and parmesan cheese, as well as with bits of prosciutto and spinach and topped with a little marinara sauce, fresh basil, and more parmesan. His thoughts went to Maria, and he raised his glass, "To Maria, *cent anni*." Everyone at the table joined in, including Brian with his soda.

The next couple of hours continued to proceed in this way. In between courses, either people would come over to the table to talk to Gennero or Nina or the girls, or one of them would visit another table. Bobby and Brian made numerous trips to the bar, and both were able to finagle small amounts of wine here and there from friends (like Sal or Mickey), who were all too willing to enter into conspiracies with them. From time to time throughout the evening's festivities, someone would catch Gennero's eye from across the room and raise their glass or just nod solemnly. Gennero would return the acknowledgment and turn back to continue in the conversation he was having.

The main entrée consisted of a superb veal scaloppini with gorgonzola sauce and a Caesar salad sprinkled with herbed croutons. After a suitable period of time to allow for digestion and more socializing, this was followed by a dessert of creamy, smooth, individual cheesecakes with mixed-berry sauce. Finally, the waiters served regular or espresso coffee with a choice of after-dinner liqueurs. Speeches accompanied the dessert and coffee, and lastly, there were sleepy and clingy, emotional good-byes and good nights.

After putting on their coats, the boys hugged Gennero. "Great-Grandpa, this was the best night ever," Brian managed to say. He was a little unsteady on his feet, and his face was flushed.

Gennero suspected that he'd imbibed a bit too much but was secretly proud of his ability to pull it off without making a total fool of himself.

"Brian, Bobby, I want the two of you to know that I'm very proud of the mature way in which you both conducted yourselves tonight. There were a lot of very important and very powerful people here tonight. They're all, each and every one of them, your friends and family, as well as mine. Treat them fairly and with the respect and affection they deserve, and they'll always be there for you. These are wonderful people. Don't let them down, and they won't ever let you down."

The boys looked at him like he was being just a little bit too serious. Nina and the girls hugged him. Rosie and Sal came over. Gennero introduced his family to Sal and Rosie. He had totally forgotten about Rosie, but apparently she had had an enormously good time, as had Sal. They all said good-bye at the door. Everyone conveyed their thanks and their congratulations to Dom, Nick, and to Joe. The valets brought around their cars, and soon Gennero was in the backseat of his Lincoln, letting himself feel fatigue for the first time.

Rosie couldn't stop talking all the way home; she was so excited about the people she had met: judges, councilmen, lawyers, so many important people, and the food, "Oh-my-god, how wonderful." She couldn't thank Gennero enough. When Sal got to Gennero's house, Gennero told him that he'd be bringing Theresa home tomorrow morning instead of on Monday and that he'd call Sal on Sunday evening to let him know when to pick him up on Monday.

Once inside, Gennero took off his coat and jacket, loosened his tie, and slipped off his shoes. In his stocking feet, he walked across the deep-pile carpeting of his living room and sank heavily into the soft, embracing comfort of his favorite easy chair. The only light was from the front hall, and in this half-light, he leaned back and took a deep breath. *It was a wonderful night, being with Nina and her wonderful brood, including Denise, so charming.* He smiled thinking about Andrea, who he hadn't seen for so long. *She looks tired*, he thought. *They work her so hard. But she looks strong and determined.* He remembered Maria's frustrated ambition to become a physician and looked forward to telling his sister about Andrea's success. He guessed that Andrea would go ahead with a residency in obstetrics and gynecology and deal with the family problems later when they came up, but it would be her decision.

He thought of the many friends he had seen tonight at the Villa Contursi and the good time he'd had. It made him feel that his whole life, and everything he had ever done, was recognized this evening by the gratifying response of so many of these friends. Everything he had done, everything he had been, seemed to have been returned to him tonight many times over. In a way, he felt complete, as if a circle had been closed, and everything was in harmony. He wished that his mother and father could have been there to witness and to experience the warmth and the intimacy of the evening. The only discordant note was Tessie. He remembered that he would have to go to the hospital in the morning to pick her up. He felt caught between hope and despair, until he told himself it will be what it will be. *And whatever that is, I'll probably be able to handle it. So . . . to bed.*

Something woke Gennero. It must have been almost time to wake up anyway. It was getting light outside, although the sun didn't seem to be shining yet. Gennero went to the window and looked out through the thin, sheer white curtains. The street outside, which passed in front of the house, was a country dirt road that curved off to his left around some trees. It was very quiet. Only some birds were chirping. Then he saw a man coming around the curve, walking along the road, apparently intending to pass in front of Gennero's house and keep on going. Gennero watched him with curiosity. There was something about him; then Gennero realized that the man was him—a younger version—maybe thirty or forty years younger. He could see the man's face, his own face, as if in a movie close-up. As the man trudged along, tired as if he had been walking a great distance, a breeze began to stir. Gennero saw the tall grasses begin to sway and the leaves on the trees begin to flutter lightly.

Gradually, almost imperceptibly, the breeze began to stiffen. Dried leaves could be seen blowing along and across the dirt road. The man, the young Gennero, reached up and held onto his hat, an old felt fedora like men wore in the 1930s and 1940s. Still, he trudged on, leaning slightly into the wind, which continued to build, now blowing debris along the road. Despite the obvious force of the wind outside, Gennero was aware that here in the bedroom where he stood watching, everything was totally still and silent. But outside, the continually rising velocity of the wind forced the young man to stop in his tracks. Not only was he unable to move forward, but Gennero could see the wind exerting a punishing and distorting force on the young man's face. The skin of his cheeks began to ripple backward under the growing pressure. The hat blew away. The skin pulled back more and more until it too began to blow away, peeled off like old shingles from an old house or pages from a newspaper.

The wind blew fiercely and relentlessly, and little by little, the man's clothes and skin began to rip off and disappear into the clouds of dust swept up from the dirt road. Finally, even the man's bones, his skeleton, were blown away. Only then did the wind begin to subside and to quietly return to the calm stillness that had existed before. All evidence of the young Gennero had been blown away, swept away. Not even his footprints were left.

There was not a single sign that he had ever been there at all. He had left no mark whatsoever. Gennero couldn't believe it. He was simply gone, all gone. Not a trace of him remained. Indeed, it was as if he had never ever existed.

Slowly, Gennero opened his eyes. He looked toward his bedroom window, at the shade drawn down to where the window was cracked open. Only then did he realize he had been dreaming. He looked at the clock. It was time to get up, and he did so, but with a terrible sadness within him.

Chapter XXXVIII

GRADY: JAMMING WITH TOMMY

Around ten thirty Saturday night, Grady walked into the pub where Karen was waitressing. He looked around and thought he caught a glimpse of her in the back. He walked toward the far end of the bar where he'd be most likely to catch her eye, slid into an empty space, and ordered a club soda. Then he lit up a cigarette and waited for Karen to see him. About ten minutes later, she approached the bar to pick up or place an order with the bartender, and she saw him. Karen held up two fingers, indicating that she'd be with him in a couple of minutes. Grady killed time by watching a muted basketball game on the TV screen overhead. Loud music played in the background, and everyone had to yell at their neighbors in order to be heard. Eventually Karen came over.

"I don't know how you put up with all this racket," he said.

"What?" Karen asked, cupping her hand to her ear.

"I said I don't know . . ." Then he realized that Karen was teasing him.

"What are you doing here? Is anything wrong?" she asked.

"Everything's cool. I was just wondering if you might have changed your mind, if you wanted to go over to Christy's to see Tommy play and meet his wife, Dolores."

Karen smiled. Her dark eyes twinkled. "As a matter of fact, the thought had crossed my mind. I can get off a little early, and for some reason, I'm feeling energized. But I really do need to relax, and the idea of going out sounds like fun."

"Good. I'll wait here for you."

"Should be about another fifteen minutes."

Grady nodded. There was no use in trying to talk over all the noise. Karen returned to her work, picked up her order at the end of the bar, and went into the back room. He finished his cigarette as he worked on his club soda and watched the silent game. Grady looked around him, at the line of beer bottles and mugs on the bar along with a few shot glasses and some mixed drinks. For almost fifteen years, booze had been an integral part of his life. Later, drugs of all kinds had come to provide alternative highs, but it had all started with booze, and a part of him remembered drinking with affection.

He'd had some good times being high or drunk. And there were still times when he missed it, even craved it. It was funny; he had no craving for any other drug, not even heroin or cocaine, certainly not any of the wide assortment of anonymous pills he'd swallowed. But alcohol, that still had a pull on him. On the other hand, in moments like this, he had sympathy for the other people at the bar. Part of him even felt superior, like he knew something that they didn't. At any rate, he felt no urge and was more than content with his clean-tasting club soda.

A few minutes later, Karen came up to him, put her arm through his, and gave him a squeeze. "Come on, big guy, take me away from all this."

Grady smiled and, putting some change on the bar, slid off of his stool. "Let's go, hotshot," he said, and he led her outside.

"I've got good news," he said. "Martinez at the warehouse needed to take off for a few hours earlier this evening and asked me to go back in to fill in for him. So I picked up thirty bucks that I hadn't expected."

"Great!"

"Point is, I'm springing for a cab."

"Wonderful. I'm looking forward to sitting down. I can imagine how my legs are going to look in another twenty years if I keep doing what I'm doing now. I think of my poor mother. She had varicose veins you wouldn't believe. She was so embarrassed by them. She ended up having surgery to have them removed."

Grady scrutinized her. "So you're saying I've only got another twenty years of enjoying your legs before I have to trade you in?"

Karen started to make a smart-ass retort and then realized that Grady had just indicated that he was planning on being around for the long haul. "Yeah, something like that," she said, smiling and giving his arm another squeeze. "And if I can get my butt back to school, I might be able to tack on a few more for you."

"That would be nice," he said. "Twenty years from now, I'm gonna be too old to go combing the streets for a replacement."

"Grady, I don't think you're ever going to be too old."

They spotted an empty cab and flagged it. It was a nice relief to enjoy the warmth of the taxi, and they snuggled together on the ride north to Christy's club on Girard Avenue. When they walked in, a big, burly guy stopped them at the door to collect their admission charge. Grady leaned over and spoke into his ear, "Fuck you, asshole, I'm not paying."

The bouncer, stunned, took a half step back to see who this crazy dude was. It was only then that he recognized Grady. "Grady Powers, you son of a bitch! You oughtn't to go doin' that to me. I might just a bopped you one by accident."

Grady gave the bear of a man a hug and a complicated handshake. "It's good to see you, Amos. My god, I didn't expect to see you still here after all this time."

"Well, I got me a piece of this place now."

"You do? You're part owner now?"

"Oh, yeah. So you see, I got to stay here and keep an eye on my investment. You know, not too many folks you can trust in this business."

"Don't I know it? Listen, Amos, this is my girl, Karen. Karen, this big, ugly dude is Amos."

"How do you do, Karen. I'm pleased to meet you." Then, with a sly wink, he said, "Anytime you want to dump this poor white boy, you just give me a holler, and I'll be there." There was a little bit more kibitzing, and Grady mentioned that they had come to hear Tommy play and wanted to sit with him and his wife, Dolores.

"I'll see right to it. Grady, it's always a pleasure to see you. You got to come by more often. We miss you. You too, Miss Karen. You always be welcome here." Then Amos waved a waiter over and told them where to seat them. The waiter led them on a weaving course through the club back toward the stage. No one was playing now. Instead, a CD was playing on the sound system. Grady and Tommy spotted each other at the same time.

Tommy got up to embrace Grady. Introductions were made all around. In addition to Tommy and his wife, Dolores, there was Rueben Ramirez, their keyboard player, and Sonny White, the drummer. Rueben was the leader of this group and was from Cuba by way of Florida and New York. Sonny was a talented black kid also from New York. All of them had been drinking pretty steadily for a couple of hours. Tommy offered to pour Karen a beer from the pitcher on the table, but she declined, saying she'd stick with soda. Tommy smiled and said sure.

The guys were on their break, and Tommy introduced Grady to them by talking about Onfire and how they had often played this club together as well as spots up in NYC. Neither Rueben nor Sonny had heard of Onfire, one of the disadvantages of the band not having done much recording.

About ten minutes later, the break was over, and the three men made their way up onto the small stage. When they started playing, Grady was surprised at the quality of their sound. Their style was a combination of the rock and roll of Onfire plus a jazzier kind of improvisation and a more traditional jazz type of structure, with each of the musicians taking turns at little solos. In addition, Rueben brought a Latin quality and rhythm to the music. The overall effect was unique and infectious.

While Grady listened, especially to Tommy on saxophone, Dee and Karen got to know each other. Among other things, the topic of Richie and Tracy came up. Grady caught their names and turned his attention to listen more closely.

"I'm not surprised that you didn't like her much," Dee was saying. "Back in high school, I don't think anybody trusted her, or if they did, they got a knife in their back. We used to refer to her as the slut of the Western world."

Karen smiled. "Yeah, I didn't pick up on that right away, but I think Grady did." She turned toward him to acknowledge his having joined in the conversation. "He sized her up as a cold, conniving bitch. Right?" she asked, looking at Grady.

"I saw her as being interested only in herself, and if she did have any interest in anybody else, it was only for what she could get from them."

"You got it," agreed Dee.

"But," Karen added, "she is drop-dead gorgeous."

"She always was," Dee agreed. "In fact, I think she got even more beautiful as she matured. I can certainly understand why Richie would have been attracted to her."

Grady and Karen exchanged glances and communicated to each other an agreement not to share either their knowledge of Tracy's pregnancy or their suspicion that Tracy had conspired with Brian to murder Richie. This was something they had to talk more about with each other before sharing it with anyone else.

Karen changed the subject and asked Dolores about herself and their daughter, her previous work as a dancer, her view of married life, living with a musician, and so on. Grady returned his attention to the trio and became absorbed in their music.

At the end of the set, the three men came back to the table for their twenty-minute break. Grady immediately complimented them on the quality of their work. "You guys really have created a very different kind of sound—really, really good. Very creative and very special. Really excellent and . . ." He couldn't stop raving. "I think you're doing important stuff here."

Rueben and the others were very appreciative. They wanted to buy Grady a drink, but he declined, coming right out with the fact that he was a recovering alcoholic and drug addict and that he was content with his club soda. They spent a lot of time talking about music, song writing, the business, what was wrong with it, the hassles, and so on. Grady was surprised to find out how much in agreement they were with his views and unexpectedly found himself comfortable with them. Eventually, Rueben invited Grady to join them in the next set. Grady declined, but they insisted and even indicated that they had a guitar on hand for a guitarist who usually played solo earlier in the evening. At last, Grady agreed.

Halfway into their next set, Tommy stepped up to the microphone and made an announcement. "Ladies and gentlemen, friends one and all . . . we are very fortunate to have with us tonight a very popular musician who is no stranger to Christy's, having played here many times as one of the founding members, the lead guitarist, and the singer of the very popular band, Onfire. Please welcome my friend, Grady Powers."

Grady got up onto the stage to a surprisingly robust round of applause. Grady figured that he had a feel for Rueben's style of playing and that he'd be able to find a way to merge with it. Tommy suggested they do an old standard they were familiar with, one the trio had played on other occasions. They started off together, and Grady easily picked up their rhythm and pace. He looked to Rueben for signals as to when to fade into the background as someone else would solo and when to start and stop his own. The number served as a good warm-up for Grady. It had been a long time since he had been on stage, but by the end of the number, he felt right at home, both with being on stage and with being part of the group.

Rueben broke right into another number, and Donny and Sonny didn't miss a beat as they joined right in on cue. Grady was taken by surprise, but apparently Rueben was as comfortable with him as he was with them. He had no choice but to go join in, and he found himself carried along by the new melodic line and the Latinized beat of the piano and Sonny's drums. When it came time for Grady's solo, he closed his eyes and let his fingers do their own thing. He imagined he was a sea bird flying over the rhythmic breaking of the waves on a long, curving shoreline.

He soared, dived, darted, twisted, rolled, glided . . . challenging the waves, caught in the breeze, fighting it, being carried by it, turning into it and away from it . . . Something told him to open his eyes. He looked at Rueben who was smiling. Rueben nodded, Grady wrapped it up, and the four of them returned to finish together in a driving ending. The house went wild. Karen was standing on her feet, jumping up and down. Grady looked around at the group. They were all clapping and smiling. Grady thanked them all, put the guitar back on its stand, and returned to the table. Dolores told him that Tommy had told her what a great guitarist Grady was but that she was just speechless, he was so good.

Afterward, on the cab ride home, Karen told him, "Grady, do you have any idea how talented you are?"

He grinned and hugged her closer. "I know that I have talent. But, you know, tonight was something different. Part of it was playing with another group, not my own, playing a style that somebody else developed. This was the first time, I think, I had to find a way to fit in, and to tell you the truth, I'm a little surprised . . . I'm very surprised, that I was able to do it as well as I did." He was silent for a moment, thinking, remembering.

"I've mostly done rock and roll in the past. I know I can do that. That's easy for me. I'm just thinking that, on top of everything else, maybe one of the reasons I stopped performing was because I was no longer enjoying it as much as I had. Tonight there was a challenge. But not only that—the music, the jazzy part of it, the improvisations, the Latin rhythm, all of it. I tell you, hon, I loved it. It was a gas."

Karen hugged him. "I'm glad it was that good for you. It was that good for everyone else. If it had been any better, I'd have had an orgasm." Grady laughed and pulled her to him. The taxi dropped them off at Karen's place, and in spite of their fatigue, they couldn't wait to make love before falling dead asleep.

SUNDAY

MARCH 7, 2004

Chapter XXXIX

Grady: Calling Mother

Sunday morning, having permission to sleep in as late as they wanted to, with no commitments and nothing that needed to be done, Grady and Karen lay curled up together under the covers in the darkened room, sleeping as if drugged. Gradually, as the sun rose higher in the sky, the room brightened, and eventually Karen opened her eyes to peek at the clock. Ten thirty. Absolutely delicious. She stretched and then turned over to wrap her arm around Grady and snuggled closer to him. She inhaled the wonderfully intoxicating aroma of their lovemaking from the night before and pressed herself into him even more and then let herself doze off again.

Grady became aware of Karen's closeness but couldn't stir himself to respond. His eyes and his body felt too heavy and leaden. But his mind, awakened and set in motion, began to recall the night at Christy's. He was genuinely surprised at how much he had enjoyed playing. Playing and interacting with Tommy again was part of it, a bridge back to the old days, a way into the old feelings they had all shared in Onfire. But he had also enjoyed Rueben and Sonny—as people as well as talented musicians. They had shared his anger at the politics and exploitation of the industry and were willing to stay independent rather than become part of a system they despised. That sharing of values had made him feel less guarded and had helped him to relax. But he had also respected their musicianship and had enjoyed their unique sound as much as anybody he had heard over these past two years. And playing again—there was a part of him that had felt a joyous release last night, as if he had suddenly found himself on the outside of a prison, albeit one of his own making. He felt a sense of freedom he hadn't experienced in a long time.

Grady realized he was waking up and turned to face Karen, whose eyes were still closed, although he knew she wasn't really asleep. Shifting, Grady put his arm under her neck, and she rested her head on his chest. He kissed the top of her head, and she responded with a weak squeeze of her hand, which lay stretched across his body. They lay like that for a while, resting, dozing, until Karen eventually said, "I've got to get up and pee. Save my place."

"Umm," he mumbled, "only if you don't take too long."

When Karen came back to bed, he made sure to open his eyes. He hated to miss a chance to see her naked. He never tired of thinking how beautiful she looked to him, and he smiled appreciatively as she slid back under the covers.

"That was fun last night at Christy's," she said.

"Yeah, I was just thinking before how much I enjoyed myself."

"You were great," she said, hugging him. "I had no idea that you could really play that well. And you fit right in with them, without any rehearsal or anything. I couldn't get over it."

"I had the same reaction. I surprised myself, I know that. And I think I surprised them too."

They were silent for a while, recalling the previous evening.

"I really liked Dolores too. She was very down to earth," Karen said.

"They all were. Good bunch. Good people."

Karen agreed. "Yeah," she said. "They were." Then after a while, she continued, "Dolores certainly agreed with you in your assessment of Tracy."

"I can't understand why a girl who is that beautiful would turn out to be such a slut. How does that happen?"

"Who knows? But I'd guess that there's a connection between her getting into drugs and becoming a whore. Either the same thing propelled her down both paths or going down one led her to the other."

Grady was silent, trying to comprehend that. "I don't know; it just surprises me. When I was in high school, the only girls who had reputations like that were the ones who weren't that attractive, what we would call dogs or pigs. All us guys had fantasies of getting laid with someone who was really good looking, but it seemed that for one reason or another they weren't all that available. But to see a woman like Tracy who is . . ." He was searching for the words that would do her justice.

"So fucking beautiful," suggested Karen.

"Yeah, so fucking beautiful; that captures it. Anyway, it just surprises me, that's all."

"I've known women like that who, because of their good looks, that's the only way that anybody responded to them. It's as if that's all they were, their looks. They were a great set of boobs or a great ass or a beautiful face, and that's all they were. So first thing you know, that's what they're thinking they are, and that's what they're offering to guys. And so they get into sex early, maybe earlier than most. I don't know. I didn't have that problem."

"How can you say that? You're fantastic looking."

"Grady, I know I'm attractive now, but you should have seen me as a teenager—tall and skinny and gangly. I had big feet. I was no prize. I was depressed. I was angry. I hated my father and tended to hate boys in general. No, hon, I was not in the popular crowd at all."

"I'm glad I didn't know you then. I waited until you ripened before I picked you."

"Oh?" she said, pretending surprise. "I thought I picked you."

"No," Grady said, shaking his head in mock seriousness. "I only let you think that you picked me. In reality, I picked you."

"Well," she said, relaxing into him, "you showed wonderful judgment."

They cuddled for a while longer, and then Grady said that he had to go to the bathroom. "Why don't you take your shower while you're in there, and I'll start breakfast," she suggested.

"Great."

"Anything special you want?"

Grady gave her a leering grin.

"I mean for breakfast," she clarified.

Grady smiled. "Eggs would be good."

"Eggs it will be then," she said, stretching, preparing herself for getting out of bed.

Later, after breakfast, while Karen was taking her shower, Grady called his mother. After a couple of rings, she finally answered the phone.

"Hi, Mom, it's me."

"Who else would it be, calling me on a Sunday? I knew it would be you."

"Well," Grady said, shrugging his shoulders, "what can I say. I guess I'm glad that you know I'm going to call."

"Oh, Grady, of course I know you're going to call me. You never fail me. Sunday is my favorite day of the week."

"Well, I'm glad, Mom. So how are you doing? How're your knees?"

"Oh, Grady, there's no use complaining, is there? These knees are what they are. They hold me up sometimes, and they groan and creak, and they hurt like the blazes."

"Is that new arthritis medicine any help?"

"Son, not even prayer helps these old knees. I just have to rest them a lot more nowadays. But even then, you know, it's hard to sleep with the pain."

Grady bit his lip. Every Sunday when he called, he half hoped that he would not have to listen to a litany of her physical complaints. He knew that it was important to her to feel that somebody cared about her pain, and he tried to fill that role for her, but at the same time, he usually ended up feeling that she was punishing him. Somehow he felt that she was blaming him for her pain, as if he were the source of her discomfort, and she was letting him know just how much of it he had caused. He'd hang up feeling guilty and resentful in fairly equal portions.

"I'm sorry to hear that, Mom. I wish there was something I could do to make you feel better."

"Oh, Grady, that's nice. I wish there was something you could do too, but just calling me is enough, although it would be nice if you could come down sometime before it gets too hot."

"I'd love to come down, Mom, you know that, but I'm falling behind on my bills as it is. I don't know when I'll be able to afford it." In the back of his mind, he remembered the conversation with Gennero, his offer to pay Grady's airfare to Florida. Grady appreciated that, and he wanted to go visit his mother, but he felt such guilt for not working regularly and for receiving disability that he had great difficulty in accepting such a financial gift— even though he knew that it would make Gennero happy to be able to facilitate such a visit.

"How are you making out, Grady?"

"Me? I'm doing great, Mom. I'm hanging in, holding it together."

"Still working your program?"

"Yeah, both me and Karen are still working our programs." It angered Grady that his mother never seemed to acknowledge his relationship with Karen. She never asked about her. The thought occurred to Grady that maybe part of the reason for that was his history with women over the years.

"I don't know if you realize it, Mom, but Karen and I are getting closer to each other." He experienced an anxious, fluttery, acidic feeling in his gut at using the word "closer." He had thought of using the word "serious," but that was way too scary. *Is that what's happening? Are we getting more "serious"?*

"No, I didn't know that. Well, that's nice. It's good to feel close to someone. I used to feel real close to your father, God rest his soul. It's a good feeling."

"Yeah, it is." Something in Grady decided to take a leap—a leap of faith, a jump off of a bridge, he didn't know what—it just came out. "That reminds me, Mom. What did Dad take all of those medications for?"

"What do you mean, Grady?"

"You remember, when I was little, in grammar school and in high school, I remember Dad always taking a lot of pills. Pain pills, I think. What was that all about?"

"Why, Grady, don't you remember? Your poor father was in constant pain. He had that accident when he fell off the ladder when we lived up in Jersey, and he was never right after that. Poor man, he couldn't sleep, walk, lie down, or sit up without being in the most excruciating pain. I don't know what he would have done without those pain medications. He probably would have killed himself, I'm sure. But he never complained. He'd never tell you, but you could see it in his face and hear it in his voice. I used to feel so sorry for him. He could never work after that accident. It seemed to take all the life out of him."

"I don't think I was ever aware of that," Grady said, half to himself.

"Your father put a very brave face on it. He tried to stay interested in his hobbies, doing those magic tricks for you and your friends, reading, listening to music, but half the time those medications made him so drowsy that he'd have trouble staying awake. It was hard for him to concentrate too long. Between the pain and the medicine, both of them got to him."

"I don't think I realized how incapacitated he was. I guess you must have felt like he wasn't there for you either."

"Is that how you felt? Like he wasn't there for you?"

Grady knew that he'd blundered in letting that slip out. "I'm sorry, Mom. I didn't mean it to sound that way. But, yeah," he finally admitted. "To tell you the truth, that is how I felt."

His mother was silent for a few moments on the phone. He pictured her stern and angry look, lips pursed, eyebrows raised. But he was surprised at what he heard.

"Well, now that you say it, I can see why you might have felt that way." More silence. "And you're right, Grady, I felt that way sometimes too, as if I had lost him and he was no longer there for me. But I knew what he was going through, and I understood. I see now that it was different for you. I guess we never explained it to you." She paused for a few moments and then continued. "There's so much that just never occurs to parents to explain. I'm sure that you had lots of questions about things that you didn't understand and that we never talked about."

Grady thought to himself, *If not now, when?* "Can I ask you something else, Mom?"

"Of course, Grady. This seems like as good a time as any to ask questions."

"Well, ever since I was a kid, I've had these dreams . . ." *My God, am I really doing this?* "In the dreams, I'm really little, maybe a year or two old, that's all. And there's a young woman in the dream. She has long, straight, blonde hair, and her name is Kelly. And in the dreams, it feels like she's my mother, and . . . I was wondering if . . . she was my mother and if I'm, like, you know . . . adopted?"

"What?"

Grady was immediately sorry that he had allowed himself to ask her. Now he'd really be in her doghouse. *How could I have been so stupid? Stupid fucking idiot!* He felt like whacking himself in the head with the phone but was afraid it would only cause more problems. He felt like he was five years old again. "I'm sorry, Mom, I shouldn't have . . ."

"You thought you were adopted?" Her putting it into the past tense gave him some hope of wriggling out of trouble.

"Well, the dreams always seemed so real. I couldn't help but wonder . . ."

"Oh my God, Grady, I can't believe I'm hearing you correctly. You actually believed you were adopted?"

"Well, you know, I wondered about it. I can't say I actually believed it," he lied. "I was just wondering about it. You know, like there were no baby pictures of me, but you had pictures of Terry."

"Yes, I know about the pictures. You always used to ask why there were no pictures of you. What can I say, Grady? Sometimes parents just get jaded with their children's exploits. We take all these pictures of our first child, but by the time the next one comes rolling around, everything isn't such a big deal anymore. And besides, taking pictures had been your father's thing. I was never interested in taking pictures. He always took them, and after his accident, well, he never took any more after that. It's not so much that he couldn't, but he simply didn't have the energy for it anymore. Anyway, Grady, to answer your question, no you are not adopted. I gave birth to you, and I have the caesarian scar to prove it. You must have seen your birth certificate. Don't you remember that Dad and I are listed as your parents?"

"Yeah, I know, but I always figured that it could have been changed."

"My goodness, you have put a lot of thought into this, haven't you? Why didn't you ever bring this up before?"

"I guess I tried to, like asking about the pictures, but I . . . truth is I was afraid of upsetting you."

"Was I such an ogre, Grady?"

"You could be pretty scary, Mom. I knew better than to set you on the war path."

"Oh, I don't know about that. You didn't seem so careful when you were in junior high and high school."

"No, you're right, but before then, I was scared to death."

She seemed to be thinking about that. "I guess I took after my mother a little bit in that regard. Now there was a truly wicked woman. And maybe," she acknowledged, "I was making up for your father not being able to play the role of disciplinarian. Everything fell on my shoulders, or at least I felt like it did. As well as being the mother, I had to be man of the house too. Maybe I was too strict with you before I stopped trying and decided to just let you go your own way. Lord knows, there didn't seem to be anything I could do to stop you. You always had such a strong will, Grady."

"So what about this young woman, this Kelly? Was there such a person? And if she wasn't my real mother, then who was she?"

"I don't know, Grady. I know she wasn't your real mother. That I know for a blessed fact. But who else she could be . . ." She trailed off into thought. "I'm trying to remember back more than thirty years, trying to remember and picture life in our house in New Jersey before we moved to Philadelphia when you were four years old. I don't remember anybody named Kelly."

She paused again, obviously trying to remember their lives back then. "I used to leave you with babysitters sometimes, so I might have left you alone with somebody. I didn't trust your grandfather to watch you, that's for sure."

"Grandfather? I don't remember him at all."

"You don't remember Grandpa Powers? Well, come to think of it, that shouldn't be too surprising. I guess you didn't see him anymore after you were about three years old. Don't you remember what happened?"

"Mom, I haven't the vaguest clue what you're talking about."

"Oh, Grady, I can't believe you have no memory of this. Don't you remember when Grandpa Powers burned down the house?"

"He burned down the house? You mean he burned down the house we were living in?"

"Actually, it was his house. Your father and I went to live with him after your grandmother died. Your grandfather wasn't the most competent of men. To tell you the truth, Grady, God forgive me for speaking ill of the dead, but I think that man had gone halfway around the bend. He was forever forgetting things and getting lost. I guess he had what we call Alzheimer's now, although he got it young.

"Anyway, one night we were all asleep, and suddenly the smell of smoke woke us up. Your father and I got up, and the whole house was filled with smoke. Your grandfather was downstairs in the living room, laughing his damn head off. The moron was burning papers in the fireplace without opening the flue or whatever you call it. Pieces of burning paper were floating around the room setting fire to the drapes, the carpets, the furniture. And the fool was just standing there laughing.

Dad and I rushed into the bedroom to get you. You weren't quite three, I think . . . you sure you don't remember any of this?"

"No, Mom, I really don't. I think this is the first you ever told me about it."

"That's hard to believe. But be that as it may, by the time we got you wrapped up, there was too much smoke and flames to go down the stairs, so we went back into our room and shut the door and opened the window. I handed you out to your father, who had climbed out onto the garage roof, and then I got out. By that time, someone had called the fire department, and they were pulling up out in front of the house. Dad climbed or jumped down, and I tried handing you down to him. I'm afraid I didn't do a very good job; I ended up dropping you. I'm sorry, Grady. I never forgave myself for that. You ended up with a concussion and were badly bruised. You spent a couple of nights in the hospital.

"Meanwhile, Grandpa had gone out the front door and was dancing around the lawn in his pajamas like it was the Fourth of July. The whole house burned down. We lost everything we had. He didn't have a dime's worth of insurance. He went into a nursing home after that. We all stayed with one of my younger sisters . . . oh my god, Grady . . . that's who you were thinking of, my sister Carrie. You couldn't say your Rs all that well and called her Ka-wi instead of Carrie. I bet that's who your Kelly is, my sister Carrie."

Grady had been following this story mesmerized. He pictured every detail of what his mother was telling him. Whether he was remembering it or not, he couldn't tell, but it all seemed vividly real to him. Now, everything made sense. The flashing lights, the damp grass, the pervasive bodily pain, even the white room with other kids and toys. It wasn't an orphanage as he had thought. It was a hospital.

"Mom, tell me about your sister. What was she like?"

"Carrie? She was my youngest sister. Let's see, she would have been about eighteen then. Yes, she had just graduated from high school and was the last one living in my father's house. Do you remember, Grady, that I had six younger brothers and sisters?"

"No, I don't think so. I knew you had some brothers and sisters, but you never talked about your family. I think I remember something about there being some kind of feud or something with them."

"Oh, yes. When my mother died, when I was fourteen, it became my job to take care of my father and raise my brothers and sisters, since I was the oldest. I'm not bragging when I say this, Grady, but I gave up everything for them. I ended up quitting school when I was sixteen. I did all the cooking and cleaning and washing and shopping. Everything. My father, your Grandfather O'Hara, was a hardworking man, Grady. He was in construction. He built houses. He worked hard and kept a roof over our heads, but he drank hard and was no use around the house as a husband or father. I don't think he could boil water for tea.

"When I met your father and got married and moved out of the house, none of them forgave me for leaving. They all accused me of abandoning them. They never gave me credit for all that I had done for them. They just kept expecting me to keep on doing it for the rest of my life. When I got married and moved out, they never talked to me again until we had to move back in with Carrie and Dad after the fire. We stayed with them for about a year until we got back on our feet, and then we moved to Philadelphia."

"And, Carrie was your youngest sister," Grady interjected. He wanted to get her back on track.

"Yes. Carrie was the last one left at home living with Dad, so she wasn't working yet. She was lucky. I mean she had her youth, a youth that I missed out on. She was full of fun. She loved taking care of you, but she had all of these boyfriends. She was real pretty; slim, long blonde hair, outgoing. Everybody liked her—Carrie O'Hara, the bell of the ball."

Grady was astounded. Here he was, thirty-four years old, and this was the first that he was hearing about his family history. His father's father, senile and burning down their house. His mother's father, a drinker too. His mother having to quit school to take care of her father and siblings. "Mom, how come I didn't know any of this?"

She took a few moments to answer. "I don't know, Grady. I guess I was so angry at them. I was angry at my mother for dying, at my father for expecting me to fill in for her, at my four brothers and two sisters for taking me for granted and never showing a bit of appreciation for the seven years of sacrifice that I made for them. And then the way they turned on me and refused to acknowledge your father. And then later, Grady, when Terry died, that was such a heartbreak. He was only a year and a half or so, not even two, and going like that. I'm sure I was depressed for a while. And then we went through that very tough time after the fire. Grady, I guess the very last thing on my mind was making an effort to bring you up to date on my family."

"Yeah, I guess so." Then, after reflection, he added, "It doesn't seem like you got a lot of TLC yourself, Mom."

"The story of my life. That's when I turned to the church. It's been the only thing that hasn't really demanded much from me, and I feel like I've gotten a lot of strength from it."

Grady understood this for maybe the first time in his life. In fact, he felt like he understood a lot for the first time in his life, including the fact that he had always seen his mother as someone who was supposed to be there for him, not the other way around. "Mom, I wish I had known all of this before."

"Why? It wouldn't have changed anything."

"Maybe not for you," he agreed. "But it might have made things different for me. I wish that I had been able to understand you better . . . both you and Dad. I hate saying this, Mom, but ever since I was a kid, I've been angry at both of you, and I think if I had understood what the two of you had gone through, that somehow it would have made a difference. I would have felt differently. Maybe I would have turned out better."

"You've turned out fine, Grady. You're a good person. You're a good son. You don't do bad things. You've had your problems, but

I can't think of anyone who hasn't had them. You've found your way through them, and you've turned out fine."

Grady thought about what he might have set in motion regarding Tracy and Brian Hoffman, and he didn't exactly feel like a choirboy.

"Yeah, well, I'm glad you think so, Mom." Grady couldn't remember ever having the feeling that his mother approved of who he was. It was an odd feeling, like realizing it would be safe to remove a suit of armor.

"Grady, I don't know about you, but talking about all of these past things has me feeling a little breathless, so if it's all the same to you, I think I'd like to say good-bye now and go rest a bit."

Grady smiled. "Sure, Mom. Yeah, it's taken something out of me too. I'll talk to you next Sunday."

"Good. I'll be looking forward to it. Be good now."

"I will, Mom. Take care. I love you."

"Love you back, son."

Karen had stayed in the living room while Grady was talking to his mother, busying herself with paying bills. She looked up when he entered the room. He shook his head in disbelief, a goofy smile spread across his face.

"You look happy," she said.

Grady grinned as he sat down on the love seat next to her. He was grinning so much his face began to hurt.

"You're not going to fucking believe this," he said, still shaking his head. "All this time, I mean practically my whole life, since . . . at least kindergarten if not before, I thought, I really believed, that I was adopted. I can't get over this. God, if I don't drink now, I never will."

"Grady, what happened? Tell me. You've got me in suspense here."

Grady laughed. "Well, I waited thirty years; you can wait thirty seconds for me to catch my breath." He leaned into the cushioned back and stretched. "Yes!" he yelled. "Fucking yes!" Then he fixed Karen with a mischievous grin and said, "I am not adopted. The dreams were real. They really happened, but I misinterpreted the whole thing. The dream that I thought was reality, well it was, but a different reality."

"Grady, I'm going to kill you," Karen kidded through gritted teeth. "I'm going to be an old lady before I find out what you're talking about. Out with it."

He couldn't stop laughing. "I know I'm busting your chops. It's just that . . . it's crazy . . . just fucking crazy. Listen to this. My grandfather, my father's father, apparently he was senile, and my parents and my sister and me, we were all living with him. And one night he burned down the fucking house, and my mother was out on the garage roof trying to hand me down to my father, and she fucking dropped me. Can you just see this? And I ended up in the hospital with a concussion and lots of bruises. Those dreams I had of flashing red lights and lying in the grass, that's where that came from. And listen to this—afterward, they went to live with one of my aunts who was only eighteen then—and that's the 'Kelly' of my dreams. She wasn't my mother; she was my Aunt Carrie, not Kelly. Everything fits." And he leaned back into the cushions, happy, drained, speechless.

Karen tilted her head to look at him. "You look like a big puppy dog." Her eyes teared up. "I'm so happy for you, Grady. You look so damned happy and so relieved."

Yes, he thought. *I am relieved. I'm not sure why, but yes, that's part of what I'm feeling.*

"Thanks," he said. "Yeah, I'm feeling good. And you're right, I'm feeling relieved too. I'm not sure what else I'm feeling. It's all too new yet. I never expected to hear anything like this, that's for sure. There's other stuff too, like her saying that I turned out all right." He sighed. "I never thought I'd hear that from her."

"Maybe you've got to let all of this sink in for a while. Don't try to analyze it. Just let it soak in."

"Yeah. Anyway, I'm glad you're here to share it."

"Me too," she said.

They sat silently for a few minutes. Grady was reliving the conversation with his mother.

"Oh, by the way," he said suddenly, "I didn't have a chance to tell you, but yesterday afternoon, I called Gennero and told him about what happened with Tracy yesterday."

Karen made a face. "Do you think that was wise?"

"Yeah, I think so. I needed to tell him. I was feeling guilty holding onto it, like I was keeping something from him. I thought he had a right to know."

"Of course he has a right to know. Only I thought we were going to let it simmer for a while, digest it and talk about it a little to see if we came up with any other ideas."

"Yeah, and we will. We're not going off half-cocked on this. I just told Gennero. He had the same reaction as we did."

"Which is . . . ?"

"That it makes sense, but that we need to think about it first before we do anything."

Karen appeared relieved. "Good," she said.

"In fact, he wants to meet with us this week, for breakfast or lunch someday. He'll give us a call. Actually, he wanted to meet with us last night, but you were working, so we made it for lunch or breakfast instead."

"That's nice. I'm looking forward to meeting him."

"You'll like him. I call him Zio, Italian for uncle. I've known him ever since I was a little kid, and he's always been real good to me. I'd do anything for him. That's why I couldn't wait. I felt like I was holding out on him."

"I understand," Karen said. "It sounds like he wants to sit on it for a while too."

"Yeah. Gennero usually isn't one to rush into things without thinking everything through."

"What do you think he'll end up doing?"

"I don't know." Grady thought for a while. "I'm not sure that I really want to know."

Chapter XL

Gennero: A New Beginning

Gennero carried the heavy weight of his sadness around with him as he plodded through the business of showering and dressing and making a light breakfast of some toast and a soft-boiled egg. He thought of doing some cleaning up and maybe even some food shopping but decided against it and instead sat down in the living room to read the Sunday paper that had been delivered. As he sat back in his favorite chair, the newspaper in his lap, a mug of hot coffee in his hand, he looked out of his living room windows at the sunny day outside. It was somewhat blustery and chilly, he knew, but the sparkling reflection of the bright sun off the windows across the street elicited an uplifting feeling of hopefulness and increased energy. Gennero let out a sigh, sipped his coffee, and began to read his newspaper.

A couple of hours later, Gennero emerged from his house and walked out to the waiting taxi, ready to go pick up Theresa. When he walked into her room, he saw the vase of flowers that he had ordered. He was glad that he had remembered to do that. They looked bright and cheerful and may have been partially responsible for the smile on Tessie's face.

"Good morning, *cara*," he said hopefully, wishing her into a good mood.

"Ciao, Gennero," she answered happily. "I was hoping that you would be coming soon. I'm all ready to go. I have everything all ready."

"Good, wonderful. Let me just check with the nurses to see if there's anything we have to sign." He said all of this as he went over to her and gave her a kiss on the cheek. "The flowers look nice," he said approvingly. "When did they come?"

"Oh, thank you, Gennero. They're beautiful. A young man delivered them this morning. I'm going to take them home with me. I'm not going to leave them here for these people."

"I'm glad that you like them," he said. "They'll look nice at home—add a little touch of spring, no?"

A nurse came into the room. "Good morning, Mr. Giantonio. All ready to take your wife home?"

"Oh yes. Anything we have to sign?"

"No, everything is all taken care of. Let me just get a wheelchair for Mrs. Giantonio. You know we're not allowed to let you walk out of here on your own feet," she said to Theresa, "so we'll give you a ride down to the front door. Do you need a hand with anything?"

Gennero looked at Tessie, saw that they had everything, and shook his head no. Turning back to Gennero, the nurse made a point of adding, "Mrs. Giantonio has all of her medications and a written list of directions. If you have any questions, Dr. Weinstadt's number is listed on the form."

It was clear that she was emphasizing this to make sure that Tessie understood that Gennero knew. Then she left to get a wheelchair. When the nurse returned, Gennero picked up Tessie's things, the overnight bag, the flowers, and followed them to the elevator. Once outside, Gennero hailed a cab, and soon, without a lot of conversation, they were back home. Gennero helped Tessie out of the taxi and paid the cabby.

As the taxi drove off, Gennero turned and took a good look at his house and at his wife walking ahead of him to the front door. He had the feeling that this was the beginning of a new era, a new stage of his life. One way or another, life was going to be different from before. No doubt, these next few months were going to center around coping with Theresa—either getting her the help that she required, setting limits with her and successfully getting her to cooperate with the necessary treatment regimen, or implementing some options, like possible separation or putting her into some kind of treatment facility or nursing home. He still wasn't sure what the possibilities were, but he'd explore them with Dr. Sacerdote on Tuesday.

Inside, Theresa was giving the place a very close inspection. "Gennero," she said, "who changed the drapes?"

"What drapes?"

"These living room drapes. These aren't the drapes that we had up before. Did you change them?"

"Why would I change drapes?" he asked, raising his hands. "Believe me, *cara*, the last thing I'd have on my mind is the idea of changing drapes. These are the same drapes we've always had."

"No, Gennero, no they're not. These are different. I can tell. Look at these flower designs; these are a different color. I would never have had this color of rose in drapes in the living room. Don't you remember? Our drapes had a burgundy-colored flower in it, not rose. Don't you remember?"

Gennero made a face. "*Cara*, to be perfectly frank with you, if I closed my eyes, I couldn't tell you what color shirt I have on, never mind what color flowers we had in our drapes. But I can guarantee you that nobody changed the damned drapes."

Theresa studied him with narrowed eyes but didn't say anything. She continued to walk around the living room and kitchen and dining room, inspecting everything carefully, picking something up, mumbling something to herself in disgust, and setting it back down. Meanwhile, Gennero took off his coat and his jacket and put Tessie's overnight bag on the steps to be brought up later. He put the vase of flowers on the hall table where he thought they added a touch of welcoming color to the house.

"Aren't you going to take your coat off?"

Tessie looked at him and nodded. "I'm sorry, Gennero. I don't mean to be difficult," she said, taking off her coat and handing it to him. "It's just that everything seems so different and strange, like it's not my house anymore. Everything looks like it's been changed. How could this happen, Gennero? Somehow, somebody got into the house and changed everything. None of this is mine,

Gennero. It's all different. It's like I don't even live here anymore, like I don't belong, like it's somebody else's house. I feel like somebody stole my life from me."

Gennero saw that she was on the verge of tears. He laid her coat over a kitchen chair and took her into his arms to comfort her, but she stiffened. It was like trying to hug a refrigerator. He stepped back and put his hands on her shoulders. As short as Gennero was, Theresa was even shorter, barely reaching five feet, even with her shoes on. He knew that any attempt to reassure her that no one had been in the house changing things would only make her angrier and feel less understood and supported. So he said nothing but only rubbed her shoulders, trying to think of something comforting to say or do.

"Tessie, if you want to get new drapes, that's no problem. We can get new drapes, new furniture, anything you want. We'll do whatever we can to make this just the way you want."

Theresa shook her head and pulled away from him.

"Would you like some coffee or tea?" he asked.

Tessie shook her head no and then said, half to herself, "I'm going upstairs to take a bath. I didn't dare take a shower in the hospital."

"Fine, *cara*. Go. Take a nice long hot bath. Relax, settle down. I'm going to be in the living room, reading the rest of this morning's paper."

Theresa went upstairs, taking her overnight bag with her, and Gennero went into the living room where he put on a CD of *La Boheme* and sat down with the paper. This time, neither the bright sun flooding the room nor the surging romantic arias were sufficient to lift his spirits. *So this is how it's going to be,* he thought gloomily. *Well, this is not how I intend to live the rest of my life.*

Gennero let himself become absorbed in the newspaper. Although he prided himself on his ability to accept reality, sometimes it took him a while. Right now, he needed to avoid being overwhelmed by a sense of futility and frustration. Nonthinking was what he needed to do to avoid the feeling of drowning. Finally, after finishing reading every section, he let himself close his eyes to rest.

Later, Gennero opened his eyes and realized he had dozed off for nearly an hour. The opera was over, and the room had darkened considerably. It was almost four o'clock. Gennero looked around. There were no other lights on downstairs, but he thought he heard Theresa upstairs, doing something. *Jesus Christ, she's been up there almost four hours. What the hell is she doing?* Gennero heaved himself up out of his chair and climbed the stairs to the second floor. As he approached the landing, he called out to her, "Theresa, what are you doing up here so long? Are you all right?"

He found her in the bedroom, rearranging all of her dresser drawers. "Oh, Gennero," she said, shaking her head disgustedly. "I don't know what we're going to do. All my things, even my underwear, my bras, my shoes, all of my jewelry that you gave me over the years, it's all gone. Nothing remains, Gennero. It's all gone." She seemed close to weeping.

"What are you saying, Tessie? It's all right there. I can see it—your panties, your slips, it's all there."

"No, Gennero. This, all this," she said, pointing helplessly to the little piles of clothing spread over the top of the bed, "it's all different—different labels, different materials. This," she said, picking up a black half-slip, "look at this. I never owned a black slip like this, with all this lace. Only a whore would wear something like this. Gennero, somebody comes into the house and does all of this. I've tried to tell you before, but you never want to listen."

Gennero hung his head, acknowledging his sin of disbelief, of nonsupport. What could he say? What could he do? "I'm sorry, Theresa. I don't know what to say. I don't know how to be helpful to you."

"I know, Gennero. I know. You are a sorry excuse for a man. Married fifty-four years, and you don't even know what to do to protect your own wife." She returned to her task of rearranging her—or somebody's—clothes.

Gennero could think only of trying to change the subject. "I thought we might have some pasta tonight. Do you want me to put the water on?"

"Sure, Gennero. You go put some water on and leave me to deal with this, this outrage. Don't you understand? This," she said, again indicating the spread of intimate clothing on the bed, "is like being raped, Gennero. Raped over and over again. And you don't do anything. Nothing. Nobody does *nienta. Absolutemente nienta*! Go. Go boil your water. I'll be down to cook your supper when I'm finished with this."

Gennero was aware of clenching his fists. But punching her would be too easy. He imagined himself reaching across the bed and connecting with his right hand, sending her back against the dresser, her back smashing painfully against the dresser's sharp-edged top, her collapsing onto the floor, jaw fractured, teeth loosened, lip split, blood trickling out. But it wouldn't solve anything and would only make everything immeasurably worse. He felt impotent. He continued to stare at her as she angrily continued her senseless task, and then he turned and went back downstairs. *The hell with her. I can make my own supper. I don't need her. If I wait for her, I could be down here for hours. Besides, if I make supper for myself, it might help her to realize I'm not totally dependent upon her.*

Gennero went into the kitchen and began to prepare for supper. First he poured himself a glass of wine and took a sip. Then he boiled some water for the pasta, took some lettuce and vegetables out of the refrigerator to make some salad, and got a jar of tomato sauce from the cupboard. He put the radio on and listened to the local news. Slowly, absorbed in his tasks, he began to relax. He was in this much more relaxed frame of mind when Theresa came down.

She had already changed into a flannel nightgown, robe, and slippers. It was only then that Gennero realized that she had only now taken her bath, that she had become obsessed with her clothing and had spent four hours at it before he had interrupted her.

Theresa looked around and took everything in. "If it's all the same to you, Gennero, I'd rather have oil and garlic with the pasta tonight instead of tomato sauce."

"Sure," Gennero said. "That'd be fine."

Slowly, Theresa moved in and began to take over the preparations. Gennero took his glass of wine over to the table and sat down and continued listening to the radio. The talk on the radio filled the space that otherwise would have remained empty and silent. Neither Gennero nor Theresa initiated any conversation beyond an occasional minor request or polite question.

"Where's your medication?" he asked. "I don't see it out."

"It's in my purse."

"Where's that?"

She sighed deeply. "My purse is upstairs in the bedroom."

"Okay," he said, getting up. "I'll go get your medicine." Then, as he was about to leave the kitchen, he turned. "Have you taken any of your pills yet today?"

"I took them earlier, upstairs."

Gennero tried to sound firm. "You remember, Tessie, you promised that you would take your medicine like you're supposed to."

She didn't bother to turn around but simply nodded and mumbled, "I know."

Gennero glared at her back and then turned and climbed the stairs. A few minutes later, he returned with three bottles of pills. He put them on the kitchen table. "I want to see you take these pills, Tessie. You understand? I want to see you with my own eyes, swallowing them. I need to be sure you're not playing the same games with me that you played in the hospital."

He watched her head bob up and down and heard the barely audible, "Fine."

Gennero sat down and read the labels on the bottles. One was to be taken four times a day, one was to be taken twice a day, and one was to be taken only once daily, at bedtime. He put that bottle in his pocket to take upstairs and got out the two pills for her to take with dinner.

Theresa glanced furtively at him to see what he was doing but didn't make any comment. Soon, she filled the plates with pasta and brought them to the table. Then she brought the two small bowls of salad and, finally, a glass of water for herself and a small dish of freshly grated parmesan cheese.

"Thank you, *cara*. Everything looks delicious."

Theresa barely acknowledged him with a mumbled thank-you.

They ate in silence. When he was finished, Gennero sat back in his chair. "Theresa, what's the matter? Ever since we got home, instead of being happy that you're home, you act sullen and resentful, like I've done something terrible to you. All I want is to make you happy, but whatever I do, it only seems to make things worse. If you hate me so much, then maybe we shouldn't be living together. I don't want to make you more upset. I know you're unhappy, but I don't think it's my fault and don't think you should be blaming me."

Theresa looked at him. Her face was colorless, almost gray, and the skin on her cheeks hung loosely. She had lost weight and become haggard looking. It was as if there were no muscles in her face to hold her skin up. Gennero thought, for perhaps the first time, that she looked old.

The briefest of smiles, a fleeting shadow of one, passed across her face. "Would you like some espresso?" she asked.

Gennero was surprised at her response. "Yes, Theresa. That would be very nice."

"I'll make some." She pushed herself up from the table and, carrying her empty plate, went to the sink to pour the water. "I'm not blaming you for my unhappiness, Gennero," she said, shuffling back to the table in her slippered feet to retrieve the rest of the dishes. "I blame you for not doing anything at all to support me."

Gennero started to protest, and she raised her hand to cut him off.

"No," she said quietly, "let me finish. I know you don't believe me. You think I'm out of my mind and need mental treatment. I know how crazy some of this sounds. But we have been married for fifty-four years. Who had the better memory, you or me? Who was the most observant of things, noticed little things, eh, you or me? Now, all of a sudden, you don't believe me? You think I'm stupid? I know what I see. I know what I remember. I know my own clothes, Gennero, my own jewelry that you bought for me."

She waved her arms around the kitchen. "I know my own house, where we've lived for all these years. You think I'm stupid and I don't know these things? No, I don't blame you for the harassment, the things people are doing to us, those sick bastards. If you opened up your eyes, you would see these things too. What saddens me, Gennero, saddens me beyond belief . . ." her eyes filled up with tears that spilled out onto her cheeks, "is that you no longer respect my opinion. What I say doesn't matter to you anymore. You take my words and throw them in the garbage. You throw me in the garbage, Gennero. That's what I blame you for." She had been standing at the table, leaning over slightly toward him as she spoke. Her voice had remained quiet. Now that she was finished, she picked up the dishes and returned to the sink, where she put them down and finished preparing the coffee.

Gennero remained still, focusing on what she said, hoping there would be something in what she said that would help him cope with this situation. He was no longer sure what to say, but he felt he had to respond in some way. Common courtesy, if nothing else, seemed to demand it.

"You're right, of course, Tessie, in reminding me that you always had a very good mind, a keen observer, an excellent memory. But we all change as we get older."

"What are you saying? Are you now saying I'm senile? I'm younger than you, Gennero. And your sister, Maria, she's older than either of us. Is she senile too? How come I'm the one who's getting senile when I'm younger than either of you?"

"Theresa, I'm not saying that you're senile. I'm only saying that as we get older, we're no longer the same as we were. I know I'm not—"

"That's right, Gennero, you're not. You're not the same as you were. When you were younger, if somebody gave me the evil eye or looked at me lewdly, you would have killed him. I know. Now, anybody can do anything they want—invade our house, take our valuable things and leave cheap imitations as substitutes, and you don't do anything. And when I tell you—Gennero, look at me— when I implore you to listen to me, just believe me . . . you give me that look like you have now, a look of disgust. Do I disgust you, Gennero? Is that how you feel about me now?"

"No, Tessie. No, you don't disgust me. I get frustrated, that's all. I get frustrated with you, and you get frustrated with me, that's all. We have trouble seeing the world through the same eyes. You see evil. I see . . . sunshine. You think I'm wrong and wonder what's wrong with me, why did I suddenly seem to change? And I think that I'm right and that you're wrong, that you have changed. And I don't understand why. Theresa," he said, leaning forward onto the table, "that's why we need help. Not just you, but me too. I need help in dealing with this. Somehow, it's as if the two of us have become stuck in two different worlds. We need help in getting back together, looking at things from the same point of view. *Cara*, we're in serious trouble. We need help if we're going to get through this."

The water started to boil, and Theresa shut off the gas and brought the pot over to the table where she inverted it to let the hot water drip down through the coffee. She went back and forth, bringing the small cups and saucers and spoons, a small bowl of sugar, and a plate with some cookies on it. Then she sat down.

"I'm trying to understand your point of view, Tessie. I really am, but it's so different from my point of view. We disagree on so much. I wish that you could try to understand things from my point of view sometimes instead of assuming that I'm against you or don't care about you anymore just because I disagree with you sometimes." Gennero sat back and sipped his coffee.

Now Theresa leaned forward, crossing her arms on the table. "Gennero, I see how sad you are. I know this is difficult for you, but it is much more difficult for me. I live in fear all of the time. Every day, I'm afraid of how someone is going to try to hurt you or Nina or our granddaughters or those sweet boys. Every day, I'm frightened, every minute. I haven't felt safe or at peace for one minute these last few years. Gennero, I feel like I'm all alone, like I'm trying to protect you and our family and—what more can I do to make you realize what's going on?

"Sometimes I think that it's impossible for you to be so stupid and that you really do know what's going on, but for some reason you don't feel free to tell me. So then I wonder, what is it that you know? Do you have some secret plan to keep us safe? Are you just pretending not to notice things? Or is it that you're part of what's going on? Which is it, Gennero? I have to know." She sat up straighter, pulling her robe more tightly around her, and lifted her cup, keeping her eyes on him all the while.

Gennero saw her inspecting him, looking for some telltale sign that would indicate whether he was telling the truth. "Theresa, I'm not plotting against you. I really don't believe that anyone is plotting against you or any of us. This is what I was trying to say before. We look at the world differently. I wish I could persuade you to think the way I do, and God knows how hard I've tried. But I can't. And I know I can't force you to think like me. And, *cara*, I understand that you've been trying so hard to get me to think like you. I understand how frustrating it must be for you to not be able to get me to think like you. But I can't. Tessie, I just can't do it. I'm sorry. I just can't bring myself to agree with you on these matters."

He took another sip of his coffee and then put the cup down and sighed deeply. "We're at an impasse, *cara*."

There didn't seem to be anything else to say. Gennero looked across the table at his wife. They both had tears in their eyes. It felt like a moment had been reached, a moment when each of them had finally become resigned to this reality. They were at an impasse. There seemed to be nowhere to go from here. They would just have to stop. Wash the dishes, watch television, go to bed, go to sleep—anything except continue to face the absolute futility of thinking anymore about the reality of their situation.

Gennero slowly got up from the table and took a cookie from the plate. "I'm going to watch some TV. You want to come too?"

Theresa shook her head. "Not yet. You go on. I'll clean up here."

Gennero lightly squeezed her shoulder as he passed behind her chair on the way into the living room. He sat down heavily on his chair and pressed the palms of his hands into his eyes. He felt like crying, but there were no tears, only a big hollow space inside of him—despair. He turned on the TV, more as a distraction than anything else. He heard Theresa in the kitchen, the light clatter of dishes and silverware being washed in the sink. Half of him watched the programs, half of him continued to replay the conversation between them. Each time it led to the same horrible dead end. He couldn't wait until his appointment on Tuesday with Sacerdote. He wished that he could talk to him now. Then he remembered his lunch date with Joey. He got his cell phone out and called Joey, setting their luncheon date at one of the restaurants that Joey would end up having some responsibility for. Then he called Sal and made arrangements for Sal to pick him up at eleven thirty in the morning.

While he had the cell phone out, he called Maria to see how she was. Mona answered the phone. Everything was fine. Artie had come over earlier in the afternoon and stayed for a while. Maria was a little tired and a little sore but better than Mona had expected. Gennero indicated that he'd be over in the afternoon after his luncheon appointment. When he got off the phone, he called out for Theresa.

"Tessie," he said when she came to the doorway, "tomorrow I have to see Joey Giantonio to talk about his taking over for me. I'm going to meet him for lunch. While I'm out, I thought I might pick up some things that we might need. You want to make me a list?"

"Sure, Gennero, I was thinking about that. We need a lot of things. We seem to be out of almost everything. I'll make out a list for you. What time are you leaving tomorrow?"

"Sal is coming by at eleven thirty to pick me up."

Theresa nodded and returned into the kitchen. A while later, while Gennero was becoming engrossed in a movie, she returned with another small cup of espresso and a couple of cookies. "I thought you might like another cup," she said, sitting down on the sofa where she could also watch the television.

"Thank you, Tessie." Gennero wasn't sure how to read this gesture. A peace overture? He took a sip. "Ah," he said, "nice and hot. Thank you, *cara*." Theresa smiled and picked up her knitting, which she usually engaged in while sitting with Gennero and watching the TV.

When the movie was over, about ten o'clock, Gennero stretched and yawned. "I'm feeling very tired tonight. I'm going to go up to bed now. How about you?"

"No, Gennero. I'm not tired yet. I'll stay and watch the news or something. You go ahead. I'll be up later."

Gennero nodded. He went over to where she was sitting and leaned over to give her a kiss good night. "I'm sorry, but somehow we'll find our way through all of this. I know we will."

"I know." She smiled sadly up at him. "Go on, go to bed. I'll be all right. I'll be up soon."

Gennero nodded and turned and went upstairs. He sat down on the edge of the bed and had to rest before reaching over to remove his shoes. He was feeling extraordinarily tired and sleepy, even lightheaded and dizzy, and wondered if all of this stress was beginning to take a toll on him physically. After all, he wasn't exactly a young man anymore. Gennero went to the bathroom and got ready for bed, deciding to leave the hall light on for Theresa for when she came upstairs. Gennero crawled into bed and curled up under the covers. He was soon asleep.

Gennero saw the flickering light in the hallway, or maybe he smelled or heard something, but when he went to look, he saw several little fires on the floor of the hallway and in the other rooms. The burning objects seemed to be Theresa's things—articles of clothing and pictures. It was as if each thing had separately burst into flames. He began stamping the fires out one by one, and when he turned around, he was suddenly out on the front lawn. More of Theresa's personal belongings were spread out around a huge tree. Again, each of these long-cherished items seemed to be spontaneously bursting into flames, and he diligently began trying to put the fires out, trying to save her belongings, all these little treasures of her life. He worried how she might feel finding her belongings destroyed, and he tried feverishly to prevent that from happening.

The tree was so huge that he couldn't see around it, so he had to hurry around it to save whatever it was that had been out of sight and hidden from view: a pair of fur-lined boots, a photograph album, a jewelry box, a scarf. He slapped at the flames with his hands, attempting to extinguish them. Then his attention was directed back to the house, to the second floor. He saw Theresa up there. Apparently she had come home from someplace. She was changing her clothes. He noticed that her breasts seemed to be much smaller, and he realized that he was no longer sexually attracted to her. He noticed that the fires upstairs were all out. He could see the charred studs and timbers. He yelled up to her that he saved most of what she wanted. They'd clean the house up and give it some fresh paint.

His hands seemed to be charred or sticky from the flames, as if his skin had melted, although his hands didn't hurt. An ember from the flames had apparently been propelled somehow onto his shirt. He felt a searing pain in his chest as if it was on fire. He put his hands to the burning pain and felt hot stickiness. He heard Theresa talking but couldn't understand her. "What?" he tried to say, but his lips didn't move. He struggled to move his lips, and the effort woke him up.

The room was dark except for the light coming in from the hall. His chest was in terrible pain. He turned his eyes downward and saw his hands on his chest and also saw, protruding from his chest, the big chef's knife from the kitchen. In the shadows back from the bed, he could barely make out Theresa, standing, leaning against the dresser. Gennero struggled to say something, but it was as if he was paralyzed, his muscles leaden. He began to understand what Theresa was mumbling.

"You left me no choice, Gennero. You said it yourself; we were at an impasse. You refused to see the danger we're in. What else could I do? I tried giving you some of my pills, but it didn't seem to do anything. You just watched more TV and went to bed. I knew that these sickos, these bastards who are tormenting us, were going to get to you sooner or later—either kill you horribly or get you to do their dirty work for them, to get rid of me. I couldn't let that happen, Gennero. I decided I'd rather do it myself than let them do that to us. I'm sorry, *caro.* I hope it didn't hurt too much."

My God, what has she done? Jesus Christ, she's gone and done it. So this is how it ends. Gennero felt himself growing weaker. He tried to lift himself up, but he couldn't. He had no energy to make the effort. He felt his mouth filling up with blood, and he let his head fall to one side, letting the fluid leak out onto the pillow through his lax lips. He tried to keep his eyes open, but it was becoming more and more difficult. He heard Theresa slump to the floor, still mumbling. He opened his eyes but couldn't see her. He let his eyes close again and felt himself flowing out onto the pillow and the bed. He knew his life was draining out of him. *This is not what I imagined dying in bed would be like.* He became angry but could not even make a fist or clench his teeth. He thought of saying good-bye, but there were too many people, he couldn't think . . . everything was fading . . . *Maybe I'm just dreaming . . . This will be a mess to clean up . . . I'll have to buy a new mattress.* Pictures of Maria and Nina, from many years ago, appeared to him, and it was with these memories of earlier and joyous times that he let go and breathed his last.

MONDAY

MARCH 8, 2004

CHAPTER XLI

SAL

Sal pulled the limousine up to the curb in front of Gennero's house and, leaving the motor running, stepped out, anticipating that momentarily Gennero would walk out of the front door. When a few minutes passed without Gennero's emerging, Sal reached in and lightly tapped the horn twice. When there was still no sight of his boss, Sal turned off the motor and reluctantly walked up to the front door and rang the bell. He anticipated some flak from Mrs. Giantonio. Gennero had told him long ago that she had misinterpreted something he had said or done and didn't want to have any interaction with him.

When there was no response, Sal rang the bell again and knocked on the front door. Leaning his ear against the door, Sal couldn't hear a thing. Reaching into his jacket pocket, Sal took out his cell phone and called Gennero's number. There was no answer. Sal then called Mr. Romano, Gennero's boss.

"Hello, Mr. Romano, this is Sal Gramaglia, the driver for Gennero Giantonio."

"Yes, Sal, what's wrong?"

"I'm over here at Mr. Giantonio's home. He called me last night and asked me to pick him up to take him to a luncheon date with his cousin, Joe."

"Yes?"

"Well, I've been here almost ten minutes now. He didn't come out like he usually does. No one answers the door, and I tried his cell phone, and there's no answer. This isn't at all like him. I think something is wrong."

Paolo waited only a moment before responding. "Sal, stay there. I'll be there in ten minutes. I'm going to call his daughter, Nina. I'm sure she'll have a key. Do you have Joey's number?"

"No, Mr. Romano."

"Then I'll call Joey and let him know what's up. You stay there, and just in case, don't let anybody in the house until I get there, or until Nina gets there. Understood?"

"Yes, I understand."

"I'll see you ASAP," he said and then hung up the phone.

While he waited, Sal periodically tried the bell and knocked on the door. He walked around the back of the house, but the back door was secure, and there was no one to be seen. A few minutes later, Paolo drove up in his little Mercedes convertible and hurried up to the front door where Sal was still standing.

"Nina's on her way with a key. Still nothing?" he asked.

"I don't like this one bit," Sal said. "This is so unlike him to keep me—or anybody—waiting."

Paolo agreed. Within a couple of minutes, a cab pulled up behind the limo, and Nina got out and hurried up to the two men. They held their breath as Nina fumbled with the key.

Once inside, Nina called out to her mother and father, without results. They took a quick survey of the downstairs and found nothing. Everything was clean and orderly, nothing out of place. The men waited for Nina to lead the way upstairs.

Again, she called out. "Pop? Mama?"

They noticed that the upstairs hall light was on.

As soon as she looked into the bedroom, her hand flew to her mouth, and she recoiled into the wall behind her. Sal and Paolo, behind her, stretched their necks to see into the room. There, lit by the stream of sun coming in under the window shade and the hall light behind them, they saw Gennero, lying in his bed, a big carving knife plunged into his chest. His head drooped their way, and blood had leaked out of his mouth, soaking the pillow with its dark red color. His eyes were closed, his hands resting on his chest near the bloody wound made by the stabbing.

"Oh my god," said Paolo. "Jesus Christ." Without stepping into the room, Paolo looked around. It was then that he saw Theresa's body slumped on the floor next to the dresser. He stepped over and tried to find a pulse but couldn't detect one.

"Sal, call 911. Tell them to send an ambulance. I'm not sure if she's alive or not. And tell them about Gennero." He then gingerly went to Gennero and tried to find a pulse on him. He couldn't detect one, and Gennero definitely looked dead.

Sal made the call, and Paolo helped Nina downstairs.

"Nina," Paolo said, "I hate to ask at a time like this, but it would be very helpful to have your father's cell phone. Do you mind if I look for it and take it?"

Without speaking, Nina indicated it would be fine.

Paolo rushed back upstairs and in a minute was back downstairs with it. "This is between us," he said. Nina nodded.

Within another minute, an ambulance arrived, and the paramedics rushed in. They were directed upstairs and soon confirmed that Theresa was dead as well. They called the police, and shortly a squad car arrived, and the house was declared a crime scene.

A detective, who Sal used to know when he was working on the force, arrived with her partner. They asked Paolo and Sal what happened, how they found the bodies, what they touched, what time this all happened. All three of them were in a state of shock, numb with disbelief and grief.

Paolo called Joey and let him know what happened. Paolo also called Dominic and told him. Sal decided to call Grady and let him know. Sal told Nina that he was at her service and wondered if she wanted to call Maria to tell her, or did she want to go over there?

Nina thanked him. Nina indicated that when they could go, she would like to go over to Maria's. Then she called her office and told her secretary what happened and that she would not be in the rest of the day. Paolo told Nina that he would be glad to help with the funeral arrangements and that he'd call her later on to discuss that with her.

Sal called Rose and told her what happened. His eyes filled with tears, and he choked up a couple of times on the phone. He told her that he'd see her later on and hung up.

Nina called Rosalie and told her that Nonna and Nonno were dead, that it looked like Nonna had stabbed Nonno and then committed suicide. Then she asked Rosalie to call Andrea at work and to tell the boys. They agreed to meet and go out for dinner. No one would feel like cooking anything.

Rosalie didn't know how she was going to tell the boys. After leaving a message for Andrea at the hospital, she called Denise and broke down on the phone.

Later, Sal drove Nina to Maria's house. Mona answered the door, all smiles, and welcomed Nina, but she was confused to see Gennero's car and driver, but no Gennero. Then she noticed the pale and drawn look on Nina's face. She knew something terrible had happened but couldn't imagine what. She went upstairs with Nina to where Maria was resting in her bed. The howl that came from Maria's throat was one of incomprehensible pain, a pain unimagined and unimaginable. The three of them held one another and cried.

Meanwhile, downstairs, in the Lincoln, alone for the first time, Sal too gave into his grief and sat slumped, his eyes blurry with tears, vacillating between deep sadness and an intense anger that someone had allowed this tragedy to happen. *How could this have possibly happened? It wasn't fair. It's not right that someone as thoughtful and respectful as Gennero should die like this. Is there no justice in this world? He didn't deserve this,* Sal thought. *He didn't deserve this at all.*

WEDNESDAY

NOVEMBER 17, 2004

Chapter XLII

Grady and Karen

Grady and Karen were sitting at the kitchen table in their new apartment having breakfast. "Are you sure that you feel comfortable with this?" Karen asked.

"Absolutely! Look, we don't really need the money for anything else, and I certainly don't have any burning desire to go out and buy a lot of shit that we don't need in the first place. What could be better than using it for your tuition so that you can go back to school to get your master's degree and do the kind of work that you really want to do? I'll bet you that if I had asked Gennero for the money so you could go to graduate school and cut back on the waitressing, he'd have gladly given me the money."

"I know. You're probably right. I just feel funny using money that he left to you to spend on something for me."

Grady smiled. "Hey, I'd probably feel the same way. Maybe that's the reason that I haven't spent any of it on myself yet. I feel like I haven't really earned it, so it's not really mine. Besides, it's not just for you, it's for us. You'll be able to work at what you want to do and make a good salary, plus you'll have benefits. You're also going to be a lot happier, and that's going to be good for both of us."

"Grady, I don't think I can be any happier than I've been this past year."

"Yeah, I know. Me too. But being a waitress isn't as rewarding as being a drug counselor."

"All right, then. I'll go ahead and register for next semester, and I'll tell them down at the pub what I'm doing. I know that they'll do whatever they can to accommodate me and give me the hours that I want. Between that and all the loot that you're bringing in, we'll be on easy street."

Grady sat back and smiled. "I don't know what feels better, being out of debt or playing in a group again. I had no idea how much I had missed that. Being with Tommy again is like old times, and Rueben is such an amazing musician. Another thing I can't get over, I haven't had one of those blackout spells since that time we had breakfast with Tracy. It's like everything is going perfectly. And then having the inheritance from Gennero in reserve . . . and to top it off, we're both sober!"

"I know, Grady. Sometimes it feels too good to be true. And then I think, hey, we've paid our dues. We've each been through some hard times. Maybe it won't stay like this. I know that we'll run into some problems. I'll have some shitty supervisors or some killer clients, and you'll have some bad gigs or whatever, but we've demonstrated that we can hack it. We know we can do bad times and come out okay. I'm not scared of the future, Grady. I'm not scared of our good luck not lasting forever. We've got it now, and we'll use it as best we can, and when it runs out, we'll just cope as well as we can."

"You know, babe, one of the things I love about you is that you've got your head screwed on straight."

Karen smiled a wide, happy smile. "I know," she said. "I love that you love me 'cause I'm smart."

"As long as you know that it's not your brains alone that turn me on."

"Oh, I know. I know."

Dom and Maria

Maria was getting ready to bake some cookies for the upcoming holidays when she heard the doorbell ring. As soon as she entered the dining room, she saw through the curtained glass of the front door that it was her cousin, Dominic.

"Well, good morning, stranger. What a nice surprise to see you."

Dom smiled boyishly. "Truth is, Maria, I wanted to surprise you."

"Well, come in, come in," she said, stepping back and making room for him to enter the front hall. "So you wanted to surprise me?"

Dom removed his topcoat and hung it on the coatrack. "I remember this coatrack from when we were kids. It's always been here in this same spot."

"Sometimes I think it's held up better than we have."

"Well, it hasn't changed at all while we have . . ." He searched for the right word, but couldn't find it and just let the thought hang in the air.

Maria led Dom into the living room where they sat down.

"Can I get you coffee, Dom?"

"No, thank you, Maria. I just had breakfast. I'm fine. The reason I came is I was wondering if you saw yesterday's *Inquirer*."

"Probably," she said. "Why?"

"I was wondering if you had read this story?" he said, handing her a copy of the newspaper opened up to a page-three article about a Haverford woman being sentenced for possession of drugs. Maria scanned the headline and shrugged again.

"No, I don't think I read that story. Why?"

"I didn't think that you would have read it. But let me give you some background." Dom then went on to tell Maria that Gennero had confided in him that he had been looking into the circumstances of Richie's death from an overdose of heroin. "Gennero wanted me to help him find out as much as I could about a woman who Richie had been involved with. Maria, Gennero was very circumspect about this, but he felt he had to let me know why this was so important to him. So he told me that Richie was really your son."

Maria absorbed this information. At first she was shocked that her brother had betrayed her. But then, very quickly, she understood and knew that Gennero trusted Dom to guard her secret. "I understand," she said.

"No one else knows about that." Dom paused and then continued. "Anyway, I looked into this girl and gave Gennero whatever I found out about her."

"I remember," Maria recalled. "Gennero was asking Richie's friend Grady about it. As I recall, Richie had been in love with some girl and caught her cheating on him, so he went and beat up the other guy pretty bad. Then, so Grady thought, Richie felt so bad about it that he turned to drugs and ended up accidentally taking an overdose. Gennero believed this, but it didn't make a lot of sense to me. But I don't know a whole lot about these matters, so what could I do? I guess we'll never know exactly what happened. Richie is dead and gone, and I guess I've made my peace with that . . . although I still haven't been able to accept what happened with Tessie and Gennero. I don't understand that at all. They say that she gave him a bunch of her tranquilizers, and then, apparently while he slept, she stabbed him through the heart. And then she took the rest of her pills and committed suicide? Why would she do that? I don't understand. I just don't." Tears welled up in her eyes.

Dom reached over and took her hand. Maria took out a handkerchief and dabbed at her eyes. "Forgive me, Dom. This happens at least once or twice a day. I know I'll come to accept it one day, just not yet." She forced a fleeting smile onto her face. "I'm okay now. Please, go on."

"Well, Maria, both Gennero and Grady continued to look into things. And they discovered that the girl that Richie was supposedly in love with was a young, good-looking girl named Tracy Malatesta. Richie learned that she was pregnant and, believing that it was his child, wanted to marry her. Gennero and Grady found out that Tracy was a heroin addict and was trading sex for drugs with a young man named Brian. The man that Richie saw her with was her drug dealer. Richie was furious not only because she was cheating on him, but because she was doing so while pregnant, with what he thought was his child.

Apparently Richie thought that she was going to stop using drugs and then would marry him. So, of course, Richie was furious that this guy was feeding her heroin and that she was endangering their baby's health in addition to cheating on him. He saw Brian as a threat to his baby's life, maybe even to Tracy's as well, and that's why he lost it and tried to kill the guy."

Maria's eyes were wide in interest. "Yes," she muttered, "that would be like Richie, acting out of love, protecting his child."

"Now it turns out that Brian had met Richie before, and he knew who Richie was, so he was able to tell Tracy who beat him up and put him out of commission. Maria, some of this is conjecture, but it is the only thing that fits the facts . . ."

"Go on."

"Gennero and Grady figured out that Tracy and Brian must have conspired to get even with Richie by tricking him into using heroin that was more pure than what he was used to. That's how he died from an overdose. They murdered him and made it look like an accident or suicide."

The mention of that word "suicide" struck Maria physically like a punch in her chest. It was the most unacceptable of any of the explanations she could have thought of—and one she secretly feared might have been the real explanation for her son's death. Now, here was another explanation, one she'd never thought of before. Murdered? Her son murdered? By these two? A drug-addict slut and her sleazy boyfriend-dealer? "Dom, you're sure?"

Dom nodded vigorously. "Yes, Maria. We're sure."

Maria turned away. She had to think. She had to do something. "Dom, what should we do? We can't just let this stand. I can't just let this be . . ."

Dom patted her hand. "Maria," he said. "It's all done. Gennero took care of it. The night before he died, Gennero was at a party at our restaurant. You were in the hospital, you remember, which is the reason you weren't there."

"Yes, I remember; it was a party for your son, Joey. Nina told me about it."

"At the party, Gennero told me the whole story. He had just found out the final bits of information that day. Gennero took me aside and told me and then he told me what he wanted to do. Everything was set in motion that night."

"What was set in motion?"

Dom pointed to the newspaper. "Take a few minutes, Maria. Read the story."

Maria read:

> Philadelphia. November 16, 2004. **Main Line Woman Receives Ten-Year Sentence:** Yesterday in Philadelphia's criminal court, Judge Vincent Carbone sentenced Mrs. Tracy Hoffman of Haverford to a minimum federally mandated sentence of ten years for drug possession with intent to sell. Mrs. Hoffman had been an elementary teacher in the Haverford Charter School until March 2004, when she and her husband were arrested. At the time, Mr. Brian Hoffman was a mortgage broker for Philadelphia First City Bank.
>
> The couple was arrested by a combined local and federal undercover narcotics strike force that arrested Mr. Hoffman in a sting operation selling heroin to an undercover strike force officer. Mrs. Hoffman was in the company of her husband at the time of his arrest and had six grams of heroin in her possession. Subsequent search of the couple's home in Haverford and of their late-model SUV at the scene of the arrest revealed quantities of heroin judged to have a street value in excess of $200,000.
>
> The Hoffmans pleaded not guilty, and defense attorney Jordan Wallach argued that persons unknown had planted the drugs. Mr. Wallach speculated that the strike force might have been motivated by the desire to claim the success of a huge drug bust and said that federal prosecutor Emelio Romano was looking for headlines to build up a resume in preparation for a

future political career. Judge Carbone threatened Mr. Wallach with contempt of court for the outburst, which made news at the time.

Under federal legislation, the home in Haverford and the automobile belonging to the Hoffmans were seized by the city and by federal drug authorities. While awaiting trial, Mr. Hoffman was found dead hanging in his cell in April 2004. After an investigation, his death was ruled a suicide. Yesterday, Judge Carbone, in sentencing Mrs. Hoffman to the state correctional institution at Muncy, Pennsylvania, a maximum-security prison for female inmates, lectured her severely on the damage she had done by betraying the trust that had been placed in her as a teacher of young and impressionable minds. Mrs. Hoffman, a stylishly dressed, attractive blonde, continued to claim her innocence after receiving her sentence.

Upon finishing the article, Maria looked up with a wide Cheshire-cat smile of satisfaction on her face. "I think I recognize a couple of names here," she said.

"Isn't it beautiful? She has no idea what happened to her. There's no way to tie Richie's death into this. It's simply the law and the justice system doing their job."

Maria looked down for a moment. When she lifted her head, her eyes were glistening. "Gennero thought of this?"

"Yes, it was his idea. At his suggestion, I talked to some of our friends and set it in motion. Maria, I know it doesn't bring Richie back, but it's all we can do to set things right."

"I know. Dom, I don't know how to thank you."

"I have an idea. Why don't you and Artie—I hear the two of you have been seeing a lot of each other lately—be my guests for dinner at the restaurant? Let me know when, and I'll set it up for you and Judge Carbone and his wife, Connie, and Paolo and his wife, Gloria, to join us. Maybe they can bring their son, Emelio, and his wife too."

Maria smiled. "That would be nice. Yes, Artie and I are making up for lost time. I've wanted to tell him about Richie but didn't want to make him sad about missing out on a son who died. But now, with this closure, I think it's time to tell him."

"I know I don't have to remind you to be discreet about how all this came about."

Maria smiled. "You're right, Dominic, you don't have to remind me."

"Right. You'll call me when you want to come to the restaurant," he said, rising.

Maria nodded and got up also. "Yes, Dom, I'll call you. Soon." Then she gave her cousin a big hug. "Thank you, Dom. Thank you so much."

Nina and Maria

It was after lunch, and Nina was sitting back in her chair, swiveled around so that she could look out over the skyline. Almost without thinking, she wheeled around, picked up her phone, and called her Zia Maria. "Ciao, Zia, it's me, Nina."

"Nina, what a wonderful surprise. How are you?"

"Oh, I don't know, Zia, feeling kind of blue for some reason. I think it might be the holidays coming. I'm not looking forward to them this year, with what happened to Mama and Pop, you know?"

"Of course. I was just telling Cousin Dom earlier today how I still cry every day, thinking about them."

"Yeah, we all miss them, especially Pop. The two of you were very close."

"Yes. We were." She said it simply, a matter of fact. But inwardly, she felt the loss intensely. She took a tissue out of her apron pocket and wiped her eyes.

"So how are you feeling? What do the doctors say?" Nina asked.

"Oh, everything is fine so far. They want to see me every six months, but when I was in the last time, about a month or so ago, the doctor said everything is fine. He wants me to keep taking the medication for a while longer, but he's very pleased."

"Thank heaven for that."

"Tell me, Nina, about Andrea and Rosalie and the boys. How are they doing?"

"Well, Andrea, as you know, decided to take the residency she was offered out in St. Louis, in obstetrics and gynecology. She's working hard, but she likes it very much. I miss her, but the truth is she's been spending so much time working that we didn't get to see much of her anyway. She'll be able to come home a couple of times a year, and we'll go out to visit her, I'm sure. Rosalie is still enjoying working for Nick at the restaurant, and she and Denise are very happy together. I can't get over how great Denise is with the boys. They just adore her. So do I.

"Oh, I almost forgot, with the inheritance that she got from Pop, Rosalie decided to buy a house. They're only looking now, but they're all excited about the process, deciding where they want to live, what kind of house, you know. The boys are looking forward to getting their own rooms, although next year Bobby might be going away to college. Pop left each of the boys a trust fund for college, so they don't have to worry at all about that, and that's a big relief to Bobby."

"It's nice to hear that so many good things are happening in your life."

"You know, you're right. There are a lot of good things going on. Even—would you believe this, Zia—Joey Giantonio introduced me to a good friend of his, a really nice man. We've been out to dinner a couple of times. I'm not getting my hopes up, but this is the first normal and intelligent man I've been with in years. I'd given up hope of ever having a man in my life again."

"Nina, I know what you mean." Maria smiled to herself, thinking of the happy and comfortable times that she'd been enjoying with Artie over these past six months or so. "So why are you so blue? Do you think it's just missing your mother and father or is it something else?"

"I don't know, Zia."

"Nina, do you remember whose birthday is in ten days?"

Nina thought for a moment. "Oh, of course, Richie's: November 17, 1970."

Maria was silent.

"You may be right, Zia. I hadn't been thinking consciously about him. His death was such a shock. I guess I've tried not to think about it. It was just so painful. But maybe you're right; between his birthday and Thanksgiving and Christmas and Andrea being away . . ."

"Nina, I have an idea. Why don't you plan on coming over here for breakfast tomorrow? Plan to stay for a while. Do I have a story to tell you!"